R☆ A☆L☆ wwww   mL

MP mv sk GOOD   DG

RM auf 1/28/17

nk

River
Rising

BOOKS BY DOROTHY GARLOCK

After the Parade
Almost Eden
Annie Lash
Dream River
The Edge of Town
Forever Victoria
A Gentle Giving
Glorious Dawn
High on a Hill
Homeplace
Hope's Highway
Larkspur
The Listening Sky
Lonesome River
Love and Cherish
Midnight Blue
More than Memory
Mother Road

Nightrose
A Place Called Rainwater
Restless Wind
Ribbon in the Sky
River of Tomorrow
The Searching Hearts
Sins of Summer
Song of the Road
Sweetwater
Tenderness
This Loving Land
Wayward Wind
Wild Sweet Wilderness
Wind of Promise
With Heart
With Hope
With Song
Yesteryear

DOROTHY GARLOCK

River Rising

DOUBLEDAY LARGE PRINT HOME LIBRARY EDITION

WARNER BOOKS

NEW YORK   BOSTON

Copyright © 2005 by Dorothy Garlock
All rights reserved.

Warner Books

Time Warner Book Group
1271 Avenue of the Americas, New York, NY 10020

Printed in the United States of America

ISBN 0-7394-5463-3

Cover illustration by Wendell Minor

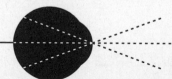

This Large Print Book carries the☐
Seal of Approval of N.A.V.H.

This book is dedicated with love to my sisters,
Mary Bruza and Betty O'Haver.
If I could have chosen sisters, I would
have chosen you.

River
Rising

RIVER RISING

Edging toward the town of Fertile
Close to flooding o'er its banks
River rising.
Passions rising.

Deep beneath the surface waters
Hidden crimes and vengeance roil.
Passions rising.
River rising.

Dammed with rocks
And damned by laws
Love, unstifled, surges forth.
River rising.
Passions rising.

Break the dam.
Release the current.
Let it wash away the past.
Let the river, clean and rushing,
Take its course,
Be free at last!

—F.S.I.

Prologue

Fertile, Missouri
1928

The woman clutched the slim tin box tightly to her chest, hurried down the street to her house and up the stairs to her bedroom. She closed the door and sank down on the edge of the bed, sucked in gulps of air and waited for her heartbeat to settle into a regular rhythm.

The vile, rotten, lying, conniving sonofabitch had hidden his dirty little secret well! She muttered her fury, unable to find words to describe just how despicable she found him to be. If he were not already dead, she would kill him again and again. She fervently hoped that he was burning in hell!

She never would have found out the sinful things her husband had done if not for the leak in the roof at the hardware store. Water had come down the wall in back of the counter. When shelves had been emptied and moved out, she had found in the wall behind the bottom shelf a box that contained not only a ledger but bow ribbons, garters, buttons, snips of hair tied with a string: his mementos. In an envelope were Kodak pictures of his bastards: a shaggy-haired boy in overalls too short for his skinny legs, a small girl with blond curls, another girl with dark braids, a tall boy standing beside a board fence and a baby in a carriage. She wondered how he managed to get the pictures.

She had told her brother, when he asked what she had found in the box, that it was her personal diary she had put there for safekeeping and that it really was of no consequence to anyone but her. She had not realized then the significance of the ledger, but she had figured it out later when she scanned the names. One name jumped out at her:

Julie Jones—July 1917—girl March 1918 named Joy. Below he had written: *I couldn't have picked a better name myself.*

Now in her room behind a locked door, she moved to the chair beside the window, opened the ledger and began to read. An hour later she was too angry to cry. Pregnancy had resulted from his intercourse—he didn't consider it rape—with twenty of the fifty-seven women and girls he'd penetrated with his mighty sword, as he had so disgustingly called it. Only a very few of his encounters had been consensual. His notes made it clear that he preferred a challenge and thoroughly enjoyed stalking the women and girls he had chosen to have his children and forcing them to accept his seed.

Her husband had kept a careful record of each conquest and was proud that only two miscarriages and the death of one of the women had been the result of his desire to procreate. He regretted the death, but his victim knew who he was and he'd had no choice but to kill the girl.

In a note written in 1917 he explained his compulsion to rape: *I will sow my seed in young females and leave behind a part of myself when I leave this earth that will go on and on into the future.* When he died, he left eighteen children and three pregnant girls. Two girls from neighboring towns had received a second dose of his sperm when he discovered that they had failed to catch the first time and the opportunity had arisen for him to copulate with them again. Behind these names he had written: *Second time was even more satisfying because the bitches knew that they were going to get plowed deep and long.*

The woman stared out the window at a boy riding his scooter down the sidewalk, then watched the iceman stop across the street, go to the back of his truck and hoist a large chunk of ice to his back. The boy was waiting when he returned to the truck and was given a chip of ice. As he skipped away, she wondered if he was one of her stepchildren.

Her hands curled around the arms of the chair. She had grieved for Ron Poole for five years, the same number of years they had been married before he was killed. He had never expressed regret that they had not had children. The first year of their marriage he had demanded sex morning and night and sometimes in the middle of the day. He had been a gentle lover, but when, after a few years, she hadn't conceived, he seldom touched her and had begun to act more like her brother than her husband.

Looking back, she remembered him as being kind to her and acting the doting husband in public. His standing in the community was important to him, and it helped to make it all the more difficult to believe that he was a rapist.

She covered her face in shame as she remembered lying in bed waiting for him to come to her, love her and satisfy her sexual hunger. She realized now that the rutting stud didn't need his wife. He was getting his satisfaction from young girls, not only here but in surrounding towns.

An idea began to form in her mind, a way that she could get even not only with him but with the stupid, careless women who had allowed him to take advantage of them. With a goal in mind she skipped a few pages in the ledger and began to make her own list.

When she finished, she realized that she knew nine of his children. They lived right here in Fertile. Some had been raised as brother or sister to the girl who had given them birth. Some of the girls had married as soon as they realized that they were pregnant and passed the children off as their husbands'. But the man for whom she had grieved for all these years had known better; and, according to the notes he had posted beside the birthdates, he had received an enormous amount of satisfaction watching their development.

He appeared to be fond of all his offspring. Beside their names he had noted physical descriptions and whether or not they appeared to be healthy. Beside two names he expressed regret that he had not been more careful when he chose their mothers. He was not pleased with the care they were being given. He was even exploring the idea that if something happened to the mothers, it might be possible for him to adopt the children.

The woman sitting in the rocking chair began to rock energetically. She felt suddenly as if she had come alive. The mantle of grief for her lost love had slid from her shoulders. She'd often heard that hate was very close to love and that nothing energized the soul as much as hating someone and seeking vengeance.

The dull and listless life she had lived since his death was over; she now had a goal in mind. It would be a few years before the offspring he had so proudly sired would be old enough to fit into her plans. But that was all right. She was in no hurry. She would spend the time getting to know each of them, and when the time came, she would be ready.

Chapter 1

Fertile, Missouri
1934

April sat in the car, her hands gripping the steering wheel, and peered at the muddy road ahead through the windshield of her Model T Runabout. Amid the heavy rain, she could see only a few feet past the radiator cap on the hood of her car. The road behind her would be deep in mud by now, so there was no point in turning back even if she could.

With a sigh of despair she turned off the motor, closed her eyes and said a little prayer. "Please, God, let someone come along to help me." Then a little voice whispered in her ear. "God helps those who help themselves."

It was impossible to see out through the isinglass on the side curtains. April worked the lever that wiped water from the windshield. During the second or so that the glass was clear, all she could see was the muddy road ahead and a fence that ran along the side. The last time she stopped she had estimated that she was about ten miles from Fertile. Surely she had come five miles since then.

She had walked five miles many times and could do so again.

The watch that hung from a gold chain around her neck said three o'clock. She had two choices. She could sit here for the rest of the day and let night come, or she could get out of the car and walk to Fertile. The days were getting shorter this time of year, and if she didn't want to be stranded out here in the dark, she had to get along.

April removed her shoes and stockings, took her valuables out of the suitcase on the seat beside her and put them in the pockets of the old coat she decided to wear. She tied her shoelaces and hung her shoes around her neck, opened her umbrella and stepped out into the driving rain.

Cold, soft mud covered her feet to her ankles. Standing beside the car, she adjusted the umbrella and gave the auto an affectionate pat.

"You've been a good girl, Daisy. You brought me this far without a single complaint. I hate to leave you, but I have no choice."

She had inherited the 1925 Model T Runabout when her grandfather died. It had served her well during her last year of nursing school and during the two years her grandmother lived following his death.

Despite the heavy downpour, only a trickle of water had seeped in around the side curtains. The top was as good as the day her grandfather replaced it shortly after he had brought the shiny new car home. Hortense, her grandmother's pet goat, had climbed on the top of it, and her sharp hooves had gone through the roof. She had hung there, suspended, until April's angry grandfather, threatening to kill her, had pulled her out. The car had been kept in the shed with the doors closed after that.

"I'll be back for you, Daisy."

April started up the road. She had gone only ten steps when her feet slipped out from under her and she fell back in a sea of mud.

"Dammit!" The hand not holding the umbrella had instinctively gone out to break her fall and was now covered with mud to her elbow. She had to use it to tip her straw hat back out of her eyes so that she could see. "Damn, damn, dammit to hell!" she swore. *Sorry, Grandma, you said not to cuss unless I just had to. Well, this is enough to make a preacher cuss.*

Rain hit her in the face as she tried to scramble to her feet only to fall back again. Finally she had to turn over on her knees and put her hand down in that soupy dark mess to push herself up. When she was back on her feet, she righted the umbrella to shield her head and shoulders from the rain and trudged on down the muddy road.

If she'd had the sense of a goose, she thought now, she would have stopped when she saw that it was going to rain. But how did she know that it had probably been raining here for hours and that she was heading into it? Her skirt was wet and wrapped around her legs, making it difficult to walk. She reached down and pulled it and the coat up past her knees. There surely wasn't anyone around to see her legs except maybe a cow or two in the fenced pasture.

After a while she found her breath coming hard and her heart beating fast from the exertion. It was tiring pulling her feet out of the sucking mud. The rain had settled into a steady downpour. She stopped to rest, and when she looked back, she couldn't see her car. Her entire world was a ten-foot radius around her.

When she came to a place where water ran over the road, she stopped and stood first on one foot and then the other. *He who hesitates is lost.* The thought came and went as she lifted her skirt and coat up past her knees, and stepped into the muddy water again. When it reached midcalf, she took careful steps, feeling her way, until she knew that was as deep as it was going to get. As she walked out of the water, she let the wet garments drop around her cold legs.

With her head bent April plodded on down the middle of the road. Rain beat against the umbrella. Thunder rolled overhead. If she hadn't been so wet and miserable when she thought about Elbert Prescott, the pharmacist back in Independence with whom she had kept company for a while, she would have giggled.

Short, plump, persnickety Elbert, who wouldn't be seen without his starched shirt and bow tie, would be horrified to see her wet and covered with mud. If not for his snooty mother's objection, Elbert would have asked her to marry him. Of course, she wouldn't have accepted; but it would have been nice to have been asked, considering the Prescotts were supposed to be the upper echelon of Independence society.

April felt just a little guilty that she had led Elbert on a bit. It had been a balm to her ego to have the most eligible man in town pay attention to her. She had been a source of gossip during her school years because she and her mother had come back to town to live with her grandparents and had been silent about her father. Many thought she had been born out of wedlock; but she knew differently, and so had her grandparents.

She was beginning to despair of reaching town before dark when the rain slackened a bit and she spotted a small house and a lean-to shed set in the middle of a pasture.

A burst of hope rose like a bubble in her heart. She would go there and ask for help. She wasn't able to find a break in the fence or a lane leading to the house. To get there, she would have to go over or under two strands of barbed wire. Without her shoes, she couldn't go over. She lowered the umbrella, removed her hat, lay on her back and scooted under the barbed strands.

After getting to her feet, she raised the umbrella again and trudged toward the house. Walking was much easier on the sod even though it was soaking wet. She thought briefly about trying to improve her appearance before she knocked on the door, but that thought fled when out of the corner of her eye she saw a large animal with horns! The beast stood perfectly still looking at her. She hurried toward the house, turning her head frequently to keep watch on the animal.

Thinking to use the umbrella to ward off the beast if it attacked, she lowered it and held it at the ready. The rain streamed down her face and filled her eyes. She blinked rapidly to keep them clear. When she was within a dozen yards of the house, the animal pawed the earth and started toward her.

"Stay back," she warned. "Stay back or

I'll whack you!" The bull, blowing steam from its nostrils, came on the run. "Get away . . . or . . . I'll hurt you." Panic made her voice loud and shrill. She raced for the porch of the small house, praying the door wouldn't be locked. When she jumped up onto the porch, a man stood in the doorway.

"Don't you dare hurt my bull! I've got every cent to my name tied up in that animal."

April turned back with the umbrella raised to see that the bull had stopped and stood looking at her. Afraid to turn her back on him, she backed toward the door. The man reached around and tried to take the umbrella out of her hand, but she held on to it.

"How were you going to hurt Rolling Thunder with an umbrella?"

"I was going to poke him in the eye."

The man eyed the metal tip. "That would have done it. I reckon the loss of an eye wouldn't have kept him from doing what I bought him for."

With the danger past, April looked up into the face of the tall man. He had laughing blue eyes and a head of sandy hair almost the same color as hers. He was grinning like a jackass eating strawberries!

"I'm stuck down on the road."

"No, you're not. You're standing on my porch."

"My car is stuck down on that poor excuse for a road."

"Oh, why didn't you say so?" Then, "You tried to drive a car down that road?"

"Evidently, or I'd not be stuck," she said irritably.

"You got a little wet, too, didn't you? And a little muddy."

"You're very observant."

"Hmmm . . . one of my better traits." He tilted his head to look at her bare, muddy feet. "You'll have to wash your feet before I can let you walk on my Persian carpet."

"Maybe I don't want to come in."

"Sure you do. I've got a kettle full of beef stew. Smell it? Besides that, I don't think Rolling Thunder likes you."

"Is your wife here?"

"Which one?" His brows drew together in question.

"Listen, mister, call off your bull, and I'll get on back down to the road." She stepped to the edge of the porch and unfolded the umbrella.

"Ah . . . shoot! Can't you take a joke? It's been boring as hell here all day."

"I'm in no mood for jokes. Amuse yourself with Rolling Thunder, not me."

"Wrong gender, ma'am."

"Oh!" With one eye on the bull April stepped off the porch.

"Come back now." The man grabbed her arm. "I'll behave. My name is Joe Jones. I don't have a wife."

"I can certainly understand why." April shrugged off his hand and turned. "Jones? Do you have brothers?"

"Yes, and three sisters."

"Your brothers' names?"

"Jason and Jack, and little Jacob."

"What does Jack do?"

"He's helping Pa farm right now."

"Does he do something else?"

"Plays baseball sometimes."

"Dr. Forbes told me about Jack Jones being an exceptional ballplayer. He said the Jones family were a decent, well-respected family." She gave him an exasperated look. "Was he wrong?"

"Doc was right. We're pillars of the community. Are you the nurse he's been expecting?"

"April Asbury, R.N."

"Well, you sure don't look like an R.N. or a P.N. or any other kind of N. You look like a half-drowned little kitty cat right now. Come in. I promise not to pounce on you."

Holding on to the porch post, April held first one foot and then the other beneath the stream of water pouring off the roof.

"I'd hate to ruin your Persian carpet." Not until her feet were free of mud did she step inside onto the wide plank floor.

Joe lit a lamp, and April could see that the one room had a cookstove, a bed, dresser, table and chairs.

"I'm warming up the pot of stew my sister sent over. You'd better get out of those wet clothes."

"Yeah, sure." April looked at him with lifted brows. He seemed to fill the small room. She felt crowded.

"I'll go out on the porch if you insist, but I'd rather stay."

"It won't be necessary for you to make the sacrifice. I don't have any dry clothes to put on."

"I'll lend you some of mine until yours dry. Now, don't get all starchy on me. I'll go out on the porch. I can't have Doc's new nurse getting sick on my account. He'd be sure to find that I had TB or cancer or something just to pay me back." Joe opened a drawer and pulled out a pair of worn work pants, a flannel shirt and a pair of socks. He tossed them on the bed. "I promise not to peek," he said as he went out the door and shut it behind him.

April had to smile in spite of herself. She didn't feel one bit threatened even if he was big as a horse. Dr. Forbes had amused her with stories about the people in Fertile. Joe and Jack Jones belonged to the Jones family who lived on the edge of town. During the summer months they had baseball games in a pasture beside their house and dances in the yard between the house and the barn.

"The boys, Joe and Jack, can spin some of the wildest yarns you ever heard." She had no trouble believing that now. Dr. Forbes had told her about Julie Jones, who raised her siblings after her mother had died. She had married a neighbor and taken the younger children with her. The children's father had married the sister of the Methodist preacher, and they'd had one child.

April wondered while she was getting out of her wet clothes why Joe Jones hadn't married. He was certainly old enough. The flirt! She rolled up the sleeves of his shirt and the pant legs, cinched the waist with her belt and put on her shoes, which she had kept dry beneath her coat. She looked at herself in the small mirror over the washbasin. She was as bedraggled as a wet hen, yet Joe Jones had still flirted with her. She bet that he'd flirt with a stump. Some men were like that. She ran her fingers through her hair and opened the door.

"Well, now, that's better. I was getting worried that Doc had pulled a fast one."

"What do you mean, a fast one?"

"He said the easiest way to build a practice was to get a pretty nurse. He's bragging that his new nurse will cause every single man within fifty miles to suddenly get sick. I had my doubts when you stumbled in here. But now . . ." He circled around her, his eyes going up and down as if he were judging a horse or a cow. "Hmmm . . ." Her dark blond hair was full of colors, curling wildly around her face and making an unruly fall down to her shoulders. "Pretty brown eyes," he murmured. "And a kissable mouth. Tall, too. I don't like to bend way over to kiss a woman." He stroked his chin. "Doc did just fine for an old . . . goat."

"Mr. Jones, Dr. Forbes isn't an old goat! And if you should be foolish enough to get fresh with me, be aware that I carry a large hatpin, and I know how to use it when I meet up with a masher who isn't smart enough to keep his hands to himself."

"Ouch! Masher, huh?"

"Yes, masher. Now, where can I hang my wet clothes?"

"Toss them on the line over the stove. When the rain lets up, I'll take you over to my pa's place, and in the morning I'll go down and pull your car out of the mudhole."

"I would appreciate that. And, of course, I'll pay you for the trouble."

"How much?" He was laughing at her. His expression was rich with the droll humor of a natural-born flirt. His eyes, beneath heavy straight brows, were so blue, so bright and vivid with laughter that they fascinated her. They were twinkling stars in his sun-browned face. There was a fine etching of spider wrinkles around his mouth. He was a good-looking man, probably well aware of it. Watching him set out bowls and spoons on the table, she judged him to be between twenty-five and thirty.

"How far did you drive today, Miss R.N.?"

"Asbury. April Asbury. I drove from Kearney. I stopped to visit a distant cousin."

"By jinks damn! I'm dining with a relative of Jesse James. They say everyone in Kearney is related to him in one way or the other."

"Sorry to disappoint you. My cousin moved there from Independence a few years ago."

"Naw?" He looked crestfallen. "Shoot! If you were related to the outlaw, it would have raised my standing at the pool hall. I might have gotten a few free games after spinning the yarn about the cousin of Jesse James spending the night at my house."

"You mean that would create excitement—"

"Sure. If you've seen the uncle of Charles Lindbergh, you're a celebrity in town."

In spite of herself, April laughed. "Do you ever get offstage, Mr. Jones?"

"Not when I'm having fun, Miss Asbury." He grinned at her and nodded for her to sit down. "My sister Julie is like a mother hen." Joe stirred the stew heating on the stove.

"Even though most of us are grown up now, she still mothers us."

"Most of you?"

"Our baby sister, Joy, just turned sixteen. She's a handful, but no more than our other sister, Jill, was at that age. Jill's married to my best friend, Thad Taylor. We own adjoining tracts of land and farm together." Joe ladled stew into a bowl and placed it in front of April. "If I'd known I was going to entertain a lady tonight, I'd have shaved."

Inhaling the aroma from the stew, April suddenly realized that she was hungry.

"I hate to leave Daisy down there on the road all night."

"Hell and damnation, woman!" Joe dropped his spoon on the table. "You didn't tell me there was another woman—"

"You didn't ask me." April enjoyed watching him jump up from the table and pull out a slicker and mud boots.

"Does she have an umbrella?"

"No. An umbrella wouldn't cover her."

"Well, hell. I don't have another slicker."

"She doesn't need one. This stew is delicious. I must get the recipe from your sister. You should eat yours before it gets cold."

"I can't sit here and eat when a woman's

sitting down there on the road. She's probably scared to death."

"She isn't a woman."

"What is she? A kid? My God but you're
a cold one."

"Let's see . . . 1925. That would make her
about nine years old."

"You left a nine-year-old kid down there in
the car by herself? I can't believe anyone
would be so stupid. My God! What was Doc
thinking of when he hired you?"

"He was thinking that he had gotten the
best nurse to come out of St. Luke's Nursing School."

"A nurse is supposed to have a little horse
sense! Who is with her?"

"Nobody, unless someone came along."

"Don't eat all the stew. I'll be back as
soon as I can."

"Daisy will be all right until morning. If I
couldn't drive her out of that mudhole, you
sure can't."

Joe turned at the door. His eyes honed in
on her and narrowed. She lifted her brows in
a silent reply and raised her empty bowl at
the same time.

"May I have some more of your sister's
delicious stew . . . please?"

"There's not a woman or a kid down there? Daisy . . . is your car?"

"The sweetest little Ford Runabout you ever did see. I'm crazy about her."

"I ought to strangle you." He began taking off his slicker and kicking out of his mud boots.

"But you won't. The Jones family are pillars of the community. You told me so yourself."

"Well, I lied. The Joneses are blood brothers to Al Capone." He bared his teeth. "We're also cousins to Pretty Boy Floyd and Bugs Moran. My great-great-great-grand-pappy was Benedict Arnold's best friend."

"Hmmm. That does change things. You are a bad lot. I've not known Dr. Forbes to make such a mistake in judgment. It makes me seriously doubt his medical ability."

"You think you're pretty smart, don't you?"

"Yes, I do. I've been told that my intelligence is above average. Let this be a lesson to you, Mr. Jones. Know the facts before you jump to conclusions."

"You think you're pretty smart, don't you?" he said again, enjoying bantering with her.

"I don't even have to think about it."

"Well, think about this—I've got one horse. I can let you ride with me, or I can make you walk along behind carrying a load like an Indian squaw."

"I'm not worried. The Joneses would not want their reputation tarnished by such a dastardly deed. I must ask your sister for the recipe for this stew."

"You wouldn't want the recipe if you knew what was in it," he growled. "Worms, grasshoppers—"

"Oh, I love worms. Have you ever had them dipped in chocolate?"

Joe lifted his eyes to her smiling face and couldn't look away.

By damn! She was something else.

Chapter 2

The night was dark, foggy and utterly quiet except for the labored breathing of the horse and the whisper of leaves in the tree-tops as the wind passed through them.

"I hope you know where you're going. It's darker than the bottom of a well out here."

"How many times have you been in the bottom of a well?"

"Are you never serious?" she asked with an exasperated sigh.

Joe chuckled. "The horse knows where we're going."

"Thank goodness for that." April tried to sit up straight and not lean back against him. "How much farther?"

"Not much. Cold?"

"No."

"Then sit still or I'll not be able to keep the

slicker around you. You're the most mule-headed woman I ever met." His voice was close to her ear. "You'd not admit you were cold if you were freezing to death."

"You've only known me for a few hours, Mr. Jones. How do you know how stubborn I am?"

"I can read you like a book, Miss April. You're cold. You're wishing you'd stayed an extra day with Jesse's kin down in Kearney and missed the rain. And you're wondering what my pa is going to say about me riding in this time of night with a pretty woman dressed in my old work clothes." When he laughed, his breath was warm on her ear. "Since my pa married my stepmother, he's been a churchgoin' man. He might get out the shotgun and make me marry you."

"Oh, no! I can't let that happen. Dozens of women will commit suicide, and I'll carry the guilt to my grave."

His arms pulled her tightly against him, and she could feel the movement of his chest when he chuckled.

Lord. She was rare. He'd not had so much fun since he'd stood by and watched a fat girl chasing his friend Thad Taylor down a street in Oklahoma. If not for the fact the creek might be flooding the road, he'd take her on to town just to prolong his time with her.

"We're almost there. Old Sam's picked up speed. He's thinking about that nice dry barn ahead and a bucket of oats."

No doubt about it, Joe Jones was a charmer. Every single woman in Fertile, Missouri, must be after him. April vowed not to be among them. When she met the right man and settled down, it would *not* be with a handsome man. Her father had been one, and, according to her grandmother, her mother had not had an easy time with him.

They rode into the yard of the Jones farm and right up to the back porch. Joe slid off the horse and reached up to lift her down. She was surprised that her legs were stiff and numb, and she had to lean against him for a minute, during which time the back door opened, letting a ribbon of light flow out across the porch.

"Jack, is that you?"

"No. It's me, Pa. I've brought a lady who was stranded down the road."

"I thought you were Jack."

April blinked until her eyes became accustomed to the light. Then she saw a stocky man, not as tall as his son. His hair was dark with wings of gray at the temple. She held out her hand.

"April Asbury, Mr. Jones. I'm sorry to impose on you at this hour, but my car's stuck, and I walked to your son's house."

"She's Todd's new nurse, Pa."

The big hand that engulfed hers was warm and callused.

"Come in. My wife is upstairs putting our son to bed. She'll be down shortly."

"Is Jack here?"

"No. He went to town this afternoon when it started to rain again."

"I'll put Sam in the barn. In the morning I'll get Jack to go with me to pull her car out of the mudhole. Here are your clothes, Miss April." He shoved the flour sack containing the damp clothing into her hand.

April entered a warm, homey kitchen filled with the aroma of freshly baked bread. The teakettle on the big cookstove emitted a thin plume of steam. A bowl of shiny apples sat on the blue-flowered oilcloth that covered the table.

"Hello." A pleasant-faced woman with soft blond hair came into the room and closed the door leading to the stairway. "Oh, my. You got caught in the rain."

"I certainly did." April held out her arms, showing the large shirt she was wearing. "Mr. Jones was kind enough to lend me something dry."

"I'm Eudora Jones."

April held out her hand. "April Asbury. I've come to work with Dr. Forbes."

"How nice to meet you." Eudora smiled and her husband smiled watching her. "Sit down and I'll make us a cup of tea. You do drink tea?"

"Hot in the winter, cold in the summer."

"It's not quite winter, but the air is cold and damp."

April liked Eudora Jones immediately. She was somewhat younger than her husband, certainly not old enough to be Joe's mother. Dr. Forbes had told her that Jethro Jones's first wife had died and Julie, his oldest daughter, who was sixteen at the time, had stepped in, run the house and taken care of her siblings.

Later, after Eudora had hung April's wet clothes on a line that stretched over the cookstove, she poured hot tea. The four of them sat at the kitchen table.

"Dr. Forbes has been without a nurse since his last one got married and moved to St. Joseph. I thought for a while we might have a nurse in the family." Eudora's teasing eyes went to Joe.

"There was no danger of that," he commented dryly. "Unless Jack would get caught in her net. She was too old for Jason."

Jethro chuckled, then said seriously, "I wish Jack would patch it up with Ruby. I'm thinking it's going to take that to settle him down."

There was a long silence that prompted April to think there was more to the story of Jack not being "settled down" and they didn't want to discuss it in front of her.

"Have you heard from Jason?" Joe asked.

"Yesterday." Eudora's eyes met her husband's before she turned to April. "Our Jason is going to school in St. Louis. Charles Lindbergh is his hero. He has this burning desire to be an airplane pilot. When he can, he wants to take flying lessons. We're very proud of him."

"He's had the flying bug since a barnstorming friend of Julie's husband, Evan, stopped here a few years ago on his way to an air show," Jethro explained. "Jason has read and studied everything he could get his hands on about airplanes since then. When he turned twelve, Evan took him to Kansas City so he could go up in a plane."

"I'm eager to meet Julie. Dr. Forbes spoke highly of her."

April felt a tinge of regret that she had never had brothers or sisters. She knew from the tone of Joe's voice and the look on his face when he spoke of his siblings that they meant a lot to him.

"Jill looks like she swallowed a watermelon." The teasing look suddenly spread over Joe's face. "Thad says she's getting as ornery as a cat with a knot in its tail."

"Jill is a small girl," Eudora explained to April. "She's carrying around quite a load right now."

"Thad's afraid to go to the field. Someone told him that first babies come early. He'll be a wreck by the time it gets here," Joe said.

"She's got a couple of weeks to go. Julie's been going over every day."

"I hope this is the last of the rain. Thad's already worried how he'll get to Julie if the creek is up. He has it all planned: He goes first to get Julie, then you, Eudora, then he's off to town to get Doc. If the roads are bad, he'll go on horseback and take an extra horse for the doc."

"Jill said that she just might stay pregnant permanently. Thad waits on her hand and foot. He'll hardly let her lift a glass of water. He has tended to the garden this summer and even helped her can beans and tomatoes."

"He's spoilin' her, is what he's doin'," Joe said.

"She was already spoiled." Jethro was grinning. "You and Jack spoiled her, then Thad took over the job."

"Did Jack take the car to town?"

"No. He walked."

"Maybe I should mosey on into town and come back with him. I'll stop by and let Doc know his nurse is here."

"Suit yourself." Jethro got to his feet. "Better take your slicker. It'll probably rain off and on all night."

Joe tied his horse to the fence in front of Dr. Forbes's clinic, then followed the walk to the porch and around to the doctor's private quarters. When he knocked on the door, it was opened immediately.

"That was quick. Are you expectin' one of your adorin' ladies? Sorry to disappoint you." Joe's grin said that he was not sorry at all.

"You s-sick, I hope," Doc grunted.

"Nope. I'm fit as a fiddle."

"Well, c-come in anyway."

Dr. Forbes was a rough-looking man with heavy shoulders and chest. He looked more like a lumberjack or a stevedore than a doctor. A few years older than Joe, he had come to town right out of medical school about nine years earlier and had taken over old Dr. Curtis's practice. He had a quick wit besides being an excellent doctor. He also had a slight stutter in his speech, which, for some unknown reason, endeared him to the ladies.

Joe kicked his boots off at the door.

"Something smells good. Have the good ladies in town brought you supper in hopes of snaring you for their daughters?"

"Daughters, h-hell. They hopin' to t-trap me for themselves."

"What are you now, Doc? Forty? Fifty? I heard your bones creakin' when you opened the door." Joe enjoyed teasing the doctor because he was only thirty-four and his once-dark hair was rapidly turning gray.

"S-smart-ass. What're you doing out on a night like this? Can't be Jill. I saw her yesterday. She's not due for a couple of w-weeks. Thad thought I should pinpoint it down to the day and hour. I'm good, b-but not that good."

"I came to tell you that your new nurse got as far as my place before she got bogged down in the mud."

"April is here?" A brief smile fluttered across Doc's face, then disappeared. "Did you t-treat her to s-some of your smart-alecky humor? If you did, I'll s-sew up that mouth of yours the f-first chance I get."

"I treated her like the gentleman I am. What do you take me for? A country clod?"

"You said it. I didn't."

"I charmed her. She fell for me like a poleaxed steer. She couldn't keep her hands off me."

"B-bull hockey! She's too smart for that."

"She's at Pa's. Jack and I will pull her car out in the morning. She'll be so grateful she'll swoon in my arms. Where's she going to stay?"

"I've put out some feelers. Shirley Poole has a room to let. Only she and her b-brother live in that big old house. I don't know if she offers meals. She and Miss Asbury would have to work that out."

"Marry her and she can stay here." Joe watched carefully for Doc's reaction. His expression never changed.

"And lose out on all the c-cakes and pies I get from the ladies who are trying to s-snare me?"

"How about Mrs. Bloom? Her son went to St. Louis to find work."

"It's a thought. I'll s-suggest it to Miss Asbury."

"How did you meet her?"

"You're awfully nosy about my new n-nurse."

"Why not? She's the prettiest thing to come to Fertile in a long time."

"She was r-recommended by a doctor in Kansas City when I went there to take a brushup course. She was working at the hospital and taking care of a s-sick grand-mother. She told me that she wanted to eventually work for a small-town doctor where she could get to know the patients. I wrote to her as soon as Miss Franklin t-told me she was quitting."

"She's a lot better-looking than Miss Franklin."

"You're just saying that because she turned you down for Harold Walker."

Joe snorted. "She made a play for every single man in town and some that were not single. Even you, for God's sake. That's how desperate she was. She caught poor old Harold when he was looking the other way."

"Why even me? Hell. I'm the best c-catch in town."

"Bullfoot! I'm the one carrying the stick to keep the women off me."

"Don't play f-fast and loose with my nurse. Hear? I want her to s-stay."

"Miss April Asbury can take care of herself. She'll have you wrapped around her little finger in no time at all." Joe headed for the door and slipped on his boots. "I'll get her car as far as our place. I think the road from there to town is hard-packed enough for her to come on in."

"Don't rush off. I was about to offer you a p-piece of Miss Davenport's chocolate cake or a dish of Mrs. Maddox's peach cobbler or a hunk of meat loaf b-brought in by Sarah Parker."

"Thanks. That's generous of you, but I'm afraid it would get out that I'm eating the treats the dear ladies bring you and your supply would be cut off. I'd better get back uptown, look up Jack and see if he's ready to go home."

"Jack's going through a d-difficult time right now."

"Pa's worried about him."

"You're a h-hard act to follow, Joe. You've got your land and a good start while he's s-still working at home with his pa. His dream of p-playing baseball blew up, and he doesn't know what to do with himself."

"I know he was disappointed. But hell, Doc, we all have disappointments. That's no excuse for trying to drown them in booze."

"He was shaken up when Ruby b-broke off with him and started going out with a fel-low who has a g-good job with the electric company."

"Jack had his chance with Ruby. She's been crazy about him since they were kids in school. I don't know why they broke up, but I suspect it had something to do with his drinking. Her folks are churchgoing people, and she was probably getting stomped on at home."

Doc stood in the doorway as Joe crossed the porch. "Hurry up and get s-sick, Joe," he called. "I'll need the money to pay my new nurse."

"If I get sick, I'll head for the vet over in Mason. At least he knows enough not to pull my teeth if I have a bellyache."

Doc chuckled and closed the door.

Joe rode his horse the two blocks to Main Street, then turned into the alley behind Hannity's, the pool hall where Jack usually hung out when he was in town. After tying his horse, he walked between the buildings to the front door.

He heard his brother before he saw him.

"Dammit, This. I've a notion to bend this cue stick around your scrawny neck."

"You're a poor loser, Jack."

Jack was playing pool with This and That, the redheaded Humphrey twins. Their names were Thomas and Thayer but they had been called This and That since they were babies, and most folks thought those were their real names. They still resembled each other but not as much as when they were younger.

The twins were strong, hardworking boys, as were all the Humphreys. They had been working with a harvest crew, but that job played out. They were home now and, like hundreds of other young men, looking for work.

"What're you doin' in town? Come to see about the prodigal son?" Jack bent over the pool table to line up a breaker shot.

"Came to see Doc." Joe took a cue stick from the rack on the wall and set up the balls on the other table. "How about a game, That?"

"What are we playin' for?"

"Nickel."

"Lord, you're cheap," Jack snorted. Joe knew his brother was on his way to being drunk. "Play the boy for a quarter."

Jack wasn't as tall or as heavy as his older brother. Thick light brown hair sprang back from his wide forehead. His smile was engaging. Until lately he had been the prankster in the family.

Jack made several plays before he spoke again. "Why'd you go see Doc? Is Jill all right?"

"Yeah. I went to tell him that his new nurse is out at the farm."

Jack straightened up and chalked the end of his cue stick. "What she doin' out there?"

"Waitin' for you and me to pull her car outta the mud."

"Tonight?"

"No. In the morning."

"I told Corbin I'd come by in the morning and help him grease his printing press."

"It won't take but an hour or two. We can take Pa's team."

"What's she look like?" This asked.

"Well"—Joe reached for the cube of chalk and studied the balls on the table—"you remember that teacher you had in high school who was so ugly she'd make a freight train take a detour through the woods?"

"Holy Moses! Not like her!"

"She's a very nice lady. She can't help what God gave her." Joe moved to the end of the table. "Doc isn't known for picking good-looking women."

"Hell," Jack said. "This one can't be uglier than the last one he had."

"You'll see."

"Doc got a new nurse?" The question came from a man who stood beside the cue rack.

"Yeah. How's things at the hardware, Fred?"

"Slow. Not like it was when I first came here back in '23. Business was booming then. That fellow Hoover about ruined the country."

"He didn't do it by himself. No man has that much power."

"I'm glad he got voted out. Roosevelt even *looks* smarter. But then, he's probably crooked as a snake's back. He'll look after his rich cronies, and to heck with the rest of us."

Fred Hazelton was pessimism personified. If there was a dark side to any subject, Fred would find it. It was probably the reason he had never married. He had come to Fertile eleven years earlier to help his sister, Shirley Poole, run the hardware store after her husband was killed.

"Sister has a room to let," Fred said. "Does the nurse have a place to stay?"

"I'm not sure. Her car is stuck in the mud out near my place."

"I'll tell Sister to call Doc Forbes."

Joe sank the last ball in the pocket and held out a hand to That to collect his nickel.

"Come on, Jack. Let's call it a night."

"Go ahead. I'll be along." Jack took a drink out of the bottle he brought from under the pool table.

"If the law catches you drinking in here, it will go hard for Mr. Dewey," Fred said.

Jack glared at the shopkeeper. "I suggest that you tend to your own damn business."

Joe saw the sign. Jack was spoiling for a fight. He wouldn't fight a soft, sissified man like Fred, but he'd cut him down verbally.

"Fred's right, Jack. We don't want to cause Mr. Dewey any trouble. He's hanging on here by the skin of his teeth, trying to support his family."

"I know that. I just don't want some prissy-ass store clerk telling me what to do."

"Let's go. My horse is out back."

"I suppose you're going to stay till I do."

"You got it right, Brother."

"Sheee-it. Let's go. I'm out of booze anyway."

Fred waited until the Jones boys and the Humphrey twins left the pool hall, then went out into the light drizzle and down the street to the house he shared with his sister.

"Sister," he called excitedly as soon as he opened the door.

"What is it?" The woman who hurried from the back of the house was tall and thin with a heavily lined face. Long gray-streaked brown hair was pulled tightly back, twisted and pinned in a knot on the back of her neck. She looked much older than her thirty-five years.

"The new nurse is here. You've got to go tell Doc Forbes about the room."

"I've already told him. He said that he'd tell her about it. That's all I can do."

"You promised that we'd get a lady roomer!"

"I'm doing the best I can."

"Joe Jones says that she's not pretty. But that doesn't matter."

"Where did you see him?"

"In the pool hall. Her car is stuck in the mud out by his place."

"I'll talk to the doctor again in the morning."

"Go early."

"Why are you so anxious for us to get a lady roomer?"

Fred started up the stairs to his room and turned back.

"Because you need someone here in case something happens to me."

"Nothing is going to happen to you. You're as strong as a horse. Aren't you?"

Fred continued on up the stairs without answering.

With a furrowed brow Shirley watched him until he turned at the landing. *Why was he so concerned about her being alone all of a sudden?*

Chapter 3

A crowing rooster awakened April. She lay for a long moment relishing the comfort of the soft bed and remembering the big red rooster her grandmother had when she was a little girl. Her grandpa had claimed him to be almost as old as he was himself and declared that only because he would be tough as boot leather kept him from lopping off the bird's head and putting him in the cook pot. Grandma had just smiled and warned Grandpa to keep his hands off that rooster. She cautioned that it was not wise of him to irritate the cook lest he leave the table with a bellyache and a running off of the bowels.

April had been weary the night before when Mrs. Jones had brought her to the room at the top of the stairs. The long drive, the trudge through the mud to reach the small house set in the pasture and the horseback ride had tired her out. She had fallen to sleep almost immediately and had awakened only briefly during the night when she heard footsteps in the hallway outside her door.

Now hearing voices below in the farm-yard, she rose from the bed to look out the window. Joe was standing at the head of a team of mules. He wore an old straw hat and an oiled slicker, and his pant legs were stuffed down into rubber boots. As she watched, a man came from the barn leading a saddled horse. Joe said something to the man, whom April presumed to be his brother Jack. The brother, laughing, put his thumb to his nose and waved his fingers in an obscene gesture. He then mounted the horse and loped him down the lane toward the road. Joe followed slowly, leading the mules.

April moved the curtains back to look at the sky. It was too early to tell if the rain clouds had passed over.

She hurried to dress, wondering when Mrs. Jones had placed her dried clothes on the chair in the room. She must have been sleeping soundly not to have heard her.

"Good morning." Eudora had just finished pouring her husband a second cup of coffee when April stepped into the cozily lighted kitchen. "There's warm water in the reservoir," she said, as she moved Jethro's plate from the table.

"Has the rain stopped?"

"For the time bein'," Jethro said. "The boys are on the way to get your car."

"Did they have breakfast before they left?"

"Oh, my, yes." Eudora laughed and placed her hand on her husband's shoulder as she passed him. "I only hope they don't kill each other before they get back."

"Don't worry about that." Jethro's eyes, blue as his son's, twinkled. "They been at each other since they were knee-high to a frog."

"I could have gone along to help." April finished blotting her face and drying her hands and placed the towel on the rod at the end of the cabinet. "It would be too bad if they pulled in the wrong car." A small laugh escaped her. She couldn't help thinking that it would serve the "flirt" right.

"Joe said you were driving a Ford Runabout. We've not seen many of those around here." Jethro got up from the table. "You ladies will have to excuse me. I have chores." Before he reached for his hat, he pulled his wife close and kissed her. "You don't plan to wash today, do you?"

"I will if the sun comes out. I'm three days behind already."

"If the sun comes out, I'll be back in to build a fire and fill the iron washpot."

"I can do it. You don't need to stop your work and come all the way back to the house. I know you want to finish digging out the stumps while the ground is soft."

"I'll be back in." He kissed her again, this time on the nose, and went out the door.

Eudora brought a pan of hot biscuits from the oven to the cloth-covered table. She poured coffee for herself and April, then sat down.

"That man," she exclaimed and shook her head. "He's just as sweet and loving as the day we were married eight years ago."

"You're very lucky."

"I know. I've got a wonderful family that I love. Jethro's children accepted me into the family wholeheartedly. I took care of my mother for many years and married late in life. I never thought this happiness would be mine. I'd fight an army for any one of them."

"Doc Forbes spoke highly of the Jones family when he was telling me about Fertile. That's how I knew that I could trust Joe to bring me here." April buttered a biscuit and lifted her brows. "He comes on pretty strong. He even assured me that the Jones family were pillars of the community."

Eudora smiled. "Both of the older boys have glib tongues. Wait until you meet Jack. He can be a little shy at first, but watch out after he gets to know you. Jason is the serious one. They are all different—from Joy, the youngest, to Julie, the oldest. Our Jacob, like Jason, loves books. He is curious as a cat. I'm surprised he didn't wake up when Jack and Joe came down. He tags after them whenever he can."

"How old is he?"

"He's six. He'll go to school this year."

"Doc Forbes told me that it was quite unusual, but the names of all the Joneses start with *J*."

"All except mine. They have threatened to change my name to Judora. Of course, they were teasing me."

April told Eudora a little about herself and

why she left her hometown to come to work for Dr. Forbes.

"I've always wanted to work with a doctor in a small town and jumped at the chance when it was offered."

"Times are not good, but this town is no worse off than any other this size. At least our bank is still solvent. Evan, Julie's husband, is on the board of directors, and he's got a good head for business."

"Does Julie live close by?"

"Evan's farm joins ours on the north. Jill and Thad live three sections over from Julie. Joe and Thad farm together. We are lucky to have the family close. They all pitch in and help one another. Joy lives with Julie and Evan. Jethro's wife died shortly after Joy was born, and Julie took care of her. She's sixteen now."

"Mama, where'd Joe and Jack go?" A small boy came from the stairway and closed the door.

"Hello there, sleepyhead. Come meet Miss Asbury. She's Dr. Forbes's new nurse."

The boy stepped forward and offered his hand. "How-do, ma'am?" He touched April's hand briefly.

"It's nice to meet you, Jacob."

"You, too . . . ah . . . thank you . . ." He looked at his mother for guidance. She smiled and nodded. "Where'd they go, Mama?"

"They went to get Miss Asbury's car. She got stuck in the mud up near where Joe lives."

"Shucks!"

Jacob was a dark-haired child with a sprinkling of freckles on his pale face. April noticed immediately that he was not as big as a normal six-year-old child would be. Her nurse's training kicked in, and she wondered if he'd had a serious illness.

"They'll be back soon." Eudora moved a box step over to the wash bench. "Wash up and come eat breakfast."

A misty rain was falling when Joe rode into the yard with Jack leading the mules. April went out onto the back porch.

"Where's my car? Couldn't you find it?"

"What kind of car was it?" Joe turned the horse toward the porch.

"It's a Ford coupe with a canvas top and sides. I left it right in the middle of the road."

"Maybe Daisy got tired waiting for you to

come back and took off on her own." The grin on his face was irritating.

She glared at him and mouthed. "You . . . jackass!" Then, "Where is it?"

"At the end of the lane. I'll give you a ride out when you're ready to go."

"Don't trust him, ma'am." Jack lifted his hat briefly. He turned to his brother. "She isn't so ugly that she'd make a freight train detour through the woods. I'm going to tell Pa you're lying again. Ma'am"—he turned back to April—"I'm Jack Jones, the reliable one in the family."

"He's about as reliable as snow on the Fourth of July. Blabs everything he hears," Joe snorted.

"How do you do, Mr. Jones? And thank you for rescuing my car."

"It was a pleasure, ma'am."

"If it was so pleasurable, why were you swearin' like a sailor when you were at-tachin' the chains to it?"

"Pay him no mind, Miss April. He's seein' the writin' on the wall and knows that I'm goin' to beat his time with you." Jack gave his brother a scornful look. "He just can't stand to take a backseat when there's a lady involved. He'll tell all kinds of windy stories so she'll favor him. If that don't work, he'll cheat—"

"How would you like a punch in the nose?"

"Boys! You're going to scare her off before she even gets to town." Eudora and Jacob had come out onto the porch.

"Whatcha doin', Jack? Can I go?"

"Right now I've got to rub down the mules, peanut. It's muddy out there, and you hadn't ought to be around the mules. See if your mean old Uncle Joe will give you a ride down to the barn."

Jacob giggled. "He ain't mean, Jack."

"I say he is. Now, who're you goin' to believe, me or him?"

Jacob turned his laughing little face to April. "They're funnin'."

"You'll see who's funnin' when you get up here," Joe growled. "If you don't believe me, I'll take a bite out of you."

Joe reached down and scooped the giggling child up and set him in front of him on the horse. It was easy to see that the two big men adored the boy and he them.

"I'll give you a ride down to your car when you're ready to go, Miss April. That is, if she behaves herself," he said to Jacob and walked the horse slowly to the barn.

Arriving at her new job was not as April had pictured it. Rain was coming down in sheets by the time she crossed the railroad tracks just outside of town. She drove slowly down Main Street and turned left as Joe had instructed. At the end of the block she saw the low square house with the wraparound porch. There was a sign in front, but it was raining too hard for her to read it.

She stopped the car and waited, hoping the rain would slacken. She didn't want to meet her new employer looking like a drowned cat. After a while she thought the rain had let up a bit and put on the old coat. Holding the umbrella over her head, she left the car and dashed for the porch. After shucking off her wet coat, she draped it over a chair and left the dripping umbrella beside it. After slicking her hair down with her palms, she followed the arrow to the side of the house and to the door marked OFFICE.

The small reception room was empty. Its cluttered desk faced the door, and there were two chairs and a handsome deacon's bench for patients.

"Hello. Anyone here?"

The only sound was the ticking of a large schoolhouse-type clock that hung on the wall above the bench. When the phone rang, it startled her. She looked at it sitting on the desk and waited for someone to come from the other room to answer it. After the third ring she picked it up.

"Dr. Forbes's office."

"Who're you?"

"Dr. Forbes's nurse. I've just arrived."

"This is Diane Ham, the operator. Is the doctor back?"

"There isn't anyone here."

"Then he's still out at the Barges'. Their little one has whooping cough. George Belmont, over at the creamery, cut his hand. I told him the doctor would be back by the time he got to the office. I can't reach Doc; the Barges don't have a phone."

"When Mr. Belmont gets here, I'll look at it. It may be something I can take care of."

"What did you say your name was?"

"I didn't say, but it's April Asbury. I would have been here yesterday, but I got stuck in the mud out north of town."

"If Doc calls in, I'll tell him you're here."

"Thank you."

April looked down at her soiled dress and knew that it would take a stretch of the imagination for anyone to accept her as a nurse. She hadn't dreamed that she would be starting her duties today. Even if she had, she thought now, there wasn't anything she could have done differently.

She wished that she looked more professional. She loved wearing her white starched uniform with the perky little cap perched on her head. She had worked hard to get the black stripe that circled it.

April hardly had time to look around and locate the supplies she would need when she heard heavy boot heels on the porch. The door was flung open and two men came in, water dripping off the brims of their hats. One had a towel wrapped around his hand.

"Where's Doc?"

"He isn't here. But I—"

"Dammit. Diane said he'd be here."

"Come into the surgery and let me look at your hand."

"Who are you?"

"Doc Forbes's nurse. I just arrived today."

"You don't look like a nurse."

"I would if I had my uniform on. If you want to wait, I'll go to the car and get it. I'll have to iron it before I put it on. That might take some time."

"Let her take a look, George."

"Dammit. Diane said Doc would be here," he said again.

"He was detained by a sick child with whooping cough."

"All right. Ya better know what yo're doin'."

The man, who removed his hat and dropped it on the floor beside the door and followed April into the surgery, had an unremarkable though pleasant face framed with a mop of dark unruly hair. His shoulders were broad, his arms heavily muscled, no doubt from lifting milk cans if he worked at the creamery. She motioned for him to sit down on the stool and put his arm on the examination table. While he was removing the towel, she scrubbed her hands at the chipped sink that had been installed in the corner of the room.

"Holy cow!" April exclaimed when she looked at the palm of his hand and the deep cut that reached from the base of his thumb to the base of his little finger. "That's a devil of a cut."

"Ya ain't tellin' me nothin'. It hurts like a sonofabitch." He peered into the face bent over his hand. "Ain't ya a bit young to be a nurse? Nurses ain't supposed to be young and pretty."

"How are they supposed to be?"

"Old and ugly and mean. Not . . . like you."

"Are you flirting with me, George?"

"Naw. Ah . . . dammit to hell!" He swore when she poured antiseptic on the wound.

"This will need stitches. Do you want me to do it, or do you want to wait for Doc Forbes?"

"Have ya ever done it before?"

"I worked for six months in the emergency room of a hospital located in a rough part of Kansas City. I've seen fingers torn off, stab wounds, patches of hair pulled from the scalp and noses bitten off. Course, I couldn't do anything about that. I've sewn ears back on, George. This little old cut is a piece of cake. But I've got to warn you. It'll hurt like a son of a gun."

"Wal, if a skinny little thing like you can do it, I guess I can take it."

She looked at him seriously. "Do you prefer plain or fancy stitching?" She cocked a brow as she waited for his answer.

"Any way ya want to go, honey. As long as I can take ya to the show Saturday night."

"Shucks, George. You're number eight on my list for Saturday night. If the seven before you chicken out, I'll call you. How's that?"

"It's a deal. Fix me up so I can play in the horseshoe tournament Sunday next. You'll not turn down the chance to go out with a champion." He winked at her.

April gathered the supplies she would need and sat down on a stool across from George.

"I pitch a mean game of horseshoes myself," she said as she began the stitches that would close the wound. "Where do you play?"

"Over by the baseball diamond. When we pitch here, there's usually quite a crowd." George gritted his teeth and looked out the window.

"I used to play with my grandpa and some of his friends on Sunday afternoons. I've been known to get five ringers in a row."

"You're kiddin'! I'd like to see that." She had his interest now.

"Maybe I'll stroll down to the park, watch your game and give you a few pointers."

"Horseshoes and baseball are big around here. I don't suppose you play ball?"

"Just in school. Do they have a women's softball team here?"

"Naw."

She looked up to see that sweat had broken out on his forehead. His jaws were clenched, and he kept his head turned away from her. April worked fast. She'd had big men faint while she was stitching them up. She clipped the last stitch and stood up.

"I don't think you should pitch horseshoes for a while. I'll be mad as sin if you ruin my pretty stitches."

"How about teamin' up sometime?"

"I'll have to see how good you are before I commit to being your partner. I've got one more thing to do here." She reached for the bottle of iodine. "It's going to hurt like a—"

"—sonofabitch."

"I wasn't going to say that, but it's all right if it makes you feel better."

The door to the outer office opened. April

heard a male voice speak to the man who waited for George.

"Howdy."

"Howdy, Doc."

"Come take a look, Dr. Forbes." April looked up as Doc came into the surgery. "And reassure George these are the best-looking stitches he'll ever have." She spoke as if it hadn't been almost a year since she'd seen him.

Doc set his bag down and looked at the hand that lay on the table.

"Fancy. R-red thread?"

"I couldn't find any. I had to dye it with iodine."

"That's a s-sneaky way of getting out of playing in the tournament, George. You kn-knew I'd win."

"Horse hockey, Doc. I could beat ya pitchin' with my left hand."

"What're ya betting?"

"A hind quarter of venison against the delivery of my first kid."

"Hell, George. You're n-not even married."

"What's that got to do with it?"

April finished with the bandage and busied herself putting away the supplies.

"Better come back in a couple d-days, George, and let me take a look at that."

"Ma'am, are ya sure ya won't go out with me Saturday night?"

"I'll put your name on the list. Thank you for asking me."

As soon as the door closed behind the two men, April smiled and held out her hand.

"It's good to see you, Doctor."

"I'm glad you're here, Miss Asbury. Joe came by last night and told me that you'd be here s-sometime this morning."

"I became stuck in the mud up by his place yesterday afternoon. He and his brother pulled my car out this morning. I need to find a place to stay."

"I've got a couple s-suggestions. There's the hotel. Nice big airy rooms. They'll give you a weekly rate, b-but it'll still cost more than living in a p-private home. Mrs. Poole has a large r-room and will give you break-fast and supper for f-four dollars a week. She and her brother run the hardware s-store."

"I prefer to stay in a private home where I will have a place to wash and iron my uni-forms."

"My laundry is d-done by Mrs. Bloom. She also w-washes for the surgery twice a week."

"It would be a luxury to have my uniforms laundered, but I'm afraid I can't afford it right now. Would Mrs. Poole allow me to do my washing there?"

"She'll be at the h-hardware store. Phone and ask her."

"If she will allow me to use the washing facilities, I'll go look at the room."

Chapter 4

The room was big, square and airy. The hardwood floor gleamed, yet the place was cozy and feminine, with twining roses on the wallpaper and an embroidered scarf on the walnut dresser. The white bedspread and pillow shams were also embroidered and edged with crocheted lace. The bed was a heavy four-poster with a thick mattress. April moved aside the white starched curtains and looked down on the backyard and a small, neat vegetable garden.

"The bathroom is across the hall between my room and the storage room." Mrs. Poole spoke from the doorway. "The hot-water heater is there. You'll need to light it a half hour before you take a bath."

April smiled at the woman who had seldom taken her eyes off her since she came into the house.

"I'll bring my things in."

"You'll take it?" Mrs. Poole seemed surprised.

"Yes. I think I'll be very comfortable here."

"Fred will be here in a few minutes. Fred is my brother. He lives here with me. He'll bring in your things."

"May I borrow your ironing board? I have to iron a uniform for tomorrow. I have my own iron, and I'll get a board as soon as I can go uptown."

"No need for that. You're welcome to use mine."

"Washing and ironing uniforms is a never-ending job. I usually keep the ironing board set up in my room all the time."

Mrs. Poole nodded. "We have supper after Fred closes the store at six. Saturday nights we're open until nine, and I take Fred's supper to him or go stay at the store while he comes home to eat."

"I'm sure there will be times when I'll not be here at six, and I won't know until the last minute."

"In that case, I'll set your supper aside."

When April returned to the car after carrying a few of her belongings up to her room, she saw a man hurrying down the street toward her.

"Miss? Miss Asbury? Here, let me help you."

On hearing her name, April turned to look at the man who must be the brother Mrs. Poole spoke about. He was a plump man with a broad, clean-shaven face. He wore a white shirt, bow tie and a dark felt hat.

"Fred Hazelton." He held out his hand. "I'm Mrs. Poole's brother. She called to say that you'd taken the room. It will be a pleasure to have you staying with us."

"I don't know how long I'll be here. It will depend on my job here with Dr. Forbes."

"Of course. Let me help you with these boxes."

"Some are quite heavy. I had to bring everything I own simply because I didn't have any place to leave it."

Even though Fred insisted he was used to carrying heavy things at the hardware, he was sweating by the time everything had been carried up the stairs to April's room.

"Thank you, Mr. Hazelton."

"You're very welcome. But call me Fred . . . please."

"Fred," Mrs. Poole called from the bottom of the stairs. "Tell Miss Asbury dinner is ready anytime she is."

"I suppose you heard that," Fred said with a chuckle. "I'm glad you're here, Miss Asbury. My sister needs a pretty young woman around. She hasn't been herself since her husband was killed. She thought the sun rose and set on him."

"How long has it been?"

"Hmmm . . . let me see. Back in '23. That's when I came here to help her with the store. It was a terrible accident. He fell from his horse. It became frightened and stomped him."

"How awful for her."

"She could have had gentlemen friends, but she discouraged their attentions."

The only time Fred took his eyes off April was when he scanned the room. He sucked his lower lip between his teeth as he backed out the door.

She was just too beautiful for words! Oh, God! Oh, God! He could hardly wait.

"Thank you again, Fred," April called.

"See you downstairs . . . April."

*   *   *

During the week that followed, April took up her duties with Dr. Forbes as if she had been doing them for years. She seemed to anticipate his needs, and they worked together as if they were extensions of each other: setting a broken leg, sewing up gashes brought on by a knife fight down in Shanty Town, bringing down a baby's fever when the child was about to go into convulsions.

Twice she had been unable to eat supper with Mrs. Poole and Fred because patients had come in just as the office was closing for the day. She had gone back to the rooming house to find a cloth-covered plate of food on the table. After she had turned down Fred's invitations, first to stay downstairs and listen to the radio, then to play cards, he had ceased to ask. April wasn't sure that she liked him. She knew that he was harmless, yet his solicitations made her nervous.

Dr. Forbes introduced her to tall, gaunt Frank Adler, the druggist and one of Doc's best friends. At his pharmacy she met one of the two town attorneys, Harold Dozier, who was a well-dressed man with faultless manners. He was single, Doc pointed out on the way back to the office, and owned several houses in town.

"I think he liked what he saw," Doc said. "I'd be surprised if he didn't come calling."

The parade of women coming by the office to look her over was a source of amusement to both her and the doctor.

"Why was she reminding you of the church supper?" April asked after one of the ladies had left. "It's three weeks away according to the note on your calendar."

Doc lifted his shoulders in a shrug.

"At least she had an excuse," April continued. "One came in yesterday and, after hemming and hawing, finally got around to asking me if I was married or engaged."

"Did she leave a pie or s-something?"

"Dr. Todd Forbes! You're spoiled."

"Yeah, I am. I guess—"

He cut off his words when the door opened. A tall, lean man came into the office. He removed his hat, revealing thick dark hair. It was hard not to notice the scar that sliced across one eyebrow onto his cheek. It showed a pale, threadlike line through his summer tan.

"Howdy, Corbin. You sick?"

"Naw. Sorry to disappoint you."

"Damn. None of my so-called friends ever get s-sick anymore. How am I goin' to make ends meet if m-my friends don't give me their business?"

Corbin shook his head and grinned. "I hear this every time I come in here." He extended his hand to April. "I'm Corbin Appleby, ma'am. Welcome to Fertile."

She placed her hand in his. "April Asbury. I'm glad to be here."

"Corbin was the police officer here until he got to be as c-crooked as the crooks. Now he owns the r-rag he calls a news-paper."

"You see why I'm not going to get sick and let him get his hands in my pockets?"

Affection between the two men showed in their ability to tease each other.

"I'm here to get a story about your new nurse, Doc. I might even put her picture on the front page."

"Paint a mustache on her. I'm afraid she's going to dry up the supply of c-cakes and pies the ladies bring me."

"So that's what's causing that little pot-belly."

"Smart mouth," Doc snorted. "I don't

have a potbelly and you know it. Go ahead and interview my nurse. But first, how's Annabel?"

"She complains of a backache once in a while."

"During this last month she's not to be lifting Murphy."

"I've already told her. Our son is two and a half," Corbin explained to April.

"A good-sized boy for his age," Doc added.

"Are you wishing for a girl this time?"

"I'll take whatever I get and pray that it's healthy and my wife comes through it all right."

"As I've told you before—women have been h-havin' babies for y-years now. You're as bad as an old woman when it comes to w-worrying."

"Boone will bring Tess over in a week or two to stay until after the baby comes. Tess was my wife's neighbor when she lived over by the big river." Corbin explained this to April while he was setting up his camera to take her picture.

When the picture was taken and the interview over, Corbin told Doc that the job of town police officer was going to be open in a few weeks.

"The council firing Burkhardt?"

"He got a job as a guard down at the state prison."

"Will they b-bring in an outsider like they d-did when they hired you?"

"They need a man with experience."

"You interested in the job?"

"No. I promised my wife I'd stay out of law enforcement. I would help train a man if it came to that."

"How about Jack Jones?"

"No one thinks more of Jack than I do. But he's been hitting the bottle pretty heavy lately."

"If he had a purpose in life, he m-might not."

"He's local. That's in his favor, but I don't know if I could talk the city council into hiring him."

"How about This or That Humphrey?"

"Too young."

"How about Joe?"

"He might take it for a while, but we need a man who wants to make law enforcement a career. Joe wants to raise cattle. Have you seen the bull he's got out at his place?"

"I have," April said. "He calls him Rolling Thunder."

"April was s-stuck in the mud out by Joe's when she first came to t-town."

"If you had to get stuck, you couldn't have chosen a better place."

"That's what *he* said." April's eyes were twinkling. "He's not lacking in confidence."

Corbin smiled. "Wait until you see him and Thad Taylor together. They'd put Amos and Andy to shame."

"Thad is married to Joe's sister," Doc explained to April.

"I hope you like it here and stay, Miss Asbury. We need someone to keep Doc on his toes."

"I plan to stay as long as he wants me. I've burned my bridges behind me, so to speak."

After Corbin had left, Doc picked up his bag. "I'll be gone for an hour or two if anyone asks for me." He was out the door before she could ask any questions.

April didn't have time to think about Doc's sudden departure. As he left, George Belmont came into the office.

"Where's Doc goin'?"

"Didn't say. Come into the surgery and let me look at your hand." George pulled his hand out of his pocket and followed her. He sat down and placed it on the table. April brought supplies from the cabinet and looked closely at the wound. "Stitches are ready to come out." She was surprised when he withdrew his hand from her touch.

"Not until you say you'll go to the picture show with me tonight." He grinned cockily. She had already noticed that he had recently shaved and was wearing a clean shirt.

"That's blackmail," she said with pretended shock.

"Yeah."

"I don't buy it. Give me that hand, or I'll give you a shot that will lay you low for a week."

"You'd do that?"

"You can bet your boots I would. I put those stitches in and I'm taking them out."

"I don't suppose you'll come to the ballpark and watch me pitch in the tournament?"

"You're not pitching with this hand, George. If I catch you, I'll take a willow switch to your backside." April continued to talk while she snipped the stitches and pulled them out with the tweezers. "I thought a grown man would have more sense than to try to pitch horseshoes not more than a week after he almost sliced his hand in two."

A smile spread across George's face. It delighted him to have this pretty young woman fuss over him. Lord, he knew that he didn't have a chance with her, but the fellow who did would be a lucky son of a gun.

"Be careful and don't pop open that cut, because if I have to stitch it again, I'll use the dullest needle I can find."

"What do I owe you?"

"One dollar. Stop back in a day or two."

"You wantin' to see me again, little sweetie?"

"Of course. You're the cutest thing I've seen in a mighty long time. I just love your big blue eyes." She batted her lashes at him.

"They ain't blue. They're brown."

"Oh, so they are. I guess I've got you mixed up with the man who cut his foot."

George was laughing and shaking his head when he left the office.

* * *

Dr. Forbes was thankful he had made his escape without having to tell Nurse Asbury where he was going. He could have made up some lame excuse about somebody being sick or injured, but sooner or later the lie would have caught up with him.

I hate the lying, pretense and conniving . . . but dear God, what else can I do?

He drove to the edge of town and then turned north on the river road, relieved that it was hard-packed clay and the rainwater had run off into the ditch alongside it. The road was slick but passable. He had driven on it under these conditions before. He drove slowly and carefully until he reached the lane leading to the house. Then he pulled the car onto it just far enough to park it off the road.

With a large paper sack in one arm, Doc walked along the grassy edge of the lane to the house that sat amid a thick group of tall pines. It was a small cabin with a cobblestone chimney. Flowers were planted in a round bed in front, and pots of flowers lined the steps leading to the porch. White curtains fluttered at the windows.

The door opened while he was toeing off

his muddy shoes. A slim young woman stood there. Doc sucked in a deep breath, and his heartbeat picked up speed. She wore a faded gingham dress and, on a face the color of ripened wheat, a broad smile of welcome. Her features were delicate and her amber eyes large, clear and shining. Thick dark hair was held back from her face with a ribbon.

Doc stood there, his eyes devouring her face, for a full minute before he breathed, "Caroline. Oh, Caroline . . ."

Chapter 5

"If it doesn't stop raining, it'll be Christmas before we get the corn out of the field."

Joe sat at the table in his sister's kitchen holding her year-old daughter on his lap while she cooked the noon meal.

"I remember the year when we had to leave it until after Christmas. Papa was afraid it was too wet and would grow mold." Julie stopped by to wipe the drool from the baby's chin.

"That year we picked just enough for seed and had to dry it on corn dryers hung in the barn loft. We let the hogs and cows eat out of the field. Had a nice fat deer around Christmastime."

"Evan said we might as well feed it this year. A bushel of corn won't be worth much. Wheat is twenty-five cents a bushel. Oats only ten cents. Thank goodness we're not cotton farmers. They're only getting five cents a pound."

"Beef and hog prices are so low that some fool suggested the government go around to the farms, pay a measly price for the animals, then kill and bury them in order to bring up the price."

"Evan told me about that. He doesn't think Roosevelt will do it, although he's determined to bring the country out of this slump."

"He has his work cut out for him. Twenty-five percent of the workforce is unemployed. A man would have to sell nine bushels of wheat just to buy a pair of boots."

"We're lucky, Joe, that we live here on a farm that's paid for. We'll at least have plenty to eat."

"Yeah, but unless prices come up, banks will be taking over those that have mortgages." Joe held his niece up and away from him. "Hell and damnation, Nancy Ann Johnson! You've wet a bucketful."

Julie laughed. "When she lets go, it's a stream. Don't worry, you'll dry."

"These are my next to good pants."

"Going somewhere? I thought you'd come to spend the day."

"I'm going to town," he growled.

"Can I go, Joe?" The voice was followed by the slamming of the door leading to the rooms upstairs.

"Hello, brat."

"Cleaning done already?" Julie asked.

"All but changing the beds." Joy set the bucket of cleaning supplies on the floor and leaned the broom against the wall. "I'll have it done before dinner. Can I go to town with you, Joe?"

Sixteen-year-old Joy Jones, the youngest of the Jones children, had gone to live with Julie and Evan when they married. Julie had taken care of the girl since the day she was born and was the only mother Joy had ever known. She was a small, slim girl with a mass of blond curls and large blue-green eyes. She had been doted on since birth, but Julie had tried hard to keep her from being spoiled by her older brothers and sister.

"Honey, I'm going horseback."

"I don't mind. We could walk. We walked to town before we got a car."

"You'd be in mud up to your knees. Besides, I might want to stay in town tonight."

"Well, shoot!"

"Do you have books to return to the library? You should have told Evan—"

"I want to see Mrs. Poole."

"Whatever for?" Julie wiped her hands on her apron and lifted Nancy from Joe's lap.

"She's helping with the Y.P. harvest party. I'm on the committee, and I've got a fantastic idea I want to tell her about."

"The young people at the church," Julie explained to Joe when he lifted his brows in question. "Joy, you didn't tell me that you were on the committee or that Mrs. Poole was in charge. I thought Opal Patterson was."

"Mrs. Patterson had to bow out for some reason or other. When Mrs. Poole took over, she chose me, Sammy Davidson, Richard Myers and Evelyn Bradbury to be on the committee. Sylvia wanted to be on it, but Mrs. Poole chose Evelyn, who doesn't know anything about parties."

"I take it you do?" Joe teased.

"I know more than a twelve-year-old. Sylvia and I can't figure out why she wanted Evelyn to help her plan the party."

"I didn't know that Sammy Davidson

went to our church." Julie pulled a clean
diaper from the clothes basket.

"He does now." Joy batted her eyelashes
coyly.

"Our little sister is out recruiting for the
Lord." Joe threw his arm around the girl,
whose head came only to his shoulder. Joy
wrapped her arms around his waist.

"You'll take me to town?"

"Sneaky little brat!" He kissed the top of
her head. "Who are you meeting in town?"

"Who knows? It's Saturday."

"You might cramp my style, brat."

"You're seeing a girl?"

"Maybe."

"Dr. Forbes's new nurse? Eudora said she
was a beaut."

"Eudora was right. She's a beaut and
smarter than a roomful of lawyers."

"Then she's too smart to have anything to
do with an old clodhopper like you." Joy
pushed herself away from Joe and out of
his reach.

"Hey, watch it. You just asked me for a
favor."

"You said no. Didn't you?"

"I was fixing to say it was up to Julie."

Joy hurried to hug him again. "Oh, in that

case, nice brother, sweet brother, handsome brother—"

"Imp!" Joe held her away from him.

Having changed Nancy's diaper, Julie dropped it in the pail of water beside the washstand and handed her daughter back to Joe.

"All right, kid, don't you dare wet on my dry knee," Joe growled at the baby, then softened his words by nuzzling his nose in her soft hair.

"I don't mind you going to town, Joy, but Joe doesn't want to ride herd on you all day." Julie returned to a pot on the stove and poked the potatoes with a two-tined fork.

"I'll stash her someplace until I'm ready to come back," Joe said.

"You're not to go wandering all over town." Julie's voice was stern when she spoke to Joy.

"Sylvia is going to the library. I'll meet her there."

"Honey, I doubt if the Taylors will go to town today. The roads are too muddy."

"They'll go in the wagon."

"All right. But Joe, you're to keep an eye on her. Toughs from the river dives come uptown on Saturday. Oh, dear, what if it storms?"

"You're a first-class worrier, Sis. I'll take care of little sister. If she gets feisty, I'll flip up her skirts and tan her behind."

"Thanks, Joe. You're the sweetest brother in the whole wide world. I've got to finish upstairs." Joy kissed him soundly on the cheek and fled.

Julie turned. Her hands were folded in her apron. "You know how dear she is to me, Joe."

"I know, but you're going to have to give her some slack. She's got a good head. She's growing up and feeling her oats."

"I know what it feels like to be sixteen, full of enthusiasm, with the world waiting to be explored. Her dreams can be shattered, her life turned upside down in a second. I don't want that to happen to her. I want her to experience all the stages of growing up, falling in love, marrying and having a family."

"You did that, Sis."

"But it was a long hard road, Joe," Julie said sadly. "I really never thought it would happen. At times I have to pinch myself. I have a wonderful, loving husband. We have two healthy children and I have Joy with me.

Jill is wildly in love with Thad. Jason is doing well and Papa is happy. I wish you and Jack would find someone to love and settle down."

"Sis, you're a romantic at heart. Love as you see it doesn't happen for everyone."

"I'm surprised that Shirley Poole is working with the young people." Julie switched the conversation because she was near tears. "She's always been so standoffish. I never dreamed that she'd be interested in doing anything with the church young people. I don't think I've ever heard the woman laugh."

They both glanced toward the door at the sound of heavy steps on the porch. Through the screen they could see Evan removing his boots.

"Howdy, Joe," he said when he came into the kitchen, but his eyes sought his wife. "Before you ask, sweetheart, I didn't forget to get the spool of thread." He reached into his pocket, then hesitated. "You did say number forty? Black?"

"Evan Johnson, I said number fifty white and you know it." She put her hand in his pocket. His hand held it there when he bent to kiss her, then allowed her to pull the package out. She peeked inside, then pinched his arm. "You stinker, you're a bigger tease than my brothers."

"What's for dinner?"

"Sauerkraut!"

"Sauerkraut?" He grasped his wife's shoulders and held her away from him. "Tell me she's just getting even with me, Joe. She knows I hate sauerkraut."

"We're having corned beef pie, if you ever turn loose of me so I can put the crust on top and get it into the oven."

"My favorite. I've trained her right, Joe." Evan plucked his daughter off Joe's lap and held her up over his head. "How's my little dumpling?"

"Better watch it. She'll drool on you." Joe stood up and shook the wet spot on his pants. "Water comes out of that kid from both ends."

"Did you wet on your Uncle Joe?" Evan crooned to the baby. "Good girl. Don't worry about his growl. He likes to growl about something."

"Did you go by Papa's?" Julie asked after Evan had sat down. "I thought you'd bring Logan home with you."

"He and Jacob were building a house out

of cardboard boxes right in the middle of the kitchen floor. They were having so much fun I couldn't take him away until they finished their project. I'll go back over this afternoon and bring him home."

"How was Jacob?"

"He's still pale, but getting his strength back. He was holding his own with Logan."

"Typhoid almost killed him. I was afraid he'd never come out of it." Julie filled the coffeepot from the teakettle on the stove. "But Eudora never lost faith. She said that God wouldn't be so cruel as to take him when she had waited so long to have him."

"I picked up some news in town." Evan bounced his daughter on his knee. "The city council is looking to hire a new police officer."

"Yeah? What happened to Burkhardt?" Joe asked.

"I hear he's put in for a job as guard at the state pen."

"I hope he works harder there than he did here. He's not the officer that Corbin was. The saloons down in Shanty Town are almost wide-open."

"Corbin will recommend Jack for the job."

"Jack?" Julie set the bowl of potatoes

on the table. "Jack doesn't know anything about law enforcement."

"Corbin volunteered to train him, mother hen." Evan winked at Joe.

"What do you think, Joe?" Julie asked.

"Corbin recommending him and Jack getting the job are two different things. But if he got it and Corbin trained him, he would be a damn good officer. One thing about our brother is that when he takes on something, he goes into it whole hog. If the town hires him, they won't be shortchanged."

"I don't know—he'd have to carry a gun." Julie went back to the stove. "Papa needs him—"

"Papa doesn't need him and Jack knows it. He needs to do something that will make him feel worthwhile. He can't mourn the rest of his life because his baseball career didn't pan out."

"I told Corbin that I'd speak to a couple of the councilmen on Jack's behalf. He's concerned about Jack's drinking lately."

"He isn't the only one," Joe said. "Jack drinks because he's at loose ends. He needs something to work for. He's been drinking more since he broke up with Ruby."

"Corbin asked me to talk to him and see

if he's interested." Evan looked at his wife to get her reaction. She was busy at the stove. "I'll do that when I go over to get Logan."

"Jobs are pretty hard to get. He'd be a fool not to go for it. Everyone thinks this depression will get worse before it gets better."

"Would *you* take the job if it was offered?" Evan asked Joe.

"I'd have to think about it. I've got my money tied up in the bull and the land I bought with Thad. Jack needs the job more than I do. He talked about going into the army, or into one of the work projects Roosevelt talked about while he was running for office. But it'll be a year before a government project gets off the ground."

"Evan, put Nancy in the high chair. Joe, call Joy to come down for dinner, and you men wash up."

"Yes, ma'am." Joe headed for the wash bench.

After putting the baby in the chair, Evan grabbed his wife around the waist and kissed her.

"Evan . . ."

"Stop worrying, little mother hen. Jack

can handle himself. He's not a kid anymore."

"Joe, stop!" Joy clutched her brother's
arm. "I'll get off here."

"I'll take you on downtown, honey, and let
you off by the drugstore." Joe loved teasing
his little sister. He always got a rise out of
her. She didn't disappoint him.

"Don't you dare!" Joy screeched. "Stop
this horse. I'm not riding into town on a
horse. Stop and let me down."

"Why? Are you ashamed of my horse?
He's not swaybacked. He's got good teeth."

"Please. Stop teasing and let me get
down."

"Well, if that don't beat all. You're just getting too uppity for words." Joe pulled to a
stop, got down, lifted his sister off the horse
and walked beside her.

"My . . . skirt was up over my knees."

"So what? You're just a kid. Nobody
would notice."

"I'm not just a kid. There would be plenty
to notice. Some girls my age are already engaged to be married."

"You thinking on getting married?" Joe
looked down at her. She was very pretty,

and in a couple of years she'd have her pick of the men in town. But he wasn't going to tell her that now.

"Silly. You know I'm not."

They crossed the railroad tracks and turned toward the feedstore, where Joe would leave his horse in a pen.

"I'll go on down to the hardware store and see Mrs. Poole."

"Hold on. I'll go with you." Joe removed the saddle and carried it to a lean-to shed.

Joy stamped her foot in frustration as soon as her brother's back was turned.

"I know the way. You don't have to come with me."

"I'll go with you to see Mrs. Poole, then take you to the library, where you'll stay until I come back for you."

Joy began to panic. How was she going to keep Joe from knowing that wanting to see Mrs. Poole was just an excuse to get to town? Oh, Lord, what if he stayed to hear her suggestions for the harvest party?

Think. I have to think of something.

She had a moment of relief when they entered the store and Fred said his sister was at home.

"Business is slow. Not many people coming to town because of the muddy roads."

"Is the river still rising?"

"It's leveled off, they say. Let's hope they don't have a lot of rain north of us. It wouldn't take much to bring her up and over the banks."

"Come on, Sis. We'll walk over to the house. See ya, Fred."

"You don't have to come."

"Are you trying to get rid of me?" Joe asked as they left the store.

"You make me feel like a baby."

"You are a baby. My baby sister. If I see a boy eyeing you, I'm going to knock his teeth out."

"You wouldn't!" Joy raised fearful eyes to her brother's face and saw his teasing grin. "You . . . polecat. You make me so mad!"

They walked the rest of the way in silence.

When Mrs. Poole came to the door, she looked first at Joy, then at Joe, who stood behind her. An expression of near fright came over her face.

"Hello, Mrs. Poole." Joy's voice trembled.

"Howdy, ma'am."

When the woman said nothing, Joy said,

"I thought of a few things we could do at the harvest party and wanted to tell you about them if you're not busy."

"Oh . . ." Mrs. Poole opened the screen door. "Come in."

Joe said, to Joy's relief, "I'll wait here on the porch."

"You're welcome to come in," Mrs. Poole said.

"That porch swing looks inviting. Take your time, honey. I'll be here."

"My brothers think that I'm such a baby," Joy explained when she and Mrs. Poole were alone.

"My brother thought the same about me when we were growing up. But we know better, don't we? I can tell that you are a very levelheaded young lady, and your brothers will have to realize that you can make some decisions for yourself. Come into the parlor, Joy. This is a rare treat for me to have a young lady call on me."

"My suggestions may not be worth much."

"I'm sure they will be a help. I've never planned a party for young people. I need all the help I can get. Sit down, my dear."

"What do you think about having the girls

bring box lunches and the boys throwing apples? The one who throws the farthest gets to choose first and so on."

"I don't know, dear. There are more girls than boys."

"Golly. I hadn't thought of that."

"We'll be going on a hayrack ride. Afterward we'll have a bonfire and roast marshmallows. Mr. Oakley, at the store, has already promised to furnish them."

Shirley's eyes searched every feature of the girl's face and carefully noticed the way she tilted her head of blond curls. *She could have been mine. It's not fair!*

"We need to plan games, Joy. Can you stop in after school one day?"

"It's hard for me to stop after school. Either Julie or Evan comes for me, or I ride with Sylvia's folks. I could come on Saturday."

"That will be fine. Plan to spend the afternoon. We'll put our heads together to make this the best harvest party the church has ever had. Maybe you and I could make cookies for the party."

"That would be fun, Mrs. Poole." When Joy stood, Shirley moved close and put her arm across her shoulders.

"It's been a treat for me to have you visit. Come anytime you're in town."

"Is the doctor's new nurse staying here?"

"Yes, but she's busy and I don't see much of her." They had reached the door, and before Joy could push it open, Shirley said, "I'm so glad you came, Joy. I'd like for us to be friends."

"I'd like that, too, Mrs. Poole. Good-bye."

Joe was waiting, and they walked down the steps to the street before he spoke.

"Well, how did it go?"

"She's nice. She invited me to come back anytime."

"Did she, now?"

"What do you mean by that? She said that I've got a level head and should be able to make some decisions for myself."

"Did she, now?"

"Stop saying that, Joe. I like her. She talks to me like I'm an adult. I'm going back there next Saturday so we can plan the games."

"Plan games, huh?"

"And make cookies."

"Uh-huh. Where to now?"

"Library, but I'd rather go to the show." They were passing the theater, and Joy stopped to look at the billboards. "Oh, look,

Joe. *Tarzan, the Ape Man* is playing." She stared in awe at the near-naked Johnny Weissmuller perched on the limb of a tree.

"You can't go to the show and leave Sylvia waiting at the library."

Joy looked up at her brother, her lower lip clenched between her teeth.

"She may not be there. It's so... muddy."

"She *won't* be there." Joe spoke even as the thought came to him. "You lied to Julie."

"No! Sylvia didn't say for sure. She was going to try to come in with her father when he came in to see Mr. Oakley. If she did, she was going to wait for me at the library."

"Come on. We'll see if she's there."

"And if she isn't, you'll take me to the show?"

"I've got more important things to do than to watch a near-naked man swing through the trees."

"I bet if it was a near-naked girl, you'd find the time to watch," Joy grumbled and hurried to catch up with her brother.

Chapter 6

Jack strained to help Corbin Appleby transfer the heavy roll of newsprint to the press and set it in place. In the back room of the *Fertile Sentinel* the air was heavy with the odor of melting lead, ink and cigarette smoke from the man at the linotype machine setting copy for the Tuesday edition.

"That son of a gun is heavy." Jack raised his voice in order to be heard over the sound of the machine.

"That's the God's truth." Corbin wiped his forehead with the sleeve of his shirt. "Thanks. Come on up front where we can talk without having to shout." He paused beside the man at the linotype and waited for him to complete a line of lead and drop it in place before he spoke. "That's the last to be set today. When you finish, you can start tearing down pages." The man nodded, and Corbin led Jack to the office.

"I'm obliged for the help." Corbin sat in a rolling chair behind a cluttered desk.

Jack shrugged. "I'm getting damn tired of this rain. Not much to do at the farm until it dries up a bit."

"I was down looking at the river this morning. I've not seen it this high. It won't take much more for it to go over the banks."

"It flooded once back during the war. It took out a lot of shacks and came up past Main Street. There's a high-water mark on the corner of the bank building."

"I've seen it." Corbin leaned back in his chair. "Just west of here they're having droughts. Figure that out."

"Too much rain is about as bad as not enough."

Both men knew they were making small talk leading up to the real reason why Corbin stopped his work and brought Jack to the office.

"Did Evan talk to you about the police job?"

"Yeah, I've been thinking I'd like to have a go at it if you think I can do the job."

"Jobs are few and far between nowadays. As soon as word gets out, there'll be fifty men here applying for it."

"Do I have a chance?"

"Better than most. You've got me and Evan rooting for you, and I think Doc will put in a good word, but your carousing the last few months may go against you." Corbin's level gaze held Jack's.

"I've been at loose ends lately." Jack's voice was neither apologetic nor defensive. It was a mere statement.

"A man is usually judged by the way he handles the rough hands he's dealt."

"And I've failed the test?"

"Not yet."

Jack's pride was pricked. "If you think I can't cut the mustard, don't recommend me. I sure as hell would hate to put you, Evan and Doc in a bad light."

"I wouldn't put my neck out if I didn't think you'd make a good officer. I'm willing to put my reputation and my years of law enforcement experience on the line and help train you. The mayor asked me to help them find a good man because I was an officer here at one time."

Jack grew still. His eyes held those of his friend as he remembered the day Corbin had told him a minor-league baseball team was coming to town to play the locals and that he was good enough to play on the Fertile team.

The man looking so steadily back at him had played an important role in his life. There was not another man outside his family whom he respected more.

"I'll not let you down." His voice was hoarse.

"I never thought for a minute that you would, once you decided that this was something you wanted to do. Now we've got to work at getting you the job."

For the next hour Corbin talked about his own training to be a military policeman while he was in the army, his service in France, coming to Fertile and the problems he'd had with one of the council members.

"Most of it boils down, Jack, to using good old common horse sense. You'll run into situations where there are no set guidelines, and you'll have to do what you think is best. Personal likes and dislikes must be put aside. A hothead has no business in law enforcement. There will be times when you will be so angry you'll want to bash in a head, but you must hold your temper and do what the law requires. Other times a good friend of yours might be breaking the law, and it would be easy for you to look the other way. You must do your duty as a police officer regardless of who is doing the wrong thing."

"I have a lot to learn."

Corbin placed two books on the desk. "Study these books. If Evan and I are successful in getting you an interview with the city council, you'll be halfway prepared for some of the questions they'll ask you.

"Now you'd better get over and see Annabel and Murphy. She's been complaining that you've not been around much lately."

A smile lightened Jack's face. "When's the baby due?"

"Pretty soon now. In a day or two I'm going to tie Doc's leg to the post on my porch."

Jack laughed. "He said that you were a pain in the butt when Murphy was born. I think he called you an *id-idiot*."

"Wait until his wife has a baby and we'll see how he acts." Corbin stood. "I'll keep in touch and let you know how things are going. There's one man on the council that's against anything I'm for, but he's on good terms with Evan. I'll let Evan handle him."

In spite of the cloudy day, the world seemed brighter when Jack left Corbin's office. He wondered what Ruby May would think about his being a policeman. He had always thought that someday he and Ruby would be married. They had known each other since before they started school. But, hell, he didn't have anything to offer her now; they'd have to live in the house with his pa and Eudora. He couldn't ask her to give up her teaching job for that.

She'd gone out twice, that he knew of, with that smart aleck who worked for the electric company. The man's wife hadn't been cold in the ground before he was out looking around. Ruby was smart. But was she smart enough to see that what he wanted was a woman to take care of his kids? She'd not fall for that smooth-talking lineman even if he did have a house and a good job.

But oh, God. What if she did?

"Well, for goodness' sake!" April sat at the desk with Doc's ledger open in front of her and struggled to read some of the scribbling he'd made during the weeks before she arrived. She figured that HC stood for house call and OC was for office call.

OC Tim M. pain pills   1.00
HC Little Phillips girl sore throat   1.00
OC cash   .50

April ran her finger down the list. There were very few charges for more than a dollar and very few notations identifying the treatment. Only occasionally was there a date beside the entry and no indication that any of the patients had paid for his services.

A half hour later, still trying to figure out Doc's strange bookkeeping, she looked up as the door opened and Joe Jones stepped inside.

"You're still here." His words surprised her.

"Didn't you expect me to be?"

"Wasn't sure. I thought Doc's ladies might have scared you off."

"Laws," she snorted. "It would take more than a few jealous cats to run me off. He's in the house if you want to see him."

"I don't. I'd rather talk to you."

She put her pencil down and folded her arms. "Go ahead. Talk."

"How do you keep that cap perched on top of your head?"

"Bobby pins."

"How do you keep that uniform looking as crisp and new as a two-dollar bill?"

"Wash, starch and iron. In that order."

"You look damn fetching in it."

"Thanks. Anything else?" She tried not to smile at him and failed miserably.

"Can't you say something nice about me?"

"Give me a day or two and I'll think of something."

His eyes were warm and friendly, and with that devilish grin on his face he was sinfully handsome. He stood with his booted feet spread, his hands in his back pockets.

"How's Daisy?"

Her mouth opened, then closed before she said seriously, "The last time I saw her she was still sitting beside Mrs. Poole's house trying to shake the wet leaves off her hat."

"She's a tough old bird."

"That she is."

"Will you go to the picture show with me tonight?"

"Well, I don't know. Are you trustworthy?"

"A pillar of the community."

"Seems like I've heard that somewhere before."

"It's true. I'll swear on a stack of Bibles."

The screen door opened and Jack stepped into the office. April hadn't even heard him cross the porch.

"Watch what you're swearin' to," he growled at his brother.

"What're you doin' here?"

"Come to ask Miss April to the picture show."

"You're too late. I've already asked her. Besides, you haven't even been introduced to her."

"What difference does that make?"

Joe slapped Jack on the back. "Give up, little brother. I've already beat your time with Miss Asbury."

Little brother? April looked from one big man to the other. Joe was taller but Jack was heavier.

"When we passed the house, Pa said you'd gone down to the paper to help Corbin."

"We?" Jack's eyes darted to April.

"Me and Joy. I got talked into bringin' the brat to town."

"I lucked out there. Where is she?"

"Over at the picture show watching a near-naked man swing through the trees."

"Who's s-swinging through the tr-trees? Relative of yours?" Doc came through the door connecting the house to the office.

"Howdy, Doc. Tarzan. Don't you read the funny papers?"

"Yeah, but I don't r-remember seeing anything n-naked in them."

"He isn't really naked."

"It's a he, huh? That's why I didn't n-notice. What're you two doing here b-bothering my nurse?"

"Well, I—" Joe was immediately interrupted by his brother.

"I came to ask her to go to the pictures with me."

"If I were she, I'd not go with either one of you."

"If you were her, I'd not ask you, Doc." Joe winked at April, who sat behind the desk disbelieving the nonsense she was hearing.

"Miss Asbury, Joe's got to look after the mutt. I'm free for the evening."

"I've got plenty of time to take the brat home and come back, Miss Asbury. I'm far more trustworthy than this kid who thinks he's a man."

"I'd like to meet this brat you're talking about."

"Oh, no!" the brothers said together.

"She's in constant motion and has been since the day she was born. She's fifteen and can look so helpless you melt. All the while she is working on you to get you to do what she wants. She's a cross between an angel and—" Jack looked at Joe to supply the word.

"Mata Hari."

"Lizzie Borden."

April laughed. "She can't be that bad."

"You think not?" Jack snorted. "The little mutt can make you believe a cow pie is a cupcake."

"She could coax the bark off a tree," Joe said, and Jack nodded agreement.

"She wheedles. She knows just how to butter you up. She tells you that you're the most wonderful brother in the world—"

"She gets her way. Most of the time."

April looked at Doc. "If all of this is true, why is she running around loose?"

Doc chuckled. "They spoiled her when she was l-little. Now they g-got to live with it."

Joe pulled out his watch. "Show is over in half an hour. I'll take her home and come back."

"No need to go to all that trouble, Brother. I'm here. I'll take Miss Asbury to the picture show."

"I believe I have some say in this great debate." April stood up. "I'm playing canasta with Doc tonight."

Two heads turned toward the doctor. He merely lifted his brows.

Finally Joe spoke. "Good idea. We'll all play. Is that all right, Doc? I didn't really want to see a near-naked man swinging through the trees anyway."

"G-guess so. If it's all right with April. I'm going down to see if the r-river's come up. Want to go, Jack?"

"Sure, but I don't want to leave April with *him.* No tellin' what he'll tell her about me."

"I'm going home." April put away the ledger and moved out from behind the desk.

"I'll walk with you," Joe said quickly and smirked at his brother.

April was not sure what to make of the Jones brothers. They were fun. She had to admit that. Joe was a good-looking devil. She'd be on her guard against him. Her mother had loved a good-looking man who enjoyed the freedom of being with women other than his wife. He had brought her nothing but heartache.

Joe walked with her to the rooming house. She stopped at the steps leading to the porch.

"Thank you for being so gallant."

"Gallant? I've not heard that word lately. What time shall I come back and take you over to Doc's?"

"You don't need to come back. I told Doc I'd come down after supper. One of his ladies brought him a peach cobbler, and he invited me to help him eat it."

"Do you and Doc have something going?"

She tilted her head to look into his eyes. He was gazing down at her without even the hint of a smile on his face.

"Inside the office he's my boss. Outside we're friends."

"Honest?" The smile that came back in a flash spread his lips and put creases in his cheeks. "I didn't want to step in and edge him out."

"You think you could?"

"I'd give it my best try."

Her heart skipped a beat. "You don't lack for confidence."

"Sure I do. At times I feel like I was fourteen again."

"Oh? Tell me."

"Not now. It's too soon." He reached for her hand, squeezed it and walked quickly back down the street.

In her room April removed her uniform and after looking at it carefully, decided that she could get one more day out of it if she pressed it. She hung it on a hanger. In her bra, panties and robe she picked up a towel and a bar of her favorite scented soap and went across the hall to the bathroom. Standing before the small mirror, she washed her face and under her arms, blotted them dry, slipped her robe back on and returned to her room.

Remembering she had left her soap in the bathroom, she opened her door to go back to get it and almost ran into Fred, who had come from the storage room.

"Oh! You scared me."

"Sorry. I was putting some things in the storage room." His voice was not quite steady, and his hand went to his perky bow tie to straighten it. "Are you about ready to come down to supper?"

"In ten minutes or so."

"See you there." Fred hurried down the hall to the stairs.

A creepy feeling wiggled its way into April's mind. The house was big and quiet. Surely she would have heard his footsteps if he had walked past her room. Something about the way he looked at her made her uneasy. It was silly, of course, but at times he made her feel as if he were seeing right through her clothes to her naked body.

April crossed to the bathroom, scooped up the bar of soap and went quickly back to her room.

Joe stood outside the movie theater and spoke to those he knew as they came out. The crowd thinned to a trickle, and there was still no sign of Joy. He went into the lobby and spoke to the doorman as he emerged from the semidarkened theater.

"Is everyone out?"

"All but a couple of kids in there necking." His grin disappeared when he saw the scowl on Joe's face. "I told them to get a move on."

Joe moved past him and into the semi-darkness. His eyes swept the auditorium. On the far side, at the end of a row of seats, Joy stood close to a tall boy. His arms were wrapped around her waist, hers around his neck. Their faces were a mere breath apart.

"Joy!" Joe barked.

The two sprang apart. Then Joy leaned close and whispered to the boy before she moved away from him and toward Joe. The boy followed.

"I was coming." She had a rebellious look on her face, and Joe wanted to shake her.

"It didn't look like it to me. Come on." He took a firm hold on her elbow.

The boy followed them outside.

"This is Sammy Davidson," Joy said.

"I know who he is. *Good-bye,* Sammy."

Sammy's smile was contemptuous, as if he knew that Joe wouldn't do anything to him right out here on the street in plain view.

He briefly thought of arguing, then thought better of it.

"Bye, Joy. I'll see you Monday in school." There was a definite tone of defiance in his voice. "And after school . . . if they have play practice." He gave Joe a smug grin.

The frown on Joe's face and the look he gave Sammy would have scared a less confident boy. But it had no effect on Sammy. He smirked and sauntered on down the street. Joe took his sister's arm and propelled her in the opposite direction.

"Did you know he was going to be at the show?"

"No."

"He's a tough little nut."

"He isn't. He's on the Y.P. party committee. Mrs. Poole chose him. She thinks I'm a good influence on him."

"Mrs. Poole's hind leg," Joe snorted. "What does she know about raising kids? She's never had one."

"She likes Sammy."

"He drinks and smokes."

"So do you."

"Don't be smart. I'm a man. He's a kid."

"I suppose you'll tell Pa and Julie."

"Don't you think they should know that

you're meeting a boy like Sammy on the sly?"

"It wasn't on the sly. He . . . just happened to be there."

"Joy! I'm not stupid. I saw him at the library when you went in to see if Sylvia was there. So don't tell me he just happened to be there. Do you kiss every boy who just happens to be in the theater?"

"No. Sammy's got a right to go to the show if he wants to. Why don't you like him?"

"I told you. He's too young to be drinkin', smokin' and hangin' around with that bunch from the river joints. I don't want his reputation rubbing off on you. Folks judge others by the company they keep."

"He's sixteen. You and Thad were younger than that when you got drunk in the barn. I saw you pukin' your heads off."

"And you ran to the house and blabbed it." Joe went into the poke corral and saddled his horse. When he came out, Joy had started walking toward home. He mounted the horse and caught up with her. "Give me your hand."

"I'll walk."

"No, you won't. It will take too long and

I've got things to do. Give me your hand or I'll get off and paddle your rear end."

"Oh, you make me so mad. The whole damn family watches me like I'm a criminal or something. I'll be glad when I'm out of school and out from under your thumb."

"So will I, little sis."

Chapter 7

When April went down to the dining room, she saw that the table had been set for two, and there was no sign of Mrs. Poole. Fred stood beside the place where she usually sat, waiting to seat her.

"Shirley is at the store," he said in way of an explanation for her absence. "She spoils me. She wants me to sit down and enjoy my meal without having to grab bites behind the counter." He sat down and passed the bowl of potato salad. "How do you find our little town after living in the big city?"

"Compared to Kansas City, Independence isn't a big city. Fertile is a nice little town."

"There's one drawback." He chuckled and placed a deviled egg on his plate. "There are very few secrets in a small town."

"I suppose you know some of them." *And you're going to tell me.*

"Well, let me see . . ." He appeared to be thinking. "It's no secret that a dozen single women in town have squared off in a cooking contest. The prize is Dr. Forbes. It's no secret that Joe and Jack Jones chase every new girl who comes to town. It's no secret that a few of them have left town in a hurry, and it's no secret that a certain merchant on Main Street visits his lady friend while his wife is in church."

"You're just a fountain of information."

Fred ignored the sarcasm in her voice and chuckled again.

"Folks come into the store and want to talk. I've no choice but to listen."

"Very accommodating of you."

Her voice was so heavily laced with sarcasm that Fred suddenly became aware that she did not like the topic of the conversation. He quickly changed it.

"There's a beautiful drive along the river."

"I heard that the road is terribly muddy now."

"Probably so. Our great-grandfather was one of the founders of Fertile. He moved his family here just after the Civil War. The railroad didn't come through until quite a few years later. He brought the goods for his store in a freight wagon."

"Really?"

"Shirley can show you pictures of how the town looked before the turn of the century. Would you like more tea?"

"No, thank you." April tilted her head to listen as the clock in the living room chimed the hour. "You'll have to excuse me, Fred. I'm expected back at the clinic in a few minutes." She placed her napkin beside her plate and stood.

Fred immediately got to his feet. "You're working tonight?"

"Book work that I didn't get done today."

"I'm surprised the doctor expects you to work evenings. I'll walk with you."

"He doesn't *expect* me to work. I want to. You needn't walk with me, Fred. Go ahead and finish your meal. After the trouble your sister went to prepare it, she would be disappointed if you didn't do justice by it."

April made her escape. When she reached the sidewalk in front of the house, she breathed a sigh of relief. She didn't want to go to Doc's so early. If Joe was there, he'd think she was eager to spend the evening with him. Yet she didn't like being alone in the house with Fred. Next Saturday night, she'd plan to skip supper or eat at Sparky's.

She wondered if she had made a mistake in renting the room from Mrs. Poole. Regret traveled through her mind as she walked the block to Doc's. The woman was nice and accommodating and the room pleasant. She had been so sure that she would like it there that she had paid a month's rent in advance. She hadn't counted on being so uncomfortable with Fred.

Doc answered her knock on the door and led her to the kitchen, where he and Jack were eating.

"Don't let me interrupt your supper. I came over early so that I could help you . . ." Her voice trailed off. "I really came early to tell you that your books are in a mess."

"You told me that today. Have a seat."

"Hello, pretty lady." Jack jumped up and pulled out a chair for April. "Have some potatoes. I fried them myself."

"Are all the Jones boys flirts, Doc?"

"Don't know. I've not s-seen Jason lately."

Occasionally April had been attracted to men, mostly professionals: doctors or businessmen who wore suits and ties. None of them compared with Joe Jones. She had never expected to be attracted to a farmer. Jack was every bit as handsome as his brother, only in a different way. His hair was darker, his face broader. His eyes, a deep blue, gleamed with a friendly light, but not the same friendly light as Joe's. Joe's smile was spontaneous. Jack's was rather forced at times.

Now, why did she think this? Was it the sadness she saw in his eyes when occasionally he let down his guard?

April pulled her gaze from Jack's and spoke to Doc. "Is the river still rising?"

"Don't think so. It's s-still level with Coleman's d-dock. If it comes up over that, it's time for folks d-down there to get out."

"It'll go over the banks if they get a lot of rain up north." Jack was suddenly serious, his eyes on Doc. Obviously Doc was worried about the possibility of the lower part of town flooding. "There's nothing we can do about it, Doc, but wait and watch. The folks living down there have been through this before. They'll know when it's time to leave."

Doc snorted and looked down at his plate.

"Ready for the cobbler?" April asked.

"You serving?"

"Sure. I'll give myself the largest portion." April had been in Doc's kitchen several times during the past week and knew where things were kept. From the icebox she took a bottle of milk.

"Shall I pour off the cream, Doc?"

"The spoon thing you put in the bottle to hold the milk back is in the drawer on the right."

April sank the spoon, shaped like a small ladle, in the narrow-necked bottle and fitted it snugly in the indentation. She poured the cream into a pitcher. After dishing up the cobbler she set their servings, the pitcher and the remaining cobbler on the table.

"Don't get on the bad side of Mrs. Maddox, Doc. This cobbler is delicious," April said after taking the first bite.

Doc chuckled and shook his head. "I feel almost guilty taking her cobblers when there's not a s-snowball's chance in hell that she'll ever find me on her doorstep."

"Are they after free doctorin'?" Jack winked at April. "Or is it because you're so handsome?"

"Horse hockey!" Doc snorted and got up to answer a knock on the door. He came back to say that he was going next door to the surgery to treat a boy's foot cut by the jagged edge of a can.

"I'll come help." April got quickly to her feet.

"No. I can handle it. Stay here and see that Jack doesn't eat everything in sight."

April and Jack finished eating, then washed the dishes. She enjoyed his company. He told her about the neighborhood baseball games they'd had in the pasture beside the house back when he was a kid, and about being asked to play on the town baseball team.

"Doc had just come to town. Your landlady's husband, Ron Poole, was on the city council and was coaching the town team. He brought Doc to the playing field. He tried out for shortstop and was pretty good. We played a traveling team out of Chicago that summer. We didn't win but had a hell of a lot of fun. After the game we all went out to the farm and had ice cream. Evan brought out his Victrola, Pa hung up some lanterns and we danced."

"It sounds like you had a very enjoyable childhood. I've often wished for brothers and sisters," April said wistfully.

Jack laughed. "Oh, we had our ups and downs like any family. Joe and I were usually kept out of mischief. We worked with Pa. Our sister Julie was the hub of the family wheel. She had to leave school when our mother took sick. After she died Julie looked after the house and the little ones."

"I was lucky enough to have my grandparents after my mother died."

"Did your father die, too?"

"I saw him last when I was four years old. I only vaguely remember him." April emptied the dishwasher, wiped the pan and slipped it under the sink. "Well, that takes care of that."

When April returned from the bathroom, where she washed her hands and ran the comb through her hair, Jack was squatted down in front of the radio fiddling with the dial.

"Doc's got a pretty high antenna. I was hoping to get Nashville and the *Grand Ole*

Opry. I like to listen to Uncle Dave Macon and his Fruit Jar Drinkers."

"I've heard of them."

"Not exactly Paul Whiteman, but fun." Jack turned the dial a few more times. "I guess we'll have to settle for *Amos 'n Andy*."

Doc came in, followed by Joe.

Doc asked Jack, "Did you eat all the cobbler?"

"It's on the table," April answered, trying not to look at Joe.

The first time she did, his eyes snared hers. "My, you look bodacious, Miss April. Doesn't she, Doc?"

"I know how to p-pick 'em. Business is booming s-since she came. My social life, too. I've even got c-company on Saturday night."

Although April knew that Joe was teasing, her heart skipped a beat and heat turned her cheeks warm. She went to the kitchen and released a breath she hadn't even known that she was holding.

"Let's finish off the c-cobbler, Joe. Then April and I will skunk you and Jack in a game of c-canasta."

"I get to partner April," Jack protested. "I was here first."

"Whine and complain. That's what I've had to put up with all these years." Joe slapped his younger brother on the back before taking a seat at the table. "I'm the eldest son. I'll partner April. Now, I'll hear no more about it."

Jack wasn't giving up so easily. "Then I'll walk her home."

"How're ya gonna do that with a broken leg?"

"Lately there's always someone wanting to break my legs," Jack complained.

"Good," Doc grunted. "More business for me."

April couldn't remember having a more enjoyable evening. Doc seemed to enjoy himself, too. She and Joe won three games out of five. When the clock struck twelve, she was surprised the time had gone so fast.

A good-natured argument erupted between Joe and Jack about who would walk April home.

"I brought Pa's car. You can take it and go on home, or you can wait." Joe took April's arm.

"I'll wait."

"Suit yourself. Come on, April. I've been waiting all evening to get you alone in the dark." His hand slid down her arms, his fingers laced with hers. Even knowing that he was teasing, April felt a thrill run down her spine.

"Don't be g-getting fresh with my nurse," Doc called.

"Doc, you take all the fun out of life."

"There's really no need for you to walk me home. I'm not afraid a bogeyman will jump out of the bushes and get me."

"If anyone jumps out of the bushes and gets you, it won't be the bogeyman. I've got a reputation to uphold." Joe's arm beneath hers held her close to him. He shortened his steps to match hers.

"I've heard about that reputation. According to Fred, it's no secret that the Jones boys chase every new girl who comes to town."

"He told you that?"

"Uh-huh, and more."

"You believed him?"

"I'm considering—"

"Stop considering and consider yourself

chased. How about me taking you out to meet Julie and Evan tomorrow afternoon?"

"Shouldn't you check with your sister first? She may not want visitors tomorrow afternoon."

"She'll want to meet *you*. I'll tell her we're coming when she and Evan stop to pick up Pa and Eudora to take them to church in the morning."

"Do you live with your father?"

"Part of the time. My place, such as it is, is out where you found me. I want to build a decent home out there someday. I put my feet under Julie's table or Jill's or Eudora's. They all feel sorry for me and feed me."

"And you manage to look as pitiful as possible."

"Of course." They walked along in silence until they came to the walk leading to the front porch of the rooming house.

"Good night. I think I can find my way from here."

"It's ending too soon. Shall we walk up to the library and see what's going on?"

"It's midnight. What could be going on?"

"They could be having a poetry reading or something. We wouldn't want to miss out on that."

"I'm disappointed. I thought you could do better than that."

"I had to think fast. We could sit for a while in the porch swing."

"It squeaks."

"I forgot that. I sat there today while waiting for the mutt. How about the porch steps? I'd like to tell you the story of my life."

"It's late. How long will it take?"

"I'll start it tonight, add on to it tomorrow and try to finish it off after we go to the pictures next Saturday night."

"You must have led an interesting life up to now." April sank down on the next to the top step and leaned back. Joe sat on the step below hers and turned so that his face was level with hers.

"It hasn't been all that exciting. I spent a couple of years in Oklahoma, working the oil fields. I got my clock cleaned a time or two until I learned there was no such thing as a fair fight with a roustabout or a wildcat driller. They are tough. They have to be to do the kind of work they do." He chuckled and squeezed her hand.

"After all that excitement you came back here to this slow-moving little town?"

"There's no place like home." He was serious. "Thad Taylor and I were going to pool our money and start a ranch down there in Oklahoma. We got homesick and decided to come home, farm and raise cattle."

"You've not regretted it?"

"Not for a second. Home and family are a man's greatest possessions."

Gone was the devilish, teasing grin. She heard the sincere tone in his voice and believed him. This was a different side of Joe. He was a man who treasured family and friends.

"Thad and I discovered the value of family while we were in Oklahoma. We were tired, sick and hungry part of the time, and no one gave a damn. We had to get out and scratch or starve."

"And you did."

"We did everything from helping a rancher skin out a bunch of dead cattle so he could sell the hides to moving outhouses for a drilling crew."

She wanted to tell him how lucky he was to belong to a large, caring family, but she didn't want him to stop talking. He told her about the Kickapoo Indian they met who had the unlikely name of Randolph Blue-feather.

"Blue took pity on us and pulled our tails out of the fire more than once. We learned a lot from him. He liked for people to think he was a savage, but in truth he was well educated and one of the smartest men I've ever known." Joe ran his thumb over the knuckles of the hand he held in his. "I'm talking too much about me. I'd rather hear about you."

"I was born in Independence, went to school in Independence, lived with my grandparents in Independence. I went to nursing school in Kansas City and worked in the hospital there until I came to Fertile to work for Dr. Forbes. Not a very exciting life compared to yours."

"Whoa! There's a lot of filling in to do. Have you ever been in love?"

"More times than I've got fingers and toes. When I was little, I was in love with the iceman who gave me chips of ice. Then it was the grocer who held me up so I could put my hand down in the candy jar. It would take all night for me to tell you about my love life. It's late and time I was going in. If

Jack goes off and leaves you, how will you get home?"

"Walk. It's only a mile."

April stood and stepped up onto the porch. She was searching her mind for something to say when he reached for her, pulling her close, and her world narrowed suddenly to that small space on the front porch.

"Will you be mad as a wet hen if I kiss you?"

"Probably."

"I think I'll risk it. It would be nice if you put your arms around my neck." When she didn't move, he said, "That's asking too much, huh?"

He lowered his head and pressed his lips to hers softly, gently, quickly, then lifted his head and looked into her face.

"That wasn't a real kiss, just a trial run." He kissed her again, this time harder and longer. "Doggie," he said when he stepped back. "I could get addicted to that. I'll be here tomorrow about two. Is that all right?" He held her hand tightly so she couldn't leave before giving him an answer.

"All right. Good night."

He smiled and her heart did handsprings. "See you tomorrow," he whispered.

She slipped inside and watched him leave the porch and go down the walk to the street.

The car was not where Joe had left it. He cussed his brother briefly, but was too happy to get very upset about Jack leaving him. The street was deserted. The clock in front of the barbershop said one-thirty.

On the way up the hill to his father's house on the edge of town, Joe relived the past few hours. He had met women of many types, but not one of them had tied him in knots as Doc's nurse was doing. She had a quick wit and a soothing manner. She possessed a dignity and a freshness he'd not discovered in another woman. Something about her made him want to be with her. Every night since he met her, he had lain awake thinking about her, wondering how it would be to have a woman like her love him.

April crept up the darkened stairway. Her heart beat in a strange and disturbing way. She went into the bathroom at the top of the stairs and closed the door before she turned on the light. When her eyes became accustomed to the light, she looked at herself in the small mirror over the lavatory and was surprised that she looked the same.

Joe had kissed her. Although he'd acted flirty, she had to believe that it wasn't a flirty kiss. She hoped that he hadn't been aware that her heart had raced like a runaway train.

Don't get carried away, she cautioned herself. *It probably meant less than nothing to him.*

She went to her room, turned the lock in the door and carefully pulled the window shades to the very bottom of the glass panes. After kicking off her shoes, she removed her dress and slip and sat down at the dressing table to clean her face. While wiping off cold cream with a soft cloth, she had the eerie feeling that she was not alone.

For a moment she was frightened. She looked around the room. The shades were down, the door locked. There wasn't room in the wardrobe to hide anyone. Feeling silly but determined, she looked under the bed. Nothing was there.

After removing her panties and bra and placing them in the dirty-clothes bag, she went back to the bed and searched under her pillow for her nightgown. It wasn't there. She reached over and snatched away the other pillow. There it was, folded neatly.

What was going on?

She was sure she had crammed her gown beneath the pillow on the side of the bed where she slept as soon as she took it off. Had Mrs. Poole been in her room to straighten the bed? But she always made her own bed before leaving a bedroom.

April slipped the gown over her head, flipped off the light and got into bed. A minute or two later she heard a muffled sound somewhere in the house and rose up on her elbow to listen. When she heard nothing else, she sank back down and let her mind wander over the magical events of the evening.

No more than a dozen feet away, on the other side of the partition that separated April's room from Fred's, Fred quickly turned out the light, lest it shine through the small holes in the wall he used to watch her. He was breathing heavily and holding his erection.

This had been the best. It had been worth staying up and waiting for her. It even

helped dull the disappointment he had felt
when she didn't take a bath or use the toilet
while he watched from the storage room
before supper.

*Tonight he had seen her walk around the
room totally naked. Her breasts, her bush,
her buttocks—he'd seen all that glorious
bare skin.*

Other times he had seen only parts of
her—her breasts without a bra and one time
when she took off her panties. He had gotten a view of the feathery bush between her
legs, but not for very long. He was looking
forward to the time when he could watch
from the storage room while she stripped
naked and took a bath.

He chuckled silently, gloatingly. He'd
seen more of her than the damn Jones
boys, who thought that they were God's gift
to women.

Fred crept back to the bed and eased
down on his knees beside it. While visions
of April, delightfully naked, played in his
mind, he slipped his erection between the
mattress and a pillow that rested on the
springs and rocked back and forth.

Chapter 8

The sky was just beginning to lighten in the east when Dr. Forbes left the house and drove toward the river. The hour before dawn was the quietest time of the morning, and the sound of the car engine was loud and abrasive to him. The medical bag that was never far from his side was on the seat beside him. Two large brown paper sacks, one from each of the grocery stores in town, were on the floor of the car.

Thank the good Lord there had been no rain for the past forty-eight hours. The road should be dry enough for him to drive right up to the house. God, how he hated having to sneak around to be with her, but if it were known that the doctor was seeing Caroline Deval and wanted to marry her, people would not allow him to treat them even if they were dying.

He prayed that in the near future he and Caroline would be able to walk hand in hand down a street and no one would gawk or sneer. It wasn't right that because of the dab of colored blood in her veins she was considered inferior or that a white man who took her for a wife was thought of as trash.

Wife.

There wasn't a preacher or a judge in the state of Missouri who would marry them even if they could obtain a license.

A month ago he contacted an agency in western Canada. He had read in a journal that many small towns in that area were in need of a doctor. He wouldn't make much money, but it would be enough to get by and support his family.

Dear God, wanting her, wanting to be with her, to take care of her, is eating me alive!

Now was not the time to try to sell his practice. But when the time came, and he didn't have any offers, he would walk away and leave it without any qualms whatsoever. He still had the inheritance from his father to fall back on. Being far from home was a small price to pay to be with the woman he loved. His sisters would understand. Of all the people in Tennessee, they might be the only ones who would see beneath Caroline's skin color.

Doc had felt a little guilty about bringing April to Fertile knowing that he didn't intend to stay here. But after observing how efficient she was, he knew he had made a good choice. She could set an arm or leg and tend most emergencies as well as he could, although she couldn't prescribe medication. If Fertile were unable to get a doctor right away, she would be able to handle most things that came up. He wouldn't be leaving the town high and dry.

Doc turned onto the river road and, careful to stay in the middle of the road, had no difficulty going the mile to where he turned into the lane leading to the house. If Caroline was awake and heard the car, he hoped that she would know that it was he and not be frightened.

He drove behind the heavy stand of lilac bushes that would shield the car from the road. He could just imagine the stink that would be created if the people of Fertile found out he was visiting Caroline Deval this time of morning. He had heard the snide remarks made about her, suggesting she made her living whoring. He'd had to keep his temper and calmly explain that her father had left her enough money to live on. God, how he hated narrow-minded, bigoted people.

Damn, he just wanted to take her and get the hell out of town with the least fuss possible. He wanted to go someplace where he could live with her openly, introduce her as his wife, make her the mother of his children.

Doc had deliberately turned the car so that the headlights shone on the shack set back in the trees. The door opened, and a large colored man came out, stood for a minute, waved his hand and went back inside and closed the door. Silas was ever watchful. He was worth every dollar Doc paid him.

Lamplight shone from the kitchen window by the time Doc got the groceries out of the car. The door was open when he reached it.

"Todd? Is something wrong?" Caroline, in a long nightdress, her curly black hair covering her shoulders and cascading down her back, stood in the doorway.

"No. Nothing is wrong. I just couldn't wait another day to see you."

She stood aside for him to enter. He placed the sacks on the table, turned and pulled her into his arms. Hugging her close, his nose against her face, breathing in the scent of her, he felt as if he had, at last, come home. Gently and reverently he kissed her lips before raising his head and looking down at her.

"Are you all right?"

"I'm fine. And you?"

"I am now that I'm h-here with you."

Her arms encircled his neck. "Oh, Todd. I'm nothing but trouble for you."

"Don't say that," he scolded. "I never started to live until I found you." He held her away from him and looked down into her face. "Did you start your m-monthly flow, sweetheart?"

She shook her head. Her large expressive eyes filled quickly with tears.

"Honey. Do you hate it s-so much?" His hands came up to frame her face.

"I'll be bringing another child into the world to be just like . . . me."

"Lord, I hope so. I hope it's just like you."

He kissed the tears from her eyes and ran

his hands down over her slender hips. She had missed one period, but he had thought she just might be late. After missing two periods it was possible that she was pregnant with his child. He couldn't help but smile to think that a little bit of him was growing inside this precious woman.

She unbuttoned his shirt and snuggled her face against his bare chest.

"Ah sweetheart. I don't w-want you to be sorry. I should have waited until I b-brought you a diaphragm. But I wanted you so and th-thought I'd die if I didn't have you." He trailed kisses over her face.

"It isn't all your fault. I wanted you, too."

"If there's a b-baby, we'll be away from here and married before it comes. I p-promise."

She looked at him with tears rolling down her cheeks. "We can't marry, Todd. You know that."

"We can in Canada, honey. Many n-nationalities are darker than you are. Up there no one will even question."

"But you'll know and . . . I'll know."

"I knew the f-first time I came here to t-treat your father. My life changed forever that day. He told me how it was to be an outcast because he I-lived with the love of his life, your mother, who had colored blood."

"My great-grandfather was white, as was my mother's father and, of course, my dear papa. Why is it that I have ten times more white blood than colored, yet I'm more readily accepted by the coloreds than the whites?"

"I don't know, honey. I think it goes way b-back to the days b-before the Civil War." He sat down in a chair and pulled her down and cuddled her on his lap. He tucked her bare feet up and covered them with her gown. "Have I t-told you about Jody, my childhood friend? He I-lived in the hills above Harpersville, Tennessee.

"Jody could run like a deer, but b-because he was colored, he wasn't permitted to p-participate in the games held each year on the Fourth of July. We thought it so unfair that my younger s-sister and I and some of our f-friends urged him to run in the footraces even if he had to start fifty p-paces behind the other runners because he was s-sure that he could win.

"Jody won that race. And much to the

chagrin of the city officials, they were f-forced to give him the p-prize."

"Was he very black?"

"Black as could be." Todd chuckled. "And feisty. He had a chip on his shoulder the size of an oak t-tree. The t-town had a stupid law that c-colored folk were not allowed in town after the s-sun went down. One time Jody was at our house, and the t-time got away from us. Instead of going around town and into the hills, he ran right down the m-middle of Main Street at dusk and thumbed his nose at the sheriff, who s-stood on the walk in front of the jail."

"What happened to him?"

"Nothing. The sheriff was a good sort. Later my sister's husband s-sent Jody away to school. He was smart, worked hard at his studies and n-now he's an acclaimed p-professor of botany at the Alabama Tuskegee Institute."

"You know, I had a sister, but she and Mama died the same day. They got the influenza during the war."

"Then there was j-just you and your papa. He g-guarded you from those who would have m-mistreated you."

"He worried that he would die and leave me, and that's just what he did."

"He lived long enough to know that I would take care of you." His voice was thick with emotion. "I p-promised him, sweetheart." He cradled her in his arms and lifted her face so he could place soft kisses on her lips. "I love you m-more than anything in the world."

"I love you . . . too." Her voice broke on a sob. "But I'm afraid of what I'm doing to you."

"Ah . . . little darlin', you've b-brought untold joy to my life. I live for the hours I s-spend with you. I don't want you to be afraid e-ever again. Silas will always w-watch out for you when I'm not here. He'll not l-let any of the river trash near you." His hand stroked her flat stomach before unbuttoning the front of her nightdress and slipping a hand inside to reverently caress a small, firm breast. "The first time I came h-here, you captured my h-heart and have been c-constantly in my thoughts."

"Papa talked about you after you left that day. He said I could trust you." A shudder went through her as if she were shaking off a shadow of old grief and fears.

"You do trust me to take care of you, don't you, sweetheart?" The longing in his voice made her heart ache. She brought his lips down to hers and spoke against them.

"With my life, my heart, my everything. Forever."

They exchanged soft, sweet kisses.

"Will you go to b-bed with me, darlin' girl? I want to love you," he whispered urgently.

"I will go to the farthest corner of the earth with you."

He set her on her feet and took her hand.

A knock on the door awakened April.

"Miss Asbury?"

"Yes."

"The operator is on the phone."

"Thank you. I'll be right there." *So much for sleeping on Sunday morning.*

April's feet hit the floor and found the soft slippers she kept there. She shrugged into a robe, belted it and opened the door. Mrs. Poole was on the stairs. April followed her to the wall phone in the kitchen.

"Hello. This is Miss Asbury."

"I'm looking for Dr. Forbes. He isn't

at home or in his office." The operator sounded as if she were offended.

"He may have gone down to check on the river. Is there an emergency?"

"Mrs. Watson has been to the house. Her daughter has a very painful boil under her arm. She's been up with her all night."

"Where is she now?"

"Here in the office."

"Tell her that I'll meet her at the clinic in ten minutes."

April hung up the phone and raced upstairs. She dressed quickly, slipped her bare feet into a pair of sandals and ran the comb through her hair. She grabbed up her purse and was out of the house in five minutes. The block to the clinic seemed extra long. A woman and a young girl got out of a car as she approached it. The girl was holding her arm over her head.

April unlocked the door and held it open for them.

"It hurts." The girl, about ten or eleven years old, had tears in her eyes.

"I'm sure it does, honey. Boils are mean. Come in here and let's see what we can do to give you some relief."

While April scrubbed her hands, the

mother helped to remove the girl's dress and to get her up on the table, where she could lie down. The boil was big, angry and, no doubt, terribly painful.

"I put the yolk of an egg on it trying to draw it to a head," said the mother. "When that didn't work, I put on a bread and milk poultice."

"Both of those are good but boils can be stubborn. Honey"—April addressed the girl—"there are two things we can do. We can put a hot poultice on it that will eventually draw it to a head, or I can nick the boil with a knife so it will drain. The poultice will take longer; the cut from the knife will hurt for just an instant, but you'll get quick relief."

"I want it over." Tears streamed from the corners of her eyes.

"You're a brave girl. I would be blubbering like a baby if I had this thing under my arm. I'll get things ready."

Minutes later April had the supplies on the cart beside the table. She had covered the sharp sterilized scalpel with a mound of gauze to keep the girl from seeing it.

"When I was your age, I had a boil on my bottom. At first I was too embarrassed to tell my grandma. Hold her arm over her head," April said to the mother. "I had to sit in school all one day on one hip because it hurt so bad. You can bet I told my granny when I got home. She fried some onions and made a poultice. I lay with that poultice all night long. When morning came, it hadn't done a blasted thing to bring that stubborn boil to a head."

April made a quick slash in the boil, and white pus shot out into the gauze she held at the ready.

"It's over, honey. It should be feeling better anytime now."

"Did yours ever come to a head?"

"The doctor came out the next morning. I had to bare my butt. I was sure that I'd never be able to look him in the eye again. But know what? When next he saw my face, he didn't recognize me. It made me wonder if he would know me if I showed him my bottom." April worked swiftly while she talked. "This may sting a bit," she said before swabbing with antiseptic. "You are a brave girl. Did you see that?" she asked the mother. "She didn't even flinch."

"I want to be a nurse . . . like you," the girl blurted.

"That would be great. You and I could talk about all the boils we'd lanced." To Mrs. Watson she said, "Keep a warm, damp cloth on it for a while to be sure it's completely drained before it closes up." Then to the girl: "Does it feel better now?"

"Oh, yes."

"Your mother will have to dab it a couple of times with iodine. It'll sting for a minute or two, but we don't want that ugly old thing to come back."

"What do we owe you?" Mrs. Watson asked when they were ready to leave.

"If Doc was here, it would be about fifty cents, but he isn't here and—"

"You did as much as any doctor could have done." Mrs. Watson placed several coins on the desk.

After her patient had left, April put away the supplies and poured boiling water over the scalpel, then placed it into the sterilizer. Before she left the office, she called the operator.

"Diane? The doctor still isn't back. I'm going home. If I'm needed again, call me at Mrs. Poole's."

When April arrived back at the house,

Fred was sitting on the front porch reading the paper.

"Good morning," she murmured as she went quickly up the porch steps.

"You're out early."

She nodded, then hurried into the house and back to the kitchen, where she hoped for a cup of coffee. Mrs. Poole, dressed for church, took a plate of scrambled eggs and bacon from the oven.

"That looks good but it's coffee I need." April reached for the percolator on the stove.

"If you would like to go to church, I'll wait for you to get ready."

"Some other time. Doc isn't back yet. I should stay near the phone."

"Where is he?"

"He may be out on a call, and he may have driven up the river road. He's worried about flooding."

Mrs. Poole sniffed. "If it floods down there, it won't be a great loss. The rats and whores will scatter. Maybe they'll settle farther downriver. The town would be better off without them."

"Fifty or more people live along the river

in Shanty Town. Wouldn't the merchants miss their business?"

"They're more trouble than they're worth. Fred has to go down there regularly to collect on bills."

April began to eat. "Doc says floodwater can get into the water wells and cause typhoid."

"I figured he was worried about something other than river rats and whores. There's a colored whore down there who services the men. They say that she could almost pass for white. I've never seen her. She doesn't dare show her face in town." Mrs. Poole whipped off her apron almost angrily and hung it in the pantry.

"The plum butter is delicious, Mrs. Poole."

"I should send a jar to Dr. Forbes. Poor man, he doesn't have a woman to do for him."

April thought of the pies, cakes and even meat loaf the single ladies in town brought him, but she wasn't about to tell Mrs. Poole that.

"He would enjoy it, I'm sure."

"Are you setting your cap for him?"

"For Doc? Heavens, no. He's my boss and my friend."

"Well, he's sure a cut above Joe Jones."

"What do you mean? Isn't Joe respectable?" There was a note of irritation in April's voice.

"Respectable, but a fly-by-night. He's flitted here and there for years. Farming now, I hear. I wonder how long that will last."

"Is there something wrong with that?"

"Not for some girls, but you're educated. You wouldn't be satisfied pulling water from a well and going out back to an outhouse."

April bit her tongue to keep from retorting. She looked at her landlady as if seeing her for the first time. Her hair was set in stiff waves and pinned in a tight knot on the back of her head. Her face was pinched, her small mouth was tight. Her head was tilted; her nostrils quivered as if she smelled something offensive.

What in the world happened to this woman to make her so bitter?

"Do you know the Jones family?"

"Oh, yes. They live on the edge of town, but never been considered town folk. Joneses have been scratching out a living out there on that rocky farm since long before the war."

"In other words, the people who live on farms surrounding the town are considered outsiders even though they trade with the merchants in town?"

"They don't pay taxes in town or contribute to the cost of running the town."

"They must pay county tax. Doesn't the county help provide services for the town?"

"I don't know how that works. My late husband was on the city council. They were always short of money."

"Sister," Fred called from the doorway. "We'd better be going or we'll be late."

"Coming. I cooked the meat for dinner last night. When I get home, all I have to do is fix the potatoes. Church is out at noon. Dinner should be ready by one."

"I won't be here for dinner."

"Oh." Mrs. Poole looked as if she had swallowed a bug. "If I'd known that, I'd not have cooked such a large roast."

April said nothing. She'd be damned if she would apologize. The woman waited beside the door as if expecting an explanation. April remained silent.

She stayed seated until she heard the

click of the front screen door closing. She got up and hurried to the front window to be sure Fred was leaving with his sister. When she saw the two of them walking side by side and Fred talking earnestly to Mrs. Poole, she went back to the kitchen to wash her soiled dishes and put them away.

Leaving the bathroom door open so that she could hear the telephone if it rang, April ran water into the tub. She was determined to bathe, wash her hair, get ready for her date and be out of the house before Mrs. Poole and Fred returned. Rather than wait for Joe to come here, she would meet him on Doc's front porch.

She mulled over in her mind what to wear while she lay back in the warm water. It was hard for her to believe that she was actually going on a date. She had gone out before, but never with a man as handsome and charming as Joe Jones.

A secret smile worked its way onto her face.

Give it your best shot, Joe. I'll enjoy being with you, but there's no way this girl is going to let you charm her into doing something as idiotic as falling for you.

Chapter 9

"Waiting for someone?"

April had been sitting on Doc's porch for a good long while before he came to the door.

"I didn't know you were back. I'm waiting for Joe. He's taking me out to meet his sister Julie."

"Is that right?" Doc stepped out onto the porch, slouched down in a creaky old rocker and lit his pipe.

"You don't approve? My landlady doesn't approve of me having anything to do with the Jones family."

"What business is it of hers? You don't have to p-please anyone but yourself. But to answer your question, it isn't up to me to approve or d-disapprove. Joe's a g-good man. So's Jack."

"Mrs. Poole was telling me that unless you live in town, you're considered outsiders. She said Joe was a fly-by-night and that he and Jack chased every new woman who came to town."

"Horse hockey."

"She also said that some of the women they chased left town suddenly. Is this true?"

"Joe and Jack are as d-decent as you'll find anywhere. I don't know where she got such cockeyed ideas."

"She has strong opinions."

"Mrs. Poole is a b-bitter woman. Pay her no mind."

"She cares even less about the people who live along the river than she does about those who live outside of town."

"There's some r-rotten apples down there, but some good folk, too. The s-same as here in town."

"Is the river any higher?"

"It's about the s-same."

"Isn't it strange? A few hundred miles west of here the crops are dying due to the drought, and here we have to worry about the river flooding."

"From what I hear, it's j-just in this area.

Western Kansas is dry as a b-bone, and so is Nebraska."

Doc leaned his head back, propped his feet on the porch rail and looked off into the distance. Apparently his mind was fully occupied. For a long while April hesitated to break into his thoughts. Finally she was compelled to tell him about her early morning patient.

"The operator called for me to come to the clinic this morning. Mrs. Watson brought her little girl in. She had a boil under her arm the size of an egg. I met her there and lanced it."

He turned to look at her. "You're a g-good nurse, April. The best I've ever had."

April was struck by the sad tone of his voice and the bleak look on his face, as if the weight of the world were riding on his shoulders.

"Thank you. Is something worrying you, Doc?"

"Only that I should have let you know that I would be g-gone for a while. I'll be sticking c-close to the office for the next week or two. I have t-two expectant mothers due anytime now."

"Mrs. Appleby and Jill, Joe and Jack's sister?"

"They're due about a w-week apart, but it's Jill's f-first and it could come early or late."

"Do you anticipate any problems?"

"No. She's h-healthy as a horse. If I'm not mistaken, here c-comes your beau."

"He's not my beau!" April stood up and waved to make sure Joe would see her and stop. She didn't want him going to Mrs. Poole's.

"You'd b-better tell him that. I don't think he knows."

"I will make it perfectly clear. No way will I fall for a good-looking flirt."

"We all hide our insecurities b-behind something. Joe does it by f-flirting."

"Joe insecure? He's one of the most confident men I've ever met. I doubt he'd back down from a tornado."

Joe came up the walk with an unabashed grin on his face. He was wearing a freshly ironed shirt, string tie and duck pants.

"Well, damn if you d-don't look pretty," Doc said.

"I clean up pretty good. You knew that,

Doc. Talk about pretty. Look at Miss April. She's about as pretty as a covey of quail."

April rolled her eyes toward the heavens. "I'm terribly flattered to be compared to a flock of birds."

"You're not impressed? She's not impressed, Doc."

"She got more b-brains than to be taken in by that old line. You'd better get a n-new one."

Joe's shimmering eyes were busy exploring every inch of her, from the green print dress with puffed sleeves, square neckline and full skirt to her bare legs and the sandals on her feet.

"All right. How's this? She's as pretty as apple blossoms in the spring." Joe's admiring gaze caused the color to rise in April's cheeks, and she hated it.

"Crab apple? Hardly flattering. Can't you think of something that rhymes?"

"She's sharp today." He flashed a dangerous, heart-stopping smile. "I'll have to watch my step. Doc, Julie sends an invitation for you to come to supper."

"Tell her thanks, but I'd better s-stick around here today."

"If you change your mind, come on out."

After she was seated in the car, April looked back to where Doc sat on the porch.

"He looks so lonesome."

"Yeah. Doc's got a heavy load right now." Joe spoke so quietly that April turned to look at him and saw the serious expression on his face.

"What do you mean 'right now'?"

"He's worried the river will flood the water wells."

"I can't help but wonder if there's something else on his mind."

"Doc's a very private man."

They were driving slowly down Main Street. The only cars parked along the street were at the hotel.

"The town buttons up on Sunday," Joe said as if he had to say something to fill the silence. "Spring Lake amusement park is open, but the dance hall is closed on Sunday. We'll go out there some Saturday night when it's really hopping." His eyes smiled into hers. "Do you like to dance?"

"I like to, but I'm not very good at it."

"That's a fib if I ever heard one. I bet you're good at everything you set out to do."

"Thanks for the confidence, but you'll

change your mind after you suffer a broken toe or two."

They rode in silence. She had not experienced silence before when she was with Joe. It made her nervous. Good Lord! She hoped that he wasn't aware that she had to open her mouth to get enough air in her lungs and how hard and fast her heart was thudding.

Settle down, silly thing, or you'll give this jellybean something to really crow about.

"Is this your car?" *Her voice was quite normal, thank goodness.*

"No. It's Pa's. I don't have a car. I go horseback where I want to go. Every cent I could scrape up went into Rolling Thunder." April saw the deviltry in his eyes as well as something warm and fluttering in their depths. "That's why I wasn't going to let you hurt him."

For a moment she couldn't breathe, then laughter bubbled out of her. She laughed, gasped, then laughed again.

"I only had a little old umbrella."

"But you had blood in your eye."

Their laughing eyes held until he had to look back at the road. April stared at his profile for several moments longer. She could see the squint lines at the ends of his eyes and the small mole on his lower eyelid. His cheeks were flat, his mouth wide and firm. A cowlick stood up next to the part in his crisp, clean hair.

He turned and caught her looking at him. She took a deep breath, afraid that if she spoke he would be sure to know how happy she was to be here with him.

Joe's hand left the wheel and covered hers on the seat between them. She was fun to be with, smart as a whip, and she could very well be the girl of his dreams. Her hair was the rich color of ripened wheat, her mouth wide and sweet, her eyes warm and smiling.

Sweetheart, I'm going to do my best to do this right. I don't want to scare you off. You may be my pot at the end of the rainbow, my life's mate, the love I've been searching for. I need to keep you close so that I can find out one way or the other if we were meant to be together.

April let her hand rest in his until he had to take it away to make the turn leading to the Jones farm.

"Eudora and Jacob will ride with us to Julie's. Pa and Jack went over after dinner last night. One of Evan's horses is ready to foal."

Fat hens scattered when they drove into the farmyard. On the porch Jacob was jumping with excitement, but he didn't run toward the car until it stopped. Then he bounded off the porch.

"Joe, can I sit on your lap and drive?"

"Not today, squirt. You'll have to sit in the back with your mama."

"Ah, Joe. Please, please, pretty please can I sit with you?"

"Of course you can." April got out of the car. "You can sit right here beside your big brother. I'll sit in back with your mother."

"Kid." Joe frowned first at April, then scowled down at Jacob, who was grinning as unabashedly as his brother Jack sometimes did. "You don't know how close you've come to getting your little backside swatted."

"Why? I said please."

"Yeah, why, big brother?" April smiled sweetly. "He said please."

Joe lifted Jacob up and set him on the seat. "Rascal, see if I make you any more slingshots," he muttered. "Or crack walnuts for you to eat."

"What did you say, Joe?" April asked.

"Nothin'." With a hand beneath her elbow he helped her up and into the car and murmured for her ears alone, "I'll get even with you later."

Eudora came from the house with a basket over her arm. Joe went to meet her and relieve her of the basket.

"Stay here on the porch, Samson," Eudora said to the big brown dog who followed her. "You know you can't go in the car. Hello, April. Isn't this a lovely day? So good to have sunshine again."

"It sure is. This is my favorite time of year. Not too hot. Not too cold."

April and Eudora chatted about weather and gardens as Joe turned the car around in the farmyard and headed back toward the road.

"As soon as we have a killing frost, the woods between the two farms will be a riot of color. I love the gathering of the harvest and the preparations for winter," Eudora said.

"I used to help my grandmother can beans, make chow-chow and shred cabbage for sauerkraut. Grandpa would take apples and pumpkins to the cellar. Have you always lived on a farm?" April asked.

"I lived in town all my life until I married Jethro. But I love living in the country."

When Joe turned into the lane, April could see Julie's house and the farm buildings beyond. The large house with its deep front porch was sparkling white; the barn and outbuildings were painted brick red. Big oak trees shaded the house and barnyard. From the branch of one hung a child's swing with a board seat. Yellow pumpkins were visible among the dried vines in a large garden, at the end of which were several heavily laden apple trees.

It was a beautiful place. A peaceful place.

By the time the car stopped, Julie was on the porch holding Nancy in her arms, and Logan was running to meet Jacob.

"Come look, Jacob. Sally had her baby." The two boys took off for the barn as soon as Jacob's feet touched the ground.

"Hello, Eudora," Julie called as she came out into the yard, her eyes on April. "Hello. I'm Julie."

"I'm April Asbury."

Julie was a tall woman with hair just a shade darker than Joe's. Her dark brows were slightly arched. Lashes, long and thick, framed light brown eyes both quick and quiet.

"And who is this?" April stroked tiny fingers. The baby turned her face into her mother's shoulder.

"Nancy Ann. She's shy until she gets to know you. Don't worry about the boys, Eudora. The men are out there, and I know Joe is dying to see what's going on."

"I'm not sure I should leave April with you," Joe said. "I'm afraid that you'll tell her all sorts of things about me."

"I'll tell her only the good things." Julie laughed, then said over her shoulder as she walked to the house, "If I can think of any. Come in, April, Eudora. Sorry to be bringing you in through the kitchen, April. Our front door is seldom used by family."

Julie settled her daughter in a canvas jumper hanging from a heavy spring suspended on a hook in the doorway leading into the pantry. As soon as the little feet touched the floor, the child began to jump.

"She's showing off." Julie smiled proudly. "Sometimes she bounces so hard her little bottom touches the floor."

The kitchen was sparkling. On the long

trestle table a white cloth was spread; in the center was a silver-based cruet set. High-backed chairs surrounded the table.

"Hello, Joy." Eudora had placed her basket on the table and was taking off her hat.

April turned to see a young girl standing in the doorway leading to the other part of the house. She was the one Joe and Jack referred to as the *mutt* or the *brat*. She could coax the bark off a tree, Joe had said. April could see why. She was beautiful: curly blond hair, large blue eyes, delicate features.

" 'Lo." Joy spoke to Eudora, but her eyes were on April.

"Joy, this is April Asbury, Dr. Forbes's new nurse." Julie made the introduction.

"And the one Joe's got his eye on." Joy came farther into the room. "You won't stand a chance if he decides he wants you."

"Joy! For goodness' . . . sake," Julie sputtered.

"I might have something to say about that," April said. "Was that Rudy Vallee I heard on the Victrola when we came in?"

"We have several of his records. Do you like him?"

"I do. And Bing Crosby and Paul White-man."

"The harvest committee is meeting this afternoon, but I had to miss it." Joy looked pointedly at April.

"Go close the lid on the Victrola, Joy." Julie spoke calmly but with enough force in her voice that the girl left the room immediately.

"How are you coming with your quilt, Julie?" Eudora asked to fill the void that followed.

"Slow. I've not had the time to work on it lately. I was hoping to get the blocks put together so the Sewing Circle at the church could quilt it this winter."

"I'll be glad to help. I've not started my wedding ring quilt yet. I'm still collecting scraps."

Joy returned and said to April, "I'm going to see the new colt. Want to come?"

"Yes, I would. I've never seen one the same day it was born."

"Evan told Logan he could name it," Joy said. "He'll probably call it something dumb like Ice Cream or Christmas or Santa Claus."

"If Evan said I could name it, I'd probably call it Birthday or Valentine's Day."

"Joy named the last one." Julie followed them to the door.

"I named her Marlene, after Marlene Dietrich, who was so beautiful in *The Blue Angel*."

The double doors of the barn were folded back. April stepped inside and followed Joy down the center aisle to the far end where Joe and Jethro stood outside a stall. Jethro was holding his small son, who sat on the top rail. He nodded a greeting.

"Come to see the new arrival? She's a beaut." Joe held out his hand to April and pulled her up in front of him so she could see over the railing. Joy crowded in between her father and Joe.

The tiny colt was standing on wobbly legs. Jack was on his knees in the straw with one arm around the foal to steady him while he wiped him with a cloth. He looked up. April smiled at him, and he answered with a cocky grin.

Joe spoke to the man standing at the head of the tired mare. "Evan, this is Miss Asbury."

"Glad to meet you, ma'am."

"It's amazing, isn't it?" Joe's voice, when it came again, was so close to April's ear that she could feel his warm breath. "Not even an hour old and he's standing."

April was more aware of Joe close behind her, his hands on the railing in front of her hemming her in, than what he was saying.

"It takes us humans a year sometimes."

"It's mine, isn't it, Daddy? I can name it, can't I? Can I come in and pet it?" Logan was so excited he couldn't stand still.

"Not yet, son. Stay out of the stall. Sally isn't used to having a baby yet, and she might be afraid you'll hurt it." Evan spoke calmly to his son.

"I won't hurt it, Daddy."

"I know that, but Sally doesn't know it yet."

"I think I'll name him Grace."

"It's a boy, silly," Joy said. "You can't name a boy Grace."

"How do you know, smarty? I don't see anything hangin' down. So there!"

"Shall we go?" Joe whispered in April's ear. "It could get embarrassing very soon."

April pressed her lips together to keep from laughing. She turned her face, and her cheek came against him. She moved her head quickly.

"There's nothing like living on a farm to teach the kids about the birds and the bees."

Joe took her hand and they walked back down the aisle. She blinked when they came out into the bright sunlight.

"This is a beautiful place."

"One of the more prosperous farms in northern Missouri. Evan is a good business-man and a good farmer. He has stud-ied every aspect of it. Uh-oh—here comes trouble."

Out of the bushes beside the barnyard, accompanied by loud honking, came two large white geese on the run, their necks stretched, their wings spread.

"Stand your ground. If you run, they'll chase you. All right, you two," he said to the geese and got between them and April. "She's not going to rob the place. Go along and find a bug to eat." He shooed at them.

The geese strutted back and forth a time or two, heads up, tail feathers twitching, be-fore they walked away as if they owned the farm and everything in it.

"Evan has seven of these critters. Two of

them are usually here by the house. They are very smart birds and great watchdogs. When a stranger or an animal approaches, they raise a racket."

"Do they have names?"

"Julie named them after presidents: Thomas, Calvin, John, Georgia."

"Georgia?"

"She couldn't very well name a female goose George." He winked at her and tucked her hand into the crook of his arm. "One night Evan heard a commotion going on out in the yard. He looked out and saw a fox. Each of his seven geese had a mouthful of fox and was pulling in a different direction. The next morning he found no missing ducks or geese, and chunks of fox fur all over the yard."

April laughed. "Poor fox. If he's smart, he'll think again before he comes back."

"A gander will be particularly mean during nesting season, but the females will not bite you unless you mess with their nest."

"That's something I always wanted to know."

"Smart mouth." He moved his hand down her arm to hers. "The reason they came out of the bushes today was because they didn't know you and wanted to protect me."

She rolled her eyes toward the clear blue sky. His grin was so endearing she unknowingly squeezed his hand and smiled back at him. Their eyes held until the sound of a motorcar coming up the lane drew their attention.

"Here's Thad and the watermelon."

"Shame on you for calling your sister a watermelon."

"Wait until you see her. If she doesn't look like she swallowed one, I miss my guess."

Jill Jones Taylor was a small girl with an infectious smile, a saucy, turned-up nose and shoulder-length dark blond hair. After the introductions had been made, Thad and Joe pushed each other around like a pair of bear cubs. Jill endured her brother's teasing and gave back as good as she got.

Thad's laughing eyes landed on April. "You look like a smart lady. You can't be interested in this dirt buster."

"Who said I was interested? I just wanted a ride out here to meet the Jones family. He tells me they are pillars of the community."

"Well, now, that makes more sense. I can tell you a thing or two about—"

"Shut up, Thad," Jill said softly.

"But, honey, you know how I hate to see a sweet, innocent girl get taken in by the Clayton County Masher. I'm just doin' my Christian duty."

"Don't honey me, Thad Taylor. You can do your Christian duty by waiting until April gets used to us before you start your shenanigans."

The day with the Jones family was one of the most enjoyable April had ever spent. She sat on the porch with them and listened to the talk about the river rising, cattle and grain prices, and the discussion between Evan and Jethro about what it would mean when Prohibition ended. Joe, Jack and Thad played catch, and the little boys chased each other around the yard.

Later they all gathered around Julie's large table for supper. It was evident to April that she loved having them there. April was surprised at how comfortable she was with the family and they with her.

Furtively she watched Joe, trying to memorize the way his sudden smile changed his expression drastically. There were moments when she forgot to be wary, and her eyes caught his. He would smile and wink. At times she knew that he was watching her, and she had to remind herself that she must guard her heart. Joe Jones could very well be the man who would break it.

She listened to his good-natured banter with his brother and sisters. Not having a sibling, she couldn't help but feel a twinge of envy.

April hated for the day to end. It was twilight by the time they piled into the cars, waved good-bye to Julie and Evan on the porch and drove down the lane to the road. After they had dropped Jethro, Eudora and their tired, sleeping son at the farm, Joe pulled her over close to him and turned the car toward town.

Chapter 10

Shirley Poole passed the plate of cookies for the third time. Two of the young people on the porch reached to take the chocolate squares. Sammy Davidson, sitting on the porch railing, shook his head.

"You said Joy was coming."

"You were there when I made the announcement, Sammy. I said if you can't come, let me know. Joy didn't say she wasn't coming, so I assumed that she was. She's only a little late. We can start without her or wait. It's up to you." Shirley sat down and smoothed her skirt over her knees. "While we are on the hayride, Mr. Oakley will build a large bonfire. He's going to donate—"

"She's not comin'." Sammy rudely interrupted and slid off the rail. "I'm not stayin'."

A giggle came from Evelyn, the youngest

member of the group. Sammy scowled at her.

"What're you laughin' at?"

"You. Ever'body knows you got a crush on her."

"That's none of your business."

"You kissed her at the movie house."

"Who told you that?"

"Richard. He said you told him. Did ya?"

"What if I did, *Dumb Dora*?" He took a can of Prince Albert tobacco out of his pocket and, showing off his skill, rolled and lit a cigarette. "Yeah, I've kissed her," he said after drawing in smoke and expelling it from his nostrils. "More than once."

During the minutes that followed, the only sound was the squeaking of the porch swing. Silently Richard and Evelyn watched Sammy smoke. Shirley Poole couldn't take her eyes off the boy. Visions of her husband filled her head. He had been so handsome, so sweet and gentle . . . Determined, Shirley smiled and broke the silence.

"Joy is a pretty girl and certainly old enough to kiss a boy if she wants to. I don't know why anyone would make a big to-do about it. Some girls her age are already married."

Three sets of eyes turned on Shirley.

"Well . . . I was young once, you know. If Joy and Sammy like each other, I see no harm in a little kiss or two. It's the most natural thing in the world."

"You . . . think it's all right for them to . . . kiss?" Evelyn sputtered.

"You don't need to spread it around." Shirley's laugh was light, more like a high giggle. "Some of the old fogies in our church might think my ideas too modern. But I understand young folk . . . and their feelings."

Sammy's eyes became wary as he watched the older woman. He breathed in the cigarette smoke and blew out a smoke ring. *Now, this is a switch. Old Mrs. Poole has always been such an old sourpuss. What's she up to?*

"Are you stayin', Sammy?" Evelyn asked.

"I'll hang around for a few more minutes, and if she ain't here, I'm long gone. I've got things to do."

"We'll schedule an hour meeting at the church after school Wednesday. Is that all right with everyone? Tell Joy tomorrow that we'll have to get someone to take her place if she can't come to the meetings."

"Maybe she got a new boyfriend," Evelyn said behind her hand to Richard.

"What did you say?" Sammy turned hard, cold eyes on the girl, and she wished that she'd kept her mouth shut.

"Nothin'."

"Anyone who butts into my territory will answer to me. Joy is my girl. Understand?" Sammy moved threateningly toward the two in the swing. "Understand?" he said again.

They nodded.

"Don't forget it. I'll tell Joy about the meeting on Wednesday, Mrs. Poole."

"Thank you, Sammy," she called as he sauntered off the porch and down the walk toward town. "We have a lot of work to do between now and the party."

Richard breathed a sigh of relief when Sammy left.

"He really likes her."

"She likes him a lot." Evelyn looked at Mrs. Poole and giggled as if she was telling something naughty. "She thinks he's really cute."

Shirley picked up the cookie tray and turned to hide her smile.

*   *   *

Joe drove slowly into town. April's shoulder was tucked behind his. He wanted to put his arm around her, but he cautioned himself about moving too fast. The day had gone far better than he had hoped. April seemed to like his family, and they had certainly taken to her. She had a quick wit, a sense of humor, and could hold her own with any of them. He couldn't imagine being serious about a woman who didn't fit in with the people he loved the most.

They crossed the railroad tracks and drove down Main Street, circled the block and drove past Doc's. A light was on in the back part of the house.

"Doc is probably listening to his radio. I'm surprised he's still single," April said quietly. "Has he ever had a lady friend?"

Joe waited until he had turned the corner before he answered.

"He has friends. Mostly couples and single guys like me and Jack."

"Confirmed bachelor, huh?"

"I wouldn't say that. Are you thinking about setting your cap for Doc?"

"Don't be silly! Mrs. Poole asked me that

today. Besides being my boss, he's my friend."

"That's a relief. I'd hate to have to beat him up."

"Oh, my. A bully. One more thing to add to the list of masher, lecher, seducer . . ."

"Am I really all of that?" he asked proudly. "I'll have to live up to my reputation and keep you out all night. What would you like to do?"

April had been hoping that he wouldn't take her directly home, although she did have a uniform to iron.

"What would *you* like to do?"

"I'd like to drive down by the river." Then he added on a breath of a whisper, "Find a secluded spot and pitch a little woo." Without seeing it, she knew that mischief danced in his eyes.

"Pitch a little woo? What on earth are you talking about?"

"Don't tell me they don't pitch woo down in Independence."

"They might if I knew what it was."

"Neck, sweetheart. You know—hug and kiss." April felt his laughter against the shoulder wedged behind his, and she hoped that he wasn't aware of how happy she was being here with him.

"I should have taken Thad's warning. I'm seeing the Romeo of Clayton County at work," she muttered as if to herself.

"We might get stuck in a mudhole if we drive the river road. This will have to do." Joe turned into the ballpark, stopped and turned off the lights. "Now, my sweet young thing, I've got you in my power." He had a villainous tone in his voice, and he twirled an imaginary mustache.

"I warn you, sir. I have my trusty hatpin."

"Oh, Lord. Be careful where you poke me." He laughed, intimately, joyously, and hugged her to him.

"Is this where they hold the famous Fertile horseshoe tournaments?"

"Right out there next to the third-base line."

"George Belmont asked me to come watch him play."

"He couldn't hit the stake if it was right under his nose. You wouldn't want to watch him embarrass himself."

"He has a good excuse for not playing well. I put six stitches in his hand." April looked out the window into the dark night. Joe fiddled with the steering wheel.

Finally he said, "We have some pretty good ball games. Our team is the best in the county. Jack plays and coaches."

"Has he heard any more about the police job?"

"He goes before the council next week for an interview."

"I hope he gets it. I'll keep my fingers crossed."

"He'd make a good policeman."

"Joy declared that she'd never speak to someone named Ruby who broke his heart."

"Joy's a pistol." He flashed a grin that crinkled his eyes at the corners. "I'm thinking that Jack and Ruby broke each other's hearts. They've been crazy about each other since high school. Did you hear Jill urging Jack to come stay a day or two? She's hoping that Ruby will drop by." His fingers were looping her hair over her ears. It was so distracting that she barely heard his next words. "Ruby teaches country school."

Suddenly he pulled her tightly against him, giving her no chance to resist. His face came to hers, and he kissed her long and hard. At first her lips were compressed with surprise, but a few seconds into the kiss they softened and yielded. The pressure of his mouth hardened—seeking, demanding, forcing her head back as his lips moved hungrily over hers. Her mind was spinning, but she managed to place her hands on his chest to push herself away.

"What brought that on so suddenly?"

"Believe me, sweetheart, it wasn't sudden. I've been trying to get up the nerve since we parked here."

"I figured you'd get around to it sooner or later. It was a bit sooner than I expected."

"Nice, though, wasn't it? I'd like to do it again." He cradled her head in one of his hands and pressed it to his shoulder. "I think you're the prettiest, sweetest girl I ever knew," he whispered with his mouth against her forehead. "I've been thinking of you as my sweetheart. Do you mind?"

She pushed away from him, holding a handful of his shirt while her eyes searched his face to see if he was teasing. There was no sign of the grin that could come so quickly to his lips. His brows were drawn in a worried frown.

"You're going a . . . dab too fast for me. I don't think . . ." Her voice stumbled to a stop. She was acutely aware of the warmth radiating from his broad chest and his body made firm and muscular by hard work.

"Right now I'm thinking about kissing you again. I've wanted to since that night you stumbled up onto my porch as wet as a drowned rat. Lord-a-mercy, you were pretty with your hair plastered to your cheeks, your chin tilted and your eyes spittin' fire."

"Drowned rat? That's something every girl wants to hear once during her lifetime." She didn't smile but she wanted to. "With a line like that, I don't know how you ever became the head masher of Clayton County."

"I'll get even with Thad for telling you that." With his thumbs locked beneath her jaw, he tilted her head and put his mouth to the sweet, soft one that was driving him crazy. He kissed her softly, almost as if he were kissing a child.

"I've waited all day to get you alone so I could kiss you." He pressed her palm to his chest. "Feel my heart? It's doing handsprings."

His mouth moved over hers with warm urgency, molding her lips to his. It was a pos-

sessive kiss. As it lengthened and deepened, his hand slid down her body, stroking
her from shoulder to thigh. A torrent of de-
sires racked her when he stroked the sides
of her breasts with his fingertips. These feelings were strange to her. She was power-
less to control them. They intensified when
his warm, wet tongue caressed her lips.
When he lifted his head, their eyes locked,
both unwavering. Her breath came raggedly
through wet, throbbing lips.

A strange desire inside of her made her
frantic. She pushed herself away from him
again.

"Hold on," she muttered huskily. "I'm not
used to this on a first date."

"This isn't like any first date I've been on,
either. It's like I'm starved for you. I'm sorry,
sweetheart, if I've gone too fast." His hands
moved down to clasp hers and guide them
upward. "Let me hold you for just a minute
with your arms around my neck."

April lay against him, her arms around
him, while her heart thumped against his.
What had turned him so serious all of a
sudden? What had inspired the intimate
kisses?

She couldn't fall in love with him. She wouldn't!

When she fell in love, she wanted it to be a cherishing kind of love that made her and her man want to be together every minute of the day and night. She wanted them to be both mentally and physically attuned. She wanted him to plant his children in her body, make a home with her, stay by her side forever and not dash off for greener pastures as her father had done.

Joe was much too handsome, much too glib. His silver tongue was much too persuasive for a girl who had never had a serious beau. Gently she moved out of his arms, but he refused to allow her to move to the other side of the seat.

"We'd better go. I've got to iron—"

"Have I blown it?"

"Blown what?"

"My chance with you."

"Because of a few kisses. We're friends, aren't we?"

Friends don't share the kisses we shared.

The words were on the tip of his tongue, but he held them back. He turned on the lights and started the car. Her casual answer didn't sit well with him. Dammit, he wanted them to be more than friends! Had he read her wrong? He was sure that she had enjoyed his kisses and had returned them.

Main Street seemed deserted when they reached it. There were lights in the hotel lobby and the telephone office. Not a word was said until he stopped the car in front of the rooming house.

"I enjoyed the afternoon very much. Thank you for taking me to meet your family."

"They enjoyed you, too." He reached for her hand and entwined his fingers with hers. "Next Saturday night is the last night Spring Lake park will be open. They close during the winter months. Would you like to go?" He leaned back so that he could look into her face.

"I'm not much of a dancer. I've never square-danced."

"We could just watch if you don't want to dance." A note of anxiety was in his voice.

"All right. We can take my car. It's been sitting there beside the house since I got here."

"Fine with me." The familiar grin was

back. "You'll not forget between now and then?"

"Not in six days. Seven or eight days . . . maybe."

"You're not doing a thing for my ego."

"Your ego doesn't need any help from me." She reached for the door handle. "I've got ironing to do before I can go to bed."

Joe got quickly out of the car and was around to the other side before she could get out. They walked arm in arm up the walk to the porch. At the door he turned her toward him, put his arms loosely around her and clasped his hands behind her back. Their faces were close.

"This is new to me," he whispered. "I've never met a girl who sends me into a tail-spin, one that I want to be with all the time."

April's breath clogged her throat, but she managed to say, "You'll get over it."

"I don't want to get over it."

She knew that he was going to kiss her again and felt extremely happy. The hands on her back slid around her and pulled her tightly to him. The lips that touched hers were warm and sweet as they tingled across her mouth. His tongue circled her lips, coaxing them to open. Her skin quivered; the tiny hairs on her body seemed to be standing on end.

"You're so sweet, taste so good. I don't know why we wasted all that time out at Julie's." He took his lips away and looked down into her upturned face. "I'd better go," he said in a husky whisper. "I'll see you Saturday, if not before."

"Good night."

April watched him until he reached the car, then she opened the door and went into the house.

From the upstairs window of his darkened bedroom, Fred waited for April to come home. Barefoot and wearing only his BVDs he slouched in his chair with the lace curtain pulled back. When the car stopped in front of the house, he got to his feet and stood beside the window for a better view. It seemed an eternity before they came up onto the porch. Another eternity before Joe headed back to the car.

Damn farmer didn't even have a car of his own.

Fred listened for the sound of the door closing and for her footsteps on the stairs. Quietly he felt his way across the dark room to the wall that separated the two rooms and waited for the girl of his dreams to turn on the light that would guide him to one of the several small holes he had drilled in the wall so he could view every corner of her room.

His heart pounding with excitement, his eyes tight against one of the holes, he watched her plug in the electric iron, then go to the vanity and look at herself in the mirror. She lifted the hair off the back of her neck before slowly unbuttoning the front of her dress, then worked on the side fastener. When the dress was off, she placed it over the back of a chair, unhooked and removed her bra. She lifted one rose-tipped breast and rubbed at the red line made by the bra.

Now wearing only a pair of wispy panties, she slipped a white uniform over the ironing board and began to iron.

On the other side of the wall, Fred watched, breathing heavily and sweating profusely. His hand slid down to his extended member. He swallowed the low moans of pleasure that rose in his throat and wished fervently that she had a hundred uniforms to iron.

Chapter 11

The first part of the week was so busy that April didn't have time to think of anything but the work at hand. Mixed in with the usual office calls were a broken arm, a man with a series of bee stings and a serious dog bite. Doc had to have the dog killed and its head sent to Kansas City to be tested for rabies.

On Wednesday Miss Davenport, the most aggressive of all the ladies striving for Doc's attention, spent three hours in the reception room waiting for him to return from an emergency call north of town. All the while, she eyed April like a hawk watching a baby chicken and repeatedly asked her where the doctor had gone and what was the emergency. Fearing the woman would track him down and waylay him, April explained that the information was confidential and then tried to ignore her, but at one point it was impossible.

April was in the back room when she heard the door open and Miss Davenport's voice, clear and precise.

"The doctor isn't here."

She hurried to the reception room to see a woman standing hesitantly just inside the door. She was holding a baby. A small boy clung to her skirt.

"Hello. May I help you?"

"I come to see the doctor, but—"

"He's out on an emergency. Is there something I can do?" April saw the disappointment on the woman's tired face.

"Mama. I wanta drink." The boy tugged on his mother's skirt.

"Shhh . . . We'll get one on the way home."

"I'm tired, Mama."

April held her hand out to the boy. "Come with me. We'll get you a drink of water."

The woman followed April and the boy into the back room. While April was getting a glass of water for the boy, she set the baby down on the examination table and took a small bottle from her pocket.

"Doctor said bring the bottle back and he'd give me more medicine for the baby's colic."

"What is your name?"

"Colson. Mrs. Gordon Colson. This is Emery." She indicated the boy. "And Lucille."

Noticing the woman's weariness, April said, "Lay the baby on the table while I get your file." She nudged the baby's chin with her fist. Lucille waved her little hands and kicked her feet. "You're quite a chunk for your mother to carry."

"We walked a long way." The boy returned the empty water glass to April.

"What do you say?" Mrs. Colson prompted.

"Thank you."

"You're welcome. Would you like a drink, Mrs. Colson?"

"I would appreciate it. Emery's right. It was a long walk."

After getting the water for Mrs. Colson, April left the room to find Doc's record of Mrs. Colson's visits. Thank goodness he had made notes.

Baby Lucille has frequent bouts of colic. Two drops of paregoric in 8 ounces of water no more than twice a day. (Paregoric in green bottle reduced to half strength.)

"Your baby suffers from colic?" April asked when she returned to the room.

"Doctor thinks it's caused by what I eat. I been tryin' not to eat gassy things."

"Oftentimes babies have colic while nursing."

"I'm real careful of the medicine I give her. The doctor gives me just a little bit at a time. He said she should grow out of it soon."

"I'm sure she will." April took the bottle with the eye dropper over to the cabinet. She filled it to half an inch, which would be not more than two tablespoons. When she turned, Miss Davenport stood in the doorway.

"You are not qualified to prescribe medication." Her voice was loud and stern. "You're only a nurse, if that. I've not seen a nursing certificate."

"This doesn't concern you. Please wait in the reception room."

Miss Davenport turned to Mrs. Colson. "Surely you'll not give your baby medicine prescribed by . . . this woman."

Mrs. Colson's frightened eyes went from April to the tall, stern-faced woman in the straw hat. The small boy, sensing the tension, grabbed on to his mother's skirt.

April's temper flared. "What goes on in this office is no business of yours. The doctor prescribed this medicine for this baby and suggested the mother come back for a refill. I suggest that you leave this room immediately. Better yet, leave the office and come another day if you wish to see Dr. Forbes."

"Oh, you would like that, wouldn't you? You want a clear field with him so you can work your crafty schemes. That dear man is too trusting to see through a woman like you. I'm staying."

"Suit yourself."

"Dr. Forbes will hear about this. If that baby has one sick day, you will go to jail. I swear it." Miss Davenport's face was red with anger.

April went to her desk to get the stick candy Doc gave to the children. "Candy for you," she said to the boy. "And one for baby sister." She walked with Mrs. Colson to the door.

"Thank you," Mrs. Colson said. Then she added in a low voice, "Tell the doctor I'll pay when I can."

"I'm sure he understands. Bye, Emery. Bye, Lucille."

"The doctor will hear about this and the sheriff, too, if that baby gets sick." Miss Davenport crossed her ankles primly and slammed her pocketbook down on her lap in a gesture that clearly meant she was there to stay.

April went back and sat at her desk. The tension in the room was thick. She mumbled a word she seldom used, pulled open a drawer and took out the ledger, but she was so angry she couldn't concentrate on the work.

When Doc finally returned, his shoulders slumped; he was tired to the bone. He had been out to a farm where a man had been cutting down a tree. The trunk had kicked back, pinning him to the ground. Doc had worked for hours trying to save him and had lost him in the end. Any death sat hard with Doc, but this man had a wife and two small children, who hovered near. At first he thought he had a chance to save the man, but it wasn't to be.

He still had Miss Davenport to deal with.

"Doctor." She jumped up as soon as he

walked in the door. "I've been waiting three hours."

"If you had an appointment, Miss Davenport, I'm s-sorry. I had an emergency c-call."

"That's all right. I understand."

April grimaced. *Now butter wouldn't melt in her mouth!*

"Well, if you'll excuse me . . ."

"Doctor I must speak to you . . . privately."

Doc gave April a look of resignation, then said, "Come in." He hung his hat on the hall tree and went into the examination room. Sweeping past April, Miss Davenport followed and closed the door.

April wondered where Doc got the patience to deal with women like Miss Davenport. She could hear their voices coming from behind the closed door. After a while the female voice became shrill. Doc's voice remained low and even. Suddenly the door was flung open. The woman, her face red with anger, came out. Looking neither left nor right, she marched across the reception room and out the door, slamming it behind her.

April looked up to see Doc leaning wearily

against the doorjamb. "If we're lucky, that'll be the last we s-see of her."

"I was tempted to set the place on fire to get rid of her."

"She was p-planning a dinner party for me, asking the bigwigs in t-town. She wanted to r-raise money to improve this place. She also w-wanted me to fire you."

"I'm not surprised at that. I wasn't exactly civil to her."

"I told her that I w-wasn't interested in her advice about my n-nurse, I wasn't inter-ested in her d-dinner party and definitely not interested in *her*. I made it c-clear that I was not in the m-market for a wife and if that was w-what she had in mind, she should set her sights on s-someone else."

April had to grin. "At times harsh words are necessary."

"She caught me at the wrong time. I lost a p-patient today. I keep w-wondering if there was something else I could have d-done."

"Doc, I'm sorry."

"I keep telling m-myself that his injuries were so severe that he might not have thanked me if I had saved him. It doesn't help much."

"It should help to know that you did your best."

Doc crossed the room and looked out the front door. "Anything happen that I should know about?"

"Mrs. Bacon called. Paul's fever is down to normal. She said you told her to watch it; and if it stays normal, you'll take his tonsils out at the end of the week."

"The kid's tonsils n-need to come out, or he'll be sick the rest of his life."

"Mr. Peterson is suffering another attack of gout. I told him to keep his foot elevated and put an ice pack on it. He swore at me and said he couldn't stand the sheet on it, how in the blankety-blank-blank could he stand an ice pack."

Doc grinned. "Pete uses some p-pretty colorful language at times."

"I believe he was slightly tipsy when he called. How old is he?"

"He m-must be darn near eighty. He was an old man when I got here nine y-years ago. It's almost six o'clock. Are you about r-ready to close for the day?"

"In another few minutes. Oh, yes. I gave Mrs. Colson paregoric out of the green bottle for Lucille."

"It's a small dose and will give the baby relief."

"Why don't you go rest for a while?"

"I think I will." Doc went through the connecting door, and April finished her notations in the ledger. It was impossible to do more work with so much on her mind.

When she stepped out the door of the office to go home, she saw a car stopped in the street. Joe, with one foot on the running board, was leaning against the side window talking to a girl in the driver's seat. Her hand was on his arm. He reached into the car and ruffled her hair. She squealed and he laughed. It was just one more unexpected event in an already nerve-racking day.

April retreated into the office, went out the back door and up the alley to the rooming house. Knowing that she had no right to feel uncomfortable seeing Joe with another girl, she chided herself for avoiding him. She should expect no less of him. He was a charmer and always would be. It was his nature, slow to temper and quick to laughter. He would still be attracting women when he was a gray-haired old man tottering around with a cane.

I have to get over him.

*   *   *

Joe and Jack parted at the newspaper office, Jack to talk to Corbin before the two of them went to the town council meeting and Joe to take his work boots to the shoe repair. When he came out of the shop, he was hailed by Evan, who had stopped his car in the street.

"Hey, Joe. Have you seen Joy?"

Joe walked over to the car. "No, but Jack and I just got to town."

"I was to pick her up at the church, but she isn't there."

"What's she doin' at church in the middle of the week?"

"Meeting to plan some kind of party they're going to have. Hop in, Joe. I thought she might have gone back to school, but she isn't there. I've been to the library, too. Julie will be getting worried if we aren't back soon."

"Did you go inside the church?"

"The door was closed and locked. I saw Mrs. Poole walking down the street and asked her about Joy. She said the meeting was over and she didn't know where Joy was. The girl with her started to say something, but the woman cut her off and propelled her on down the street. I got the idea that she was in a hurry."

"She wasn't concerned?"

"Not a damn bit."

"Let's go back to the church. She may be locked in."

Evan drove slowly along the street, searching on one side, Joe on the other.

"Julie told her to wait at the church and I would pick her up when I finished my business at the bank. I'm a little late, so I expected to see her sitting on the step."

They drove past the lumberyard, then the pastor's house next to the church. After passing the church, they reached the corner and turned. Joe looked back over his shoulder and saw a flash of something blue.

"Hold it! There's someone behind the church."

As soon as Evan stopped the car, Joe got out and hurried to the back of the building. When he reached the rear and saw the pair in a tight embrace, there was no doubt in his mind that the girl was Joy. The boy was crowding her up against the wall, his body pressing intimately into hers. Their arms were around each other, and, oblivious to the world around them, their lips were locked.

"You . . . horny little . . . bastard!" Joe's hand fell heavily on the boy's back, grabbed a handful of his shirt, jerked him back and off his feet. "I told you to stay away from her."

Sammy came up off the ground with his fists flying. "Sonofabitchin' asshole—" He landed a blow on Joe's cheek before Joe grabbed his arm and twisted it up behind his back.

"Don't try to fight me, boy. I'm already tempted to beat you to a pulp."

"Leave him alone!" Joy shouted.

Joe's temper went up another degree when he saw that his sister's hair had come loose from the barrette and her blouse had pulled from her skirt.

"Shut up and get in the car," Joe snarled. "Evan's waiting."

"I don't have to mind you."

"You sure as hell do. Now, get!"

"I won't until you turn him loose."

"Dammit, Joy! I've had about all the sass I'm going to take from you. I told you that this little pup is trash. Didn't you hear a word I said?"

"You're not the boss of me. I choose my own friends."

"Friends? This randy little polecat has only one thing in mind, and that's to get in your pants."

"You're nasty! And . . . I hate you!"

"That's too bad." Joe jerked on the arm he was holding behind Sammy's back. "If I catch you with her again, you'll lose a few teeth. Now, get the hell outta here, or I'll start working on it right now."

"I'll get even. Just you wait. You won't think you're so all-fired smart when I'm through with you." Sammy moved away from Joe but didn't leave. "Don't let him break us up, Joy."

"I won't. He's . . . just a bully." Joy burst into tears.

"I should have told Julie that I caught you with him at the picture show. I was stupid enough to think you'd learned your lesson." Joe took her arm and began walking her toward the car.

"I'm sorry, Sammy. I'll see you in school."

"It wasn't her fault," Sammy, following close behind, spat out suddenly. "Stop being mean to her."

"Mean? I've not even started." Joe

shoved Joy in the car. "Go on, Evan. Take the brat home. I have a few more things to say to this tough guy."

"If you beat him up, I'll never speak to you again," Joy yelled as the car moved away.

Joe turned frosty eyes on Sammy. He had to give the kid an A for courage. He was standing his ground.

"How old are you, Sammy?"

"Eighteen."

"If you're eighteen, how come you're in Joy's class at school? You're sixteen at the most, or else you're so dumb you've been held back a couple of grades."

"I've not been held back!"

"It doesn't matter how old you are, you're a dumb, stupid, hell-bound kid unless you change your ways. Smoking and drinking and hanging around with that bunch down by the river is a sure path to the pen, and I'll not have my sister's name dirtied by associating with you. Is that clear?"

"You can't stop me from seeing her."

"Use your head, boy. She's not for you. Now, I don't want to have to get rough with you, but I will."

"Just try it." Sammy moved away, turned and thumbed his nose. "I've got friends, too, and they're as big and tougher than you."

Joe watched Sammy as he walked down the street. In a way he felt sorry for the kid. His mother practically lived in the beer joints. His father was off following the harvest with a thrashing crew. It was just as well. He'd never given the boy the time of day. Joe was surprised Sammy had gotten as far as he had in school. He was sure that it wasn't due to encouragement at home.

Deep in thought, Joe walked back toward town. Sixteen was a tough age, the age when a boy thought he was a man. He remembered his own teen years when he'd been sure that he was smarter than his pa, but deep down the fear of disappointing or shaming him or the family had kept him in line.

The sound of a car horn brought his attention to the Ford coupe that pulled up and stopped beside him. The smile that was never far from his lips appeared when he saw the dark-haired girl at the wheel.

"Where ya goin', rancher?"

"Miss Ruby May, a sight for sore eyes. What are you doin' in town?"

"Came in to pick up some supplies. Where are you going?" she asked again.

"Heading for Doc's."

"What's important at Doc's beside his pretty new nurse?"

"Oh, my. Word does get around. You've been talking to Jill."

"I was by there last night."

"Jack didn't mention seeing you. He—"

"—wasn't there last night. Get in. I'll drop you at Doc's."

"Are you still seeing that lineman from the electric company?" Joe eased his lanky frame into the seat beside her and closed the door.

"Why? Are you going to ask me out?"

Joe laughed. "I have to sleep in the same room as my brother when I stay at Pa's. I don't want my head bashed in."

"Funny, Joe. Real funny."

"I'm not laughing and neither are you. He's crazy about you, and seeing you with that lineman is tearing him apart. He's ornery as a steer with a sore tail."

"Give it a rest, Joe. He knows what to do about it." She stopped the car in front of the clinic and Joe got out.

"Thanks for the ride. See you, Ruby." Joe

slapped his hand down on the top of the car, stepped back and watched her drive away before he bounded up the steps to the clinic and stopped short. The door was closed. He walked around the porch and stuck his head in the door of Doc's quarters.

"Hey, Doc. You in there?"

"I'm here. Come on in."

Doc was sitting at the table, his surgical instruments laid out on a cloth. He was carefully honing a scalpel.

"I heard what happened out north of town." Joe straddled a chair. "Damn shame."

"Yeah. Makes a fellow realize how uncertain I-life is."

"It'll go hard on his family."

"Yeah," Doc said again. Then, "What're you d-doing in town in the m-middle of the week?"

"Came in with Jack. He's going before the council tonight. Met up with Evan. He was out looking for Joy. She went to a meeting at the church after school."

"Find her?"

"Out behind the church, leaning up against the building smooching with Sammy Davidson."

"From your tone, I take it you're m-madder'n a pissed-on s-snake."

"You're damn right I am. Sammy drinks, smokes and hangs around with a tough, lazy crowd. Joy is sixteen and going through the know-it-all stage. The more you say against him, the more she takes up for him."

"Maybe you're making too m-much of it. What does your pa s-say?"

"He said we all went over fool's hill. Now it's her turn."

"Good way to look at it, I guess."

"Evan saw Mrs. Poole while he was looking for Joy. Her attitude didn't sit well with him. Later he wondered if she knew Joy was with Sammy."

"Why would she lie about it?"

"Do you think she knows about Joy?"

"If she did, she would've m-made a move right after Ron was killed."

"I guess you're right. Sammy's a horny little bugger. He had her squeezed right up against the building."

"If she wasn't protesting, d-don't blame it all on Sammy." Doc carefully put his instruments back in the case. "Speaking of h-horny . . . how did the date go with April?"

"Great. I have a date with her this Saturday night."

"Hmmm . . ." Doc grinned. "I guess she's not as smart as I thought she was."

Chapter 12

Julie took the pan of cornbread out of the oven and glanced out the window to see Evan's car come up the lane. She hummed happily. Her favorite time of day was when the family was gathered around the supper table, sharing the happenings of the day.

"Wash, Logan, Daddy's home," she said to her son playing on the kitchen floor with his Lincoln Logs.

"I'm making a barn, Mama."

"You can leave it there and finish it after supper."

Evan came in, his eyes seeking his wife. She was the love of his life. He thanked God every day that she was his. It gave him extreme pleasure just to look at her.

"Hi. Supper is about ready."

He went to her, kissed her raised lips and

nuzzled her neck before going to the high chair, where baby Nancy was pounding on the tray with a spoon to get his attention.

"How's my pretty girl?" He laughed and dodged the spoon that made a swipe at his face.

"I'm making a barn, Daddy."

Evan squatted down to look at his son's building project. "I see you are, and you're doing a good job of it."

At the sound of the screen door closing, Julie, with a smile, turned to see Joy standing with her back to the door, her arms folded across her chest. She had a mutinous look on her face, and her eyes were red from crying. The smile faded from Julie's face.

"Hi, honey. Supper's ready."

"I'm not hungry." Joy started for the door leading to the upstairs rooms but stopped when Julie called her name. "What?" she spat and turned with such a belligerent look on her face that Julie was instantly alarmed.

"Would you like to tell me what is wrong?"

"No, I wouldn't. *He'll* tell you. *He* was in on it."

"For goodness' sake." A flood of dread swamped Julie. She wrapped her hands in her apron. "Tell me what?"

"I might as well tell you before *he* does. *He* and Joe were spying on me and caught me kissing Sammy Davidson. Joe threw Sammy to the ground and threatened to beat him up. He's twice as big as Sammy. He's just a bully and I hate him!"

Julie's eyes went to Evan, who had turned his back and was pumping water into the wash dish.

"You . . . were with Sammy Davidson?"

"Yes, Sammy Davidson. Joe doesn't like him because his mother drinks. Sammy can't help that."

"Did you go to the meeting at the church?"

"Yes, and if you don't believe me, you can ask Mrs. Poole."

"Then where—"

"Behind the church. There," Joy said and glared at Evan. "I've told her so you won't have to."

"Stop your sarcasm toward Evan right now," Julie said sharply. "I'll not put up with it."

"It's all right with you if they spy on me, embarrass and humiliate me in front of my friends. Isn't it? You don't care. I'm just a kid with no feelings at all. I hate both of them."

Joy's voice was getting louder and more shrill as the words tumbled from her mouth. "I don't have to mind you or them. You're just my sister."

"That's enough, Joy." Evan spoke forcefully when he saw the stricken look on Julie's face, then softened his tone. "Watch what you say."

"I don't have to mind you," Joy repeated. "So don't be telling me to hush up. I don't have to live here. I'll go live with Papa."

"You'll do nothing of the kind." Julie seemed to come out of her shock. "You'll stay right here. We'll discuss this after supper. Logan, wash your hands."

Evan saw that Julie was near tears and moved the box step with his foot so Logan could reach the wash dish, then moved the high chair closer to the table.

During the meal Evan made an attempt at normal conversation. When he wasn't talking to his son, he told bits of news from town.

"Downriver in Whittier county they've built a dam of sorts by piling rocks halfway across the river. That's why the water hasn't gone down. The supervisors are protesting, but I don't think it'll do any good until we have a good rain up north and the bottom edge of town floods. Then maybe the governor will do something."

"Can they do that?"

"They're doing it. It'll take some straightening out, but politics works slowly. What I'm afraid of is that someone might think a stick of dynamite would be quicker."

After a lengthy silence Julie asked Joy, "When did they decide to have the harvest party?" The girl hadn't taken her eyes off her plate since she sat down.

"I don't know."

"You went to the meeting. Wasn't it discussed?"

"Are you trying to find out if I lied about going to the meeting?" The eyes that met Julie's were filled with resentment.

"No," Julie said softly and bit her lips to keep them from trembling.

The pause in conversation that followed was filled with Logan's chatter. He talked and talked, and not one time did his mother tell him to hush and eat his supper. He chattered happily, unaware that the others at the table were completely miserable.

Silently Joy helped to clear the table, and she dried the dishes as she did each night.

Then without a word she went upstairs to her room. Julie washed the children and put them to bed while Evan went out to check on the new foal and to make sure the door to the hen house was closed.

Later, in the privacy of their bedroom, she cuddled in her husband's arms and let the tears flow. He held her while she cried, then wiped her cheeks on a corner of the sheet.

"I don't know what to do," she said when she was able to talk. "Just a few weeks ago she was saying that Sammy was wild, and she didn't know why Mrs. Poole wanted him on the committee."

"Joe caught them the other night at the picture show. They were kissing in a dark corner. He told Sammy to stay away from her."

"Why didn't he tell me?"

"He thought that would be the end of it. I don't know much about girls, but it might be natural for boys and girls to neck a little. Joe thought Sammy had more than a little neck-ing on his mind. He said the boy is running with a wild bunch, drinking and smoking and doing a little bootlegging. He could be heading for the pen if he doesn't change his ways."

"Oh, my land. Why would she be attracted to a boy like that?"

"Maybe she feels sorry for him."

"I've always known that someday I should tell her the circumstances of her birth. I thought that maybe she would understand after she had children of her own. If she found out now, it would crush her."

Evan kissed her forehead and rubbed his hand up and down her back.

"Do you think Mrs. Poole knows?" Julie asked after a lengthy silence.

"I wouldn't think so. It's been ten years since her husband died. If she knew, she would have said something before now."

"I guess you're right."

"Honey, you're just frazzled to the bone. You've about stripped the garden. The cellar is full of beans, tomatoes, pickles, beets. I can't even name the different kinds of jam you've put up. Can't you let things go for a while?"

"All I have left to do is chowchow. I'll pick the green tomatoes in the morning before the children are awake."

"You will not. You'll stay right here in bed and have a good long rest. I'll have the tomatoes picked before sunup."

"How was I lucky enough to get you?"

"I was the lucky one. Now, go to sleep before I give in to the powerful urge I have to make love to you."

"I wouldn't mind."

"You're too tired and I can wait."

Lights from a car coming up the lane flashed into the room. Evan got quickly from the bed and looked out the window as the car turned into the yard behind the house.

"It's Thad's car," he said and reached for his trousers.

"It must be Jill's time." Julie slipped her dress on over her nightgown and followed Evan down the stairs. By the time they reached the kitchen door, Thad was pounding on it.

"You'd better have a damn good reason for getting me out of the bed," Evan said when he opened the door.

"Jill's got pains. I didn't want to leave her, but I've got to get Doc. Can you take Julie over?"

Julie crowded in front of Evan. "When did they start?"

"She's had a backache all day. The pains didn't start until she went to bed. I've got to get Doc," he said again and turned away.

"Thad," Evan called. "You take Julie and go back home. I'll go get Doc."

"Thanks. She's hurtin' and she's scared."

"I'll be ready in a few minutes, Thad. I'll get dressed and tell Joy we're going," Julie said on her way up the stairs.

Thad was sitting in the car when Julie and Evan came out and closed the door. He started it moving as soon as Julie was in the car.

"Don't drive like a wild man with my wife in the car," Evan cautioned.

"Just go get Doc, Evan. Tell him to hurry," Thad yelled and drove out of the yard.

Doc was sitting on his porch and Joe was perched on the porch rail when Jack arrived.

"Well, do we call you Marshal Jones?" Doc asked.

"Not yet." Jack grinned. "Damn, I hate waiting. I wish they'd just say yes or no."

"With a half dozen fingers in the pie, it'll take some time."

"Corbin heard what the other men had to say and thinks I've got a good chance. Two of them are from out of town, and both have done police work. But Corbin's promise to train me carries a lot of weight."

"Did they say when they would make the decision?" Joe asked. He knew how much this job meant to his brother and dreaded to see the letdown if he didn't get it.

"Corbin said they would have another meeting in the morning. Frank Adler has to sleep on every decision he makes. He was on the council when they hired Corbin. Corbin had been a military policeman during the war, so he didn't go into the job stone-cold like I'll be doing."

"Don't shortchange Frank," Doc said. "He's probably got more brains than the rest of the council put together. He's impressed with a man who is competent and trustworthy. Experience is important, but it won't be his only consideration."

"Have you talked to him about this?" Joe asked.

Doc evaded the question by saying, "Frank's an old friend."

"If I don't get the job, I'm thinking that I might join the army or the navy. I sure as heck don't want to go to California and pick peaches."

"Ruby was in town for a while tonight."

Joe saw his brother go still when he mentioned the girl he had assumed to be his until just a few weeks ago.

"Doesn't she teach country school?" Doc asked.

It was Joe who answered. "Yeah. First grade through sixth. She stays with a farm family near the school. She said she was in town for supplies."

Jack moved toward the porch steps. "I'm goin' home. You goin'?"

"Guess I'll have to unless I want to walk. You've got the keys."

"Come on, then. Papa wants to pick corn to dry for seed tomorrow."

They were leaving the porch when Evan's car came around the corner and stopped in front of the house. The lights went off and Evan got out.

"Evan. What's up?" Joe called

"I came for Doc," he said as he went up the steps to the porch. "Thad says Jill's having pains. He took Julie back to the house. He's as nervous as a dog passing peach pits. If he wrecks the car with my wife in it, he'll be passing a mouth full of teeth."

Doc stood up. "Did he say what kind of pains and how often they came?"

"He said she'd had a backache all day and tonight pains. He was so shook up he didn't know if he was coming or going."

"I'll get my bag and go out."

"I'll go with Doc. I've got to keep an eye on Thad. He might do something stupid . . . like get into a pissin' contest with a skunk," Joe said with a cocky grin.

"I'll go home and wake up Pa and Eudora," Jack said. "She might want to go over. They'll need someone to stay with Jacob."

Two pairs of interested eyes followed the three cars out of town. Sammy and his friend Tator Williams stood along the board fence surrounding the lumberyard.

"Wonder where they're goin'?"

Tator was a small-caliber hoodlum who had known Sammy since he was a three-year-old playing on the floor of a bar, waiting for his mother to remember he was there and take him home. As a ten-year-old, Tator had known, even then, that it wasn't right for the child to be there.

The kid had survived. He had guts. And now at sixteen he was as tough as he had to be to get along. His ma was a no-good slut, and his pa cared no more for him than a fart in the wind. Hell, even Tator had screwed Marla Davidson a time or two, and she was almost old enough to be his mother.

"That was Evan Johnson that went to Doc's house," Sammy said. "I'll not forget that car in a hurry. First chance I get I'll poke my knife in his tires."

"I thought it was Joe Jones you was mad at."

"I am. I'll get even. I don't know how yet but I will."

"I know how you can make him pay."

"Yeah?"

"He's got a bull out at his place that he's mighty proud of."

"Yeah?" Sammy said again.

"Yeah," Tator said and laughed. "The bull wouldn't be much good without a pecker, would it?"

"I'd rather it be *his* pecker I cut," Sammy growled. "I'll get even with him for the way he treated me in front of Joy."

"You got the hots for that little skirt, don't you?"

"That's no business of yours."

"You been in her pants yet?"

"No."

"What's holdin' ya up, boy? I told ya to go

right for the good stuff. Don't give 'em a chance to say no. If ya can get your fingers in there, your tally-whacker is sure to follow. She looks the type to spread her legs at the drop of a hat."

"Don't talk about her like that!" Sammy blurted angrily. "She's a nice girl. She can't help it if her brother's meaner than a dog shittin' tacks."

"Ha! If she's such a nice girl, what's she doin' hangin' around with a slimy little piece of horse hockey like you?" Tator slapped Sammy playfully on the back so hard that he staggered. "Boy, has that little blond piece of ass got you by the balls?"

"She's not that kind of girl."

"She *has* got you by the balls." Tator hooted with laughter. "I know how to cure that. We'll make a trip down to see that white nigger gal that lives on the south river road. I've not been there for a while. A bunch of us used to go down and pound on the door just for the hell of it."

"Why do you call her a white nigger?"

" 'Cause she don't look like a nigger."

"Then how do you know she is?"

"Everybody know that her ma was colored and her pa was white. They say that if she likes you, she'll give you a potion that'll keep you hard all night long and randy as a buckin' bronco."

"Who said that?"

"Some fellers who've been there. Only trouble is gettin' by the big colored bastard that guards her. If enough of us come onto that nigger, we could put him out of commission long enough to get to the whore."

"Count me out."

"Jesus. What's the matter with you? You goin' soft or somethin'?"

"I want no part of rapin' a woman, colored or white."

"Ya stupid kid. Ya can't rape a whore. Ya wouldn't have to do any of the rapin'. I'd take care of that. Ya can go along and watch, or are ya too sissy to even watch?"

Sammy started walking down the road toward the river. Tator lumbered alongside of him.

"Don't call me sissy again, Tator, or this knife in my pocket might find *your* tally-whacker some dark night."

"Hell and damnation!" Tator swore and muttered under his breath. "You've changed, and I don't like it."

Chapter 13

During breakfast April had to endure over-friendly overtures from Fred. He had come, smelling strongly of aftershave, to the dining room shortly after she had sat down at the table. His lips were strangely red for a man's; and they had smiled continually, giving her the creepy feeling that Fred knew something she didn't know.

After eating only a buttered biscuit smeared with blackberry jam, April had excused herself to go back upstairs to finish getting ready for work, hoping Fred would leave the house before she went back downstairs. But he had been waiting on the porch to walk with her.

There were times when she didn't let Fred's attentions bother her; but this morning she was edgy, and it took considerable willpower not to be rude. She was extremely glad to be rid of him when he tipped his hat and turned to go to the hardware store.

Sparky, from the diner, was in the surgery when she reached it. Doc was closing a cut on his thumb with stitches.

"Good morning," April said cheerfully. She always felt comfortable in these sur-roundings doing the work she loved. She peered over Sparky's shoulder. "Doc's put-ting in some pretty fancy stitches."

"It's just a little cut, but the woman got all excited and made me come have Doc look at it." There was an apologetic tone in Sparky's voice.

"Smart woman. You could get blood poi-soning with a cut like that."

April was pinning her starched cap to her hair when Sparky left. Doc came into the re-ception room and sank down in a chair.

"You look beat. You've not been to bed, have you?"

"Jill Taylor gave birth to a boy last night. It was a long, hard labor. I just got back an hour ago."

"Mother and baby all right?"

"Yeah, but Thad's a nervous wreck. He

swears that he'll never get her pregnant again."

April laughed. "I've heard that before."

"Joe was threatening to kill him if he said 'never again' one more time, which didn't help matters at all. I finally told Evan to take both of them out and put them to work chopping wood or digging a ditch."

"Sounds to me like you had an exciting night. Why don't you go take a nap? I'll come get you if anything comes in that I can't handle."

"I'll do that after I go to the post office."

"I'll go to the post office—"

"No but thanks. I need to move around."

Doc left the office before April could say more. If he had a letter from Canada, she would be sure to be curious about it. Not that the nosy postmaster wouldn't spread it all over town that the doctor had a letter from out of the country. He hated to keep his nurse in the dark about his intentions, but he wasn't ready to tell her that he had his feelers out to find another position.

"Mornin', Doc. I'm a little late with the mail this mornin'." The postmaster was running the American flag up the pole in front of the small white building that had served as a post office since the town was founded back in 1910.

"Better late than never," Doc replied and went into the building. He was followed closely by the eagle-eyed postmaster.

There were several letters in Doc's box. He looked at them hurriedly and stuffed them in his pocket.

"Ya got one there from up in Canada someplace—"

"Yeah, it's from a fellow I met in medical school. We keep in touch."

"Is he a doctor up there?"

"Yeah. Guess I'd better get back to the office."

"Doc, have ya got time to look at this sore on my eye?"

Doc gritted his teeth and turned back to the man. He pulled down the lower lid and peered at the small red lump in the corner of his eye.

"Looks to me like you got a sty. Not much you can do for it until it comes to a head. If you want to hurry it along, put hot, wet cloths on it. When a little yellow spot appears, squeeze it gently and get the pus out. Should be all right then."

"Thanks, Doc."

"You're welcome." Doc hurried out the door like he had something really important to do. It seemed to take forever to get to the privacy of his own house. As soon as he was inside, he threw his hat in a chair and slipped his finger beneath the flap of the envelope with the Canadian postmark.

He hastily read the letter and swore. The position had been filled, but there was another position open in a town near Vancouver. The clinic administrator had been kind enough to furnish the name and address where he could apply.

Doc put the letter back in the envelope and took it to his bedroom. He threw it on the bureau and sank down on the bed, resting his arm over his eyes to shut out the daylight. His body was bone-tired, but his mind was even more so.

Caroline, Caroline, my love—

Damn, damn, dammit! He would rather take her to an English-speaking country, but he might have to take her to Mexico. One thing was sure, he would find a place where they could be married before their baby was born, or he would die trying.

He moved to swing his legs over the side of the bed. He wished that he could live here in this town with his love. He had friends here, and he was fairly certain that the Jones family would accept Caroline. But as for the rest of the town, it was impossible to even think about marrying her here, even if he could find a preacher who would perform the ceremony. He would not only lose his license to practice medicine, he would be arrested and put in jail for marrying a woman with even a speck of colored blood.

Doc lay back down, closed his eyes and daydreamed of holding Caroline in his arms. The last thing he had ever thought of doing was to fall in love with her. It had crept up on him, and before he knew it, she occupied every corner of his heart. He loved her desperately. Now she was pregnant with his child. He couldn't help but be glad, yet deep down he knew that he should have prevented it.

It would take three or four weeks for a letter to get to Vancouver and back. That's all the time he could allow before considering going to Mexico. He went to his bureau, took out paper, pen and a bottle of ink. With the letter from Canada in hand he settled down at the kitchen table to write to the address in Vancouver. When he finished, he slapped his hat on his head and headed back to the post office.

It was a relatively quiet day in the surgery. Miss Fowler, one of the single ladies who had her sights set on Doc, came in with a jar of pickled peaches. A small red bow had been pasted atop the jar. She asked if Dr. Forbes was in. April felt pity for a woman who so blatantly chased after a man.

"He had a long night out at the Taylor place delivering a baby. He's taking a nap. We can't afford to have the doctor worn-out in case we have an emergency."

"Oh, well, I can come back later."

"I'll tell him you were here."

George Belmont came in as Miss Fowler was leaving.

"Howdy, pretty lady," he said loudly, and April flinched when Miss Fowler turned and gave her a disapproving look.

"Hello, George. What brings you out in the middle of the day?"

"Wanna tell you I'm pitchin' in the horseshoe tournament this Sunday afternoon." He held out the hand she had stitched a week or so ago. "Take a look. It's as good as new." She took his hand in hers and looked at it from all angles.

"It does look good. I did a heck of a job. I'd appreciate it if you would recommend my stitching to your friends. I do hands, arms, legs, even heads on occasion."

His homely face broke into a grin. "You've got my business from now on. How about comin' and watchin' me pitch?"

"I just might have to do that. Shall I bring my needle and thread in case that cut pops open?"

"I'll expect a kiss if I win," George said as he went out the door.

Later, April spoke on the phone with a woman whose baby was cutting teeth.

"I wouldn't be alarmed at that, Mrs. Lawrence. Sometimes babies will have loose bowels while teething. Have you tried rubbing his gums with the flat handle of a spoon to help the little teeth come through? Another thing you can do is tie a thin slice of peeled apple in a cloth. Let the baby chomp down on it. The little flavor in the apple will make him want to bite down. Is he running a fever?"

"No, ma'am."

"If he does, it's not because of teething. It

means that something else is going on, and you should bring him in to see the doctor. I'll tell the doctor you called."

After hanging up the phone April went to the back room to eat the crackers and cheese she had brought for lunch. When she heard a knock on the back door, she peered through the screen to see a large colored man clad in overalls standing with his hat in his hand.

"Hello."

"I wants to see Mistah Docta."

"Are you sick or hurt?"

"No, ma'am. Just wants to talk."

"He was up most of the night. He's sleeping right now. I'm his nurse. Is there anything I can do?"

"No, ma'am. I wait till he wakes up."

"Would you like to come around and wait in the reception room?"

"I sit here on dis step, ma'am, if'n ya don't mind."

"I don't mind." April finished her lunch and tidied up the surgery.

An hour later Jack came in. He was all smiles.

"Don't tell me." April stood up. "You got the job."

"I got the job."

"Congratulations." She came from behind the desk and kissed his cheek. "I'm so happy for you. You'll make a crackerjack of an officer, I just know you will."

"I'm excited, but I couldn't show it in front of the council when they told me. Here I can let my hair down. Where's Doc? I wanted to tell him first off. Corbin already knows. Doc put in a good word for me. I want to let him know that I won't let him down."

"Doc's sleeping. He was out at your sister's most of the night."

"Yeah, that's right. I got a new job and a new nephew all in one day."

April looked at the clock. "He's been sleeping about three hours. I should wake him or he won't sleep tonight." She went through the door connecting the surgery to Doc's house and knocked on his bedroom door. "Doc?"

"Yeah."

"There's nothing really pressing. I just thought you might want to get up now."

"I'll be there in a minute or two."

When Doc came into the surgery, his hair was damp and combed and he had on a fresh shirt. He stopped when he saw Jack sitting on the edge of the desk.

"Grinning like a jackass could mean only one thing. You g-got the job."

"Yeah, I did. I want to thank you for putting in a good word for me."

"I didn't really say you were all that g-good, but rather that you hadn't robbed a b-bank or killed anybody that I knew of."

"Well, thanks for saying that much." Jack stood and extended his hand.

After the men shook hands, April remembered the man sitting on the back step.

"Doc, there's a colored man waiting to talk to you. He didn't want to come in."

"Colored man?" Doc's attention was immediate. "Where?"

"On the back step."

Doc hurried to the back door. "Silas? Is something wrong?" he asked anxiously as he motioned the man to go with him out into the yard behind the house.

April looked out the door to see Doc listening intently to what the big man was saying.

"I wonder who he is," April said to Jack. "Doc seems to know him."

"He lives down along the river."

April went into the reception room when she heard the outside door open. Joe stood there. His smiling eyes met hers, then went past her to Jack.

"Hey, Brother. Just because you're the new policeman doesn't mean you can hang around my girl." Joe stuck his hand out, clasped Jack's and then banged him on the shoulder.

"You heard about it, huh?" Jack was all grins.

"I went by the paper and Corbin told me."

"Starting Monday, I meet with Corbin and the district marshal. I'm anxious to get started. There's a lot I've got to learn."

"You'll do fine. You always were too smart for your britches." Joe's eyes caught April's. She was watching the exchange. "Of course, if you get stuck, you can always call on your big brother to pull you out of a hole."

Jack laughed. "Yeah. I haven't forgotten the time you and Thad pulled me out of a hole, then hung me in a tree by my overalls and didn't come back for an hour. Julie was fit to be tied when I didn't show up for the noon meal."

"If I remember right, Pa made me do your chores for a week."

"Jack," Doc called from the door. "Joe. I didn't know you were here. Will both of you c-come out here for a minute?"

Joe winked at April as he followed his brother out the door. Doc and the colored man waited beside Doc's car.

"Joe, Jack, this is Silas. He t-tells me that for the past two nights men have been c-coming to Miss Deval's, pounding on the door and making lewd s-suggestions. One man called the other Tator. Do you know anyone b-by that name?"

"Tator Williams," Jack said. "Sammy Davidson has been hanging around with him."

Joe looked at Doc's worried face. He had known for some time that Doc made frequent trips to see Caroline Deval.

"If they k-keep it up, someone is going to get hurt, and it isn't going to be Caroline Deval," Doc said irritably. "Silas has a shotgun, and he'll use it if they t-try to break in."

"I don't have any authority until I'm sworn in, Doc. But when I am . . ."

"Why don't I have a talk with Tator and Sammy?" Joe could see how important this was to his friend, and it made him wonder if Doc had feelings for Miss Deval other than that of doctor and patient. Joe had only seen the woman from a distance. She had been working in her flower garden when he passed by. He had heard that she never left the house.

"Be careful with the shotgun, Silas," Jack cautioned. "Even if you were defending Miss Deval, folks would get all stirred up if you shot a white man."

"I knows that. I holler 'nd run at 'em wid a big stick. Little missy, her was scared."

"Caroline isn't the kind of w-woman folks think she is. They shun her and talk about her, and they don't know what they're t-talking about."

Joe didn't think he'd ever heard Doc so agitated.

"A woman shouldn't have to put up with that. If she lived here in town, they wouldn't dare. I'll look up Sammy and Tator as soon as school is out. Sammy will head right for Shanty Town."

"I'll go with you," Jack said.

"Better not, Brother."

"Why not? You think to handle both sorry pieces of shit by yourself? I know Tator. He's got the brains of a pissant, but he's sneaky as a fox creeping up on a henhouse."

"You'd best wait until you're sworn in. I might have to beat the hockey out of Tator or do something else against the law. I don't want you near. Word might get out you had a hand in it."

"I'll go with you," Doc said. "I'm getting d-damn tired of having to p-pussyfoot around." He didn't explain what he meant. Joe and Jack looked at each other and didn't ask. "Meanwhile, I'll take Silas h-home." He went in the back door to get his medical bag—he never left the office without it. "Tell April I'll not be gone more than an hour," he said as he passed Jack.

Chapter 14

Joe had never seen Doc in such an agitated state. He drove the car down the river road hitting the ruts so hard that Joe had to hold on to the side door. When he turned to look at Silas in the backseat, he was doing the same. The car took a quick turn into the lane leading to a small house set back from the road. As soon as they reached it, Doc slammed on the brakes, stopped the car and got out.

"Back in a few minutes."

Joe caught only a glimpse of the girl who opened the back door. Doc went inside. The door closed behind him.

"How often do men come here, Silas?" Joe and the big colored man got out of the car and stood beside it.

"Jist sometimes. Dey come lots after missy papa die."

"Have they ever broken in?"

"Naw, sir. But scare missy good. Mistah Doctah say I'm ta get 'er out the back and hide 'er in the woods if dey gets so worked up dey 'bout to break in."

"I've not seen Miss Deval in town. Does she ever go out?"

"Her don't go to town. Mistah Doctah bring what she need."

"Why doesn't she go out?"

"She scared of folks."

"That's not right. She shouldn't be afraid to go to town."

"Naw, sir."

The back door opened and Doc called, "Joe, will you c-come in here?"

"Sure, Doc." Joe took a deep breath, surprised by the request.

Doc held the door open. "There's s-someone I want you to meet."

Joe removed his hat and stepped into a neat and cheerful room with a cloth-covered table, braided rug on the floor and crisp white curtains at the windows. Doc closed the door, then moved to the side of an incredibly beautiful girl. Clouds of dark curly hair surrounded a pale face. She was small with dainty features, sweetly curved red lips and large golden eyes.

The words *calm* and *serene* came immediately to mind when he looked at her. But the calmness was a mask; Joe was certain of it when he saw the vein throbbing in her throat. *She is filled with anxiety.* He didn't know why he thought so, but he was sure that she was sublimely unaware of her beauty.

"This is Caroline Deval, Joe." Doc's arm encircled the girl and brought her close to him. "Honey, this is Joe Jones. I've told you about him and his brother Jack."

"Pleased to meet you, ma'am."

"I intend to m-make her my wife." The blunt words fell into the quiet room. On hearing them the girl looked quickly up at Doc.

Joe's eyes went first to the worried frown wrinkling Caroline's brow, then to Doc, who stood waiting with a defiant look on his face, his hand caressing her upper arm.

"Congratulations, Doc. You sure picked a beauty."

"I think so. Caroline's great-grandmother was colored." For once he didn't stutter. He spoke loud and clear and waited for Joe's reaction.

"Yeah?" Joe didn't know what else to say.

"That means that she's considered a colored and easy pickings for the scum who hang around the river dives."

"Don't worry about Tator Williams. I'll take care of him."

"You know what would h-happen if word got out that I'm going to marry her?"

"Yeah," Joe said again. "Folks can be pretty stiff-necked about some things."

"I'm trying to find a p-position in Canada." Doc had decided to put all his cards on the table. "Caroline and I can be m-married there."

"I wish you and Miss Deval all the best, Doc."

"Then you're still my friend?"

"Hell, yes. Beggin' your pardon, ma'am. Why wouldn't I be? Sometime I'll tell you about Radna, a lady I met over in Rainwater, Oklahoma. She had a dab of colored blood. It made no difference to my friend Blue-feather, a Kickapoo Indian who was as rich as sin. He wanted Radna."

Doc's shoulders seemed to slump with relief. "Thank you, Joe." He put both arms around Caroline and hugged her to him. "Somehow I knew that you'd understand," he said, looking over her head.

"I'll do what I can to help you, Doc. Does April know that you're planning to leave?"

"No, and I feel guilty about that. I can't tell her or anyone yet. I told you b-because it's getting harder and harder for me to protect Caroline, and o comohow I know that I could put my trust in you."

"You got it, Doc. Jack would feel the same."

"Honey." Doc turned the girl in his arms so that she was facing Joe. "I want you to know Joe Jones. Take a good look at him in case he ever comes and tells you that I w-want you to go with him. Understand?"

"But . . . Todd . . ."

"You can trust him, sweetheart. He's been my friend for a long time. If the t-time should come when I can't c-come for you myself, I'll s-send Joe."

"Silas—"

"I'll tell Silas. Did the men threaten him last night?"

"One of them threatened to do bad things to him when he told them to go away."

"Did you see the men, Miss Deval?" Joe asked.

"No. But one of them was bad. He yelled nasty things. The other one was younger. He kept trying to get him to leave."

"It very well might have been Tator Williams and Sammy Davidson. I'll put the fear of the devil in them when I catch up with them."

"Honey, I've got to get back. Mrs. Appleby is expecting her baby, and April needs to know where to find me."

"I'll wait outside." Joe headed for the door. "It was a pleasure meeting you, Miss Deval. Congratulations to you and Doc. He's one of the best men I've ever known."

"Thank you, Mr. Jones."

After Joe had gone out and closed the door, Doc held Caroline away from him so that he could look into her face.

"What will your nurse think . . . when she hears about me?"

"I don't know, honey. She seems to be a sensible person. She's never expressed her views on mixed marriage. It makes no difference to me if she approves or not."

"Do you like her?"

"She's a crackerjack nurse."

"Is she pretty?"

He kissed her on the nose. "Not as pretty as you. I'm sorry you were s-scared, darlin' girl. If anyone tries to break in the h-house, Silas will shoot over their heads. If they don't leave, he's to get you out the b-back, hide you in the woods and c-come for me."

"I'll be all right, Todd. Don't worry. I've got the little pistol Papa gave me."

"I don't want you to even h-handle that gun unless someone breaks down the d-door and is coming into the bedroom. Then sh-shoot the bastards! Oh, Lord. I hate it that you're h-here and I can't be with you." He cradled her face in his hands and kissed her lips again and again. "I love you, sweetheart. I love you so m-much. It won't be long until we can b-be together."

"I love you, too. I hate it that you worry."

"Are you feeling all right?" He smoothed his hand down over her flat stomach. "Have you b-been queasy in the morning?"

"I was one morning. I ate a cracker and it went away."

"Do you n-need anything? Are you d-drinking the milk I brought out? If you need ice, s-send Silas down to Earl's ice-house."

Her smile was beautiful. "Yes, Papa."

He returned her smile. "My feelings for you are f-far from fatherly, my sweet girl."

"I know. I wish you could stay, but I know you have to go."

"Now that Joe k-knows about us, I may be able to come out more often. He's f-fallen tail over teakettle for April. I don't know yet how she feels about him. I figure he'll be hanging around the o-office quite a bit, and I can slip away. He'll know where to find me if I'm n-needed. I'll let you know as soon as I h-hear from Canada. Kiss me again before I go."

Several minutes later they stood at the door. "Good-bye, s-sweetheart. Keep the doors locked."

"I will. Bye."

He reached the car where Joe and the colored man stood leaning against the hood.

"You did the right thing to come get me, Silas," Doc told him.

"Yessah."

Joe went around and got into the car, but he saw Doc slip a bill into the hand of the big dark man before he got behind the wheel. Doc didn't speak until they were back on the river road.

"I've a f-favor to ask."

"It's as good as done."

"In the top bureau drawer in my b-bedroom there's a letter from my s-sister, Jesse, who lives in the hills just above Harpersville, Tennessee. Her name is Mrs. Wade Simmer. I have written to her about Caroline. It would take a l-load off my mind if I knew that if something should h-happen to me, you would put Caroline on a train and s-send her to Jesse."

"I hope and pray that nothing will happen to keep you and Caroline from spending your lives together; but, God forbid if something did happen, you've got my word on it. I'll get Caroline to your sister if I have to take her there myself."

"Thanks. It's a relief that s-someone knows how I feel about her. It's b-been over a year now. I have hopes of a position in Canada. We can m-marry there, but if that doesn't come through within the next couple of m-months, I'm t-taking her to Mexico."

"You'd never know by looking at her that she had colored blood."

"Folks around h-here know. Her father worried about w-what would h-happen to Caroline when he was gone. I assured him as he lay d-dying that I'd take care of her. I'd already f-fallen in love with her."

"I kind of remember when they came here. There was talk about a white man living with a colored woman. The girl didn't go to school. I heard that her father had been a teacher in some college back East. He taught her?"

"Yes. He was a well-educated man and gave up his career when he took Caroline's mother for his c-common-law wife. She died while Dr. Curtis was h-here. Deval loved her and he loved their daughter. It almost killed him w-when he lost her. For some men t-there is only one woman. I can understand his f-feelings for her."

"Jack is still here," Joe said as Doc turned the corner and stopped behind the clinic. "I'll take Pa's car and wait for Sammy to get out of school. Then he and I will have a talk with Tator."

"They hang with a tough b-bunch."

"I can be tough, too."

"I'll go with you. If Jack s-stays in town,

he'll know where to find me if I h-have an emergency."

"No deal, Doc. I'd rather keep you out of it. I'll not face Tator where his buddies can back him up. He'll not be so tough without them. This will be just between the three of us, and it'll be their word against mine." He grinned at Doc. "I learned a few things working with the toughs in the oil fields. They think you're out of your mind if you fight fair."

"I don't want you to get hurt f-fighting my fight."

"It's not just your fight. If they succeed in harassing Miss Deval, they'll go on to bother other women who are without protection. It could be April next. They need to be taught a lesson."

Joe parked the car in an area near the school where it wouldn't be conspicuous and waited for Sammy. Shortly after the school bell rang, Joy and her friend Sylvia Taylor, Thad's sister, came out surrounded by a group of their friends. Sylvia's father was waiting. They got into his car, and Joe breathed a sigh of relief. *One obstacle out of the way.*

A minute later Sammy came out alone and headed for town. Joe started the car and trailed him a few blocks. When the boy came to an intersection, Joe turned in front of him, forcing him to stop.

"You tryin' to run me down?" Sammy hit the hood of the car with the flat of his hand.

"Get in. I want to talk to you."

"Go blow it out your—"

"Watch it, boy. You're on shaky ground as it is. Get in, or I go to the state marshal and tell him a few things."

"Tell him . . . what?"

"I think you know what."

"He'd not do nothin'."

"How about the school principal? You want to be in the school play, don't you? I doubt you would be if I had a talk with him. Want to risk it? Get in."

Sammy jerked open the door, got in the car and slammed the door shut.

"Break the window on my pa's car and you'll be shoveling shit out of the barn for a month to pay for it."

"Whattaya want?"

"Where's Tator?"

"Whattaya want to know for?"

"I need to have a little chat with the two of

you." Joe moved the car on down the street and turned to go toward the river. "Will he be at Earl's?"

"How would I know?"

"You'll know. We're going there and you're going in. If he's there, you bring him out."

"What's the matter, tough guy? You 'fraid to go in?"

"No. Earl is a pretty square fellow for a bootlegger and runs a fairly decent juke joint. He'd not let your pals gang up on me. The Feds are watching him, and I don't want to bring any trouble down on him."

"Like what?"

"Like when I smash Tator's nose all over his face and kick your ass from here to Sunday. The Feds are sure to hear about a fight and use it as an excuse to close Earl down."

"You're a real shit."

"Maybe, but I don't go out and harass defenseless women." He stopped in front of Earl's. "Now, get out and see if Tator is in there. Tell him he won the prize at the picture show or anything else you can think of to get him out here."

Sammy glanced back at Joe just before he went in the roadhouse. Joe kept his eye on the door, wondering if the kid would sneak out the back. But Sammy came out and he was alone.

"Earl said he's fishin' down by Lone Tree."

"Get in."

"I've got things to do."

"They can wait. Get in, or I'll get out and put you in."

Sammy jerked open the door and plunked himself down in the seat. He was careful not to slam the door.

"You sure like to throw your weight around. How are you up against someone your own size?"

"You're about to find out." Joe drove slowly along the river road, his eyes searching the riverbank. "There's our boy," he said when he spotted the man sitting with his back against the only tree along the bank for twenty yards. His chin rested on his chest, his relaxed arms at his side. The fishing pole had fallen from his hand. "Perfect. Just perfect."

"Whattaya mean? Whattaya gonna do?"

"I haven't decided yet." Joe stopped the car. "Don't slam the door. We don't want to wake the boy . . . yet."

Sammy followed Joe across the grassy

area to where the river, running high, was almost to the bank. Tator had a line in the water, but there was no sign of a cork. He was sleeping soundly with his mouth open. Joe squatted down beside him, picked up a long blade of grass and tickled his nose.

Tator made a half-effort to brush it away and continued to snore. Joe looked around. If a dried cow pie had been in sight, he would be tempted to poke it in his mouth. Lucky for Tator, all that fell within his sight was a dandelion. Joe reached for it and pulled it from the soft ground. Without hesitation he shoved the root ends that were covered with dirt into Tator's open mouth.

Instantly awake, Tator jerked his head up, his hands went to his mouth to grab the plant, he coughed, gagged and spat out dirt. Joe stood back and watched. Tator rolled to his knees and got to his feet.

"Why'd ya do that for?"

"Couldn't resist. Looked for a cow pie—"

"You sonofa—"

"Don't say it. I'm going to hit you anyway, but if you put that name on my mother, I just might put you out of commission for a mighty long time."

Tator's eyes rolled to Sammy. "What's got his pecker in a knot?"

Sammy lifted his shoulders. "I ain't here 'cause I want to."

"Tired, Tator? Didn't you get any sleep last night?"

"Whatta you care?"

"I care. Believe me I do. I heard you called on a lady last night."

"Lady?" Tator's loose lips curled in a sneer. "I didn't call on no *lady*."

"You and Sammy called on Miss Deval. You said some pretty nasty things—"

"She ain't no lady. She just a nigg—"

Joe's rock-hard fist connected with Tator's nose, knocking him off his feet. Blood spurted down over his mouth. Tator bounced up off the ground, his fists ready.

"Come on, you mule's ass. You can talk nasty to a woman. How about talkin' nasty to me? I'm just itchin' to bust your mouth. Won't hurt your looks none. You're already as ugly as a pile of cowshit."

Fury overrode Tator's judgment. He lowered his head and charged. He had taken only two steps when Joe's fist connected with his mouth and smashed his lips against his teeth. His eyes crossed and he backtracked a couple of steps before he hit the ground.

"Lip off again about Miss Deval so I can hit you again. You don't even have to get up. I've got no scruples 'bout hittin' a man when he's down."

"What's she to you? You screwin' 'er?"

Joe shook his head in disgust, reached down and with his hand beneath Tator's arm jerked him to his feet. He waited for him to regain his balance, then hit him again. This time his fist landed squarely in Tator's left eye.

"It's more fun hitting you when you're standing," Joe said, looking down at the man sprawled on his back. "I like seeing your butt hit the ground."

Tator wiped his bloody nose on the sleeve of his shirt and glared at Sammy. "Ain't . . . ya goin' to do . . . anythin'?"

"What can I do? He outweighs me by fifty pounds. I told you not to go down there and pester that woman."

"You was chickenshit last night and you're chickenshit now."

"I might be, but I ain't got a busted nose," Sammy said angrily.

"Get up, Tator. We got to have a serious talk."

" 'Bout what?" Tator got slowly to his feet.

" 'Bout the cell waitin' for you down at the state pen."

"They'd not send me to the pen for screwin' a nigg—"

Joe's fist smashed into his right eye so fast Tator didn't have time to even get his hands up.

"You're a slow learner, Tator. But it's all right. I wanted an excuse to hit you in the other eye. Two black eyes, a busted nose and a mouth lookin' like the asshole of a jackass for a week or two. I think I'll send Corbin down to take your picture for the paper."

Tator curled up on his side and covered his face with his hands. He was smart enough to stay on the ground.

"There's your hero, kid," Joe said to Sammy. "He's a big man when he's harassing a defenseless woman, but he's not got the guts to stand up and fight like a man." He nudged Tator with the toe of his boot. "If I ever hear of you going near that woman or talking nasty to any woman, you'll find yourself going downriver facedown. Understand?" Joe waited, then said, "I'm not leaving until I know you understand. If you can't talk, nod your stupid head."

Tator nodded.

"Take a good look, Sammy. That's what you'll be in a year or two if you don't change your ways: a lazy, ignorant, whiskey-soaked sot who isn't worth the powder it would take to blow his brains out."

"What I'll be ain't nothing to you."

"You're right and it's nothing to my sister. Don't you forget it." Joe glanced at the river before he headed back to the car. "Better bring in Tator's line. He might have a fish he can trade to Earl for a pint of booze."

Chapter 15

It was six-thirty. April had deliberately stayed late in the hope of avoiding having dinner with Mrs. Poole and her brother. She didn't mind Mrs. Poole so much, but Fred was beginning to irritate her enough that it was getting hard to be polite to him.

Doc had little to say when he and Joe returned from taking Silas home. Knowing when to talk and when to keep quiet, April worked silently and didn't bother him with unnecessary conversation.

"I'm leaving, Doc. Good night," she called, placing her nurse's cap on the desk. She slipped into the light jacket she wore because the evenings were cool and turned out the light. She was locking the door of the clinic when George Belmont and his friend Russ Story came walking by.

"Ready for our date?" George called as she stepped off the porch.

"Our date?"

"Yeah. We was going to go out to supper tonight. Remember?" He winked and grinned cockily, showing the space between his two front teeth.

"Why . . . I guess I did forget. Hold on a minute while I call and tell Mrs. Poole that I won't be there for supper." She welcomed the excuse not to return to the rooming house until after the evening meal.

The look of surprise on George's face kept her smiling while she made the call.

"Something has come up, Mrs. Poole, and I'll not be there for supper. I'm sorry I didn't call sooner."

"Well . . . I'd made bread pudding with raisins just because it's your favorite."

"That was nice of you. I must go now. Good-bye." April refused to feel guilty and happily left the office.

George and his friend were waiting beside the steps when she returned. They were in their work clothes, she in her nurse's uniform, so no one could possibly think that this was a prearranged date.

"This isn't a date, George," she said when

she joined them on the sidewalk. "I'll pay for my own supper."

"Now, what would folks think if I took a lady to dine and she had to pay for her own supper? My reputation would be ruined in this town."

"What reputation?" Russ snorted. He was a short man with sandy hair and a receding hairline. His eyes were small and close together beneath heavy brows that met at the bridge of his nose. His mouth was wide, his lower lip curled, and his teeth tobacco-stained. He appeared to be slightly older than George. He had been with George when he came to the clinic the day she arrived.

April walked down the street between the two men. She was comfortable in their company. George was fun to be with and was well aware that she didn't take him seriously. She chatted with the two men about nonsensical matters until they reached Sparky's.

"Well, howdy." Sparky's voice boomed in the small room when they came in the door. "Come in, folks. Take either one of the tables over by the window. I'll be with you in a minute." It was Sparky's favorite joke because there was only one table beside the window.

Several men at the counter turned to look at them, and Sparky's voice boomed again.

"Seat the lady and behave yourself, George. See that he does, Russ. Miss Asbury's special around here. He gets out of line, ma'am, just yell. I'll be on 'im like a goose on a June bug."

Looking as pleased as a boy with a new slingshot, George pulled out her chair. After she was seated, the men took chairs on either side of her. The white oilcloth cover on the table was scrupulously clean. Salt and pepper shakers and a small vinegar cruet sat in the middle of the table.

The menu was posted on a large chalkboard behind the counter. The choices were: liver and onions or hot beef sandwich with mashed potatoes and gravy for twenty-five cents or T-bone steak for thirty-five cents. Fresh apple, peach and chokecherry pies were on the menu, too. Mrs. Sparky was famous for her pies.

"All right, folks, what'll it be?" Sparky, in a white apron and white shirt, his sparse hair slicked down, came from behind the counter. He was carrying two glasses of water in one hand and one in the other.

April was suddenly hungry. "I want the hot beef sandwich and a glass of iced tea."

Both men ordered the liver and onions.

"You orderin' onions and courtin' a girl?" Sparky snorted and looked down his nose at George. "I'll have to take you back behind the barn and tell you a thing or two 'bout courtin' women."

"I didn't know you were an authority on courtin', Sparky." One of the men on the stools turned to look at the group at the table.

"Well, I am. Ask Mrs. Sparky. I bowled her over with my courtin'."

"That right, Mrs. Sparky?" the man called.

"Right as rain," she called back. "He chased me till I caught him."

Her remark brought laughter from the men at the counter.

"Make mine the hot beef sandwich." George looked irritated.

"Me, too," Russ said.

"Both of ya courtin' her?"

"They are not courting me," April said quickly and laughed. "They're trying to get me on their horseshoe team. They're tired of losing."

"Well, I can understand that. Neither one of 'em could hit the side of a barn, much less a stake. My old dog, Peanuts, could outpitch 'em."

"You've had your fun, Sparky," George growled. "Get back to business, or I'll go to the kitchen and tell Mrs. Sparky a thing or two about the time we went over to Mason for a tournament."

"You do that, you sneaky polecat, and I'll put saltpeter in your gravy." Sparky added the last in a whisper. "You still wantin' the liver and onions?"

"Naw. I'll take the hot beef."

"Three hot beefs, hon," Sparky called. "With a side order of fried onions. I ain't wantin' these two crackerjack horseshoe pitchers to go away mad. They'd throw our next game for pure cussedness."

"Sparky's got the runnin' off at the mouth," George explained when Sparky went to the kitchen.

"He must like you, or he'd not rib you so hard." As April spoke, Jack Jones came in the diner and hung his hat on the peg beside the door.

"Howdy, Marshal," Sparky called.

"Not yet. I've not been sworn in." Jack looked around and saw April seated at the table with George and Russ Story. "You sneaky polecat," he said to George. "What are you doin' here with my girl?"

"I ain't heard that you've got strings on her."

"We're keepin' it a secret. Right, April?"

"Hello, Jack." April smiled up at him. "Are you working tonight?"

"I'm not sure. Corbin went home to see about Annabel. He's as nervous as an ant on a hot stove."

"That's pretty nervous."

Sparky brought two plates of food to the table. "Howdy, Jack. Whattaya havin'?"

"That looks pretty good," he said, eyeing the pile of bread, beef and potatoes covered with thick, rich gravy.

"Grab a seat, and I'll tell the missus to dish ya up some."

"I'll sit at the counter. George is givin' me dirty looks. He's scared I'm goin' to sit down here."

The meal was delicious, the atmosphere relaxing, even if Russ Story didn't enter into the conversation. April could feel his eyes on her throughout the meal but nevertheless enjoyed herself. When they were ready to leave, she waved good-bye to Jack and to Mrs. Sparky, who returned the wave from the kitchen. She would have offered to pay but was afraid of embarrassing George.

"Thank you, gentlemen," she said when they were standing on the walk in front of the diner. She looked from one man to the other. Russ grunted and grinned but said nothing.

"It was our treat to have the best-lookin' woman in town take supper with us," George said with a wide smile.

"It's nice of you to say so even if it's not true. I'd better be getting on down to the clinic to see if Doc is there in case Corbin Appleby comes looking for him."

"I'll walk with ya. Didn't ya have someplace to go, Russ?"

"No," Russ said firmly and took his place on the other side of April. George mumbled something that resembled a swear word under his breath.

As they neared the clinic, April could see the light was on in the reception room.

"Doc may have an emergency." She hastened her steps. At the walk leading up to the porch of the clinic, she stopped and called, "Thanks again for supper. Good night."

"She's here." Doc was speaking into the telephone when she opened the door. He replaced the receiver on the hook. "We need to get a b-boy to Mason to the hospital."

"All right. What do you want me to do?"

"Go with him and his pa. He c-could go into shock before he gets there. I'd go, but Annabel Appleby is h-having pains, and I don't dare leave t-town. I saw Jack earlier. I'll get Diane to find him." He picked up the phone.

"He's at Sparky's," April said. "Or was a few minutes ago."

He spoke to the operator, then said to April, "He can take my car. These f-folks don't have one. Berle," he said after hanging up the phone, "I'll get w-word to Mrs. Thacker."

"Thanks, Doc." The man was so shaken his voice trembled.

Ten minutes later they were speeding out of town. Berle Thacker was in the front with Jack, and Berle's eight-year-old son, Buddy, was in the backseat with April.

Buddy had been playing with the fireworks his father had stored in a shed. They exploded and severely injured his hand and lower arm. Doc was hoping the doctors at the hospital would be able to save the boy's hand.

"How far to Mason?" April asked Jack.

"We should make it in about thirty minutes."

She held the boy's head and shoulders in her lap. The shot Doc had given the boy had temporarily put him to sleep. His hand and arm, encased in a bloody bandage, rested on his chest.

Mr. Thacker was chastising himself for leaving the fireworks where Buddy could get to them, knowing how fascinated children were with explosives.

"There were just a couple of Roman candles and a few cherry bombs. I thought to set them off after the harvest party when the young folks came back from the hayride."

"He might have found them no matter where you put them. I remember how Joe and I used to pester Pa to buy a few firecrackers," Jack said. "The ones he bought were each so small they would hardly lift a

tin can off the ground. But altogether they
would be pretty powerful."

The car sped through the dark night stirring up a cloud of dust in its wake. April was
aware of passing through two small towns.
Then she heard Jack tell Mr. Thacker that
Mason would be the next town. She hoped
and prayed the boy's hand could be saved.
She envisioned the hurt of a small boy being unable to play baseball, roll a hoop or tie
his shoes.

It seemed an incredibly long time before
the lights of Mason came in view. Jack
seemed to know just where to go, and minutes later he was turning the car into the
drive at the hospital. Mr. Thacker carried his
son into the building, with April following
close behind.

Although her nurse's uniform was wrinkled and bloodstained, she was able to
command enough authority to get the boy
immediate attention. After she had given the
attending physician the necessary information, there was nothing for her and Jack to
do but wait.

"Was the hospital where you worked this
big?" Jack asked when he and April were

seated in chairs in the hall outside the surgery.

"It was much bigger. It had five floors, and the emergency area covered half of the bottom floor. They needed the space. Kansas City is a pretty rough place, as are all big cities nowadays with so many bootleggers and speakeasies."

"Don't forget the bank robberies."

"Times are hard and people get desperate."

"Do you miss that life?"

"Heavens, no! I love being in a small town where everyone knows everyone and there isn't so much meanness."

Jack's laugh was without humor. "That's Fertile, all right."

"Would you rather live someplace else?"

Jack's grin was sheepish. "I guess not. What did you do in that big hospital?"

"I worked on the floor for one year and one year in the emergency room. It was a busy place, especially at night. We had knife and gunshot wounds. People to patch up after fights."

"No time to sneak off in the corner and take a nap, huh?"

"Did you read about the Union Station

Massacre last June? I was working that day. A team of FBI agents were escorting Frank Nash, a convicted mobster, when the shooting started. Four officers and Nash were killed. Others were wounded and brought to the hospital. One of the gunmen was captured, a man named Adam Richetti. Pretty Boy Floyd escaped."

"You don't miss the excitement?"

"Not that kind of excitement."

They talked for a while about the Thackers and how they would cope if Buddy lost part of his hand and about Doc.

"A good doctor knows his limitations," April said. "Doc knew that he didn't have the skill or the equipment needed to save Buddy's hand. Had there not been the option of bringing him to this hospital, he would have done his best."

"That's about all you can ask of a man."

They were quiet for a while, occupied with their own thoughts. Jack was thinking that April was a very nice girl with a level head on her shoulders. He studied her through half-closed eyes. She was pretty with her shiny, bouncy hair, wide-spaced eyes and her full-lipped, kissable mouth. He wondered why he had no desire to kiss her.

Ruby May.

There was no room in his heart for any other woman. The vision of her dark, laughing eyes, her slender body that fit perfectly against his, arms that wound around his neck and lips as eager as his own floated into his mind. The thought of another man kissing those lips almost tore the heart out of him. He couldn't remember a time when he hadn't loved that sweet girl. When they were younger, he hadn't known that it was love he'd felt for her. He just wanted to be with her all the time.

Hell, now that I have the marshal job, I'd have something to offer her, if it wasn't too late.

Jack suddenly became aware that April was looking at him with puckered brows. He would have been surprised had he known that she was thinking that he was a terribly nice man, but he didn't set her heart fluttering. He had some of Joe's mannerisms and would make a wonderful friend, but he didn't have Joe's personality and playful eyes that spoke of more to come . . . if she dared.

She was brought out of her reverie when

Mr. Thacker came through the swinging doors.

The surgeon had had to take off two of Buddy's fingers and part of his palm. He was able to leave the thumb, the forefinger and second finger. The boy would have to stay in the hospital for at least a week. Mr. Thacker would stay with him for the first few days. He walked with them to the car, thanking them all the way. April got in and looked over her shoulder to see Jack press some bills into the man's hand.

"We'll go directly to your house, Berle, and tell Mrs. Thacker. If you need a way back to Fertile, call Doc. Miss Asbury will get ahold of me or Joe. One of us will come get you."

"That was nice of you to offer to come back and bring him home," April said as they drove out of town.

"I'm just an all-around nice fellow," Jack said and grinned.

It was two o'clock in the morning when Jack stopped the car in front of the clinic. Doc came off the porch and met them on the sidewalk. April filled him in on Buddy's condition.

"It's what I h-hoped for," Doc said. "He'll

learn to cope with the loss of two f-fingers. I feared he m-might lose them all."

"You didn't get a call from Corbin?" Jack asked.

"Oh, yes, and I hurried over there. Annabel has backache, not r-regular pains. Corbin's as n-nervous as a mouse in a roomful of cats."

"I'll walk April home, Doc, then come back and bed down on your couch."

"I was going to s-suggest that." Doc looked up at the big harvest moon hanging high over the treetops. "Don't linger. My n-nurse needs her sleep."

Chapter 16

Fred was in a grumpy mood after only three hours' sleep and didn't appreciate his sister's criticism. He ignored her remarks about the stubble on his chin and sat down at the breakfast table.

"Are you going to shave before you go to the store?" she said for the second—or was it the third—time.

Refusing to answer, he helped himself to the bowl of scrambled eggs, reached for a biscuit and began to eat. He was tired and didn't feel like sparring with her. He had waited until after two o'clock for April to come in; and when she did, she was with one of the Joneses. He thought it had been the newly appointed police officer.

It was beyond him why the city council would hire a dumb farmer to keep law and order in town. It was even more puzzling to him why a girl like April, who was everything a woman should be, would risk letting her reputation be besmirched by keeping company with a clod with manure on his shoes.

This morning, instead of undressing in her room, she had taken her nightdress and gone to the bathroom. He hadn't dared to leave his room and go to the storage room, where he could watch her, because there was the chance that she would catch him in the hallway. Besides, he knew she wouldn't stay long in the bathroom. It was too late for her to take a bath.

Fred doubted that he would see her this morning. He had dressed while she was in the bathroom, then he'd had to come down to breakfast in answer to Shirley's persistent calls.

"Did you hear April when she came in last night?" Shirley asked.

Fred finished buttering his biscuit before he answered with a blank face that supported his lie.

"No. Did you?"

"It was after two o'clock. I'm beginning to doubt the wisdom of renting a room to her. No decent girl stays out with a man until two in the morning. I looked out the window, and I'm sure it was the younger Jones this time. She's playing the Joneses against each other, or I miss my guess."

"She may have a perfectly good reason for being out that late."

"And cows can fly!" Shirley snorted and got up to get the coffeepot. April came in while she was filling Fred's cup.

"Morning." April looked refreshed in spite of her short night of sleep.

Shirley murmured a greeting.

Fred, however, said cheerfully, "And a good morning to you, Miss April." He felt a stirring in his private parts as he remembered seeing her lying naked on her bed.

"It's cool this morning. Fall is here."

"Is the house too cold for you?" Shirley asked and moved the plate of eggs toward April. "I suppose we could light the gas heater in your room."

"No need for that. I like it rather cool." April knew immediately that Shirley was miffed about something by the tone of her voice and the way she avoided looking at her. It had been her intention to tell the pair why she had been out so late last night, but she decided that she didn't owe them an explanation about her comings and goings.

"We'll be having a cold supper tonight," Shirley said. "I'm meeting with a committee from the church."

"The kids again?" Fred asked and raised his brows.

"Why do you say it like that?" Shirley demanded. "This party is very important to them."

"Sure, sure."

"You don't think what I'm doing is important, do you?" his sister barked.

"Yes, I do, Sis. It's just that—"

"Just what?"

"You don't have much time for the store anymore."

"That's what I'm paying you for."

April glanced at Fred and saw the red that came up to flood his face. She had thought that she could never feel sorry for him, but she did.

"I've got to run." April gulped down the last of her coffee and moved her chair back from the table. "Don't count on me for supper tonight, Mrs. Poole."

"Another date?" Shirley asked, her mouth twisting. "Which Jones is it this time?"

April turned and looked the woman straight in the face. "It will be with both of them, if I can manage it. See you later, Fred." She waited long enough to see Mrs. Poole's mouth tighten before she headed for the stairs.

Take that, you old busybody.

As soon as April was out of hearing, Fred said, "What's put a bee in your bonnet this morning?"

"That girl . . . traipsing around at all hours of the night . . ."

"What she does outside this house is none of your business, Shirley. She only rented a room here and has the right to come and go as she pleases."

"Not so, Brother. I'll not have a harlot living in my house."

"Harlot? Whatever gave you that idea? Are you out of your mind?"

"Are you out of yours? You are, if you think you're going to get a piece of . . . *that.*"

Fred stood up and looked down at his sister. "I'm warning you, Shirley. If you do anything to make Miss Asbury move, I'll leave here. I'll leave you to run your precious store by yourself. You can count out the nuts and bolts, cut glass, move around the spools of barbed wire, and—"

"Ha." Shirley cut off his tirade. "Where could you make a living anywhere else? You'll not leave here. This is all you know. You've had your living handed to you on a platter for the past ten years. I could have hired a hundred clerks to take your place."

"Then I suggest you start looking for one."

"Come down off your high horse and go shave before you open the store." She gave him a look of dismissal.

On hearing her words, Fred's nostrils flared with anger. "I'm tired of you running roughshod over me, talking to me in front of folks like I'm a servant. I've put ten years of my life into running that store for you—"

"I don't . . . run roughshod over you."

"Yes, you do. Maybe you should see what it would be like without me. I'm not going over there today, Shirley. If you want your damn store opened, go open it yourself."

Fred left the room. In a complete state of shock Shirley managed to get up from the table and catch him as he mounted the stairs.

"Brother!" She grabbed his arm. "What do you mean you're not going—"

"Just what I said. I'm not going to open *your* store, and I'm not shaving today."

"I'm sorry. It's just that . . . I don't know what's gotten into me lately."

"You were sour even before Ron was killed, and it's worse now since you've been meeting with those kids."

"I have to help them!"

"Are you sure that's all there is to it?"

"I'm sure, Brother. Please, don't let us quarrel."

"It's up to you, Shirley."

"I'm sorry that I took my spite out on you. I wish I'd never rented a room to that woman."

"Does she remind you of what you could have done if you hadn't married Ron?"

"He . . . was a good catch."

"So were you. You had the store Papa left you. What did Ron have?"

"Papa would have left it to you if you had been here."

"That's all water under the bridge."

"As this should be. You'll go to the store?"

Fred hesitated for a moment, prolonging

his sister's anxiety. When he finally spoke, it was with a new dignity.

"I'll go. But you'd better heed what I said about Miss Asbury and about embarrassing me in front of people, or I'll catch the next train out. Then try to hire someone to run *your store* who won't steal you blind."

"I'm sorry. I truly am. I didn't realize—"

"I know. You didn't think I had enough backbone to stand up to you. But I do and don't you forget it." Fred moved on up the stairs feeling better than he had in a long time.

Saturday was usually a busy day at the clinic, and today was no exception. By noon Doc had already seen four patients and pulled a wisdom tooth. As a rule, he tried to avoid anything to do with dentistry, but the young man was suffering excruciating pain and begged Doc to pull it. The tooth broke, and Doc had to dig out the roots. By the time he was finished, he was sweating and cussing and the young man was almost faint with relief that the ordeal was over.

"Now you see," Doc grumbled to April, "why I h-hate anything to do with teeth."

Corbin called. He wanted to make sure

that Doc would be in town today. On the heels of that call came one from Annabel, Corbin's wife, telling Doc that Corbin was being ridiculous and that she was not going to have the baby today and that he needn't plan his day around the event.

Doc was grinning when he hung up the phone. "I don't know who is w-worse, Thad or Corbin. Which reminds me, I'll be g-gone for a while this afternoon. I need to go out to the Taylors and check on Jill and the baby, even though Thad would have been in h-here if either one of them had as much as sneezed."

"Have they named the baby? I forgot to ask Jack last night."

"Joe said they n-named him Thomas Joseph, but will call him T. J. Poor little cuss."

"Why do you say that?"

"It will be hard to live up to Thad's expectations that he be the next Thomas Edison and Joe's that he be a circus clown and Jack w-wanting him to be the next Babe Ruth."

After Doc had left, April put the back room in order and had sat down to work on the records when Mrs. Maddox came in with a basket on her arm.

"Hello, Mrs. Maddox."

"Hello. Is Dr. Forbes busy?"

"He isn't here. He went out to the Taylors to check on Mrs. Taylor and her new baby."

"Well, shucks! I brought him a pumpkin pie, you see. Pumpkins are especially good this year."

Mrs. Maddox, a short, plump little woman with a head of thick brown hair, was the most pleasant of the women who brought treats for the doctor. She was a widow with three half-grown children. They lived on an acreage outside of town.

"He'll enjoy it, I'm sure."

"Maybe it's just as well that he isn't here." Mrs. Maddox had lowered her voice, although there was no one else in the office. "You see, as a loyal friend of Dr. Forbes, I feel it's my duty to let you know what's going on. This is strictly confidential, you see. I would hate for Dr. Forbes to think that I was carrying gossip. But, you see, Hattie Davenport"—she spat out the woman's name as if it were nasty in her mouth—"is going around saying the most awful things about you and the doctor."

"Really?" April tilted her head in a listening position.

"You see, she's saying that she came here and waited two hours to see the doctor and you would never tell her where he'd gone or when he would be back. Meanwhile, you were seeing patients and dispensing medicine as if you were a doctor and not just a nurse. You see, she's saying that she doubts that you even have a nurse's certificate. She said that she is watching the child you gave medicine to and intends to turn you over to the sheriff if the child takes sick."

"Miss Davenport will have to do what she feels is right." April was beginning to wonder how many more times the lady would say "you see." She wished that she had counted them.

"Hattie is telling everyone that Dr. Forbes was rude to her, you see, and asked her to leave when she questioned him about you giving the child medicine. She told at Church Circle how you were in the house with him . . . late at night." She whispered the last few words.

"How would she know that?"

"She swears that someone saw you and

Dr. Forbes through the window, you see. But she refused to name the person."

"Miss Davenport has been quite busy."

"That isn't all, you see." She lowered her voice even more. "Hattie is telling around town that Dr. Forbes's car has been seen at that colored . . . ah . . . woman's place down on the river."

"And what if it was? The doctor treats folks down there as well as in town."

"She's making it sound like he's going there for . . . well, you know . . ."

"Well, for goodness' sake!" A flood of irritation washed over April. "Surely anyone with any sense at all wouldn't believe vicious gossip."

"Don't be too sure. Hattie belongs to everything in town, you see. Her daddy was a game warden here for years before he was elected county treasurer. Her mother died a long time ago, and now that her daddy is gone, you see, she wants to marry Dr. Forbes; but I'm guessing she must be ten years older than he is. She's no spring chicken," she added firmly.

"Evidently Dr. Forbes doesn't want to marry her, or he'd have asked her."

"Hattie is blaming you for breaking them up."

"Me?" April wanted to laugh but didn't. Malicious gossip was nothing to laugh about. "There was nothing to break up, Mrs. Maddox."

"I just wanted to warn you, you see," she said quickly when she heard footsteps on the porch.

"That was kind of you," April managed to say before Joe stepped through the doorway.

"Hello, ladies." Then, "Am I interrupting something?"

"No. Hello, Joe. Do you know Mrs. Maddox?" April's voice was a little strained.

"Sure I do. How are you, Mrs. Maddox? And how is Harry?"

"Harry's fine. He helped the Davidsons put up hay this summer." Mrs. Maddox used the full volume of her voice and stepped back from the desk.

"Is he going out for basketball again this year?"

"Oh, yes. He loves to play, you see."

"He was pretty good last year."

"He put up an iron hoop off a barrel up on the barn, you see. Every chance he got this summer he was out there throwing a ball through it."

"That's a great idea. Didn't he score the winning basket in that last game? Everyone in the stands was on their feet." He turned to April. "Harry was only a freshman and he won the game."

April watched Joe chat with Mrs. Maddox. The woman beamed when he praised her son. *He knows just how it's done. He could probably charm the bark off a tree if he set his mind to it.*

Mrs. Maddox took the cloth off the basket she had placed on the desk and took out a pie.

"Holy smoke," Joe exclaimed. "That looks good. Pumpkin, isn't it?"

"With walnuts on top," Mrs. Maddox said proudly.

"That Doc is a lucky son of a gun."

"It's for all of you. I thought you'd like a little treat in the middle of the afternoon, you see." She spoke to April, then her eyes went to Joe.

"Me, too?"

"Of course, you, too."

Joe flung his arm across her shoulders.

"This woman knows the way to a man's heart."

"Behave yourself, Joe Jones." A rosy glow covered Mrs. Maddox's plump face. "I've known this rascal since he was in short pants."

When April glanced at him, Joe winked at her. "Tell her something good about me, Mrs. Maddox," he said, his eyes still holding April's.

"He's a good, honest, hardworking man."

"That sounds terribly dull." April put a note of boredom in her voice.

Mrs. Maddox laughed up at Joe. "He's one of my favorites, you see."

"You'd better stand in line with half the women in town."

"She's the jealous kind," Joe said confidentially as he walked Mrs. Maddox to the door.

"Thank you for the pie," April said and stood up. "I'll see that you get the pan back."

"I'll stop by in a day or two and pick it up."

Joe stood at the door and watched Mrs. Maddox until she crossed the street. When he turned, April was putting away one of the ledgers.

"Hello, April."

"Hello, Joe."

"I haven't seen you for a week."

"Has it been that long?" For a minute it seemed she couldn't breathe. There wasn't enough room in her chest. She wanted to appear nonchalant. Actually her bones had turned to jelly and her muscles to mush the instant he walked in the door.

"Seems like months to me," he said quietly. After a brief silence, while he watched her tidy the desk, he said, "Lucky Jack got to be with you last night. It's just my luck that I wasn't in town when Doc needed a driver."

"I thought you came to town every night."

"Not every night, although since you've been here, I find myself looking for an excuse to come to town."

"What's your excuse today?"

"I came in with Julie and the brat. She left Logan and Nancy with Eudora. Evan had to go to Mason."

"Shame on you for calling your sister a brat." A smile tugged at the corner of her mouth.

"I left the brat at the church and Julie at the grocery store. Joy's giving Julie some anxious moments right now."

"I don't know much about kids, but surely it's just a stage she's going through."

"You haven't forgotten about tonight, have you?"

"No. I told you we'd take my car. It hasn't been farther than around the block a time or two since I've been here."

"Want me to take a look at it?"

"It might not be a bad idea. I'd hate for us to get out of town and have something go wrong."

"I'd not hate that at all." His grin was back. His eyes flirted with her. He was in his teasing mode once again. "Are you going to cut the pie?"

"Not until Doc gets back. After all, Mrs. Maddox brought it to him."

"You don't seem to be quite so chipper today. Is something bothering you?"

She opened her mouth to deny his observations, then closed it. "How could you tell something was bothering me?"

"I don't know. It was a feeling I had when I first came in and saw Mrs. Maddox bent over the desk whispering to you."

"And you thought that we were up to no good." She tried to make her voice light.

"No, I didn't think that." His hand reached for hers. "A trouble is only half a trouble when shared."

"Where did those words of wisdom come from?" She tried to appear nonchalant.

"I'm not prying." His fingers worked between hers. "Did Mrs. Maddox say something that disturbed you?"

April sighed. "You're very astute. I didn't realize I was so easy to read."

"You'd make a lousy poker player, sweetheart. What did Mrs. Maddox say to upset you?"

"Only that Miss Davenport is spreading rumors around town about Doc."

"What could anyone say about Doc that was bad? He's one of the straightest shooters I've ever known."

"Three things, according to Miss Davenport. Number one, he's allowing me to practice medicine without a license. Two, I've been alone with him in his house late at night. And three, he's visiting a colored woman down in Shanty Town for what Mrs. Maddox said was—her words—'you know.'"

"Did Mrs. Maddox believe any of this?"

"I don't think so. She thought we should know the rumors going around. I kept telling myself that she may be making this up. She is trying to catch Doc herself, although she hasn't been as blatant as some of the others."

"I don't think she'd make up something like that. She's a nice lady raising three kids by herself. She's done a good job so far."

"I should tell Doc. He has the right to know what has been said about him. I hate to do it."

"I don't think that it will bother him too much except the part about you."

"Miss Davenport is a vicious cat!"

Joe laughed. "Honey, there's one in every town."

Chapter 17

"You don't have to come in."

"I want to. Perhaps there's something I can do." Julie got out of the car.

"Do you think I lied about a committee meeting?" Joy's young face set in lines of resentment.

"I don't think that at all. I want to offer to help."

Julie followed Joy into the church. She had an uneasy feeling that Mrs. Poole's influence was overriding hers. It seemed to her that the woman was taking more than a casual interest in a fifteen-year-old girl.

Mrs. Poole met them at the door and nodded a greeting to Julie.

"Hello, Mrs. Poole. I know you must be busy this last week before the party. Is there anything I can do to help?"

"Thank you, but we'll not be needing any help. Come along, Joy, we've been waiting for you." Coolly dismissing Julie, she put her arm around Joy and drew her to the front pew, where Sammy Davidson sat with Richard Myers.

"I'll be back by three o'clock, Joy," Julie called.

"You'd better make it four," Mrs. Poole said over her shoulder. "We have a lot to do today."

Julie backed out the door feeling like she'd been slapped in the face with a wet rag. Mrs. Bradbury was coming down the walk with Evelyn. After Evelyn had gone into the church, Julie exchanged a few pleas-antries with her mother and headed for her car. The woman placed a hand on Julie's arm to detain her.

"I'm puzzled about something, Mrs. Johnson. I'd like to talk to you about it."

"Puzzled? I don't understand."

"I'm wondering why Mrs. Poole chose Evelyn and Richard Myers to be on this committee. Evelyn is only ten years old and Richard is eleven. I doubt that they are con-tributing anything to the planning of the party, but Mrs. Poole wants them at every meeting. All the planning must be falling on Joy and Sammy Davidson. Then again, I think Sammy is also a poor choice. He seldom used to come to church. He attends more often now that he and Joy are friends."

"I thought that myself at first. But Sammy needs the influence of the young church group. That may be why she chose him."

"Shirley Poole has made it perfectly clear that she has absolutely no use for anyone who lives in the area along the river. She considers them trash."

"Some of them may be, but some are good folk trying to make a living like the rest of us."

"Mrs. Poole hasn't given any of us the time of day for quite a few years. She seemed to have turned in on herself until just lately when she took an interest in planning the harvest party."

"She's been having a lot of committee meetings."

"I feel sorry for Sammy. Everyone does. But that doesn't mean I want Evelyn associating with him. Dorie Myers feels the same about Richard. She's afraid that he will take up some of Sammy's wild ways."

"Joy doesn't seem to think that Sammy is as bad as people make out."

"She should know, I guess. Evelyn says they spend a lot of time together at school."

Julie left the church with a lot on her mind. She drove to Mr. Oakley's store, parked in front and sat in the car for several minutes before she got out. Evan had taught her to drive the first year they were married, and promised to teach Joy when she graduated from high school. Now Julie wasn't sure that she wanted him to.

Where had the time gone? It seemed such a short time ago that Joy was a little girl running though the house, teasing Jason and annoying Jill. She was a happy, bubbly child bestowing kisses to friends and relatives who grabbed her up in their arms. It was hard to relate that Joy with the sullen, resentful girl she had become of late.

Oh, Lord. What if Mrs. Poole knows! What if she has a plan to reveal her late husband's crimes and expose their results? All these years, while the town held Ron Poole in high esteem, Julie held the secret close to her heart—the secret she shared with her brothers, her father, Corbin Appleby and Dr. Forbes. *Would Mrs. Poole jeopardize her*

*husband's reputation? The reputation she
has nurtured since his death?*

Thank God for her dear, wonderful Evan.
Whatever happened, she wouldn't be alone.
Her pa had been a good father to Joy. Both
the men in her life, Julie thought now, had
loved and provided for her. The only times
Evan had harshly corrected Joy were when
she had been disrespectful to her.

Wearily Julie went into the store and
placed her order with Mr. Oakley. While
waiting for him to fill it, she wandered
around the store but couldn't keep her mind
off her worries about Joy. As soon as her
groceries were stowed in the car she drove
the few blocks to Dr. Forbes's office.

When Julie entered the office, she found
Joe sitting on the edge of the desk talking to
April.

"Hi, Sis. Looking for me?"

"Now, why would I do that? I knew that
wherever you were, there would be a pretty
girl nearby." Julie smiled fondly at her
brother. He took her hand and drew her
close so he could fling an arm over her
shoulders.

"Hello, April. Is my brother making a pest
of himself?"

Before April could answer, Joe said, "I'm trying to talk her into running away with me."

"Someday some girl is going to take you up on that."

"Not this one," April said with a nervous laugh. "I'm not in the market for a ladies' man."

"What caused you to think that I'm a ladies' man?"

April glanced up to see that the smile had gone from his eyes. He was studying her with such intensity that even his sister glanced up at him.

"Maybe I should have said flirt. You should have been here to see him charm Mrs. Maddox," April said to Julie with a lightness she didn't feel.

Damn the man for getting her flustered.

Sensing her brother's unease, Julie laughed. "He was a charmer even when he was two, toddling around in three-cornered pants."

"How do you know? You were only four."

"We can argue the point later, Brother. I came to see Dr. Forbes. I can see you anytime." Julie gave her brother a playful jab in the ribs with her elbow.

"What's the matter? You sick?" Joe looked anxiously into her face.

"No, I'm not sick. Do I have to be sick to talk to my old friend?"

"Doc isn't here," April said. "He went out to see Jill and the baby."

"I was there this morning and they were all right," Joe said.

"It's just a follow-up. Doc knew that Thad would be here faster than you could say scat if either one of them as much as sneezed. Mrs. Appleby is due any day. When her time comes, Doc wants Jack to take Mr. Appleby out in the country and dump him about twenty miles from town. By the time he walks back, it will all be over."

"That sounds like Doc. I'll stop and see him another time. I just thought as long as I had to wait for Joy, I'd chat a minute."

When Julie left, Joe followed her out to the car.

"What's bothering you, Sis?"

"You always knew when I was worried about something."

"You're easy to read."

"Only to you and Evan. It's Mrs. Poole. I don't like Joy being with her so much, but I don't know what I can do about it."

"Don't borrow trouble."

"I'm trying not to. But Joy has been so difficult lately."

"What does Evan say?"

"He says that she's had a good upbringing and that she's just trying to spread her wings. He's being terribly patient with her. But the other night she went too far, and he was harsh with her for the way she talked to me. He told her that if she did it again, she would be confined to the house; and there would be no harvest party for her. She looked at him as if she hated him but was smart enough to keep her mouth shut. Several times lately, she's threatened to leave and go live with Papa."

"Pa wouldn't put up with her shenanigans. He'd not let her sass Eudora, either. Do you think Sammy is putting these ideas in her head?"

"I don't know. She is so . . . rebellious. She finds fault with everything I do or say."

"If Sammy keeps going the way he's headed, he'll find himself down in the state reformatory. The company he keeps is about as rotten as it gets. I've told the boy to stay away from Joy, but there's not much we can do until this party thing is over." Joe

decided not to tell his sister about Sammy
and Tator Williams harassing Miss Deval.

"The party is next Saturday night."

"Joy has always been a good kid."

"Until now. That's what puzzles me."

"She's going through the difficult time of
not being quite a kid and not quite an adult.
We have to hope that she'll grow out of it.
Remember Jack's rebellion? He ran off,
thinking he'd play ball in the big league.
Corbin found him over on the big river and
brought him home."

"I told Joy I'd be back to pick her up at
three. Mrs. Poole said make it four. It's
three-thirty. I think I'll go and sit in on the
last thirty minutes of the meeting. Joy won't
like it, but I don't care."

"Atta girl!" Joe's infectious smile was
back.

Julie looked at his handsome face. He
had always been so dear to her. She loved
all her siblings, but she loved him most of
all. Until she met Evan, he was the one she
depended on when she was suddenly given
the responsibility of making a home for her
brothers and Joy and Jill. He had helped to
shoulder the work and ease her worries.
She prayed that he would find a woman

who would share with him the kind of love she had with Evan.

"Are you serious about April?" she asked quietly, watching his face.

"I like her a lot. But she doesn't take me seriously. It may be because I'm a farmer, and she's used to men wearing suits and ties."

"She doesn't strike me as the kind of girl who couldn't see beyond a pair of overalls."

"I've wondered if she doesn't have a crush on Doc. If she does, she's in for a disappointment."

"Why would you say that? It seems to me they would be well suited to each other."

"Doc is in love with someone else. That's for your ears alone."

"Really? I didn't know he was keeping company with anyone."

"Forget I mentioned it."

"You know I will. Hattie Davenport has all of a sudden decided that Doc is a low-down skunk." Julie smiled. "She has chased him unmercifully for years. She must have decided that he can't be caught and has turned against him."

"I wonder what set her off. It wouldn't take much."

"There are several stories making the rounds. I'll tell you about them later. I want to get back to the church before the meeting ends. Are you going home now?"

"I'm staying in town. I have a date with April tonight."

"Well, put your best foot forward until she gets to know you. Then she'll love you. How could she not?"

Joe bumped her chin with his fist, then opened the car door for her. "Methinks you're prejudiced."

"I admit it."

Joe watched her drive away. He hated to see the worried lines in her face. She was entitled to be happy with her three children and Evan after the pain she endured seventeen years ago. Joy had better straighten up and stop acting like a spoiled brat, or he'd be tempted to take her out into the woods and shake some sense into her even if she was sixteen years old.

Julie opened the church door softly to keep from creating a disturbance. She stood in shocked surprise for a moment when she realized that the quiet, dimly lighted church was empty.

The meeting was over.

Where was Joy?

Then she heard a slight noise coming from the front of the church and took a couple of hesitant steps down the aisle. Although the light coming through the stained-glass windows was subdued, she saw the top of a blond head rise up, then disappear behind the back of a pew. Julie walked down the carpeted aisle toward the altar and stopped in shocked silence.

Joy was stretched out on the bench, and a boy was lying full length on top of her. They were in a tight embrace oblivious to anything around them.

"Joy!" Julie gasped.

The boy came upright immediately and stood like the uncertain adolescent he was. Julie could see that their clothes were still intact, but he'd had his hand beneath her blouse. Joy sat up and swung her feet to the floor. Her cheeks were flaming. Her busy hands hurried to tuck her blouse into the waistband of her skirt.

The cold look on her face chilled Julie's heart.

Joy spoke first. "Spying on me? Well, now you know. I'm a slut."

Sammy turned to her. "You are not!" The words burst from him furiously.

"You'll never make *her* believe I'm not. So why try?"

"We'd better . . . go. I told Eudora I'd be back for Nancy by four."

"Aren't you going to rant and rave at me? Or are you going to wait and do it in front of Pa or that wonderful, saintly husband of yours?"

"Shut up or I'll slap you!" Julie's hurt disappeared and anger took over.

"It wasn't her fault. It was mine. I forced her."

"I could see that. You were having a hard time holding her down." Julie looked the tall boy in the eye until he looked away. She got behind the two and crowded them down the aisle toward the door. "How long has Mrs. Poole been gone?"

"Not long. She isn't like you. She knows that boys and girls need some time alone."

"Did she say that?"

Sammy held open the door and they went out.

"She knows the old biddies here at the church wouldn't approve—"

"Get in the car, Joy."

"Bye, Sammy. I'll see you at school Monday."

"Get in the car, Joy."

Joy put her hand on Sammy's arm. "If either of my brothers touches you, have them arrested."

"By who? Your brother is the police now. They'll be laying for me. Don't let them break us up."

"I won't. Don't let them catch you by yourself. They're bullies, both of them." Joy sent a resentful look at Julie and climbed into the car.

Julie held herself together until she had the evening meal started. When Joy was in her room, Nancy dozing in her swing and Logan playing in the yard, she sat down at the kitchen table, put her head on her bent arms and gave way to the tears that had been choking her.

April took down the ledger to continue her work after Joe had left. She had given him the keys to her car, and he was taking it to the filling station to be serviced.

"Tell Mr. Wallace I'll be by later to pay," she called as he went out the door.

She heard him talking to someone on the

porch and thought that maybe Doc had come back. But when the door opened, Harold Dozier came into the office. She had met the attorney on several occasions after Doc had introduced her to him in the drugstore. A few days ago they had chatted briefly at the post office. He was a quiet, tidy man, always neatly dressed. Today he wore a white shirt, blue silk tie and dark suit. He lifted his hat off his head when he came in, careful not to disturb his hair

"Hello, Miss Asbury."

"Hello."

"It's a nice cool day. Fall is in the air." He stood in front of the desk tapping his hat against his thigh.

"It sure is. Soon the frost will be on the pumpkin." April smiled.

"And the fodder in the shock," he quoted.

"So says Mr. James Whitcomb Riley."

He smiled, and April noted that his face changed dramatically. He really was a nice-looking man . . . when he smiled. His eyes were dark, as was his hair. It was parted near the middle and combed back. His complexion was olive. Not a big man, but he was taller than she was.

"How are you liking our town?"

"I like it fine. The people are friendly."

"I was sure that you'd be ready to head back to the city by now."

"I've always wanted to live in a small town, and I'm not one bit disappointed."

"I was a little disappointed when I first came here, but after a while the town grows on you."

"You're not from here originally?"

"No. I'm from St. Louis. I came here three years ago to practice with my father's old friend."

"Did you wish to see Doc Forbes? If you did, he isn't in right now. He should be back in an hour or two."

"I was going to pretend that I came to see Dr. Forbes, but in truth I came to see you. I was wondering if you'd like to go out to dinner and a show. We could drive over to Mason. I know this is short notice, but—"

"Thank you for asking me, but I have plans for tonight."

"Some other time, then? Doc will vouch for me."

"I'm sure you're trustworthy."

"Next Saturday night?"

"Well . . . yes."

The smile appeared again and stayed

while he spoke. "I'll look forward to it." He was at the door when it opened and Joe came in. "Hello again, Joe."

"Leaving, Howard?"

"So it seems," he said pleasantly. "I'll see you in the middle of the week, April." Howard carefully placed his hat on his head, nodded to Joe and left.

"What was that about?"

"What do you mean?"

"He seemed terribly pleased about something."

April shrugged. "Did you tell Mr. Wallace I'd stop by and pay him?"

"No."

"No?"

"He doesn't charge pretty girls for servicing their cars."

"Joe. You're lying again."

"Okay. He doesn't charge *beautiful* girls for servicing their cars."

"You are the most irritating man!"

"It's part of my charm. Why was Harold Dozier looking like someone had just died and left him a million dollars?"

"You'll have to ask him."

"Was he in here trying to chisel in on my territory?"

"Joe, you don't have any territory here."

"Yes, I do, love." He bent and kissed her quickly. "You just don't realize it yet. See you tonight."

He was out the door before she could reply.

Chapter 18

Doc drove down the dusty road toward Shanty Town. He had hurriedly left the Taylors, refusing their offer of a meal, because he was anxious to see Caroline.

When he turned into the narrow lane leading to the house, he saw a flash of pink amid the cornstalks behind the privy where Silas had planted three short rows of popcorn. He stopped the car in his usual place where it would be shielded by the lilac bushes.

Caroline was waiting for him.

She wore a sweater over a ragged old skirt. Her hair was covered with a three-cornered pink cloth. To him, she had never been more beautiful.

He strode to her and without a word took her in his arms and held her close. He closed his eyes for a minute, savoring the feel and the smell of her. She was his life, the air he breathed, his joy, his treasure. His love for her knew no bounds. At times like this he would give ten years of his life to be with her for one whole day. After kissing her tenderly, sweetly, he held her away from him so he could look into her face.

"Are you all right?"

"I'm fine. I'm glad you're here."

"I'm glad I'm here, too. Have you been lifting that b-basket?"

"No. I've been picking the popcorn and shucking it. Silas carries it to the house, and I take the kernels off the cob."

"What are you going to d-do with it?"

"After I get it off the cob, we'll put it in a flour sack. Silas talked to the man at the grocery store. He'll take some of it in trade."

Doc pulled her to him again and gritted his teeth in frustration. He didn't know how much longer he'd be able to endure not being with her, taking care of her.

"Has Mrs. Appleby had her baby?" Caroline asked as they walked to the house.

"Not yet. It will be any day now. Has anyone b-been around?" He was reasonably sure she hadn't been bothered, or Silas would have been in to tell him, but he wanted to hear it from her.

"No. Don't worry." They stepped into the house. She turned and smoothed the lines in his face with her fingertips. "Don't frown, my love. Everything will be all right."

"I worry every minute I'm away f-from you. I want to be with you . . . all the time. I want everyone in the whole wide world to know that you are mine."

"I'll be just fine. Silas is here—"

"I'm j-jealous of Silas."

She laughed. "I'll wash my hands and fix you a glass of cold tea. We've got ice."

"Is the man who d-delivers respectful?"

"Silas comes in, and I stay in the other room."

Doc took some money from his pocket and stuffed it down in the can on the counter and replaced the top.

"You don't need to do that. We have plenty."

"Are you still having m-morning sick-ness?"

"Not often now." She laughed a delightful happy laugh. "But this baby wants me to know he's there."

While she washed and fixed the tea, Doc

went to the car for his medical bag and the sack of supplies he always brought with him.

Later, when she lay on the bed, he took his stethoscope from his bag and listened to her heartbeat, then moved the instrument down to her abdomen. After a minute or two he smiled, as he heard for the first time the heartbeat of his child.

"He's there, s-sweetheart. Want to hear him?" He placed the earpieces of the stethoscope in her ears and watched the expression on her face. Her beautiful eyes widened and filled with wonderment as she looked up at him.

"He's all right?"

"Strong for three m-months." He put the stethoscope back in his medical bag and ran his hand gently down over her slightly rounded abdomen. "I don't want you to b-be afraid. I'll be with you."

"I'm not afraid. It's grand knowing that I have a part of you with me."

"Sweetheart, I'll w-wait another couple of weeks for the letter from Canada; and if I don't h-hear from them, I'll start making arrangements for us to g-go to Mexico. It's always warm down there. We'll find a place along the coast so you can play b-barefoot in the sand."

"Todd, you're giving up so much."

"We've been over this a h-hundred times. I've no life without you, sweetheart. I'll dig d-ditches in Mexico to make a living for us if necessary." Her eyes filled with tears. "Now, don't cry. I can't l-leave if you cry."

"Why are you so good to me?"

"Because I love you. I've n-never loved a woman before. I think of you every minute of the day and night. The only reason I'm not living with you h-here in the cottage is because I need to keep my medical p-practice until we leave here. It isn't fair, sweetheart. But many things in l-life are not fair."

His words reminded her how generous was his love, how benevolent, and she felt guilty because all she could give him was all the love in her heart. She tried to put into words how she felt.

"Your love is a gift I never expected to be mine." She kissed him softly and gently. "It's easier for me to understand our circumstances than for you. All my life, I've known that I was set apart."

"Where we are g-going you won't be. I promise you."

Later, when Doc was ready to leave, their kiss was tender and sweet. They lingered in the warmth of each other's embrace: his chin resting lightly on her head, their arms wound around each other, reluctant to be separated, avoiding the last good-bye.

"I have to go," Doc whispered.

"I know. I'm grateful for having you this little while."

She stood in the doorway when he went to the car. He turned to blow her a kiss.

"And one for the baby," he called, sending another kiss across the yard.

She smiled and waved, hoping that he couldn't see the tears in her eyes.

"Well, well, well."

Crunched down in the bushes on the edge of the cottonwood thicket, Tator Williams snickered. The snotty doctor had the hots for the nigger wench—and she *was* one even if she did have white skin. Why had the doc taken her into the house if not for a quickie?

Tator had been waiting for the big brute who guarded her to leave her alone in the corn patch. The beating Tator had suffered at Joe Jones's hands had made him more determined than ever to screw the bitch. He had to, or lose face with Sammy and the rest of the bunch who'd heard his bragging.

Now he sat with his back to a tree trunk and mulled over how he could best use this information. Most folks in town and some along the river thought the doctor got up every morning and hung out the sun. Tator had to admit that he wasn't as snooty as some in town. He had treated Shanty Town folks regardless whether they could pay or not. He had come into the dives after midnight to patch up drunks after a knife fight and had stayed the night when Tator's old granny was dying.

Would anyone believe me when I told them the doc was screwing the nigger bitch?

Tator got to his feet to look again toward the corn patch. The big colored man was carrying the basket to the house, which meant she'd not come out anymore today. Tator slunk through the woods to the path along the river. He'd look for Sammy and tell him what he'd found out. The kid was smart; he'd know just where to drop the news so it would do the most good.

He found Sammy at the run-down house

where he lived with his mother and his pa, when the man was around. According to Marla Davidson, her husband was working with a thrashing crew. More than likely he was on a freight train trying to get as far away from her as he could. He didn't seem to have much use for his kid, either; and now that Sammy was big enough to fight when he got out the strop, Arlo Davidson was only home when he was completely down-and-out.

"This place looks like a hog pen." Sammy's angry voice reached Tator as he approached the house. "Why don't you get off your butt and clean it up?"

"If you want it cleaned, clean it yourself." Marla's voice was slurry.

"You don't want to do anything but sit and guzzle that rotgut."

"That school is ruinin' ya. You've been puttin' on airs like ya was the banker's kid. And I don't like it."

"That's too bad. You straighten up and act decent, or I'm out of here."

"Ha! Where'd ya go? How're ya goin' eat? Nobody's gonna hire a snot-nosed kid."

"Hello? Anyone home?" Tator asked the

foolish question as he opened the screen door and went in.

"Come on in and make yourself at home," Sammy said sarcastically.

"Hi Tator." Marla had a silly grin on her face. "What happened to your nose? It's all swelled up."

"Ran into a tree."

"You silly boy." Marla laughed long and loud. "Get him a glass, Sammy. He needs a drink."

"Go put some clothes on. I can see everything you got, and so can Tator."

"Tator don't mind. Do you, Tator?" she asked coyly.

"Course not. I've seen tits before."

Sammy gave both of them a disgusted look and stomped into the back room.

"Who shoved a burr up his ass?" Tator got a glass out of the dishpan, dried it on a cloth and helped himself to the bottle on the table.

"He come home from town that way. I don't know what gets into him sometimes. He thinks this place ain't good enough for him no more."

"He's just feelin' his oats. That Jones girl's

got him in a lather. Once he screws her, he'll
be over it."

"What Jones girl?"

"Shut your mouth, Tator!" Sammy's voice
rang out loud from the doorway.

Marla turned her bloodshot eyes to her
son. "Ya screwin' girls? Jesus! I didn't think
ya was old enough."

Tator laughed. "How old was you,
Marla?"

"I was fifteen when I had him. I don't care
how many girls he screws, but if he knocks
up one of 'em, he ain't movin' her in here."

"Jesus Christ," Sammy yelled. He
grabbed his old straw hat, slammed it down
on his head and stomped out, slamming the
door.

"See what I mean?" Marla shook her
head and poured herself another drink.
"Ain't no reasonin' with him no more. Can't
even talk to him. Yep, associatin' with those
highfalutins at school is what's ruinin' him."

"I'd best go and calm him down." Tator
gulped his drink and hurried out the door,
ignoring Marla's call asking him to come
back later. He caught up with Sammy as
he reached the road. "Wait up. Where ya
goin'?"

"None of your business. Stick around. She's drunk enough to take you to bed."

"I'm not interested."

"No? You screwed her once. She bragged about it."

"I was drunk. Slow down. I got something to tell you."

"I don't want to hear it."

"You will. You won't believe what I saw down at the white nigger's."

Sammy stopped and turned. "Have you lost what few brains you have? You'd better stay away from there if you want to keep the nose on your face and the teeth in your mouth."

"Nobody saw me. I stayed in the woods."

"You still have in mind to get in her pants?"

"Hell, yes. I ain't scared of that clodhopper. He's got no right to tell *me* what to do."

"I don't want to know what you're planning."

"Yes, you do. You'll never guess who was calling on the river whore. None other than the upstanding, holier-than-thou, God-fearin' Dr. Forbes. He parked his car behind the bushes and took her in the house. Whattaya think of that?"

Sammy looked disgusted. "I don't think anything of that. She might have been sick."

"She wasn't sick. She was out pickin' corn."

"You said half the men in town went callin' on her. Doc's a man, isn't he?"

"I tell you, it wasn't like that. He *sneaked* in."

"Why're you wanting to get the doc in trouble? What's he done to you?"

"Nothin' that I know of. I'm just thinkin' that if we let him know that we know he's screwing the bitch, he might throw a few dollars our way."

"Keep me out of that! Hear? Do what you want; but if I were you, I'd give some thought to what Joe Jones said. Next time he'll not stop at bustin' your nose."

"I've figured out a way to fix him."

Sammy started walking again.

"Where ya goin'?"

"Anywhere to get away from *her*."

"Don't ya want to know how I'm goin' to get even with big-shot Jones?"

"You're determined to tell me. So tell me."

"I'm goin' to de-nut that bull of his so all he'd be good for is ground meat. A feller told me how to do it."

"I suppose the bull will just stand still and let you cut off his nuts."

"I need your help, Sammy."

"Count me out. I'm not ruining any animals. That's sick!"

"That's revenge! After what they've done to you, ain't ya wantin' to get back at 'em? They think you're trash, boy, not good enough for their sweet, innocent little darlin'. You're just shit to them. Do ya think that girl wants a man her brothers can make dance on a string?"

At the mention of Joy, Sammy's eyes narrowed and his fists clenched, and Tator knew that Sammy was at least willing to listen to his plan.

Chapter 19

April was relieved when she returned home after closing the clinic to find the house cool, quiet and without either Mrs. Poole or her brother. She found the matches on the shelf in the bathroom and lit the hot-water heater. After setting the timer for twenty minutes she went back to the bedroom, removed her soiled uniform and lay down on her bed to wait for the water to heat for her bath. She was almost asleep when the timer went off.

Later, while relaxing in the tub, her head back, her eyes closed, she thought about the night ahead with Joe. *Lord help me to be on my guard.* Joe Jones was handsome, charming and all the things she had sworn to avoid when she chose her life's mate. The fact that he was a farmer with few prospects of ever being well-off were of no consequence to her. She could love a poor man every bit as much as a rich one. But she would have to know without a shadow of a doubt that he'd be faithful and not be constantly seeking the thrill of seducing another woman, as her father had done.

The thought struck April that should she marry a man such as her father, she would not even have the option her mother had, because she didn't have parents who would welcome her and a child.

Her grandparents had loved her—doted on her, in fact—but it was not the same. Now that they were gone, she was alone. She would not let her yearning for a family of her own lead her to make the mistake her mother had made. She would not bring a child into the world to know the pain of a father's abandonment.

April was satisfied that she had taken the first step to get out from under Joe's spell by agreeing to go on a date with Harold Dozier, although she was not looking forward to it. Doc had said that Harold was a well-bred man, a good catch, and several women in town had been after him. She had always avoided getting involved with a man because she hadn't trusted any of them. She had been afraid to risk her heart as her mother had done.

She had known men at the hospital who loved their wives and children; men who were faithful and dependable. She wanted to think that emotionally she had moved beyond her troubled childhood and was now able to judge a man without comparing him to the philanderers she had known.

Suddenly she was brought back to the present by a scratching sound on the other side of the wall in the storage room. She listened, her head cocked to one side, but heard nothing more and decided that it was probably a mouse scurrying across the boxes piled against the wall. She didn't want mice in the boxes she had stored there and would ask Mrs. Poole to set a mouse trap.

After finishing her bath she shaved beneath her arms and leisurely dried and powdered her long slender legs by propping each foot up on the edge of the tub. Feeling wonderfully clean and relaxed, she slipped on her robe and went back to her room.

Fred, his heart pounding, his throbbing and painful erection wrapped in his handkerchief, leaned his forehead against the wall in the storage room and gave himself up to the glorious feeling brought on by seeing his angel naked as the day she was born. When it was over, he put the hand-kerchief in his pocket and buttoned his trousers. When the door to April's bedroom closed, he peeked out into the hallway, grateful for the foresight he'd had days ago when he oiled the hinges on the storage room door.

With his shoes in his hand he scurried past her room and down the stairs. In the kitchen he grabbed up the sack of sand-wiches Shirley had left for him on the table. Careful to make no noise when he opened the door, he went to the porch, where he sank down in a chair and breathed deeply in an effort to calm himself.

He had seen all of her from the top of her beautiful head to the tips of her toes. She had been even more beautiful than the pic-ture hidden in his closet of the woman lying naked on a sofa.

April's skin was soft and pink, her cone-shaped breasts tipped with rosy nipples, her long slender legs and thighs topped with a nest of dark curly hair. He had seen more of April than he had of the woman in the coveted picture. The dark-haired beauty was holding a fan over that part of her that he most wanted to see.

Thank God he had come home when he had. He would not have known she was in the house if he hadn't heard the water running in the bathtub. Knowing that Shirley would stay at the store until he returned, he couldn't allow this golden opportunity to slip away. Holding his breath for fear April would hear his labored breathing, he had sneaked up the stairs to the storage room to watch his angel bathe.

In a languorous daze Fred put on his shoes and sat for a few minutes longer reliving the past half hour. Then, not daring to linger longer, he left the porch with a secret smile on his face and walked jauntily down the path toward the store.

As April was dressing, she heard Shirley come up to her room, then almost immediately go back downstairs. She briefly considered leaving the house before Joe arrived and meeting him at the clinic, where he had parked the car. If at all possible, she wanted to avoid an embarrassing scene with Mrs. Poole. The woman was perfectly capable of making a sarcastic remark, and she wasn't sure how Joe would respond.

Why did Mrs. Poole dislike the Jones family? And why didn't her dislike seem to include Joy, Joe's sister?

The woman had the right to like or dislike anyone she pleased. She was only April's landlady, and April didn't owe her an explanation for going out with Joe or any other man. If Mrs. Poole was rude to Joe, April had the option of immediately giving notice that she was moving. Having made up her mind to face her less-than-congenial landlady, April went downstairs.

She had on a fashionable forest-green suit and matching turban that she hadn't worn many times and not at all since she'd been in Fertile. Knowing that the night would be cool, she carried a light coat over her arm.

Shirley was not in the kitchen or the parlor. From the dining room window April could see that she was in the backyard, the far corner, searching for onions or acorn squash amid the dried remains of the garden.

After checking her image in the hall mirror

to make sure her slip wasn't showing, April went through the house and stepped out onto the porch as Joe was coming up the steps.

"Well, don't you look pretty." He removed a dark felt hat and smiled. She answered his smile with one of her own.

"You don't look so bad yourself."

"Thank ya, ma'am. I'm putting my best foot forward." His eyes teased her. "I don't usually wear this suit except to weddings and funerals and less often than that, the hat." He put it back on his head and tilted it.

"You made an exception for me?"

"I'm trying to impress you so you'll realize what a fine fellow I am." He tipped his head and gazed at her with teasing scrutiny.

"I'm impressed, I'm impressed." She had to laugh at his antics. He had a boyish appeal that was hard to resist.

"Ready to go?"

"If you are."

"I don't have to face the wicked witch?"

"Not if we hurry. She's in the backyard."

"Then let's go." He grasped her elbow firmly, and they went down the porch steps to the walk.

April had been with Joe only a few min-

utes, and she had already forgotten her resolve not to let him charm her. When he
tucked her hand in the crook of his arm and
covered it with a warm callused hand, she
smiled up at him, feeling lighter than air.

"We make a handsome couple," Joe said,
his gaze provocative.

"I'm glad you think so. I bet you say that
to every girl you take out."

"You wouldn't believe me if I told you how
many girls I've taken out this past year." His
smile was wicked.

"I'd believe you. I saw you with one of
them the other day." April wished the words
back as soon as they left her mouth.

"Yeah? When was this?" They had
reached her car. He backed her up against
the door and put his hands on each side of
her, caging her in. His eyes were strangely
grave.

"It was a few days ago. I came out of the
clinic, and you were leaning against her car,
talking to a very pretty dark-haired girl."

"That was Ruby, Jack's girl. Why didn't
you come out and meet her?"

"I didn't want to interrupt. Anyway, I was
in a . . . hurry." April stammered, annoyed

with herself. She pushed on his chest. "You look like a Chicago gangster in that hat."

"I thought I looked dashing." A smile lit his handsome face again. "How many Chicago gangsters have you seen?"

"None. But I've seen plenty of Kansas City gangsters, and I imagine they're not much different."

"I don't think I've ever seen a gangster. But I saw a killer over in Rainwater, Oklahoma. He turned out to be a relative of sorts."

"You're kidding. Aren't you?"

"No ma'am, I'm not. I'll tell you about it some dark night when we're sitting in the car after I've kissed you senseless." His blue eyes shone with amusement. He opened the car door and helped her into the car, then went around and slid behind the wheel. He gave her his special smile, the one that crinkled the corners of his eyes and curled his lips, the one that made him look sleepy, dangerous and . . . something else. She wasn't sure what.

"Mind if I drive?" he asked and started the car.

She laughed. "What if I said yes, I mind?"

"I'd say it's too late, babe."

"Where are we going?"

"To Mason, if it's all right with you. They have two picture shows. We'll have a choice of which show we want to see."

"That's fine with me. Do we have enough gas? I've not bought any since I've been here."

"We have plenty. Wally and I changed the oil and checked the tires. Fool that I am, I didn't leave much chance of us getting stuck out on some dark road."

She laughed at his irritated expression. "I'll stop by in a day or two and pay him."

Joe gave her a sidewise glance but said nothing. She had an allure that baffled him, challenged him more than any woman ever had. He turned on the headlights and drove out of town. Once the lights of the town were left behind, he reached for her.

"Come over here and help me drive."

"There isn't room for both of us behind the wheel."

"Want to bet? I'd put you on my lap, if I could." His hand tugged on her arm, and she moved over until her shoulder brushed his.

"I've not ridden in this car with someone other than my grandfather driving."

"Closer." His voice was low-pitched and urgent.

She disliked the command so charmingly uttered, but she moved, the gearshift jabbing at her knees. Her pounding heart numbed her senses. She wavered only temporarily, torn by doubt and self-recrimination, before settling her thigh snugly against his, calling herself weak and cowardly, wondering how she could be so foolish to yield so easily to his charm.

How could I allow myself to want to be close to him, touch him, have him smile at me?

"Now, tell me about the relative in Rainwater. I thought all the Joneses were upright and respectable."

"We are, darlin'. We are," he drawled. "My brother Jack is now a real sworn-in policeman; my pa is a model citizen; my sisters are married to fine, upstanding, dependable men. As for myself, I'm—"

"—the town rake!" she murmured sweetly, gazing at him with lifted brows.

"There you go. Complimenting me again."

"There's a black sheep in every family. I have one in mine."

"I don't want to talk about the black

sheep. I'm too happy just to be . . . alone in the dark with you." He put his arm around her and tucked her shoulder beneath his. "I'm good at driving with one hand."

"I imagine you've had plenty of practice." Her voice held a small annoyance.

"Not as much as I'd like, but I plan to become an expert," he whispered and pulled her closer.

He was so delightful to be with that the car ate up the miles to Mason before she knew it. It had seemed much farther the night she came here with Jack. When they drove into town, Joe had to remove his arm from her shoulders so he could shift the gears, and she moved slightly away from him.

"Shall we go by the shows and see what's on before we go to the restaurant?"

"We don't have to do both—have dinner *and* see a show."

"Yes, we do. This is a real date. I want you to know that I know how to treat a lady." He turned down Main Street and slowed in front of the blazing lights of the Tower Theatre. "It looks like *The Thin Man*, with William Powell and Myrna Loy. Have you seen it?"

"No. Have you?"

"I seldom go to a show. This is going to be a real treat, sitting in the dark, holding your hand."

"Be serious," April said as the car moved on down the street and stopped where neon lights spelled out CAPITAL THEATRE. She read the billboard: "*It Happened One Night*, with Clark Gable and Claudette Colbert. Oh . . . Clark Gable—he's sinfully handsome!" She turned to look at Joe and found his face close to hers.

"I don't like him. I like Claudette Colbert," he said with a pout. "But I guess I can put up with him for an hour or two. Shall we see this one? I'll go see when the next show starts." At her nod he pulled the car to the curb and stopped. "Don't drive off without me," he said as he got out. When he returned, he took her hand before he spoke. "The next show starts at eight. We've got plenty of time, but I'm afraid it'll go all too fast."

When they entered the restaurant, April thought surely that this was the fanciest one in town. The walls were white with touches of gold here and there. Green plants were tastefully arranged in the corners and along the window ledges. The tables were covered with snowy-white cloths. A small vase of flowers sat in the center of each. Ceiling fans spaced throughout the room stirred the air lazily. Well-dressed patrons dined quietly.

The man who showed them to their table looked like a movie star in his black suit, white shirt and bow tie and dark slicked-down hair. After leaving the menus on the table he bowed slightly from the waist and backed away.

April glanced down at the prices on the menu and gasped. She glanced at Joe and found him looking over the bill of fare as if he frequented expensive restaurants every day. She folded the menu and laid it aside.

"You've decided?" he asked.

"On the chicken and dumplings." It was one of the two cheapest choices listed.

"Sure you wouldn't like to have a steak or one of these fancy French dishes?"

"Absolutely sure. I've been hungry for chicken and dumplings. I've been after Sparky to put it on his menu."

"I thought you ate your meals at Mrs. Poole's."

"I do sometimes."

The waiter returned, and Joe ordered for both of them. He had chosen ham and sweet potatoes. April mentally figured how much this date would cost Joe. The meals and the theater tickets would ruin a five-dollar bill, and he had filled her tank with gas. That would be another dollar. She felt guilty because she knew that she must make more money at her nursing job than he did. But it would never do with a man like Joe even to discuss what this date was costing him.

So what to do? *Be suitably impressed and make sure that he enjoys himself as much as possible.*

The dinner was delicious. They smiled at each other across the table and spoke of nonsensical things. Her admiration for him grew. She realized that Joe Jones was the kind of man who could fit into any society, rich or poor, educated or ignorant, shy or outgoing. He was completely comfortable with himself.

April enjoyed the movie. She thought that Joe enjoyed it, too. She heard him chuckle from time to time. He pulled her arm through his, held her hand and toyed with her fingers, which was distracting. All too often she caught him looking at her instead of the movie screen. When it was over, they filed out of the theater with the other talking and laughing patrons.

"Now for the good part," Joe said as he helped her into the car.

"Good part? I thought the movie was the good part."

"Not on your life, sugarfoot," he said as he slid under the wheel. "The good part is when we get back to Fertile, park and neck."

April laughed. "You're the limit."

Joe drove slowly back to Fertile, his arm holding her close. They talked about the movie.

"Hanging that blanket up between them was silly." Joe glanced at her, expecting an argument.

"I suppose you liked that part the best."

"No, I liked it best when she was standing along the road showing her leg so they could get a ride."

April burst out laughing. "I should have known."

The banter went back and forth until they reached town.

"Why don't we drive on out to your father's or wherever you're going to stay and I'll drive myself home?"

"I'm spending the night on Doc's daybed. I'll go home in the morning, unless you want to go have breakfast with me."

"Thank you, no. I plan to sleep until noon."

"Not going to church?" He stopped the car on the edge of town.

"Will my reputation be ruined if I don't?"

"Not with me. And that's all that should count." He put his hat on the seat on the other side of her. "Can I take that thing off your head? It looks pretty . . . but for what I have in mind it might get in the way."

"Should I be frightened at . . . what you have in mind?" Her heart was racing, her senses in tumult, as she removed the turban.

"Maybe. I have this powerful urge to kiss you." His voice was low, rich and deep.

She didn't know what to say for a moment. "No," she finally said, trembling slightly. "I'm not scared."

His face was close, his voice low and heated, "Then let me kiss you . . ."

She was lost. His mouth was delicate at first, offering butterfly kisses on her lips and cheeks, on her earlobes and temples, on the warm pulse of her throat, then settled on her mouth with infinite possession, making her feel lusciously heated. She kissed him back, and a new tremulous feeling flared deep in the pit of her stomach. Pleasure inundated her senses, warmed her blood, and she felt overwhelmingly happy.

He lifted his head, almost drawing a moan of protest from her, and tilted her head back. She saw the sensuous curve of his mouth, then he was kissing her again. Her eyes drifted shut. His lips were soft, shaping hers. Both of her hands were clinging to his shoulders. He covered one with his and moved it down to press her palm against the heavy thump rocking his chest.

"Scared yet?" he murmured against her lips.

"Huh-uh." It was all she managed to say before he was kissing her again.

"You should be." The faintly muttered words came when he lifted his head again. He wrapped both arms around her, his heart thundering against her own. "Ah, sweetheart, I'm right on the verge of falling in love with you."

"Oh, no. You mustn't!" She could barely speak.

His mouth found hers again. He gently

caught her lower lip between his teeth and applied delicate pressure.

"Why not? Couldn't you ever love me in return?" His voice was suddenly rough, anxious.

She said the first thing that came into her mind and hoped that she sounded casual. "I don't know you well enough."

"What don't you know?" His tone was concerned, his gaze perplexed.

Instead of answering his question, she said, "People don't fall in love after a couple of dates."

"Some do."

"Not me. I'm too realistic for that." Biting her lip, she pushed herself out of his arms. "It must be after midnight. We'd better be getting on."

Joe started the car and turned on the headlights. He drove slowly along the road that ran parallel with the river.

"I really had a good time . . ."

"So did I." His grin was back, but his mind was riveted on her words. *Not me. I'm too realistic for that.* He felt a heaviness in his chest. He forced a lightness he didn't feel when he said, "We'll do it again sometime."

He didn't seem to expect a reply. She

looked out at the rolling river, wondering what she could say to keep the evening from ending on a less-than-happy note. She wanted to cry. Wrapped in her own thoughts, she was startled when he put his foot on the brake and stopped abruptly.

"Godamighty! Look at that. The river is up over Callahan's dock, which means it's over the banks in the low lands. It's rained up north, and the fools downriver haven't taken out that rock pile." Joe moved the car along slowly. "The bank is lower here than any-where along the river for ten miles in either direction. It's not been over Callahan's dock since the flood of the early twenties."

"Does that mean it'll flood now?"

"Looks like it. Doc's worried about the water wells and . . . folks down here." As he spoke, they could see flashes of lightning in the northern sky. "I'll wake up Doc, then go tell Jack and Corbin. Jack is staying at the hotel until he gets settled in a room."

"Leave me here at Doc's. There might be something I can do," she said as they ap-proached the clinic. "Then take the car and do what you have to do."

"What I want to do is kiss you again." He turned to her after he had shut off the motor.

"And I want you to," she said softly and never meant anything so much in her life. She wanted to feel the pleasure again, the strength of his arms around her, the hardness of his chest against her breasts, the sweetness of his mouth.

One hand slid up her back to close lightly over the nape of her neck. She felt his heart hammering, his breath soft on her hair. She had never felt this connection with anyone else, this rightness, as she leaned into him.

"Honey . . . sweetheart.   You're   so damned sweet I can't resist you."

The kiss lasted for a long while, a fragile kiss, tender at first and then not tender at all. She felt a warm glow inundate her senses, and inexplicable joy. When he lifted his head, she wasn't ready for the kiss to end.

"This evening has been like all my Christmases rolled into one," he whispered against her forehead.

"I enjoyed it, too."

He opened the car door and got out. They walked up the path to Doc's porch with arms around each other.

Chapter 20

It was to be a night that April would not soon forget. She stayed at Doc's while he and Joe went to look over the situation along the riverbank.

"There isn't anyone in the area who can read the river like Oran Callahan," Joe explained. "Callahan has lived on the river all his life, and he must be in his sixties. He taught his boys the ways of the river, and they are good fishermen. They've made their living catching and selling fish."

Doc drove slowly along the river road, the car's headlights reflected on the water that was coming up into the yards and filling the ditches. Lights were on in the houses as the concerned families prepared to leave their homes should it become necessary.

Some were experiencing their first flood.

Others remembered the flood of the early 1920s when the water rose until it reached the main street of Fertile. They'd had to live in makeshift shacks on higher ground until the water went down. Then came the back-breaking work of clearing away the river silt and salvaging what was left of their homes.

They found Callahan in his hip boots, with a lantern and the bamboo pole he used to measure the depth of the water.

"How fast is it comin' up?" Doc asked.

"Fast. That you, Doc?" The grizzled fisherman squinted at the men standing on the road.

"Yeah. Joe Jones is with me."

"It don't look good, Doc. Folks ort to be packin' up. Judgin' by what's comin' down-river, they've had a real turd floater up north. That rock pile in the river down at Calmar has got the water backin' up. Them fellers ain't got no more brains than a stump."

"Didn't the court tell them to clear the dam out?"

"They was told. But they're a stubborn bunch and paid no mind a-tall. There'll be trouble if folks are flooded out because of it. They ain't goin' to stand for it."

"Trouble in more ways than one," Doc

said. "All the water wells along here will be contaminated. People will be coming down with typhoid."

"My boys is bringin' the boats in. We'll use 'em to help folks that gets stranded."

Doc and Joe went back to the car. "I'll take you back into town, Joe. I've got to get to Caroline."

"I'll get Jack and Corbin. I'm afraid some of the hotheads down here will make a trip downriver to blow up that rock barricade. I've heard talk of it, and this just might push them to act."

"Hell, I hadn't thought of that. I'm going to get Caroline and take her to my place. And I don't give a goddamn what anyone thinks."

"Have you told April?"

"Nobody but you."

"You won't be disappointed in April. I'd bet my life on it. If you need any help, just say the word. I'll be there and so will Jack."

"Thanks," Doc said gruffly.

As soon as Joe got out of the car in front of the hotel where Jack had a room, Doc made a U-turn in the middle of the street and headed back toward the river road. Joe went up the steps and into the hotel lobby. He had to pound the bell on the desk before a bleary-eyed night clerk came from behind a screen.

"Is Jack Jones here?"

The clerk stretched and yawned before he answered. "May I ask who wants to know?"

"No, you may not. Is he here?"

"Is this police business?"

"That's none of your damn business. What room is he in?" The man's attitude was causing Joe's temper to rise.

"I have to know if this is an emergency before I can disturb him."

"Hell and damnation. Have you got shit for brains? Unless you want your head shoved up your ass, tell me what room he's in."

The startled clerk stood back from the fury in Joe's face and murmured, "You don't have to be so . . . rude. He's in 206."

Joe took the stairs two at a time, went down the dim hall and pounded on the door of his brother's room. Seconds later it was jerked open. Jack stood there shirtless and shoeless, his hair standing on end.

"What the hell—is something wrong? The folks . . . ?"

"Nothing wrong with the folks. The river's rising—fast." Joe took off his coat. "Do you have a pair of old pants and a jacket I could borrow? This is my churchgoing suit."

Jack threw clothes to him from a drawer. "Tonight was the big date?"

"Yeah. We discovered water coming over Callahan's dock when we came back from Mason."

"The hell it is!"

"Doc and I went down to Callahan's. He was out measuring and said it was coming up fast. It's almost up to his back porch. He's higher up than some, which means some folks are sitting in water right now."

"What am I supposed to do about it?"

"Keep the peace. Help those who can't help themselves."

"Shit. I don't know if I'm ready for this."

"Got a pair of shoes I can borrow?"

"You can wear my old boots if you want."

"I want."

The brothers left the room. As Jack passed the desk, he picked up the phone. The operator came on immediately.

"This is Jack Jones, Flora. The river is rising up to flood stage. Call Corbin Appleby and tell him I'm on my way down to his place. Call and let the mayor know about the river. We may need volunteers. Dr. Forbes already knows. I'll get back to you later."

"What happened to Diane?" Joe asked as they left the lobby.

"She doesn't put in the hours she used to. She has a night operator now. Flora Jones." Jack grinned.

"Jones?"

"We're not the only Jones family in the world. This one is a beautiful redhead. She came here from Des Moines a week or so ago, but I think her home is somewhere in Minnesota."

"She's a long way from home."

"You should give her a look."

"I'm taken. Look at her yourself."

"I might as well. I always did like red hair."

"What about Ruby?"

"Ruby's given me nothing but a cold shoulder. If what she wants is a dumb-ass like that lineman she's keeping company with, then to hell with her."

"You don't mean that . . . do you?"

Jack didn't answer the question. Instead,

he said, "Burkhardt left the police car in terrible shape. Wally, down at the station, is working on it. Meanwhile, I walk."

"April said I could use her car. We left it at Doc's. Let's cut through here and get it." They crossed the street and walked between the drugstore and the theater.

"You're getting pretty cozy if she's letting you use her car."

"I'm working on it."

"Making any progress?"

"I think so."

"Does Harold Dozier know that? He's taken a shine to her and bragging that he's got a date with her next Saturday night."

Joe stopped in his tracks. "He what?"

"I heard him telling Frank Adler at the drugstore that he has a date with her. He didn't know yet where they were going, but they were going to talk about it in the middle of the week. He was pretty pumped up about it."

"It's news to me." Joe felt like he'd been kicked in the stomach.

If it was true that she'd agreed to go out with Harold, why hadn't she mentioned it when he suggested they do a repeat of their date? He thought that she understood they would go out again next Saturday night.

April had responded to his kisses as if they meant as much to her as they did to him. He hadn't taken her for the kind of girl who kissed lightly or played the field looking over the prospects. If that was the case, Harold would win hands down. He was a lawyer, made good money, owned a nice house, belonged to the town's upper crust.

What the hell do I have to stack up against that?

April had been watching out the window and opened the door as soon as Joe and Jack were on the porch.

"The city car is out of commission. Does the offer of the use of your car still hold?" Joe asked without preamble as he stepped into the house. Jack crowded in behind him.

"Of course."

"The town will pay for the gas. If not, I will," Jack said.

"Don't worry about it."

"Doc will be back in a while," Joe said.

"I'll stay until he gets here. I've already told Flora. I don't want her calling me at Mrs. Poole's this time of night." She looked directly at Joe, but he avoided her gaze by bending to tie the laces on a pair of well-worn boots. He had changed clothes and no longer looked the well-dressed, well-mannered man who had taken her to dinner.

"Doc had personal business to attend to," Joe said. "He'll have someone with him when he comes. Someone who is *very important* to him. Remember that."

April's professional expression slid over her face to keep him from knowing how confused she was by his words and his attitude. Why was he acting like this? This was a Joe she had not met before. His face was as stern as his voice, which was so set she thought it would crack if he smiled. He hadn't looked at her once since he came in the door.

"Is this person ill? Shall I get a bed ready?"

"You'll know when Doc gets here," he said with a note of irritation. "We'd better go, Jack. Corbin will be waiting—"

"You have the keys to the car," April said. "Keep it as long as you need it."

"Thanks," Jack said as he followed Joe across the porch.

What in the world was the matter with

him? He hadn't even said good-bye. April didn't have time right then to speculate on Joe's strange behavior.

The phone rang. It was Corbin Appleby.

"Doc isn't here, Mr. Appleby. Joe and Jack Jones were just here and said he would be here shortly."

"My wife is having back pains, and I want to be sure he's where I can reach him if we need him. There will be plenty of people to help get the folks out of the river bottom without Doc pitching in."

"Shall I have him call you?"

"Just tell him to stay put, and I'll call if I need him."

April smiled at the nervous tremor in the usually composed paper editor's voice. After assuring him that she would deliver the message, April tied a dish towel about her waist and washed the dirty dishes in the pan on the counter, dried them and put them away.

While she was sweeping the kitchen floor, she had three phone calls. Flora phoned to tell her that a call had come from Blackton, a town in Iowa fifty miles to the north. The chief of police wanted the word passed to Officer Jones that it was raining cats and dogs up there. April smiled at Flora's description and promised to tell Doc when she saw him or send word if the chance presented itself.

Another call came from Flora asking to have Officer Jones call in if he came back to Doc's. There had been a domestic disturbance he might want to look into.

A man who identified himself as a volunteer fireman phoned to ask if Dr. Forbes needed any help. April thanked him, took his name and told him that she would have Dr. Forbes call if he was needed.

Joe's caution that Doc was bringing someone who was very important to him suddenly registered in April's mind. Doc had been here almost twelve years and knew the people along the river as well as he did those in town. He was probably bringing an elderly person who lived alone. He would want him or her to be comfortable. She went to his bedroom and found there was nothing to be done there. The bed was made; the room was neat. She checked the bathroom and found it the same.

Back in the living room, she sat down in the chair beside the window and slipped off her shoes. It was two o'clock in the morning. She wondered, with a smile, if Mrs. Poole was staying awake waiting to see what time she came home.

The headlights of Doc's car forged a path down the lane. River water had already come up to the back of the house. He drove in and stopped near the front door. A light shone from the window, and the door opened before he reached it.

"It's Mistah Doctah," Silas said over his shoulder and held open the door.

Doc went straight to Caroline, who was putting things in a trunk Silas had lifted up onto a table. She turned and threw her arms around him. Her beautiful eyes were anxious.

"I knew you'd come."

"It's going to be all right. You're coming to my house."

"I can't do that. No, Todd." She shook her head. "Take me someplace else."

"Hush, now. You're coming home with me, and that's all there is to it."

"No, please. You'll be ruined and I couldn't stand . . . that." Her voice had a sob in it.

"Caroline," Doc said firmly, "you and our

baby are coming home with me." He put his hands on her shoulders and drew her to him. "Sweetheart, your place is with me. Don't argue. We've got a lot to do and not much time to do it. Now, what are you doing here?"

"I'm putting Papa's things in the trunk. Silas says he'll put the chairs on the table and the trunk on it so it won't be ruined if the house floods."

"We'll take the trunk with us."

"I've got to save Mama's wedding ring quilt, her picture album and Daddy's mother's and father's pictures." She climbed up onto a chair to take the pictures off the wall.

"No climbing." Doc was behind her and lifted her down. He removed the pictures and placed them in the trunk. He grabbed the pillowcases off the bed. "Put clothes and things you want to take with you in these. And hurry, honey. The water is coming up fast. Silas and I will take care of the trunk. Is there anything out at your place you want to take, Silas?"

"Naw, suh. I got it right here in my pocket."

Doc filled the trunk with pictures, books

and Caroline's miniature cedar chest, which held her treasures: the things he had given her and the necklace made from her mother's hair. There was a little room left in the trunk, so he packed Caroline's china coffee service between the folds of the quilt before he closed the lid.

Silas set everything that water would ruin up off the floor and onto tables, counters, and chest. He even rolled up the braided rag rug Caroline had made one winter and shoved it through the hole leading to the attic.

A half hour later they were ready to go. When Doc opened the front door, he stepped out into water. Telling Caroline to wait, he and Silas carried the trunk and the pillowcases to the car. The trunk wouldn't fit in the backseat, so they set it on the top of the car. Silas would stand on the running board and hold on to it to keep it from sliding off.

Doc returned to the house, swept Caroline up in his arms and settled her in the car.

"Come on, Silas. We've done everything we can do here."

"I come back, Doctah. Don't want nobody breakin' in."

"If they do, they do. You can't stay here, man. There's a place for you with me and Caroline. Come on before the water gets so high we can't get out of here."

Silas climbed onto the running board, and Doc backed down the lane to the road.

Chapter 21

"A car is stopping out front now, Mr. Appleby. It may be Dr. Forbes. He's bringing in a patient. Shall I have him call you?"

"In five minutes or I'm coming down there."

April smiled at the threat in his voice. The man was in a panic. She hung up the phone and went to open the door. Doc was coming up the steps with a young woman.

"I'm glad you're back, Doc. Mr. Appleby is about to blow a fuse."

"Annabel having pains?"

"Ten minutes apart."

"It's just my luck that she'll deliver tonight." Doc pulled the young woman up beside him. "April, this is Caroline Deval, soon to be my wife." He put his arm around the beautiful girl, whose eyes were large and apprehensive. "Sweetheart, this is April Asbury, the nurse I've told you about."

It seemed to April that five minutes passed before she could take her next breath. She had never received such shocking news delivered so calmly. However, she quickly recovered.

"Hello, Miss Deval." The training in the trauma center helped to keep the shock from her face as she held out her hand. "I'm happy to meet you."

The girl shyly extended her hand but said nothing.

"Caroline will be staying here with me." Doc paused to get April's reaction, then said, "I want to keep her presence here as unobserved as possible in order to prevent any unpleasantness."

April nodded. The girl, slim and beautiful with dark glossy hair, large amber eyes and dainty classic features, looked as if she were ready to flee. She held tightly to Doc's hand. She glanced once at April, then fastened her eyes on Doc's face.

"It's going to be all right, honey."

"Tell her," Caroline whispered.

Doc looked into her face for a long while, then his hand went up to caress her cheek.

She turned her lips to his palm. It was plain to April that the doctor had deep feelings for the girl and she for him.

"She wants me to tell you that she has colored blood and that most of those who live in Shanty Town know it. She's afraid that if it's known that I love her and want to make her my wife, I will be ruined in this town. I'm hoping that she and I can leave here before that happens."

April didn't know what to say. She had never faced a situation like this. She could only go on instinct and do her best not to stammer.

"Is she afraid that . . . I'll . . . be unkind?" April spoke to Doc while looking at Caroline. "Please don't worry about that. I might be jealous because . . . you're so pretty." She smiled and added the last in an attempt at humor. Neither Doc nor the girl smiled.

"You know what folks will say about a young lady staying here . . . much less Caroline."

"There's no reason for them to know . . . if she's willing to stay out of sight. Oh, I almost forgot. Call Mr. Appleby. He said to call in five minutes, or he'd be up here."

"I don't want that to happen. I'll make the

call." As he passed the door, he spoke to Silas on the porch. "I'll help you bring in the trunk in a minute."

April seldom felt big and gawky when with another woman, but she did standing beside this girl. She wanted to say something to ease the tension between them.

"You're very pretty. I'm not surprised that Doc fell in love with you."

"Thank you."

After a silence April, determined to make conversation, asked, "Did your house flood?"

"Yes, ma'am." Her eyes clung to Doc, who was speaking on the phone to Corbin Appleby.

"I'll be down in a while, Corbin. It isn't doing Annabel any good for you to shout the house down. She's not going to have that baby within the next thirty minutes. Go hold her hand, tell her you're sorry you got her into this fix and tell her to breathe deeply." Doc hung up and rang the operator.

"I'm going to the Applebys. Yes, Mrs. Appleby is having her baby tonight. If you have an emergency, and I'm thinking there could be some with all the folks moving back from the river, Miss Asbury will be here. If it's

something she can't handle, she'll call me."
Doc hung up the phone.

"Silas, let's bring in the trunk." Doc went
out onto the porch, and shortly after, he and
Silas, the big colored man who had come
looking for him the week before, carried in a
trunk. They took it into Doc's bedroom; then
Silas went back to the car and brought in
two stuffed pillowcases. Doc put those in
his bedroom, too.

"Come in here, honey, and I'll show you
where your things can go." With an apprehensive glance at April, Caroline went to the
bedroom.

April felt like a fifth wheel. If she hadn't
heard Doc tell the operator that she'd be
here, she would leave. So many thoughts
were spinning around in her mind they
crowded out, for a moment, the hurt and
disappointment she felt when Joe gave her
the cold treatment.

Oh, Lord. What would Miss Davenport,
Shirley Poole and others do if they found
out Caroline was here in Doc's house? Was
she the colored "whore" Mrs. Poole had referred to who didn't dare show her face in
town? Doc would not only be ruined in this
town; newspapers would pick up the story,

and his medical career would be over. He evidently knew the risk and was willing to take it.

It must be wonderful to have a man love you so deeply that he'd chance so much to be with you.

April could hear the murmur of Doc's voice, then he and Caroline came from the bedroom.

"If you have any problem with this, now is the time to say so," he told April.

She chose her words carefully. "You have the right to choose the woman you want as your wife. I thought we were friends as well as employer and employee. As your friend, you can depend on me to support whatever decisions you make as long as they are not hurtful to someone else."

"Marriage between me and Caroline will be illegal. I could be arrested—"

"Maybe in the eyes of the law it's illegal. I doubt that it is in the eyes of God."

Doc's shoulders seemed to slump in relief. "See, sweet girl, I told you it would be all right." His arm pulled Caroline close. Then to April: "You and Joe are the only ones who know about me and Caroline. It's only fair that I tell you that I have applied for a job in Canada. I should know in a week or two if I get it. If I don't, I will be leaving anyway."

"Will another doctor come to take your place?"

"In time. I don't know how soon. I would appreciate it if you'd consider staying on and taking care of emergencies and sending those you can't handle to the doctors in Mason."

The phone rang. April went through the door into the clinic to answer it. "The doctor is out right now, Flora. Tell them to bring him here, and I'll do what I can until the doctor gets back.

"A man sliced his thigh with a knife," she explained when she returned. "An accident. It may be something I can handle; if not, I'll call you. You'd better get going before Mr. Appleby calls again."

"You'll be all right here with April." Doc's voice was soft when he spoke to Caroline. "Silas is here. When I get back, I'll fix him a place to sleep in the shed out back."

Caroline stood quietly behind Doc's chair after he had left, her hands held tightly to the back. She looked uncertain and scared. April's heart went out to her.

"I would like for us to be friends. I think
the world of Dr. Forbes. Not as a sweetheart," she added quickly, "but as a friend,
a person I respect a great deal. I'll do anything I can to help him . . . and you." When
the shy girl didn't reply, April continued. "I'll
be here in the clinic." She indicated the
open door. "You may want to turn the light
off in the living room and on in the bedroom
or kitchen. I checked the shades. No one
can see in."

"Thank you, ma'am." Caroline's voice
was barely above a whisper.

"Please call me April. May I call you Caroline?"

Caroline nodded, then said, "I'm worried
for Todd. I'd leave if I could."

"It would break his heart if you did. He
must love you very much."

"My papa was disowned by his family because he loved my mama."

"How long have you been alone?"

"Papa died last Christmas Day."

"That must have been hard. My mother
died on Thanksgiving Day. You're lucky to
have Doc. He is one of the smartest, kind-
est men I've ever known. He'll take you

someplace where you can be happy together."

The slamming of a car door and quick steps on the porch sent April scurrying into the clinic, closing the door behind her. A short, stocky woman came in, breathing heavily.

"I can't get him out of the car. I think he fainted."

April grabbed up a bottle of smelling salts and followed her to the car. The man who sprawled in the backseat was large. His belt was buckled beneath a protruding belly. A bloody towel was wrapped around a leg that looked to be as big as the branch of an oak tree. When she leaned into the car, she caught the unmistakable smell of alcohol. When she waved the bottle under his nose, he sat up, his arms flying out like a windmill. It was then that April realized the man hadn't fainted. He was drunk.

It was going to take more muscle than she and the woman with him had to get him into the clinic. April called out to the man sitting on the floor at the far end of the porch.

"Silas, will you help us?"

"Yes'm."

"He won't like that a-tall," the woman said when she saw Silas. "He don't have no truck with coloreds."

"He will this time," April said firmly. "Or he'll sit there and bleed to death. Silas, grasp him under the arms and pull him out."

"Whatsha doin'? Get 'way, nigger. I'll kick your black ass—"

"Calm down," April said patiently. "We've got to get you inside so I can look at your leg."

The man's arms flailed, trying to hit Silas, and he hit her instead. "Hey, stop that!"

"Get . . . 'way! No black sonabitch is . . . touchin' me. No split-tail, neither."

"Hush up!" April's temper flared.

"Don't ya tell me . . . to hush, ya up-pity . . . bitch." The eyes fastened on her were hate-filled. "Shit . . . eatin' nigger— ain't goin' to push me."

"Shut your filthy mouth! You're damn lucky he's willing to help a drunken mouthy sot. Now, settle down and let Silas help you, or your wife can take you back where you came from. It doesn't make a damn bit of difference to me."

"Shee-it—"

"Why're ya talkin' to him that way?" the woman said. "Can't ya see he's hurt?"

"I can see that he's drunk and has a nasty mouth."

"That ain't none of your business if'n he's drunk. Where's Dr. Forbes?"

"The doctor is away delivering a baby. If you don't want me to help him, I suggest that you take him to a doctor in Mason."

"Who're you anyway?"

"Dr. Forbes's nurse."

"You don't look like no nurse."

"Well, I am. And I'm well qualified to take care of a cut. What's it going to be? I've got more to do than stand here and argue with a drunk."

The woman leaned in the car. "Hon, ya gotta let the nigger help you, or we'll have to drive to Mason, and the road may be flooded by now."

The man cursed continually as Silas pulled him out of the car and supported him with a strong arm while he hopped on one foot up the steps and into the clinic.

"Bring him back here, Silas, and help him up onto the examination table."

Flat on the table, the man glared up at

Silas. "Get the hell out. I ain't carin' for nigger stink."

"Stay, Silas." April removed her suit coat
and pulled on one of Doc's white jackets. "I
might need you to hold this big-mouth
down while I sew him up. Take off his
shoes," she said to his wife, and she un-
wrapped the dingy blood-soaked towel
from around his leg. The gash was long and
deep across the front of his thigh. "Take off
your pants."

A grin came over the whiskered face. "Ya
wantin' to see what I got in 'em?"

"I know what ya've got in 'em, and I imagine it's about as insignificant as the rest of
ya." She mimicked his speech. "Are you
taking them off, or do I cut the leg off your
britches? Silas, hand me the scissors."

"Don't ya ruin my britches. I'll take 'em
off."

April flung a sheet over his middle and
began to load the cart with the supplies she
would need to clean, stitch and bandage
the wound.

"What did he cut himself with?" she
asked the woman, who hovered over his
head after she had pulled off his britches.

"Skinning knife. He was skinning out a couple squirrels he killed today."

April poured the antiseptic directly into the wound. The man would have jumped off the table if she and his wife had not held him down.

"Bitch!" he shouted.

"Call me that name again and you'll regret it. Do you understand me?" She glared directly into his eyes, her lips tight with anger. "You don't scare me a bit. I've treated far tougher than you; so button up your foul mouth, or I'll slap some tape over it."

Thirty minutes later she was wrapping a bandage around the man's thigh. She'd had to call on Silas to hold the leg still while she closed the cut with twelve stitches.

"You'd better bring him back day after tomorrow," April said to the woman; she had stopped talking to the drunk. "Doc will want to be sure there is no infection. I'll give you a few pain pills, but don't give them to him until he sobers up. I'm not sure how they'd mix with alcohol."

The woman helped him back into his pants and to sit up on the side of the table.

"For the record, what is his name?" April asked the woman.

"Gilbert. Morton Gilbert."

"You owe Dr. Forbes two dollars. If you don't have the money now, you can stop by later and pay. Now, will Mr. Gilbert be kind enough to permit Silas to help him back in the car?" April knew how to use her voice to cut, and she did that now.

"You don't have to be so snotty about it," Mrs. Gilbert snarled.

"Silas, help him to the car, please. I want him out of here. If he falls and breaks open the stitches, I'll have it to do all over again." April was tired to the bone. It was three in the morning, and her patience was at an end, especially with the ungrateful drunk.

She was cleaning the surgery when Silas returned.

"Dey gone."

"Thank you for helping. I'm sorry you had to suffer his insults. I wanted to sew up his filthy mouth."

"Yes'm." Silas's lips parted in a grin, showing two rows of exceptionally white teeth.

"Did Caroline's house flood?"

"Yes'm. Water come up fast. We was gettin' ready. We knowed Doctah would come."

"I'm sure you're tired. If you want to lie down, there's a daybed in the storage shed. I'll stay with Caroline until Dr. Forbes gets back."

"Yes'm. She scared of folks. She don't see nobody. Don't go nowhere since her papa die."

"I thought that might be the case. I hope she's not afraid of me."

"She poor little scared girl. She not what folks say," Silas said softly. His eyes bespoke intelligence and integrity. He had such a quiet, gentle way with the girl that April sensed he loved her as if she were his own daughter. It was no wonder Doc trusted him to guard her.

"Ignorant people can be cruel." April reached for the phone when it rang. "Hello? Hello, Doc. Has Mrs. Appleby had her baby?"

"Not yet, but Corbin has had a fit or two."

April was too tired to laugh. "I sewed up a six-inch gash in Morton Gilbert's thigh. We did not get along well."

"He was drunk and mouthy?"

"You know him, then. My bedside manner went out the window. I'd not been able to manage without Silas to bring him in."

"Everything all right?"

"Just fine. I'll bed down on your couch until you get back."

"It may be an hour before Annabel gives birth. I'll be back as soon as I can."

"I'll be here, Doc."

April turned off the lights in the clinic. She and Silas went into the other part of the house. Caroline was curled up in Doc's chair. April kicked off her shoes and sank down on the couch.

"Doc called. He thinks it'll be an hour before Mrs. Appleby has her baby." April stretched. "I'm tired. I bet you are, too. Why don't you lie down back there on Doc's bed, Caroline? He'll wake you up when he comes home."

Caroline's questioning eyes went to Silas. "Ya needs to rest. Doctah say so. He be sour-mouth if'n ya don't." She got up like an obedient child. "I be on dey porch. Missy nurse be here." He spoke gently.

On impulse April said, "I'm glad you're here, Caroline. Don't worry. Doc knows what he's doing, and he's got friends here who will help him."

Caroline nodded, then disappeared into the bedroom.

Chapter 22

Corbin had met Joe and Jack on the front porch and told them his wife was going into labor. He said that he was waiting for Dr. Forbes and that a team of mules couldn't pull him from this house until his wife and baby were safe.

"The people down there are a tight-knit group and will help each other," Corbin said. "If a crowd gathers, it will happen uptown. Hang out on the edge of it, but let your presence be known. Joe can mingle and find out what's going on. Don't let them rile you and don't try to handle a group of fifteen or twenty men alone. I called Marshal Sanford to ask for help. He wasn't in his office, but the deputy will relay my message. I'm sure that he'll either come himself or send help."

Jack listened carefully to his friend's advice on how best to handle the refugees from the flooded river bottom.

"No one complained at first because it raised the river and fishing was better. Fewer of the fish went on downriver."

"I'll be surprised if a bunch of hotheads don't go downriver and attempt to blow out that damn rock pile. I can't say that I blame them. The district judge told the town of Calmar to stop dumping rocks in the river and to take out the ones they'd put there."

"Evan said they are claiming the river straddles the county lines," Joe said. "And they've not had orders from the northwest district to take out the blockage."

"It'll come out one way or the other. I'm hoping it can be done in an orderly way. If not, someone could be killed."

"We best get going. Give my regards to Annabel and tell her that I want a girl this time," Jack said as they were leaving. "She can name her Jackiebel."

"She'll go for that, I'm sure." Corbin grinned, then said, "Good luck, Jack. You're getting a dose of law enforcement real quick, but I'm confident you'll handle it."

The brothers were quiet as Joe drove out

of town and turned north on the river road. Water hadn't come up over the road at that point, but the ditches alongside it were full. As they moved along the road, Jack stood on the running board and hopped off to meet every car and truck filled with families moving out. There were several wagons piled high with belongings and kids, and pulled by teams. The men looked grim, angry. Some of the women were crying and trying to calm the excited kids.

"Are all your folks out?" Jack would ask. "If you don't have relatives to go to, you can camp in the park, on the baseball diamond or the school yard."

As they neared the end of the residential section of Shanty Town, Jack got back into the car. "There's only a couple more houses down this way. I don't see any lights. We have to drive down there anyway to find a place to turn around."

Joe stopped the car when they came to a place where the water was halfway across the road.

"We'd better turn around here if we can. I'd hate to have to back up all the way to town." Joe cocked his head to one side. "Did you hear—?"

"I heard a shout." Jack got out of the car. "Hey! Hey!"

"Somebody's running this way."

"Hey! I need help!"

Joe stood on the road in front of the car and watched a boy run toward him.

"I can't get my mama out!" He was so breathless he could hardly talk.

He came into the lights of the car barefoot, with wet rolled-up pant legs. He bent over and put his hands on his knees, taking in great gulps of air. Then he raised his head and looked at the two men in front of the car.

"Oh, shit. It would have to be you."

"Catch your breath, Sammy," Joe said. "Is your mother in the house?"

"Yeah. The water's not up to the bed— yet."

"Is she sick?"

"She's drunk. I can't get her up."

"Is the water up over the road down there?"

"Not all the way."

"Can we drive down there?"

"Yeah. The road isn't flooded yet."

"Do we dare drive farther, or shall I walk back with Sammy?" Joe asked Jack.

"If the water isn't up over the road, we can drive. It would save time. But we'd better make it snappy."

Joe got behind the wheel. "Hang on to the running board, Sammy." He started the car and, after skirting the water, picked up speed until they came to another place where water was halfway across the road. He slowed the car to a crawl until they were on high ground again. "How much farther?" he yelled to Sammy.

"Stop when you get to the big trees on the right."

After they had stopped, Joe looked toward the house. It was a good two hundred feet from the road. Jack's flashlight shone on the water surrounding it.

"No need for both of us to get wet." Joe took off his shoes. "I'll go. See if you can turn the car around. You know where the lane is, so lead the way, Sammy."

The water that came up to midcalf was cold. Joe followed along behind the boy, feeling his way toward the faint glow that came from inside the house. His tender foot struck a rock, and he swore.

"Do you have electricity, Sammy?"

"No. I left the kerosene lamp on."

"Then we don't have to worry about electric lines falling in the water."

"Smart-ass lineman came out and turned the electricity off at the pole."

"Can't blame him. He had his orders." Joe stepped in a hole and almost fell. "Dammit to hell." He swore loud and long as he tried to regain his balance. His pant legs were wet all the way up to his crotch. It was damned uncomfortable. He decided then and there that if he could, he'd blow that rock pile down at Calmar clear to hell.

They sloshed along until they reached the house. Sammy had closed the door in a failed attempt to keep out the water. A foot and a half of river water and mud covered the floor. The boy had made an effort to save a few things by piling them up on the table and the kitchen cabinet. Blankets and bedding had been thrown up over the exposed rafters in the kitchen.

"She's in here." Sammy picked up the lamp and pushed through the water to a small room off the kitchen.

His mother lay sprawled facedown on a bare mattress. The bed took up most of the room, with just a walking space between it and a chest of drawers. Sammy set the lamp on the chest and hurried to pull his mother's dress down over her bare buttocks.

Joe jerked a blanket from the end of the iron bedstead and spread it over the woman. With Sammy's help he rolled her in it, then lifted her up and flung her over his shoulder.

"If there's anything here you want, kid, you'd better get it now. I don't think you'll be back for a while."

"I already did. My clothes and my schoolbooks are in a sack tied in the oak tree out by the road."

"Yeah? That was smart."

"I'm not the dumb-ass you think I am."

"That remains to be seen."

Joe felt his way out of the house and down the lane behind Sammy. Marla Davidson was a small woman; but by the time they were halfway to the road, she was taking on weight, and he began to breathe heavily. He labored through water and mud the last dozen yards, feeling as if each of his feet weighed a hundred pounds.

Jack had turned the car around. He opened the jump seat and helped Joe ease the woman into it. Sammy had disappeared as soon as they reached the road. He loped toward them now with a gunnysack that he flung in back with his mother.

"Let's go. You'd better drive, Jack. Sammy and I will ride on the running boards. We're wet and muddy. I don't want to mess up April's car."

Joe, riding on the outside of the car, his feet bare, his pants wet, could feel the cold seeping into his bones. In several places water covered the road and splashed on his feet when they passed through it. It was not deep yet, but at the rate it was coming up, it soon would be. When they reached the lower area, where the houses were grouped closer together, Callahan and his boys were using their boats to check the houses to make sure all the people had reached high ground.

Joe yelled, "Everyone out down here?"

"Just about," Callahan yelled back.

After they had left the river road, Jack stopped. "Where to, Sammy? Do you have relatives in town?"

Sammy stuck his head in the car. "Pa has some, but they don't have any truck with us. Maybe Ma's sister will take her. She lives down by the old blacksmith shop. She'll be mad as a hornet because Ma's drunk."

"If her sister won't take her, I can take her to the jail until she sobers up."

Sammy bit his lip. "That might be best."

"Where will you go?"

"I'll manage. Just find a place for Ma."

Joe never thought he'd feel an ounce of pity for Sammy Davidson, but he did when the boy followed along behind as he carried his mother into the courthouse, then down the steps to the jail in the basement. Jack unlocked a cell, and Joe placed Marla on a narrow cot and tucked the blanket around her.

"She'll be all right here for the rest of the night," Jack said to Sammy. "But come morning, I'll have to let her out or file charges against her for public intoxication."

"I'll be back in the morning." Sammy walked quickly out of the building to the car and retrieved the gunnysack. "Thanks," he said to Jack and took off down the street.

The streets of Fertile had never been so busy this time of night. It was still more than an hour before dawn. Men had brought their families up to high ground and had gone back to salvage what they could. Women were sitting along the curbs. Children, scared at being snatched from their beds and brought to town, were standing close to their mothers or older siblings.

Jack, awed by the sudden responsibility of keeping the peace amid this chaos, kept an eye on the sky in the northwest, hoping the rain up north would travel east and not south. He didn't know what he'd do with all these people if it should rain.

"You'd better go up to my room and change out of those wet britches," he said to Joe.

"I was just thinking about it. You'd better come along. That horse's ass behind the counter might not let me in your room."

The hotel lobby was full of people when they reached it. The face of the man behind the desk was red with anger as he argued with a man who held the hand of a small girl. His wife was beside him carrying a sleeping baby.

"I don't give a gawddamn what the policy is." The man slammed his hand down on the counter. "You've got rooms to let, and I want one for my family, or I'll crawl over this counter, and when I get done with you, you'll look like hammered shit!"

"I can count." The clerk had a superior look. "The owner of this hotel made it plain to me that some rooms were for two occupants only. Other rooms have cots. They are taken. The only rooms left are for two."

"What's the problem, Tom?"

"This jackass won't rent me a room because of the kids."

Jack moved behind the counter. "Sign the register, Tom." Then to the clerk, "You've got seven keys here." He pointed to the keyboard. "Which rooms are vacant?"

"Now, see here. You've no right to come in here and tell me how to run this hotel."

"*Some*body better tell you. You're doing a piss-poor job of it." Jack plucked a key off the board and slammed it down on the counter. "Number ten."

"Thanks, Jack." Tom picked up his daughter and with his hand behind his wife ushered her toward the stairs as another man stepped up to the counter.

Jack took his own room key off the peg and tossed it to Joe before he spoke again to the clerk.

"First come, first served. It doesn't matter if there are six to a room. Understand?"

"You'll hear from the owner."

"The owner is in Kansas City and doesn't give a damn about what's going on here. Now, am I going to have to stand here and see that you don't turn anyone away because of your damn fool policy?" When the clerk didn't answer, Jack spoke to the man who had signed the register and handed him a key. "Hi, Pete. Were you able to get your animals out?"

"When the water came up, I turned them loose. Couldn't leave 'em there to drown."

"You'll have help rounding them up when this is over."

"It'd be over damn quick if I could get a stick of dynamite in that rock pile down at Calmar."

The man behind him agreed. "As soon as I get my wife and kids settled, I'm thinkin' to make a trip down there." He reached for the register and signed his name.

"The district marshal will be here in the morning," Jack said. "He'll be able to handle the folks down at Calmar without any trouble. The judge told them to dismantle that rock pile. The marshal will take care of it."

"Yeah? Well, they've took their sweet time 'bout it, and now it's too late. I had a hundred Plymouth Rock layers that will be scattered all over the county 'cause I had to let them out. Do you think the sonsabitches down at Calmar care that I'll have a hell of a time feeding my kids without those layers?"

"Yeah, I know," Jack said. "It's enough to make a preacher cuss, but I think we should wait for Marshal Sanford before we take action. He'll be here in a few hours."

Joe returned wearing his own clothes and waited with Jack until the last room in the hotel was rented. The lobby was still full of people, sitting on the floor and on the couches.

"Put up a No Vacancy sign," Jack said to the clerk.

"They're wrecking the lobby!" the agitated clerk shrieked. His hands fluttered as he shooed a small boy away from the newspaper rack.

"You'd be smart to keep your mouth shut." Jack leaned close to speak to him. "The men here are about to lose everything they have in this world. They're facing winter and don't know if they'll have homes for their families or be able to feed their kids. They're in no mood to take crap off a slick-haired little jelly bean. Do you get the message?"

The clerk lifted his chin in a defiant response.

"All right," Jack said. "Don't call me if you spout off and someone puts a fist in your mouth."

"I'm entitled to protection just like everyone else."

"Yeah, well, I can't be in two places at one time. Guess where I'll be. You're on your own, mister."

Jack picked up the phone and rang the operator. "I'm back on the street, Flora. If you need me, turn on the signal light."

After they had left the hotel, Jack looked toward the signal light that hung in the middle of Main Street.

"Flora tried to signal me last night, and the damn bulb had burned out. I got one this afternoon at Poole's Hardware and replaced it."

"You climbed up there on a ladder?"

"There's extra wire over on the pole. I had someone out stopping traffic when I let the fixture down. He put in the new bulb, and I pulled it up." Jack slapped his brother on the back. "I'm glad you're with me tonight, Joe. This is more than I counted on."

"You seem to be doing all right so far."

"I can't keep an eye on everything without a car. It'll be a day or two before Wally has the police car ready."

"April won't mind you using hers."

"I wouldn't want to use it without asking her."

"She said keep it as long as you want."

"That meant you and not me."

"I'll drive if it makes you feel any better."

"It would. Let's go back to the courthouse and get it. I should look in on Mrs. Davidson anyway. I'm supposed to be the jailer, too."

"It's a *county* jail. Doesn't the county provide a jailer?"

"No. The district jail is in Mason. When Corbin was the police here, he talked the county into giving Fertile the space in the basement for a jail."

The brothers walked down the steps to the cubbyhole Jack used as an office, then on through it to the cells. It didn't seem that Mrs. Davidson had moved.

"I felt sorry for the kid," Jack said as they made their way back up to the street. "Hell of a note when a young kid has to see his mother like that."

"Sammy is a tough little nut. He's on his way to being a no-good if he keeps running with bums like Tator Williams. The two of them were out pounding on Miss Deval's door the other night and talking nasty. I put a few lumps on Tator's head and gave Sammy a scare. I hope he learned from it."

"Is he still hanging around Joy?"

"I'm not blaming it all on Sammy. I think it's as much Joy as it is him. She's going over fool's hill and won't listen to anything Julie says to her."

Jack chuckled. "I kind of remember when I thought Pa was the stupidest man alive."

When they were in the car, Jack said, "Let's stop by and see if Annabel has had her baby. Lord, I hope so. If everything seems all right, Corbin would be free to help. I'm afraid there'll be trouble before morning."

Chapter 23

When April left Mrs. Poole's the night before to go on a date with Joe, she never imagined it would be six o'clock in the morning before she returned.

Doc had come back a couple of hours earlier to report that Mrs. Corbin had had a healthy baby girl.

"Mother and child are d-doing fine; Corbin is a nervous wreck and swearing that he will n-never put his wife through that torture again." The corners of Doc's mouth lifted slightly; he was too tired even to chuckle. He was anxious to see Caroline and went through the connecting door. He reappeared a short time later and seemed to be relieved.

"She's sleeping. How did it go? Are you all r-right with this, April?"

"As I told you before, Doc, you needn't worry about me. I'll do whatever I can to help you and Caroline. She's worried about what her being here will do to you."

"No one needs to know she's here. When we're ready to leave, I'll get Joe to d-drive us to Mason or somewhere else to catch the train."

April thought about the conversation as she opened the door to be confronted by Mrs. Poole. The woman's face was a picture of disapproval. Her eyes traveled over April's disheveled appearance: Her skirt was wrinkled, her blouse was opened at the neck and partially pulled from her skirt. Her hair was pushed carelessly back from a weary face.

"This is a fine time for you to be coming in."

"Yes, it is. I need to take a bath and get ready for work."

"Well, I never! You're as cool as a cucumber."

"How did you expect me to be, Mrs. Poole?" April made an attempt to pass the woman, who blocked the hallway.

"I never expected an unmarried woman to come waltzing in here after she'd spent the night with a man, a man with Joe Jones's reputation for rutting with every woman that he can get his hands on, and acting as brazen as you please."

"If I spent the night with Mr. Jones, it wouldn't be any of your business. I don't have to account to you for my actions."

"As long as you live in my house, it's my business."

"Sister." Fred came quickly into the hall.

"Stay out of this, Fred." Shirley's voice was harsh.

"Don't forget what I told you. I meant every word of it."

April had never heard Fred speak so determinedly to his sister. She didn't know what was going on between them, and she didn't care. She was so exhausted that she could hardly put one foot in front of the other.

They'd had several accident patients at the clinic, as was bound to happen with so many people moving about late at night. A car had run over a boy's foot and broken his toe. Another child had his fingers crushed in a car door. A man came in with his shoulder thrown out of joint. April had put stitches in the leg of the drunk and in the arm of one of

Callahan's boys and was so tired she was in no mood to put up with Mrs. Poole's accusations.

"When my rent is up at the end of the month, Mrs. Poole, I'll be moving out." She stepped around her and went up the stairs.

"It's just as well. I won't tolerate sluts living in my house."

April turned. "*What* did you call me?"

Shirley, with chin high, stepped into the other room. Fred looked up at April, where she stood on the stairs.

"She's upset. She didn't mean that. Please . . . don't go." He had such a sorrowful look on his face that for a second April felt pity for him.

"I can't stay here, especially after that." April went up the stairs to her room, and Fred went to the kitchen to confront his sister.

"What in the world is the matter with you? Why did you say that to her?"

"Any woman who stays out all night with a man is a slut to my way of thinking. She's man-crazy is what she is. She's had men panting after her like a bitch in heat since the day she came here. I'll not have that kind of woman living in my house. Look at you. Defending her. You've had your tongue hanging out just like every other man in town. 'Good morning, April,'" she mimicked. "'How are you, April?' 'Let me get you some coffee, April.'" Shirley's voice was heavy with sarcasm.

Fred looked at his sister for a long while and wondered why he had not realized before that she was sick and twisted where women were concerned. He understood now why she didn't have women friends. Not even the church women came to call. She avoided waiting on women when they came into the store.

Shirley continued her tirade. "I know what kind of woman she is. I knew the first time I set eyes on her. Her kind attracts men like flies to honey. They know what they'll get if they get her in the dark. She's been out all night with Joe Jones. Couldn't you tell by looking at her she's been lolling around in a bed somewhere?"

"She may have been working at the clinic." He managed to keep his voice even, but he was trembling inside with rage.

"All dressed up fit to kill?" Shirley scoffed. She was full of indignation and determined to vent. "Women like her were after my Ron while he was alive. They'd rub up against him, flirt with him, entice him. But he paid them no mind. He was a real gentleman." Shirley paused in her rant. Then she said, "You'd better get to the store. With all the trash in town the windows will be broken out, and they'll be in there stealing us blind."

Fred stood looking out the window while he drank his coffee.

"Did you hear me, Fred? I don't want that trash from Shanty Town hanging around in the store. It was time to clean up the mess down there. I hope that uppity nigger whore drowned in her bed. It would be too good for her."

Fred set his empty cup on the table, left the room and took his hat and coat off the hall tree. Without a word to his sister he went out the door. He didn't trust himself to stay any longer in the same room with her. He wasn't sure what he was going to do. Shirley had ruined the one beautiful, exciting thing in his life. If April moved, his life would go back to the dreary existence it was before she came.

There were as many cars in town at seven in the morning as there usually were on a

Saturday night in the summer. Groups of men stood on street corners. The talk was of the flood and the rock pile down at Calmar. Fred paused on the fringe of one of these groups and heard someone say the water had come up over the road in front of Callahan's and that he estimated the river had risen four feet but had leveled off now.

Fred reached the hardware store to discover that someone had unloaded household goods on the sidewalk in front. A woman and two children sat on boxes beside them. He nodded politely to the woman and hoped that Shirley stayed at home until after the woman and her belongings had been moved. The poor woman didn't look like she needed any more trouble.

Inside the store Fred walked to the rear and turned to look back at the rows of barrels, filled with oak handles ready to be joined with rakes, hoes or spades. Some of the barrels held chains. There were tubs of nuts and bolts, screws and small tools. Hanging on hooks were hammers, ball peens and sledges, which he had carefully greased to prevent rusting. Screwdrivers, pliers, handsaws, all were displayed and within easy reach. At one time he had taken great pride in displaying the merchandise in the store, but his sister had gradually taken the joy out of his accomplishment.

He sat down on a stool behind the counter and rested his chin on his palms. He had a lot of thinking to do. He saw his lonely life stretched out before him. The only socializing he had was at the billiard parlor once a week. Shirley had spoken so disparagingly about every woman he mentioned that he had given up thinking he would ever marry and have a family of his own. He had nothing to offer a woman anyway. Shirley could take his job with the snap of her fingers. Without a job and a place to live he would be out on the road like the bums who came though town every day on the freight trains.

He recalled the time when he was friendly with Sarah Parker. She was a small, neat woman who, for a short while, stopped in the store a couple times a week. He had enjoyed her visits. They were beginning to get to know each other, and he was on the verge of asking her out. Then, after she had bought a shallow baking pan, she brought him a plate of sugar cookies. Shirley had been so outrageously rude to her that she stopped coming by. Then for weeks Shirley ranted about Sarah, her immediate family, her ancestors, her personal appearance. Sarah had been a little on the plump side, but she'd had a pretty face and a pleasant way about her.

Fred walked to the front window of the store and looked out onto the street. The woman was still sitting on the box with her two children snuggled close to her. Her home was under water, she was guarding the total sum of her possessions, but she had someone who loved her.

Fred sighed and retreated again to the rear of the store.

Feeling utterly humiliated that Joy's brother, that uppity Joe, had been in his home and had seen his mother dead drunk, Sammy had spent the rest of the night hunkered down on the sidewalk in front of the barbershop. What rankled him the most was that he'd had to ask for the Jones brothers' help. But, hell, he couldn't go off and leave her out there with the water rising. If it had come up another foot and a half, she would have drowned.

Lord, he wished he could leave this place. He'd heard a man could make a living in California picking peaches. He'd catch the next freight train out if it weren't that he couldn't bear the thought of leaving Joy. She was the only one who didn't think he was trash because he lived in a shack along the river, with a drunk for a mother and a pa who was as worthless as a pile of pounded shit.

Sammy dozed off and on throughout the early morning hours. Then Tator came along and kicked him awake. He sprang up.

"What the hell did you do that for?"

"Ya want to go with us down to Calmar and take out that damn rock pile, don't ya?" Tator was carrying his rifle over his shoulder as if he were marching off to war.

"They're taking guns?"

"Damn right we're takin' guns, and a-nuff dynamite to blow that sonofabitch pile to hell and back." Tator was so excited he could hardly talk. "Come on, if you're goin'. Leave your stuff here. Nobody'll bother it."

There were three truckloads of men headed for Calmar. Tator and Sammy were in the last truck. Most of the men standing in the back of the truck were older. Only a few had guns. All were grim-faced. Sammy was thrilled but a little fearful, too. The truck stopped along the bank upriver a short distance from where the makeshift dam had formed a small lake. They were piling out of the truck bed when they heard the explosions, three in all, and saw the rocks fly up and then settle in the river. A cheer went up from the men from Fertile, and several fired shots in the air.

"Shit!" Tator stamped his foot. "We missed it."

Sammy, with Tator lagging along behind, followed the men as they walked toward a group gathered around a big black touring car. The district marshal was there as well as the Joneses and Corbin Appleby. Jack Jones was shaking hands with a man in a gray Stetson hat. Joe Jones was beside him.

Tator was a half dozen steps behind Sammy. Sammy turned to tell Tator to come on so they could hear what the marshal was saying. Tator, standing on spread legs, was jacking a bullet into the chamber of his rifle.

"What're ya doin'?" Sammy yelled.

"Now's my chance to get even with that

sonofabitch. They'll think it was a stray bullet." He raised the rifle to his shoulder.

"No!" Sammy dived toward him, but Tator
had already pulled the trigger.

April left the house without seeing Mrs.
Poole. She was badly in need of a cup of
coffee but would not have gone to her
kitchen for one if her life had depended on
it. Never had anyone slandered her charac-
ter as Mrs. Poole had done. She didn't think
she'd be able to wait until her rent was due
to move out of the house.

She walked up the street to Sparky's but
didn't even open the door when she saw the
crowd of people inside. She went on down
the street toward the clinic. People gawked
at her in her white nurse's uniform, perky
white cap perched on her head, white shoes
and stockings. She smiled and spoke to
those who were bold enough to make eye
contact.

When she reached the clinic, Doc was in
the surgery with a woman and small child.
April stayed in the reception room, knowing
that Doc knew she was there and would call
her if he needed her. After the woman had

left carrying a small girl, Doc lounged in the doorway.

"You didn't need to c-come right back."

"I couldn't stand to stay a minute longer at Mrs. Poole's, Doc, but I've got to get a cup of coffee soon."

"Caroline is m-making breakfast. I locked the front door and the sh-shades are drawn."

"Is she all right?"

"She was as bright as a new p-penny this morning." His smile was reflected in his eyes. "It's so damn good h-having her here w-where I can see her and know she's all right."

"I'm happy for you, Doc. Why don't you go have breakfast with her? But first bring me a cup of coffee . . . please."

Doc laughed. "I never knew you were one of *those*."

"I am definitely one of those. I can't even see straight without my morning coffee. It goes back to my nights working on the floor at the hospital in Kansas City. I would never have survived without it."

April drank from the large cup Doc brought her. The strong coffee hit her system, stirring her brain to activity so that she was able to greet the woman who came into the clinic with civility.

"Morning, Miss Parker."

"Morning. Is Dr. Forbes in?" Sarah carried a plate wrapped in a cloth.

"Yes, but he's sleeping. He has been up all night and just now got to lie down to catch a few winks. I'm sure you'll understand that I'd rather not wake him."

"Well—I brought him some sugar cookies. He said they were his favorites."

"That was sweet of you. I'm sure Dr. Forbes will think so, too, when he wakes. He had a terribly busy night. If you would rather bring them back another time . . ." April left the sentence hanging.

"No." Miss Parker set the plate on the desk. "Just tell him I was . . . thinking of him and thought he might want a bit of home cooking."

"I'll be sure to tell him. He will be pleased, I know. Can I return your plate?"

"Oh, no. You needn't do that. I'll pick it up in a day or two."

April didn't feel a bit sorry for the lie she had told and made a to-do about putting the carefully wrapped plate on the cabinet behind her desk. She hoped fervently that

Doc wouldn't come charging through the door and into the clinic until after Miss Parker had left.

Thank goodness the phone rang.

April smiled a dismissal, and the woman reluctantly left the office.

"Dr. Forbes's office."

"April, this is Julie Johnson. Have you heard from Joe, Jack or Evan?"

"No. Is something wrong?"

"I don't know. I'm worried. They followed the gang that went down to Calmar determined to blow up the dam that caused the flooding. They took shotguns."

"I didn't know a gang had gone down there, Julie."

"Corbin Appleby sent word to Evan. I don't know what the four of them think they can do if the men won't listen to them. Marshal Sanford was supposed to meet them on the outskirts of Calmar. I hope he did."

"I've not seen Jack or Joe since early this morning."

"I thought perhaps you might have heard something. I'm at Papa's. Joe and Jack were here before daylight to get Papa's car. Joe said they had been using yours, and he wanted to take it back."

"He left it here at the clinic. I'll call you if I hear anything, Julie."

"If Eudora will watch Nancy and Logan, Joy and I may walk into town. If we do, we'll stop by."

As soon as April was off the line with Julie, she called the operator. "Flora—"

"This is Diane. Flora was on duty all night and by now is dead to the world."

"Dr. Forbes and I were wondering if you've heard anything about what's going on down in Calmar." April felt slightly guilty using Doc's name.

"I shouldn't pass along what I hear, but it may be helpful for Dr. Forbes to know that about ten minutes ago the operator there at Calmar heard an explosion down on the river—several explosions, in fact. I talked to her again just now, and she's heard nothing more.

"Got to go," the operator added. "The board's lighting up."

"Thanks, Diane."

April hung up the phone and for a minute held her fist tightly against her chest as if to press away the dread that something had happened to Joe . . . or Jack or Mr. Appleby, the new father. Oh, dear Lord.

What if Joe . . . was hurt? Damn, damn him. He had grinned his way into her heart. She didn't want to love him . . . but she did.

How had it happened so fast?

That easy grin of his that could melt the hardest heart, the careless way his hair fell down over his forehead, the teasing light in his eyes, were dear to her. He had tried so hard to convince her that he was a suave gentleman when they went to the restaurant before the show. She wished that she had told him that she didn't care about *suave*. That he was perfect just the way he was.

She suddenly felt as if she had been hit by a strong cold wind while standing naked on a high cliff. A cold hand stroked her spine. Up until he had come back with Jack to ask to borrow the car, she had been sure that he felt about her as she did about him. His kisses had been sweet, tender, loving, then passionate, as if he couldn't get enough of them.

What had brought the change in his attitude toward her? Had she done something, said something? The only conclusion that she could reach was that he had talked to Jack about her and decided that she could be getting too serious about him and that he should break it off.

When the phone rang, April grabbed it.

"This is Diane. I heard from the operator in Calmar. Dynamite was used to blow out the rock pile, and the water is flowing through. The river up your way should be going down. One man was shot, another was injured by flying rocks. Several were hurt in fights."

"Who was shot?"

"I don't know, but they're bringing him to Dr. Forbes."

"Thanks, Diane. Dr. Forbes will be ready."

April hung up the phone and dropped her head into her hands and prayed, "Please, God, don't let it be Joe."

Doc carried a plate of food to Silas, who took it and sat down on the back step to eat. Back in the kitchen, Doc pulled Caroline into his arms and kissed her, then held her away from him so that he could see her face.

"How's my pretty girl?"

"Fine when I'm with you."

"You're going to be with me f-from now

on. Can you stand to be in here for a couple of w-weeks?"

"What if people find out I'm here?"

"We'll cross that bridge when we c-come to it. But they won't find out if we are c-careful. I hate having to hide you away. I want the whole world to know that you are mine."

Caroline and Doc had just finished breakfast when April knocked on the connecting door, then opened it and came into the room.

"Doc, the Calmar operator phoned Diane to tell her that one of our men has been shot. They are bringing him here."

"Who was it?" Doc quickly got up from the table.

"She didn't know. She said that there were a few other injuries, but nothing serious."

"How about the rock pile?"

"They blew it up with dynamite."

"The water will be g-going down. I've got to warn the people not to d-drink the well water until it's been boiled." He went to where Caroline still sat at the table and kissed her. "I'll be b-busy for a while, sweetheart."

"Don't worry about me. I'll find something to do. I've got all that yarn you bought for me to make things for our baby." She whispered the last two words in his ear. She needn't have whispered; April had already backed into the clinic and softly closed the door.

Chapter 24

Doc sent Silas to Callahan with a note asking him to warn people not to drink well water until after it had been boiled. He called the mayor, the drugstore and the postmaster asking them to pass the word to anyone who came in. Diane had agreed to call merchants, as time permitted, telling them to inform their customers. Then he and April began to ready the surgery to receive the injured.

While at the hospital in Kansas City, April had often prepared for emergencies but on a larger scale. Now she worked automatically. When all was ready, she made a trip into Doc's quarters to use the bathroom. Whenever she was nervous and anxious, her bladder seemed to fill faster than at other times. She found Caroline sweeping the kitchen floor. Something spicy was cooking on the stove.

"Do you like to cook?" April asked.

"When I have someone to cook for. I don't like cooking just for myself."

"My cooking skills are limited to frying eggs and making oatmeal. My grandmother thought it was easier to do it herself than to teach me."

When Caroline smiled, April could understand why Doc had fallen in love with her. He had been chased by the single women in this town for nine years, and a pretty, sweet, fragile girl like Caroline had won his heart despite the odds against their having a happy life together. April sighed and wished that they didn't have to leave Fertile, not only because she and Caroline could be friends but because her own future was uncertain now. When a new doctor arrived, he might bring his own nurse, and she would be out of a job.

Back in the reception room, she thought briefly of calling Julie Johnson but decided against worrying her needlessly should the injured man not be her husband or brother. She went out onto the porch and looked up the street toward town. The October sun was bright but the air was cool. April wished for a jacket, but not even a fur coat would've warmed her enough to take away the cold dread that lay in the pit of her stomach.

She had seen what a gunshot could do. A single bullet could sever a spine, puncture lungs, liver . . . heart. Gut shots were the worst and usually ended in a slow death. She had seen patients with face wounds from a sawed-off shotgun. The work she and the doctors had done to save a life had not been appreciated when the patient saw himself in a mirror.

That Joe would suffer such a fate was unthinkable. Handsome, smiling, full of life—

All thought left her when the big black touring car came down the street and pulled up in front of the clinic. Corbin Appleby was out of the car the instant it stopped, and he opened the back door. Evan, Julie's husband, hurried around to help him lift the injured man out of the car. April saw the light brown hair and knew it wasn't Joe, but Jack. She couldn't help the flood of relief that swamped her and immediately felt guilty. Joe crawled out of the car and took his brother's shoulders. The three men carried Jack into the surgery and gently placed him on the examination table.

Jack was conscious and gritting his teeth in pain and swearing. His shirt was unbuttoned. A hand pressed a bloody white cloth against his side.

"Hell of a . . . note," he gasped.

"Yeah. Too bad it wasn't your hard head," Doc said, calmly removing the makeshift bandage. "It would have made my job easier."

April took the bloody cloth from him and realized it was the white shirt Joe had worn the night before. After dropping the shirt in the laundry bag, she unbuckled the belt on Jack's britches. With a jerk of her head she motioned for Joe to take off his boots while she worked on the buttoned fly. With that done she flipped a folded sheet over his privates and pulled his britches down over his hips. Joe pulled them off and then stepped back out of the way.

Doc worked to mop the blood from the wound, then, communicating without words, April helped him turn Jack to his side. Jack swore and squeezed his eyes tightly shut.

"You're lucky. It doesn't look like it hit any

vital organs. That's the good news. The bad news is that it's still in there and has to come out. Know what it was?" Doc asked without looking up.

"A .22 rifle bullet," Corbin said.

"It's lodged in his back. How ya doin', boy?" Doc patted Jack's shoulder and moved out of his sight. "Got to put you out for a while. I can sock you in the jaw, use ether, chloroform, or give you a shot of Novocain. Which shall it be?"

"Had ether once. Made me sick as a dog."

Doc mouthed something to April, and she began to prepare an injection of Novocain. The room was quiet while they worked. Doc would murmur a request, and an instrument would be in his hand instantly. At one time the clinic door opened and Corbin slipped out. After a low murmur of voices, he came back into the surgery and stood quietly beside Joe and Evan.

Although April was conscious of Joe's watching, she worked with Doc as if her hands were an extension of his. When the area in Jack's back was deadened, Doc made an incision and removed the bullet. He dropped it into a pan with a clunk. April handed him the tools he needed as he cleaned and stitched the wound.

With some of his anxiety eased now that Jack was in Doc's capable hands, Joe watched April and marveled at how calm and efficient she was. She was pretty, smart, educated—and no doubt had been on dates with well-fixed men who had cars of their own and didn't have to use hers.

A woman like April was used to men like Harold Dozier, who had clean fingernails and no manure on their shoes. She would never be serious about a hayseed who had only a few acres of land, a mortgage and a bull.

His pride surfaced. He didn't want a woman who couldn't love him for himself and not for what he had. He'd get over her. But it had better be soon because the ache was eating a hole in his heart.

Julie came breathlessly into the clinic. One word was all she could manage. "Jack!"

Evan met her and pulled her close. "He's going to be all right."

"They said he was shot."

"He was. Doc said it didn't hit any vital organs. He's almost finished with him."

"Where was he hit?"

"In his side. The bullet didn't go all the way through. Doc had to take it out of his back."

"I want to see him."

"In a little while." Holding his wife, Evan noticed Joy standing beside the door. Tears were running down her cheeks. He held out one arm. "Come here, honey."

Joy rushed to him. He held both sisters until Joe came out to tell him they were finished and Julie could come in. Jack was still under from the whiff of chloroform April had given him before Doc cleaned out the bullet hole and probed to be certain it was safe to close the wound.

He was covered now with a blanket. April was standing at his head smoothing his hair off his face. They would watch now, she explained, to see that he didn't go into shock from loss of blood.

"Are you sure he'll be all right?" Julie asked and grasped Jack's hand, pressing it between both of hers.

"You can never be one hundred percent sure about these things. There's always the danger of infection, but they got him here in good time. He's healthy and should recover without any problems." Doc spoke as he put the used instruments into the sterilizer.

"When is he going to wake up?" Joy moved to the other side of the table and took Jack's other hand.

"It won't be long now." April brought a chair for Julie and a stool for Joy, then stood back while the family gathered around.

Julie looked up at her husband. "Who shot him?"

"Tator Williams. The way I understand it, he was aiming at Joe. Sammy Davidson ran at him, spoiled his aim, and he hit Jack."

"Sammy did that?" Joy shot a quick glance at Joe.

"The kid wrestled with Tator and kept him from getting off another shot until some of the men got there and took the gun away from him. Marshal Sanford took Tator to the district jail."

"Why was he shooting at you, Joe?" Julie's worried frown went from her husband to her brother.

"He'd been acting smart with some of the women down there along the river. I told him to stop it. He lipped off, and I gave him a few aches and pains."

"How did you know he was doing that?" Julie asked.

"Doc told me. He knows what goes on down there. Any more questions?"

Joe's mood was not the best. It didn't sit well with him that his brother had almost been killed because of him. If the marshal hadn't been there, there wouldn't have been enough left of Tator to send to jail. He reasoned now that it was probably better this way. They'd put old Tator on the chain gang, and he'd have to work for a change. Joe had said a mere thanks to Sammy and would say more later. It took guts to run at a man with a loaded rifle.

Doc took Corbin off to talk about his fear of a typhoid epidemic if people drank from their water wells after they had flooded.

"I'll get on down to the newspaper and make up some signs," Corbin told him. "I'll have a notice in the paper, too, but it'll be three days before the paper comes out."

"Lord, I pity all the people who have to clean that river mud out of their homes, find their animals and salvage what they can. It'll be tough."

"We're fortunate that Marshal Sanford saw trouble coming and had a court order to remove the rocks, or it could have been much worse. Evan is going to talk to the governor and see if we can't get help for the people down there."

"I wish him luck," Doc said dryly. "It'll be like getting blood out of a turnip."

"I've got to get home. Annabel was sleeping when I left early this morning. She'll be awake by now and wanting to know what's going on."

"What name do I put on your daughter's birth certificate?"

"If I have my way, we'll call her Lee Ann. I've got to get Annabel to agree." Corbin grinned sheepishly. "She's been threatening me that if we had a girl, she would name her Corbaleen."

Doc chuckled. "That's awful. Try and convince her to see it your way."

After Corbin had left, Doc stood on the porch for a minute, then took the key out of his pocket and went to the door of his quarters. He couldn't wait another minute to see Caroline.

April's head was bent over the ledger on the desk when Joe walked past. She didn't raise her head to look at him, so he didn't say anything. He walked out the door and headed for Main Street. He was eager to go home, but he had something to do first. He was uncomfortable still wearing his Sunday suit without a shirt. It was the only thing he'd had to use as a bandage when Jack was shot.

Lord, would he ever get over the fear he felt when his brother fell at his feet hit by a bullet meant for him? Damn Tator Williams. He'd always known that Tator was the biggest turd in the shit pile, but he'd not thought of him as a murderer. Now he wished that he had put his ass up between his ears when he had the chance.

Joe was stopped as he made his way down the street to answer questions about Jack. People were concerned. Jack was well liked and most of them were pleased that he had the police job. None asked why Tator was out gunning for him. If they had, he would say what he'd told the marshal. They'd had a little set-to, nothing he thought was serious.

He crossed the street when he saw Sammy and a couple of small boys sitting on the iron steps at the side of the bank building.

"Speak to you a minute, Sammy."

"Sure."

"We gotta go, Sam. Pa'll be needin' help." The boys skirted around Joe and took off down the street.

Joe sat down on the steps. "I didn't mean to run off your friends."

"They're not my friends. They're just little kids."

"I want to thank you for what you did today."

"Wasn't nothin'. I'd not want Tator to shoot a cat."

"It was something to me."

"Yeah, well, we're even. You got my ma out. I owed ya."

"You didn't owe for that."

"Yeah, I know. You'da done the same for a sick dog."

"Where is your mother? Did her sister take her in?"

"Yeah. She didn't want to but she did. I got to get out to the house and clean it out so she can go back."

"Can't she help you?"

"Are you kiddin'?" Sammy looked at him as if he'd lost his mind. He sat with the gunnysack he'd tied in a tree now resting between his knees.

"I need to go eat something. Want to go?"

"No."

"Why? Have you stopped eating?"

"I don't want to go, all right? I need to get out to the house." Sammy got to his feet and flung the sack over his shoulder.

"I asked you to go with me because I wanted your company and not because of what you did for me."

"Listen, Jones." Sammy turned on him like a spitting cat. "I don't take charity, especially not from you, not from any of the Joneses. We're even, understand?"

"If that's the way you want it. I'd appreciate it if you didn't mention that you and Tator had been to Miss Deval's and that that was the reason I busted Tator's nose."

"You must think I'm a half-wit. Why would I tell? People would realize that I was with him. I'm not proud of doin' that."

"I'm glad to hear it." Joe stuck out his hand. "Thanks, Sammy. I'm obliged. Not many grown men would tackle a man with a loaded rifle."

Sammy looked at Joe's hand, then slowly put his in it. "Wasn't anythin'. Bye."

He hurried off down the street as if he had somewhere important to go. Joe watched him. He felt sorry for the kid, but he still didn't want him hanging around his sister. Maybe without Tator he'd straighten up, but then again maybe not. His folks were not worth shooting. The kid had an uphill climb.

Joe was almost at the corner when he saw his sisters and Evan coming down the street toward Sparky's. He stood on the corner and waited for them. Soon he was surrounded by men inquiring about Jack and what he thought should be done with Tator Williams for shooting him.

"The marshal will see to it that Tator gets what's coming to him. As to why he was shooting at me or Jack, you'll have to ask him."

"It's a dirty shame is what it is. Jack was doin' his job . . . not pushin' anybody around."

"I'll tell him you asked about him."

Joe crossed the street. As he approached his sisters and Evan, he could see the worry on Julie's face and tears in Joy's eyes.

"What's the matter? Did something happen?" he asked anxiously.

Evan answered, "No." Then: "He's not awake yet."

"Doc is going to keep him there tonight in that small room back of the surgery. I'm going back to sit with him." Julie was clinging to her husband's hand. "Evan will pick up the children and take them home."

"Isn't it the nurse's job to look after Doc's patients?" Joe's brows were raised and he spoke bluntly.

"April was there nearly all last night. She only got a couple hours of sleep on Doc's couch."

"Is the romance off already?" Joy still had not forgiven her brother for his treatment of Sammy.

"What romance, brat? You've been reading too many stories in the *True Confessions* magazine."

"You had a crush on her. Don't deny it."

"It's the way with crushes. They come and go."

"Aren't you ashamed now how you treated Sammy? He saved your life and Jack's."

"Let it go, brat. But stay away from him.

He's too rough and tough for you. He acts like a twenty-five-year-old and he's only sixteen."

"Look at the people uptown." Julie changed the subject when she realized that Joy was preparing to argue. "If the stores weren't closed, I'd think it was Saturday and not Sunday."

"We're going to get something to eat," Evan said. "Want to come along, Joe?"

"No, thanks. I've got Pa's car. I'll take it back and get out of these clothes. He'll want to come in and see Jack. I hope he hasn't heard about him being shot."

"Will you be coming back to town with Pa?"

"I'll ride over and tell Jill. Then I'll come back in and sit with Jack tonight," Evan said.

"No. I'll stay. You didn't sleep at all last night."

"I am kind of dead on my feet. I'll get a few hours' sleep, then we'll see."

Chapter 25

In the middle of the afternoon Jack became aware that he was lying on a narrow bed with rails on each side and that his sister was sitting beside him.

"Sis—"

Julie jumped up. "Oh, honey. How do you feel?"

"Like someone shot me in the belly."

"It was in the side. Doc said the bullet went through the fleshy part of your side. You're going to be all right."

"Was anyone else hurt?"

"No one but you. The marshal took Tator Williams to jail."

"Why'd he shoot me?"

"It's a long story. Joe will tell you. You scared me to death." Julie put a kiss on his forehead as she had done when he was a small boy.

"I'm awful thirsty."

April appeared beside Julie. "You're back with us. I'll get some cold water; drink only a sip at a time, or you might throw it up."

Julie held the glass for her brother and told him as much as she knew about what was going on.

"Annabel had a baby girl last night. But I guess you knew that, or Corbin wouldn't have been with you this morning. Folks are leaving town and trying to get back to their homes. I can't even imagine how they must feel. Having to clean out all that river mud, find your livestock and make a meal for your family.

"April said that people have been calling here to find out how you are." Jack didn't open his eyes, and Julie realized he had fallen asleep.

The clinic was usually closed on Sunday except for emergencies, but this had been an extraordinary day. People had been in and out all day. April hadn't had a chance to tell Doc about what had happened that

morning at Mrs. Poole's or that she was going to look for another room.

Just before suppertime Doc spoke to
Julie. "Jack will be all right if you w-want to
go get s-something to eat."

"Evan will be back after he does the
evening chores. He said he'd bring me
something. Sparky usually closes at noon
on Sunday."

"He'll stay open as long as his f-food
lasts. Some of the folks won't be able to go
right back home and f-fix a meal."

Later, Doc followed April out onto the
porch, and she was able to tell him about
her plans to move out of Mrs. Poole's
house. He was quiet for a minute, then
spoke with his customary calm.

"There is s-something eating at that
woman. When I first c-came here, Mrs.
Poole was quiet and p-pleasant. I felt so
sorry for her when her husband was killed.
He was the center of her life. But g-gradu-
ally over the years she has become bitter. I
don't know h-how Fred puts up with her."

"He's kind of strange, too, Doc."

"He's probably so glad to have a pretty
young woman around. He's overfriendly."
Doc chuckled.

"For some reason she finds fault with everything I do, and she hates the Joneses."

"If you can w-wait another week, you can m-move in here. I can't leave until the d-danger of an epidemic from the water wells is over. Then I'm taking Caroline away."

"Won't you wait until you've heard from Canada?"

"I can't depend on that. I'm thinking s-strongly of going to Mexico and taking a chance on finding a p-position. I was there once. Life is simple there, and Caroline would like the w-warm weather."

"Any village or town would be lucky to have you, Doc."

After a moment of silence April said, "Julie can't spend the night here with Jack without using the bathroom. She'll have to come into your part of the house."

"I thought of that. I was hoping Joe w-would come back and s-sit with him."

"He didn't get any more sleep last night than you did."

"If s-someone has to discover Caroline, I'd j-just as soon it be Julie."

"Caroline's a lovely girl, Doc."

"Thank you for understanding. It's much m-more than I had hoped for."

A car came around the corner and stopped. A girl with dark hair hanging to her shoulders got out and hurried up the walk to the porch.

"Jack?" The name burst from her. "Is he all right? Is he here?"

"Hello, Ruby May. I w-wondered when you'd show up. Yes, he's here, and y-yes, he's about as all right as a man can be who has caught a .22 rifle b-bullet."

Tears of relief flooded the girl's eyes. "Can I see him?"

"Sure. Have you met April? April, this is R-Ruby May Jacobs, Jack's g-girl."

"I don't know if I'm his girl . . . anymore, Doc." Ruby could hardly talk for the sobs.

"Well, s-straighten up and don't I-let him see you bawling over him."

She grabbed his hand. "If I didn't already love Jack, I'd fall in love with you."

"You'd have to get in line behind a dozen women in town," April said. "Come on, I'll take you to Jack."

Julie stood up and moved out of the way when Ruby came through the door. The girl had eyes only for the man lying on the narrow bed. Jack opened his eyes as she bent over him.

"Ruby?"

"Yes, Ruby, you dolt. Why did you have to go and get yourself shot?"

"I didn't do it on purpose."

"I know." She held his hand between both of hers and brought it to her cheek.

"Why're you cryin'?"

"Because . . . because when I heard that you had been shot, it scared the living daylights out of me. That's why."

"I never thought you'd care."

"Not care? It about tore the heart right out of me. If this is what being a police officer means, I don't know if I'll be able to stand it."

"You haven't kissed me yet."

She held her palm beneath his chin and kissed his lips again and again.

"Oh, Jack. I've missed you . . ."

"You . . . had the lineman."

"Don't mention him. I love you. I've loved you since school days when you'd give me a ride home on your horse. You love me, too. I know you do."

"If I tell you, you'll get the . . . big head."

"Tell me anyway, you lunkhead."

"I love you, Ruby May. I've been sick over losing you."

"You never lost me, sweet man. I just went away for a while. But I'm back and I'm staying."

"I'll have this job. Corbin is going to take over until I'm on my feet. If we marry, you'll be out of a job. They'll not let a married woman teach."

"There's no *if* about it, buster. We're getting married even if we have to live in a one-room shack down on the river." She kissed him hard on the lips.

"Getting bossy already. But you always were . . ." He was smiling and she kissed him again. "I kind of like that. Suppose you can do it again?"

"Greedy little pig," she teased. "There's going to be a lifetime of kisses. You're not getting away from me again. I've been too miserable."

Julie had come into the reception room to give Jack and Ruby May time to be alone.

"They're back together?" April asked.

"And I'm so glad. Both of them have been wretched."

"Doc said they've known each other for a long time."

"Since they could walk."

"It's nice to have roots."

"Do you think Doc would mind if I used his bathroom?"

"I'm sure he wouldn't mind. I always stick my head in the door and call out before going in." April opened the connecting door a small way. "Doc, are you decent? Julie wants to come in."

"Almost d-decent. Tell her to wait a minute, then come on in."

When April heard the bedroom door close, she nodded for Julie to go in, then went back to her desk. She had no more than sat down when Jack's father and stepmother arrived. She took them back to where Jack lay and apologized for the lack of chairs.

"We'll be here for only a few minutes," Eudora said. "Keep your seat, Ruby May."

April almost groaned aloud when she got back to her desk. Miss Davenport stood ramrod-stiff just inside the doorway.

"What can I do for you?" April asked pleasantly.

"Nothing. I want to see Dr. Forbes."

"Won't you sit down?"

"No, I won't sit down. He's in his rooms,

but he refused to answer the knock on his door."

"How do you know he's in his rooms?"

"I saw him at the back door giving a plate of food to that nigger who's been hanging around."

"Well, for crying out loud."

When Miss Davenport headed for the connecting door, April sped across the room and stood in front of it.

Julie opened the door from the other side. She was startled to see April and Miss Davenport confronting each other.

"Hello, Hattie."

"Miss Davenport to you, Julie Johnson. It seems I've caught you. And you a married woman! For shame! You needn't think you're the only woman he's got on the string. There was another one in there this morning. *She* fed the nigger out the back door." The longer she talked, the shriller her voice became until in the end she was almost shouting.

"What in heaven's name are you talking about?"

April said, "Miss Davenport has been spying on Dr. Forbes, Julie. She thinks that you are one of the women he keeps in his rooms."

Julie gasped. "She's . . . crazy!"

"Crazy, am I? Well, we'll see who's crazy. You just wait until the women in this town discover—"

"Please leave, Miss Davenport," April said firmly. "We have a patient in the surgery. If you wish to speak to Dr. Forbes, I'll ask him to come to the porch."

"That won't be necessary. I've seen all I want to know. His name will be mud in this town when I get through with him."

"Oh, my," April said after the irate woman had flounced out the door.

"What got into her? She's always been opinionated and hateful, but I've not seen her this bad."

"You know what they say about a woman scorned. She tried desperately to snare Dr. Forbes. He continued to dance away, trying not to hurt her feelings. Finally he had to tell her that he wasn't interested in her. She's out for revenge." April glanced out the window to see Miss Davenport walking angrily up the street.

Julie's eyes met April's and held them. "What Dr. Forbes does in his own home is his business and his alone. I'm glad it was I and not Miss Davenport who used his bathroom."

April studied Julie's calm face and knew that she had seen the evidence of Caroline's presence.

"He loves her, Julie."

Julie nodded. "I smelled the scented soap in the bathroom and saw the pile of yarn and the knitting needles. I'm glad he's found someone to love. He's a good and decent man."

"I agree. Only Joe and I know. I'm not sure about Jack."

Julie nodded again. "Do you think Doc would let us move Jack?"

"I'm sure he'd be against a move just now. Maybe tomorrow. It would be better, however, if a male member of your family sits with him tonight. He will more than likely need to use the bedpan."

"I hadn't thought of that."

"I would stay with him, but I didn't get any sleep last night, and I'm afraid that I'd fall asleep and he would need me."

"Joe didn't get any sleep, either."

"Nor did Doc."

"I'll ask Pa to stay part of the night. I'll

take Eudora home, and Evan will come back and relieve Pa." Julie touched April's arm. "Don't worry about it. One of us will be with him throughout the night. And I agree, it should be one of the men." She smiled. "If they have to use the bathroom, they can go out the back door."

It was dusk when April unpinned her nurse's cap and placed it on her desk. She was tired and hungry but had decided that she would starve before she ate another meal at the rooming house. She knocked on the connecting door, opened it and called out to Doc.

"I'm leaving, Doc."

"Come in, April."

She stepped into the room and turned the key to lock the door. Doc and Caroline were in the kitchen. As she walked through, she saw the yarn and the knitting needles on a chair.

"Sit and eat, April. Caroline has made s-something she calls a macaroni skillet. I think it's edible," Doc teased, his eyes on her, loving her.

Caroline blushed and swatted his arm. "You like it. You ate enough of it."

"It smells good."

Caroline looked pleased. "It's just bacon, onions, green pepper, tomatoes and macaroni. Anyone can make it. Even Todd."

They were so happy together it made April yearn to have such happiness herself.

Before she and Doc went back into the surgery, she thanked Caroline for the meal and told her Doc was lucky that she was such a good cook. She could tell by the way Doc smiled that he was pleased.

"Doc, Miss Davenport was here," April said as soon as they were alone. "She was watching the back door and saw Caroline give Silas breakfast. She saw you give him his supper. She as much as accused Julie of being one of your 'women' when she came from using the bathroom. She's sure to cause trouble."

The smile left Doc's face. "What did Julie s-say?"

"Julie is all right with it. She knew someone was there because of the scent in the bathroom and the pile of yarn in the chair. She understands and will say nothing. We decided that it would be best if the men in the family spent the night with Jack."

"They can take him h-home tomorrow, then you or I will have to go out a couple t-times a day to check for infection and change b-bandages."

"What can we do about Miss Davenport, Doc?"

"Nothing. I'm going to Mason t-tomorrow to see a doctor I know and find out if he w-would be able to care for patients here until another d-doctor can take over. I hate leaving you, April. I can pay you for a m-month or two."

"Don't worry about it. Go and make a life with Caroline. You two deserve to be to-gether."

"Thank you." His voice was husky. He squeezed her arm and walked into the sur-gery, where the Jones family were gathered about Jack's bed.

Fred was troubled. He waited until the up-town crowd had thinned and the streets were almost vacant before he put on his hat and left the store. He had spent the day searching his conscience and had come to the conclusion that he wasn't much of a man.

When he first came to Fertile, he'd been so pleased to be in charge of the store and a respected merchant that he had allowed his sister to browbeat him. Until now he'd been nothing more than her flunky.

But that was the least of his self-disgust. He hoped to God that no one ever found out that he had become so perverted that he spied on Miss Asbury. The only excuse he could find for himself was that the spying was the result of his urgent sexual needs. And in order to gratify them, he had stooped so low as to invade the privacy of a very nice young lady.

Fred had stood in the window and watched the farmer hurry down the street to his wife sitting on the box in front of the store. She stood up as he approached, and he enfolded her in his arms and nuzzled the side of her neck unashamedly to show his love and affection for his family. The little girl wrapped her arms around one of his legs. After hugging his wife, he picked his daughter up in his arms and whispered something that made her giggle.

The man was poor and tired, and he probably didn't know how he and his family would survive the winter, but he was still far richer than most others would have imagined, Fred thought with regret. He was loved.

Because Fred coveted his position in town and feared his sister, he had been denied the chance to have a wife and family. He had found an outlet for his craving for sex in the fantasy world of dirty pictures and magazines and then the eventual act of spying on Miss Asbury, of which he was now sincerely ashamed.

Fred entered the house, hung his hat and coat on the hall tree and headed for the stairs. Shirley called out from the kitchen.

"We're having a cold supper."

He continued up the steps to his bedroom and, after locking the door, went into the closet, where he had scraps of wallpaper and paste. He worked for half an hour carefully covering the holes he had made in the closet and bedroom walls. When he finished, he went to the storage room and restacked boxes covering the hole that had allowed him to see into the bathroom.

"What are you doing?" Shirley's voice broke the silence just as he lifted the last box into place. "That's my stuff in those boxes."

"No. Your boxes are over there by the window. These are my boxes, and I will stack them any damn way I please."

"Well, who stepped on your tail?"

"You, Shirley. You've been stepping on it since the day I came here ten years ago."

"That's a lie. I gave you a job, a place to live." Fred moved past her and went down the hall to his room. Shirley followed, still talking. "Without me you'd still be back there in Springfield sweeping out old man Gipson's grocery store or riding a freight train looking for a handout."

"And without me, Shirley, you would have lost the store years ago."

"I taught you everything you know about that store, and this is the thanks I get?"

"You've said that a million times already."

"I'll say it a million more. It's Ron's store. Not yours."

"Ron is dead. He's not been running the store for the past ten years."

"It's my store, and you'll run it the way I tell you to." Her voice was so loud it hurt his ears.

"I've decided to move out. I'll still run the store for you if you want me to, but tomorrow I'm going to look for a room elsewhere."

"You're moving out?" she shouted. "My home isn't good enough anymore?"

"I need a place of my own," he said patiently.

"You want a place where you can get that slut in bed with you. That's what you want!" Shirley's eyes were flashing hatred, and her face was set in harsh lines. The corner of her mouth lifted in a sneer.

"Get ahold of yourself, Shirley. You're saying things you may regret later."

"I've seen the way you look at her. Sniffing 'round like a cur dog after a bitch."

"Hush up!"

"If you move, you'll never set foot in my store again."

Fred reached into his pocket and handed her the key.

Chapter 26

Doc awakened to the sound of a rooster announcing the break of day. There was just enough light in the room for him to see the clock on the table beside the bed. Six o'clock. The days were getting shorter this time of year.

He felt the warmth of Caroline snuggled against him. He caught the hand lying on his chest and brought it to his lips, being careful not to awaken her. It had been pure heaven to sleep with her in his arms. They had made love last night—more than once. Not having to leave her had been wonderful. The cozy bed had been their world. He had cuddled her in his arms; they had whispered their love for each other, and he had told her of the future he planned for them.

She had stiffened when he explained that

he wanted to take her home to Tennessee to meet his sisters before they found a place where they could be married.

"Ah, don't be afraid, sweetheart. They will love you. I know it or I wouldn't take you there. I want you to know them, and I want them to know you, should something happen to me. I need to know that my wife and my child will have relatives who will take care of them." He held her tightly to him and moved his hands up and down her back.

"If something happens to you, I will not be able to bear it."

"You would, sweet girl. You would have the babe to care for."

"I should go back to the house with Silas," she whispered.

"No. You're going to be by my side from now on. You're my wife even if we are not legally wed. This is my baby." He stroked her belly with the palm of his hand. "Both of you are staying with me."

His kisses became deeper and more urgent. Desire thickened the part of him nestled between her thighs.

"Lord, honey. You make me as randy as a billy goat."

She laughed softly. "I'm glad."

Caroline nipped his chin and gasped when his skilled fingers found the center of her physical pleasure and danced around it. Unable to wait, she shifted into position so that he could enter her. The small sounds that came from her throat were music to his ears. Their joined bodies united their souls. A warm glow inundated their senses as she took pleasure in him as he did in her. At that moment happiness magically erased all of the problems that faced them.

Afterward, they held each other and dozed, unwilling to break contact, happily knowing they had a lifetime together.

The shrill ringing of the telephone brought a groan from Doc. He said a few cusswords under his breath and leaned over to kiss Caroline one last time.

"I wish we could stay here together like this forever, but it's not to be," he whispered.

The cold morning air hit his naked body when he left the warm bed. He slipped into his old flannel robe and went to answer the phone.

April dreaded going back to Mrs. Poole's. But when she reached the house, thankfully, neither the landlady nor her brother was in sight. She hurried up the stairs to her bedroom before one or the other of them should appear from one of the back rooms and confront her. After locking her door, she placed the back of her only chair beneath the doorknob.

From pure habit she checked to see if she had a clean uniform for the next day before she stripped and fell into bed. She was so tired that she was asleep almost the minute her head hit the pillow.

April came slowly out of a deep, sound sleep to hear a loud voice and a pounding on a door; not hers, but Fred's. The high-pitched tone of Mrs. Poole's voice suggested that something had frightened her. She sounded almost frantic. April swung her feet to the floor and then recognized the shocking words the woman was saying.

"You sonofabitch! Whorin' dog! Ungrateful shithead! You're not fit to kiss a mule's behind." After a pause she continued. "Money from my store paid for every stitch of clothes on your back; and when you leave, you'll take only what you brought when you came here. Understand me? You'll leave here buck naked!"

April stopped in the middle of the room to listen. Fred had opened the door and was talking to his sister in a low, calm voice.

"Go back downstairs, Shirley. I'm coming down and we'll talk. There's no benefit to waking Miss Asbury."

"Asbury? Don't you mean Ass Bury! It's what you want to do, isn't it? Bury yourself in her ass. Don't be shocked, Brother dear. I know what men want—all they think about. It's puttin' that thing that dangles between their legs in some slut."

"Stop that nasty talk," Fred said sternly. "You're making a fool of yourself. Come on downstairs."

"Turn loose of me, you . . . you . . . ass kisser. I'll talk any way I want to. This is my house. Ron wanted me to have a nice house. And it's mine. Do you hear? I've let you stay here, and this is the thanks I get. You'll be sorry you treated me like this. You'll be sorry . . ." Her voice faded as they went down the stairs.

April didn't realize that she had been holding her breath until she let it out through her teeth. What had happened to set off Mrs. Poole? She couldn't be drunk this

early in the morning. She must be having a
breakdown . . . going out of her mind.

April knew she had to get out of there. On
her way to the clinic she would stop by the
hotel to see if they had a room. Last night,
she'd heard, it had been crowded to overflowing. If she couldn't get a room there,
she would stay at the clinic until there was a
vacancy.

Feeling it safe to go to the bathroom, April
hurriedly gave herself a quick wash and
brushed her teeth. She dressed for work.
Then, after wiping off her white shoes with a
damp cloth, she went to the storage room
for her suitcase. She packed it and left it lying open on the bed. Today she would find
someone to help her move.

For a minute or two she had a pain in her
heart when Joe came to her mind. She
didn't want to think about him or the way he
had made her feel. He was a classic flirt,
and she was right on the verge of falling for
his line, his sweet grin and the look of affection in his blue eyes.

He'd had to try out his technique on the
new woman in town, and when she suc-
cumbed to his attraction, he had cast her

off, dismissed her from his mind because he feared she would become a nuisance.

She was lucky that he had shown his true colors before she had been foolish enough to go to bed with him. She didn't know if she would have been able to resist the spell he cast over her when he held her close and kissed her.

It was quiet when she opened her bedroom door. She paused to listen before proceeding. Then, as she reached the stairs, she heard the crash of something against the wall and Mrs. Poole's shout.

"You are not leaving this house!" The words were punctuated by another crash.

"Stop that, Shirley. Calm yourself. The way you're acting makes me more determined than ever to get out from under your roof. You've gone off the deep end. Just look at yourself. You've not slept."

"I was afraid to sleep, you fool. She catches me unaware, she'll cut my throat."

"Are you talking about Miss Asbury?"

"I'm talking about that slut. She wasn't satisfied to have the Joneses. She wanted Ron and you."

"You're talking crazy, Sister. Ron has been dead for ten years. Why don't you let me call Dr. Forbes? He could give you something to quiet you down and let you sleep."

"How dare you say I need that sawbones! Hattie Davenport says he keeps women down there so he can rut anytime, day or night. He's not touching me."

April walked briskly to the kitchen. Shirley was beside the cookstove. April moved around the table so that she could face the two of them.

"Mrs. Poole, I'll have all my things out of your house tonight. You can think what you please about me, it doesn't matter. But I resent greatly your slurring of a good and decent man like Dr. Forbes. I'll not waste my breath defending myself to you because you have made up your mind. I'm only sorry I ever came here in the first place."

"I didn't want you. *He* did. Now he's leaving. It's your fault—you're a slut, a whore, just like the whores who were after my Ron, making him do . . . things to them."

April realized the woman was out of control. Her shoulders twitched; her eyes were hate-filled; saliva ran from the corner of her twisted mouth. Just wanting to get out of there, April left the kitchen and headed for the front door.

"Miss Asbury." Fred lightly touched her shoulder and stepped in front of her. "She's not herself. It's like she's fallen to pieces. I've never seen her like this."

"I understand your need to defend her, and I agree that she's having some sort of mental breakdown. You should urge her to seek treatment. You must understand that it will be impossible for me to stay here after the accusations she made the other morning and now this."

"She's upset because I'm moving out. I should have had my own place years ago."

"That's between you and your sister and has nothing to do with—" She glanced up at his face. He was looking over her shoulder.

"Sister . . . no!" One of Fred's arms swept April aside, the other shoved Shirley back. She took a couple of fumbling steps, bounced against the post at the bottom of the stairs, then over onto the floor. She lay there facedown in a tangled heap, her head at an odd angle.

The butcher knife was still in her hand.

"Good Lord!" April breathed. "What in the world was she going to do?" Her nurse's training kicked in. She knelt beside the woman and felt for a pulse, almost sure that she would not find one. Shirley's neck had been broken. April looked up at Fred, who was holding his arm where his sister had cut him with the knife, and shook her head.

"She . . . she was going to stab you. I pushed her too hard!"

"How were you to know she'd fall as she did? Let me see your arm."

"It's all right. Oh, God. What have I done?"

"You could bleed to death," April said firmly. "Let me see your arm!"

She pulled his hand away, then yanked up the bloody shirtsleeve to see a cut on the top of his forearm. No artery had been sev-ered, as she had first believed. She hurried to the kitchen and took a clean dishcloth from the drawer. When she returned, Fred was staring down at his sister, tears rolling down his cheeks. April wrapped the cloth tightly around his arm.

"This will make do until Doc can put in some stitches. I've got to call him." Fred was in such a state of shock she wasn't sure he had heard her. Keeping her eye on Fred, she went to the phone in the hall, rang for the operator and asked her to ring Dr. Forbes. It seemed forever before he answered. "Doc, this is April. Come up to Mrs. Poole's right away. There has been an accident."

"It's urgent?"

"Very."

"See you in a few minutes."

When she hung up, she rang Diane again. "Please ring Mr. Appleby."

"Have you heard about the new baby?" the operator said. "It's a girl. A big one. Weighed eight pounds."

"I've heard," she said crisply, not wanting to prolong the conversation. When the male voice came on the line, she said, "Mr. Appleby, this is April Asbury, Dr. Forbes's nurse. Will you please come to Mrs. Poole's? There has been an accident. Doc is on his way here now."

"A police matter?"

"Yes, sir."

"I'll be there as soon as I can."

The shock was wearing off and reality was setting in. Fred was kneeling beside his sister sobbing. When he reached to pick up her hand, April put her hand on his shoulder.

"Don't touch her until the doctor and Mr.

Appleby get here. I had to call him. He's substituting until Jack is able to take over again."

"I pushed her too hard. She's not been herself for weeks, and she just went kind of crazy when I told her I wanted to move out. I never dreamed she'd blame it on you. I just wanted a place that was mine." Fred continued to babble. "Oh, Lord, I'm sorry. I wouldn't have hurt her for the world."

"It was an accident, Fred."

"She didn't like women. She didn't have a woman friend that I knew of, and she avoided them when they came in the store. I never thought she'd hurt you or anyone else. I wish I hadn't urged her to rent the room."

April heard footsteps on the porch and opened the door before Doc could ring the doorbell.

"It's Mrs. Poole, Doc. She fell against the post and over onto the floor. I knew right away that her neck was broken."

Doc came in and knelt down beside the woman. He lifted her head, let it fall back, then felt for a pulse in her neck.

"What's she doing with a b-butcher knife in her hand?"

"She was going to stab me. Fred pushed her out of the way, and she fell. She hit the post first. I heard her head hit the floor. It may have struck the bottom step first."

Fred was sitting on the stair steps, his head in his hands.

"Did she cut him?"

"A gash on the arm. It will need a few stitches. Mr. Appleby is on his way. Doc, she's been ranting and raving for a couple of days. Fred said that she's never acted like this before. She may have been having a nervous breakdown."

"Why was she going to s-stab you?"

"Fred wanted to move out and find a place of his own. For some unknown reason she blamed me. She accused me of being after Fred and after Ron, her deceased husband. She has a very low opinion of women and said some nasty things."

"Ten years ago Corbin and I had to t-tell her that her husband had been killed. He was s-stomped on by a frightened horse. It was sad. It was as if the l-light went out of her, and she was n-never the same again."

"She must have really loved him."

"Here's Corbin," Doc said when a car stopped in front.

April told Corbin about Mrs. Poole's strange behavior the morning after she had spent the night at the clinic and about pounding on Fred's door this morning. She repeated word for word what the woman had said about her and about Doc having women in his rooms.

"There isn't a doubt in my mind that Fred saved me from being stabbed in the back. He has a gash on his arm from the knife. He shoved her back, and she stumbled and fell against the post. He's blaming himself, thinking that he pushed her too hard. It was an accident."

"It would seem so. Is there anything you want to add, Fred?"

"I told her last night that I wanted to move out and find a place of my own. The way she looked at it was that I didn't appreciate what all she had done for me. I never thought she'd take it so hard."

"What do you think of her mental state, Doc?"

"That's not my line of w-work. But as an observer, I'd say she was not in her r-right mind."

"I don't see any need to drag her reputation through the mud. She is dead. It was an

accident, pure and simple. The facts leading up to the accident will be left out of my
report. I'll put a notice in tomorrow's paper
that Mrs. Poole had an accident, she stumbled on the stairs and fell. It's not far from
the truth." He looked at Doc. "Would you
have believed it ten years ago that we'd be
doing this, Doc?"

"No. But it's b-best now just as it was
then."

Corbin reached down and took the
butcher knife from Shirley's hand and spoke
to Fred. "Do you want me to stop by and
speak to Herman?"

"I guess so. He's the one who buried
Ron."

"He was on the city council with Ron
when I first came to work here. He's the only
funeral director in town now. There was another one before the depression hit, but he
pulled out."

"I would appreciate it. I need to put a sign
in the window at the hardware store saying
it will be closed until after . . . after . . ."

"I can take care of that," Corbin offered.

Fred dug in his pocket and pulled out a
ring of keys. "There's a second set of keys

to the store in Shirley's apron pocket. Would you take them out before she . . . goes?"

Corbin knelt down, took a ring of keys and a single key from one pocket and a small purse from the other. He gave both to Fred.

"I need to get back," Doc said. "I haven't checked on Jack since midnight. You need to come down to the clinic, Fred, and let me look at that cut. April thinks you'll need a couple of stitches."

April said, "I'll stay with Fred until the undertaker comes. Then I'll stop at the hotel and see about a room." She spoke to Fred. "Is there anyone you want me to call?"

"No. Our folks are gone."

Fred continued to sit on the stairs after Doc and Corbin had left. He sat with his elbows on his knees, his face in his hands. He looked terribly alone, but April was sure that as soon as word was out, the neighbors would be coming in.

"Do you mind if I make coffee, Fred?" It was something to do while they waited for Mr. Sellon, the undertaker.

He looked up. "Go right ahead."

April left an hour later and walked briskly down the street to the hotel. The night clerk was still behind the desk. When April asked for a room, he looked her up and down.

"Do you have luggage?"

"Of course, I have luggage. Will you have a room by this afternoon or not?"

"Name, please."

"April Asbury."

"You're a nurse?"

"How could you tell?" Her voice was heavily laced with sarcasm.

"The white dress and shoes."

"Why, of course. How astute of you."

"Fifty-cent deposit."

"I didn't bring my purse." April rolled her eyes to the ceiling. "I'll go back to the clinic and bring you fifty cents."

"What are you doing here?"

April jumped back when she heard Joe's voice close to her ear. "I could say the same to you."

"I used Jack's room last night. How is he this morning?"

"I've not seen him." Her knees began to shake. "I've got to run. I'll be back with your deposit," she said to the clerk and headed for the door.

"Wait a minute." Joe took her elbow in his hand. "Why do you need a deposit?"

"I'm taking a room here and he"—she jerked her head toward the clerk—"wants a deposit."

Joe walked back to the desk. "Why does she have to make a deposit on a room?"

"Because it's the rules. The owner said not to rent rooms to women who come in without luggage, or the good name of the hotel will suffer."

Joe leaned over the counter to say softly, "You're a real honest-to-God prick. When she comes back to get a room, you'd better have one, or I'll kick your ass up between your ears. Got it?"

April had gone out and down the hotel porch steps by the time Joe caught up with her.

"Why are you moving out of Mrs. Poole's?"

"Mrs. Poole had an accident this morning. She's dead. I can't stay there with Fred."

He caught her arm and stopped her. "Say that again."

"I said it once. That should be enough. Mrs. Poole fell on the stairs and broke her neck. Is that plain enough?"

"Yeah, I guess it is. It's too bad."

Joe kept pace with her as she hurried toward the clinic. The merchants were opening the stores. The barber was sweeping the walk in front of his shop. He yelled at Joe.

"How's Jack doin'?"

"All right last night. I'm going to see him now."

"Let me know. Folks will be askin'."

"Were you there when it happened?" Joe asked when they had passed the shop.

"Yes."

When she said no more, he asked, "Will you need help getting your things over to the hotel?"

"No."

"Is Harold Dozier going to help you?"

"I imagine he would if I asked him."

"Well?"

April stopped and glared at him. "Why the questions?"

"I want to help you if I can."

"Your help isn't needed. And you needn't worry that I took your little flirtation seriously."

She continued walking. Joe stood on the

corner and watched until she reached the clinic. He felt as if he had been punched in the gut. Damn that woman. What in tarnation was she talking about?

Chapter 27

By the time she reached the clinic, April was feeling weak and trembly and very nervous. Part of it was because she'd not had anything to eat this morning, but the larger part was the fact that Mrs. Poole had wanted to kill her and then had died as the result of it. Death was never easy to accept and especially one as sudden and violent as the one this morning. An old adage came to April's mind:

Life is uncertain and death is sure.

Meeting Joe so unexpectedly had not been kind to her already strung-out nerves. It was typical of him to show up and stick his bill into her business. She was perfectly capable of handling the desk clerk, who was sure to be a relative of the owner of the hotel or he wouldn't have the job.

She had known that she would have to see Joe at some time, but why did it have to be this morning when she had enough on her plate already to deal with. And what did he mean about Harold Dozier?

Oh, Lord. I had forgotten that on a sudden impulse I had agreed to go out with him next Saturday night.

April desperately wanted to go away somewhere and cry, but she stiffened her backbone and anchored her cap with its one black stripe to the top of her head with bobby pins. With a smile on her face she went into the surgery, where Doc was changing the bandage on Jack's side.

"Good morning," she said in her best professional voice. "You look like you could run a footrace this morning."

Jack was clenching his teeth. "I was better until this old sawbones started poking at me."

"He needed s-something to complain about, so I thought I'd help him out a bit." Doc continued dabbing at the wound with a pad. "Think you're up to the r-ride home, or would you like to stay here a day or two?"

"I could make it home on horseback. This

is the hardest damn bed I've ever lain on. And I'm about to starve to death."

"It's your own fault. I offered to b-bring you some bread soaked in m-milk."

"I need solid food, Doc. I've not eaten since yesterday morning."

"Did you ever hear s-such whining?"

"I was sure that Ruby's visit last night would sweeten him up. They looked pretty lovey-dovey to me."

Jack grinned. "It was worth getting shot for."

"I liked her. If she wasn't so nice, I would probably hate her because she's so pretty."

Jack looked pleased. "She is pretty, isn't she?"

"Yeah," Doc said. "But not very s-smart."

"Come on, Doc." April winked. "Jack's bound to have a few good qualities. Dogs like him."

"Dogs like anyone who f-feeds them." Doc finished with the bandage and moved the cart away from the bed. "Jethro coming to get you?"

"Him or Joe."

"You're to get right in bed and s-stay there. Mind what Eudora tells you. She's had n-nursing experience. If you get an infection, it'll mean a t-trip to the hospital in Mason, and I don't need to tell you that it's a r-rough ride."

"I'll do everything you say, Doc. Promise."

"If you do, it'll be the f-first time," Doc grumbled, but he smiled. "Take care of yourself, or Ruby'll be a w-widow before she's a bride."

The front door squeaked, and Joe appeared in the doorway of the surgery. April ignored him and put away the supplies Doc had been using.

"I want to go by Sparky's and get some breakfast." Jack lifted his head so he could see his brother.

Joe looked at Doc. "Pay him no mind," Doc said. "Take him home and tell Eudora to feed him a soft diet."

"Get my britches, Doc."

April went back to the reception room while Joe and Doc helped Jack into his clothes. When they were ready to leave, April held open the door while they walked him slowly out to the car. Joe did not look at her or speak to her until after Jack was settled and the door closed. Then as he walked around to the driver's side, he glanced up to where she stood on the porch.

"I'll be back."

Doc followed April back into the clinic. "Have you had breakfast?"

"I had coffee with Fred."

"Caroline will fix you a p-plate."

"I don't want to bother—"

"Fiddlesticks." Doc went through the connecting door and returned minutes later with a cup of coffee, a slice of toast and a dish of oatmeal balanced on a big platter.

"Thank you. That coffee smells good."

"Sit and eat."

Doc paced the room, then went to look out the door. April could tell that he had something on his mind and waited for him to unload.

"Caroline and I plan to l-leave at the end of the week. By then the water wells will have been t-tested, and if there is a chance of an epidemic, the p-proper authorities will be notified. I had a chance to talk to Evan l-last night. He has agreed to—or rather he insisted upon buying the house and equipment in the clinic. He is sure that if and when a new doctor comes, he will get his m-money back. This is a big load off my mind. He's going to take care to see the h-house Caroline had is s-signed over to

Silas. She wants it that way." Doc turned and looked at her. "I'm sorry to h-have to leave you, April. It wasn't fair of me to b-bring you here knowing that I wasn't g-going to be able to stay in Fertile."

"It was worth it to me just to know you and Caroline. I'll be fine. I've got a little inheritance from my grandmother that I've been holding on to. I'm better off than most folks."

"I fell in love with Caroline a year ago w-when her papa died. At first I thought that I just felt s-sorry for her, then I knew I had deeper f-feelings. Now I can't imagine my life without her."

"Not everyone finds a love like that," April said wistfully.

"Any collections that c-come in after I'm gone are yours. It will help a little to make up for my taking advantage of you."

"No, Doc. When you are settled, send me your address and I will send them on."

"It will not be m-much. Folks who can pay have already paid. I was h-hoping that you would stay here, that you and Joe—"

"No, Doc," she said quickly again. "Joe just wants to flirt around. He doesn't want anything permanent. And I could never love a man who has his eye out for every woman who comes along."

"You think Joe's that kind of man?"

"Oh, yes." The little laugh stuck in April's throat. "He's got a practiced line that draws women like flies."

"Hmmm. I guess I hadn't noticed. I don't r-remember him being stuck on anyone around here for any length of time. Not like Jack. He's never b-been able to see anyone but Ruby."

"That's just it. Joe plays the field."

"Well . . . you know what you want. I've known him for a long t-time. I've never heard of him leaving b-behind a string of broken hearts. The entire Jones f-family are as decent as any you'll ever meet."

The phone rang. It was Mr. Appleby asking if Doc was there. He wanted to bring over Mrs. Poole's death certificate for him to sign.

Continuing his conversation with April, he said, "After Corbin leaves, I'm g-going to Mason to see my friend and ask him to c-come to Fertile one or two days a week until a doctor can be f-found. I'll tell him about you and how c-capable you are. As soon as Caroline and I are gone, you can m-move into the house until it's s-sold to another doctor. I don't think it will be any time soon. This is not a very p-prosperous community right now."

"I'll stay at the hotel until then. What reason shall I give for your sudden departure?"

"I'm going to Tennessee to see my f-family. That's the truth. I'll take Caroline there to m-meet my sisters before we leave the country."

April stacked her breakfast dishes on the platter.

"It's strange about Mrs. Poole. She hated the Jones family for some reason. She accused me of all sorts of things with . . . both brothers. She lost her mind. That's the only reason I can think of for her to take such a personal interest in my affairs."

"News about her d-death will spread all over town like wildfire. As s-soon as folks know you were there, they will ask you a million questions."

"I can say that I didn't cause her to fall, because I didn't."

"You're lucky Fred saw w-what she was going to do."

"He seemed quite content when I first went there, but I can understand his wanting to move out and have a place of his own. Mrs. Poole was not easy to live with."

"It will be a b-big funeral even though Mrs. Poole wasn't very f-friendly with any of the other m-merchants. Folks here in Fertile t-turn out for one of their own. The stores will close."

When Corbin arrived, April went to the back room. She changed the linen on the bed Jack had slept on and put the instruments in the sterilizer. She could hear the men talking in the reception room and wondered how much Mr. Appleby knew about Doc's affair with Caroline.

Corbin was still there when April went back to her desk.

"The marshal is sending a man up here to help out until Jack gets on his feet. He gave me permission to deputize Joe if I should have more than I can handle."

"Folks d-down in Shanty Town should be too b-busy cleaning up to get into t-trouble."

"There are always a few," Corbin said.

"How's the new baby?" April asked.

A huge smile came over Corbin's face. "She's beautiful. She has dark blond hair like her mother and big blue eyes."

"What does her brother think of her?"

"Not much." Corbin laughed. "He wanted to know when she was going home." He put on his hat. "I've got to get this over to the courthouse. Are you doing all right, Miss Asbury? What happened this morning was horrible for you."

"It was. But I'll be all right."

Shortly after the noon hour, desperate to use the bathroom, April rapped on the connecting door and called out to Caroline.

"Come in."

When April came from the bathroom, Caroline was working with a pile of yarn, rolling it into balls. She had been crocheting.

"My grandmother used to crochet," April said. "I have a crocheted tablecloth she made. I never got the hang of following a pattern. About all I could make was a chain."

"I just finished these." Caroline shyly held up a tiny pair of blue booties. "Todd hasn't seen them yet."

"They're so little." April held them in the palm of her hand. *Oh, my Lord. Caroline is pregnant! No wonder Doc is desperate to leave here.* "Caroline, has Silas been to the back door?"

"A little while ago. He's getting some things I left out at the house."

"The back door is locked now?"

She nodded. "And the front."

"I'll not let anyone in through the connecting door, but if I rap on it, go into the bedroom and lock the door. Someone may come in to use the bathroom besides me."

"It's what Todd told me to do."

"I'd better be getting back. Doc said that he'd be gone for a while."

"He told me what happened this morning. I'm sorry you had to go through that."

"Thank you. I hope I never have to endure such a thing again."

April went back and sat down at her desk. She was a little ashamed for feeling sorry for herself. Caroline was pregnant, and there was no one in the world who cared for her except Doc and an old Negro man. But she was lucky, too, to be loved by Doc. A wave of loneliness swept over April, and tears filled her eyes.

Who in the world cares diddly-squat about me?

*   *   *

April's premonition that something unpleasant was going to happen materialized in late afternoon. She heard the sound of sharp heels on the porch and looked up to see Miss Davenport and two other ladies come into the reception room.

April stood. "The doctor isn't here."

"I know that. I saw him leave. I also saw a woman in the back door talking to that Negro who hangs around." Miss Davenport went to the connecting door and rattled the doorknob. "Locked like the front and back doors are locked. What is he hiding? People in this town don't lock their doors." She looked at her two companions to verify what she was saying.

"What the doctor does in his living quarters is no business of yours, Miss Davenport."

"It's the business of the women of this town to know that the doctor who touches their bodies is a man beyond reproach. If he has nothing to hide, why is he keeping the doors locked?"

"Ask him when you see him." April moved over in front of the connecting door.

"I think not," Miss Davenport said. "I want to see this hussy he's keeping in there. Come on, girls."

"You will not go in there!"

"Get out of the way."

"Miss Davenport, I will hurt you if I have to. You've no right to break into Dr. Forbes's house." April looked past her to the other two women. "Don't let her goad you into this. It's illegal and you could be arrested."

"This house was paid for by the tax-payers," one of the women said.

"That's not true. The doctor paid for this house."

"But Hattie said—"

"Hattie is wrong!"

Miss Davenport's anger was causing her to lose control. She attempted to push April aside.

"Don't push me!" April balled her fist and drew it back.

"I'm going in there!" When her hands came out to grasp April's shoulders to shove her aside, April kicked her on the kneecap.

Miss Davenport screamed and fell back. Her friends caught her and helped her to a chair.

"She broke my leg!"

"I told you that I'd hurt you. Now, get out of here or I'll call the law."

"You . . . you bitch! I'll make you sorry you were ever born. I'll find out what you're keeping in there that you don't want anybody to see."

The front door opened and Joe stood there. Miss Davenport continued to rant. "I'll run you out of this town and . . . the high-and-mighty doctor, too. Even Shanty Town won't have you when I get through with you."

April ignored Joe and went to the phone. "Are you going or do I call Mr. Appleby? He's been deputized by the marshal."

"Come on, Hattie. Let's go."

When she had difficulty getting to her feet, Joe went over to help.

"Don't touch me, you . . . you sidewinder!"

Joe lifted his shoulders and backed away. The two women helped Miss Davenport to the door, where she turned and glared at April.

"I'll not forget this."

"I hope you don't, and maybe you'll think before you try to break into someone's house."

"He's got someone in there. It's probably that slut from down on the river. All the men from Shanty Town used her; now it's his turn."

"Leave!" April shouted, her patience at an end. When the door closed behind them, she glared at Joe. "Why did you have to come? What do you want?"

"I told you I'd be back." The tone of his voice, soft, smooth, almost a caress, was her undoing.

April swallowed, her stomach clenched in a rush of mingled emotions. She burst into tears, sank down in her chair and buried her face in her arms.

"Ah . . . sweetheart." He knelt down beside her chair. "You deserve a good cry. Most women would have buckled under your load long ago." His hand smoothed the hair back from her wet cheek.

"I kicked her. I've never done such a thing." April sat up but kept her hands over her face. "She pushed me . . . tried to get into Doc's rooms. I couldn't let her go in there."

"Of course not. But why did she want to?"

April pulled the handkerchief from her

pocket and wiped her eyes. She felt miserable about letting herself go in front of Joe—of all people. She straightened her shoulders and checked to see if her cap was in place.

"She's been spying and saw Caroline giving Silas a plate of food out the back door. I don't know why she thinks it's her business, but she does. She was here yesterday demanding to see the woman Doc kept in his rooms."

"And you were determined she wasn't going in. Good for you." Joe's hand was now massaging the back of her neck. It felt so good she didn't have the strength to tell him to stop.

"She wanted Doc, and he had to tell her that he wasn't interested. She turned mean and has been spreading rumors about him. Mrs. Maddox told me the day she was here."

"Where's Doc?"

"He went to Mason. He should be back soon."

"Caroline all right?"

"Seems to be. She's an awfully sweet girl. Doc wants to leave by the end of the week."

"He told me."

"I'm scared of the responsibility I'll have until they can get another doctor. There's so much I don't know."

"You'll do just fine. Isn't that a steel rod I feel running up and down your back?" Joe's fingers traced her spine.

"I don't want Doc to know of my doubts. He deserves to be happy."

"I won't tell him if you don't."

"Do you know someone who will wash my uniforms? I can't wash them at the hotel."

"I bet Mrs. Maddox would do it."

"She wouldn't have to iron them. I can do that."

"When do you need them washed?"

"This is my last clean one. I can make it do for tomorrow unless something unforeseen happens."

"After we take your things to the hotel tonight, I'll take them to her."

"I'm only taking my suitcase. Fred will let me leave the rest of my things there in the storage room until I move in here."

"Feeling better now?"

His gaze anxiously searched her face. His lovable grin was gone. His handsome face was creased with concern for her. She

could scarcely draw a breath. All the reasons for wanting to put distance between
them faded into oblivion. She wanted him
because he was Joe, and he made her feel
as no other man ever had, or probably ever
would. No man had stirred her desire and
her heart as he did.

April nodded slowly. He picked up her
hand and brought it to his lips.

"I don't want you to go out with Harold
Dozier."

"How did you know about that?"

"He's been bragging. Word gets around."

"I had forgotten about it until you mentioned his name this morning. Don't you
like him?"

"He's all right. I just don't like the compe-
tition."

"You're much better-looking than Harold."

"Thanks." He grinned but the smile faded
quickly. "I don't mean in looks. He's got
so much to offer a woman, and I've got so
little."

"You think I choose my friends by what
they've got?"

"No. I didn't mean that. I mean . . . I just
wish I had more to offer, and you might . . .
just might . . . see me in a different light."

"If you were Mr. Rockefeller and had all the money in the world, I would still have to know your heart. I want a man who wants me and only me. I don't want a flirty man who chases off after every pretty skirt that comes along."

"You think that I'm that kind of man." He made the statement with undisguised bewilderment.

"Your reputation precedes you."

He was quiet for several moments, then he said, "I didn't realize that people thought I was . . . flirty." Without a doubt he was absolutely sincere. "I tried too hard with you, is that it?"

"No. I've not had many . . . boyfriends. I've tried to be cautious and not get involved with someone I thought would break my heart." April never dreamed that she would be talking to him like this.

"And you think I could do that?"

"The danger is there."

When footsteps sounded on the porch, Joe stood, but not after first squeezing her hand.

Fred stood in the hall near the front door. He had just admitted Herman Sellon, the funeral director. It was early afternoon, and already the kitchen table was loaded with food brought in by the neighbors. Even as he greeted Herman, his mind was wondering whom he could bring in to deal with it.

"Fred, I know this is hard for you to think about right now, but we need to settle a few things about the funeral, and I need to get Mrs. Poole's burial clothes."

"Burial clothes?"

"Undergarments, dress, stockings and shoes. Miss Thompson from the beauty shop will fix her hair. She'll finger-wave it. That seems to be the style Mrs. Poole wore."

"Come upstairs to her room. I've not been in there since . . . the accident." Fred's voice became husky.

Herman followed Fred. At the top of the stairs they went into Shirley's room. It was neat as always. The bed was made, and nothing appeared to be out of place. Fred opened the wardrobe.

"Should it be black?"

"Not necessarily." Herman looked over the selection. In the back of the wardrobe he spotted a pink dress with small white flowers. "This one would be nice."

"I don't think she's worn that one since Ron was killed. It may not fit."

"If you want to bury her in it, it'll fit."

"All right. Now for undergarments." Fred opened a bureau drawer, found nothing but gowns and handkerchiefs and stockings. He pulled out the stockings and opened the next drawer and removed a petticoat and underpants. A small tin box caught his eye. He lifted it out and recognized it as the box she had taken from behind the shelving they'd had to tear out when the roof leaked. He placed it on top of the bureau and closed the drawer.

"Is this all you need?"

"Does she have another pair of shoes?"

Fred found the shoes and they left the room.

After he had showed Herman out, Fred sat down beside the window and looked out onto the street. What would he do now? His sister was so unpredictable: She might have left the house and the business to distant cousins in Alabama. Should that be the case, he would have only what he had saved out of his wages. She had never allowed him access to the store's bank account. He hoped there was enough ready money there to pay the funeral expenses.

His life had changed drastically in just a few days' time. And, he realized suddenly, it all started when the river began to rise.

Chapter 28

April spent the next two nights at the hotel. She took one of her evening meals with the Jones family after she had gone to the farm to change Jack's bandages. Joe had not been there. Jack made it a point to tell her that he was expected later.

"Coming to the wedding?" Jack asked with a wide grin.

"Wedding? Is someone getting married?" April acted uninterested and packed her supplies back in her bag.

"You know perfectly well who's getting married. Ruby and I are going to have a Christmas wedding. She's giving notice that she'll be leaving her job at midterm. God, I can't believe it. I could almost kiss Tator Williams for shooting me."

"That's dumb; and if you don't stop mov-

ing around, you'll still be here in bed on
Christmas, and Ruby will have to find another joker to marry."

Jack laughed and held his side. "You're
good luck, April. I got my job after you came
here. I couldn't ask Ruby to marry me until I
got a job. Corbin said the city council will
hold it for me, and I'll get part of my pay
while I'm out because I was shot in the line
of duty."

"Well, hey. I wonder if I could get a job like
that."

Eudora came to the door. "Dinner is ready
when you are, April. I've got a tray ready for
Jack. He'll probably want to wait until Ruby
gets here to feed him. She's spoiling that
boy."

April enjoyed being with the Joneses, but
she left as soon as the meal was over, saying that she needed to be back in town before dark.

The next night she ate with Doc and Caroline.

Doc was outraged that Miss Davenport
had tried to bully her way into his quarters,
and he laughed heartily when April told him
that she had kicked her in the kneecap.

"I was told that was the place to kick if

you couldn't reach the crotch," April said
dryly. "I've never had to do it before."

"I wish I could have s-seen it."

"No. You wouldn't have wanted to be
there. That woman is jealous and mean and
determined to get into your house."

"I've never given her the s-slightest encouragement."

"You've eaten her pies," April said, and
she winked at Caroline.

"I didn't ask her to bring them," Doc
grumbled.

"She accused me of breaking her leg. Her
friends had to help her up out of the chair
and out the door. I won't be surprised if she
spreads the rumor that I'm Lizzie Borden
reincarnated."

"Or Calamity Jane," Caroline said and
giggled. Her shining eyes went to Doc. He
gripped her hand proudly.

April had heard that Miss Davenport was
now circulating the story that the woman of
ill repute in Doc's house was from Shanty
Town, but she didn't tell Doc and Caroline
that.

In just two days Joe had managed to
ease himself into the position of a friend. To
her surprise, April discovered that she

missed his winks, his engaging grins, his sly caresses. Since he had caught her crying, he had acted the perfect gentleman at all times and had done absolutely nothing that could be considered flirting with her.

He insisted on helping her when she moved her clothes, her ironing board, iron and toilet articles from Mrs. Poole's house to the hotel and had taken her soiled uniforms to Mrs. Maddox to wash. Not another word was said about the dreaded date with Harold Dozier Saturday night.

Joe spent considerable time with Doc, going with him when he called on some of his longtime patients and checking on the new babies. April was glad that Doc had such good friends as the Joneses, Evan Johnson and Corbin Appleby. She knew that he felt guilty about leaving the patients who depended on him, but his desire for a life with Caroline was a stronger impetus.

Fred had been more than accommodating. He had offered to sleep at the store if April wanted to stay at the house. But after all that had happened there, April couldn't get out of the house fast enough. She gratefully accepted his suggestion, however, that she leave some of her belongings in his storage room for the present.

April was seeing Fred in a different light. When she lived at the Poole house, he had almost made her skin crawl when he looked at her. Now there was a new expression in his eyes, a sadness at the loss of a sibling and his part in the accident that took her life. He had lived in the shadow of his domineering sister for a long time, and now that he was free of her, he seemed to be at a loss.

"You saved me from serious injury if not death, Fred. I'll never be able to thank you enough."

"I couldn't let her stab you with that knife. I thought it strange that she had such a dislike for you right from the start. I'm sorry you had such a terrible time. I only wish that I had realized Shirley was as . . . troubled as she was."

"We can always look back and think that we could have done things differently. But what is done is done, and all we can do is move on."

April dreaded going to Mrs. Poole's funeral but felt obliged to go because she had lived in her house. Doc, however, had no such obligation and would stay in the clinic while she was gone. Most people in town were shocked at Mrs. Poole's sudden death. Out of respect the merchants up and down the streets closed their businesses for the afternoon service.

On the day of the funeral April went to the hotel and changed from her uniform into a black, belted dress and matching turban. Julie, Joy and Joe were at the clinic when she returned and invited her to go to the services with them. Joe wore his suit, white shirt, tie and brown felt hat. He was so handsome she had to force her eyes away from him.

When they went out to the car, April stepped ahead of Julie and slid into the backseat with Joy. Joe silently helped his sister into the front seat. April avoided Joe's eyes when he went around and got behind the wheel. The church was full when they arrived. Joe ushered April and his sisters into a pew, careful to place them between him and April to dispel any notion that they were a couple.

Of the four of them Joy was the only one who sincerely grieved for Shirley Poole. She had liked the woman, liked the attention she had given to her. Although she was sorry for any death, April was sure that the majority of the people there, like herself, had come because it was expected of them or out of respect for Fred.

"Mrs. Poole would have wanted us to have the harvest party," Joy said as soon as they were outside the church. "I don't see why we can't."

"I've talked to some of the others," Julie said patiently. "We all think that it wouldn't be appropriate. You can wait and have a Christmas party."

"That's a long time off." Joy sulked all the way to the cemetery.

After the short burial service they got in line to offer their condolences to Fred, who stood beside the coffin. He acted with surprising dignity as he was greeted by the townspeople. April and Joy now waited for Julie, who had stopped to speak to someone she knew. Mrs. Maddox stopped to speak to April and lifted her brows and smiled when Hattie Davenport and her two friends, their noses in the air, sailed by.

Sarah Parker, a pleasant woman in her late twenties who had been one of the ladies to bring treats to Dr. Forbes, paused to say a few words. She had been ahead of April in line to speak to Fred, and April noticed that he held her hand for an extra length of time. She now wondered if they had ever been interested in each other. If so, Mrs. Poole would have put the kibosh on it.

April knew that Harold Dozier, standing with a group of men on the edge of the crowd, had been watching her. She avoided making eye contact with him. As soon as Miss Parker moved away, he came toward her. She glanced toward Joe and saw that he was looking over the shoulder of the man he was talking to. His eyes were on her.

"Hello, April. You look nice today. Black becomes you."

"Thank you."

"Big turnout today. I'm surprised."

"Why? Mrs. Poole lived here for a long time."

"What I mean is, she was not very . . . sociable. But folks in Fertile are very forgiving when one of their own passes away."

April's first thought when she viewed Harold's brown double-breasted suit, striped shirt with gold cuff links and brown felt hat was that he probably had fifty dollars' worth of clothes on his back. His shoes were the latest style and as shiny as a new penny. He had flashed a ring with a dark onyx stone when he put his fingers to his hat brim in greeting her. He was dressed to impress.

"She had been working with the young people at the church."

"Ah, yes, I heard that. She was a good woman. We will miss her." Harold, his ex- cuse being to avoid people who were pass- ing behind him, stepped closer. "I've been going to come by the clinic and see how you were making out after your terrible or- deal. I hear you've moved into the hotel."

"It's only temporary. I'll find lodgings soon. I'm in no hurry."

"Let me help you with that. I—"

April interrupted. "No, thanks. I'm not sure yet what I want."

"Well, I see that most everyone is leaving. May I give you a ride back to the hotel?"

"Thank you, but I have a ride."

"All right. I'll see you Saturday evening. I'm looking forward to it."

April nodded. *But I'm not.*

Joy had left her when Harold ap- proached. She had spied Sammy and hur- ried to where he stood beside a tall marker.

He had tried to dress appropriately in dark britches and a white shirt. His coat was much too large for him.

"Hi, Sammy."

" 'Lo. Your brother's watchin'."

"I don't care; let him watch. I heard what you did the other morning. It was a brave—"

"It wasn't anything." He leaned nonchalantly against the tall tombstone.

"Yes, it was. Don't be stubborn."

"All right, it was. Satisfied?"

"I thank you. The whole family thanks you. You deserve a medal."

"Well, now, ain't that somethin', a kid from Shanty Town deservin' a medal," he said in a sarcastic drawl. "I don't need any thanks from the Joneses."

"You got 'em anyway. You're acting like a clobberhead. Did your house flood?"

"Yeah, but I've 'bout got it cleaned out."

"Why haven't you been in school?"

"I had things to do."

"Like cleaning?"

"Yeah, and finding the chickens and keeping my ma sober," he said angrily.

"Why're you mad? I know your mother drinks."

"You and everybody else in town." He straightened up. "I've got to go."

"Why'd you come?"

"She was decent to me. Thought I was smart enough to be on the party committee. Why did you come?"

"I liked her even if she was a little strange at times."

"Well, you'd better be going. Here comes the *big brother,* and I don't feel like getting busted in the nose today."

"Let him come. He won't dare hit you! Don't you like me anymore, Sammy?"

"Why do you say that?"

"You're not very friendly, and I have to pull every word out of you," she whispered as Joe came up beside her.

"Hi, Sammy. How did you find things at home? Did you get moved back in all right?"

"Yeah."

"Did you find your livestock?"

"Didn't have anything but a few skinny chickens."

"We got to go, mutt," Joe said to Joy and tugged on her arm. "April and Julie are already in the car. See you around, Sammy."

"Bye, Sammy. Will you be in school to-morrow?"

"Maybe."

Sammy watched Joy and Joe walk toward the car. Joe had his arm over her shoulder. It wouldn't be long now before they would turn her against him. He had been thinking for a while now that he was wasting his time staying here, going to school, hoping he could amount to some-thing. What he'd better do was hop a train, go to California and get a job picking peaches or oranges or something.

He might be lucky enough to get in the movies and get rich. Now, wouldn't that just chap the folks around here? He'd come back to this one-horse town and thumb his nose at everyone in it but Joy. If she wasn't married, he'd take her away with him.

Yes, that's what he'd do as soon as his pa came back. He'd hop a train out of here. There was nothing for him here but the con-tempt of folks because he was the son of a drunk from Shanty Town.

Sammy waited until most everyone had left before he approached Fred.

"Sorry." It was all he managed to say. But

in saying it he felt that he had repaid Mrs. Poole a little bit for her kindnesses to him.

Julie didn't mention to Joy that she had seen her talking to Sammy. But she told Evan that night as he held her tightly in his arms. Her head was on his shoulder. He pulled her thigh up across his and eased his legs between hers.

"She's still got a crush on him. I don't know what to do about it."

"She'll get over it."

"I'm not sure. She's very protective of him and proud that he tackled the man that shot Jack."

"All the Joneses root for the underdog. It's their nature."

"I don't understand the attraction."

"Some people might wonder what you see in me," he teased and pulled her thigh up over his arousal and held it there.

"Be serious. You know I married you because you're so ugly I was afraid no other woman would have you, and I did love your dear mother."

"And I played on your sympathy because I was determined to have the sweetest woman in ten counties."

"Only ten?"

"Maybe eleven."

After several long kisses Evan said, "Doc really loves that girl. I hate to see him go, but I understand. I'd take you and run if I couldn't live with you here."

"Corbin knows, doesn't he?"

"Yes, and Joe and Jack. April, of course. Joe is taking them to the train in Kansas City on Saturday. Doc has boxed up some things he wants Joe to ship to him later on when he's settled."

"I've not met Caroline, but Joe says you can't tell she has colored blood. He said she was a beauty and seemed to be well educated. I guess her mother was known to be colored. Her father, a college professor, met her back East and came here thinking they could live peacefully together."

"He should have known better than to bring her to Missouri," Evan said. "But like most Easterners, he probably thought Missouri was wild and unsettled and that Indians were running around all over the place."

"Does Doc have a destination in mind?"

"He's mentioned going to Canada or Mexico, but he's going to Tennessee first to see one of his sisters. He wanted to give

Joe his car, but Joe wouldn't accept it without paying for it." Evan chuckled. "Joe didn't want to ask Wally down at the filling station what it was worth, so he asked me. He doesn't want to take out a loan, but as soon as he gets the money, he'll send it to Doc."

"Joe's unhappy right now."

"How do you know that, mother hen? He seemed all right to me."

"He's in love with April. I have the sense that he's feeling inferior. She's got a good job, and he's struggling to make it with mortgaged land and a bull."

"Not Joe. He's the most confident fellow I know."

"Something happened the night the river came up. He doesn't tease her, hardly even looks at her. Not at all like he treated her the day they came out here. He was very careful today at the funeral to keep his distance. That's not like him."

"Now that Jack has made up with Ruby and is getting married, you want Joe to have a girl. Next it will be Jason and Joy. How about Evan?" he whispered against her lips. "Give him some attention. He wants a girl, too."

"He's got a girl and he gets plenty of attention."

"Right now I want my wife before Nancy wakes up and demands her attention." He moved her thigh back and forth over his erection, sought her lips and kissed her deeply. "I love you, Mrs. Johnson. Have I ever told you that?" He reached for the hem of her nightgown.

"Only about a million times, but it isn't enough. I love you, too; and if you'll help me get out of this thing, I'll show you."

Chapter 29

"I'm leaving you my b-basic medical books, April. Another doctor will h-have his own, and Joe can s-send mine to me later on." Doc had been carefully boxing the instruments that he would take with him.

For the past two days April had carried a notebook and pencil and tried to soak up every bit of information Doc gave her.

"I've seen you in action. You're b-better than you think you are," he said when she expressed doubt about being able to take a culture to send to a laboratory for testing.

"I'm afraid, Doc, not about an emergency—I've had training for that; but something like a typhoid or whooping cough that I won't know how to handle."

"All you can do is the b-best you can. The doctor in Mason w-will know you are here alone. Call him. He'll t-tell you what to do until he gets here."

They'd had only the usual run of patients since the flood. Doc had made several trips to Shanty Town and reported that the folks had taken his advice and were boiling the water they used. There were no reports of fever aside from the usual flu symptoms.

Joe had come in for a few hours every day. He was helping his father with chores on the farm. Next week they would start picking corn, and he would have even less free time. He never tried to engage April in personal conversation, and she began to wonder if he had found someone else he was interested in. She tried not to feel hurt. It was what she had expected, wasn't it?

On Friday night, the last night he and Caroline would be there, Doc invited Joe and April to supper. Caroline had cooked a meal of baked chicken and dressing, gravy and rice. April hadn't been aware that Joe would be there until after she had been to the hotel to change out of her uniform.

Her face reddened when Doc opened the connecting door from the clinic and she saw Joe sitting on the couch. He was wearing his tan twill britches and blue collarless shirt. She was glad that she hadn't dressed up too much, but wore a plain blue skirt and blouse with a red sash.

"Something smells delicious."

"Hello, April," Caroline called from the kitchen.

After nodding to Doc and Joe, April went to where Caroline was scooping dressing into a bowl.

"Here. Let me do that." April took over the task, and Caroline placed the chicken on a platter.

It seemed to April that she had known the girl longer than a week. They had become fast friends in a very short time. She was smart and had far more general education than most people April knew. Most important, Caroline was one of the nicest, most compassionate people April had ever met. There didn't seem to be anything she couldn't do, from cooking a superb meal to making her own clothes, crocheting, knitting, cutting hair. She was going to be a wonderful helpmate for Doc.

On top of all that, she loved him to distraction.

On impulse April hugged her. "I wish you were going to be near so we could be friends. But you'll be happier away from here."

"Distance can't keep us from being friends, April. Maybe someday you and Joe can visit us."

"If I'm ever able to visit you, it will not be with Joe."

"You would come and leave him behind?"

"We'll not be together. Joe isn't that kind of man. He likes to play the field."

"Play the field?"

"He flirts with all women. Goes from one to the other. He's not great on commitment."

"Todd doesn't think so. He thinks Joe's in love with you."

April's heart lurched on hearing the words; then her common sense took over. Regarding women, men seldom see the faults of their good male friends.

"Doc is one of the smartest men I know, but he's wrong in this case. Shall I take this bowl to the table?"

April was able to project a cheery mood throughout the evening. Caroline and Doc were excited, and she was determined not to put a damper on their excitement. Their plan was to load the car and leave before dawn. Joe was driving them to Kansas City to catch a train that would take them to Harpersville, Tennessee. Doc would send his sister a wire before boarding the train.

"Move into the house t-tomorrow, April. I'll call Diane at the telephone office and tell her that I've b-been called away and that you w-will be here to take any emergency calls." Doc chuckled. "Diane will s-spread the word so folks won't think I just d-disappeared in the river."

"The whole town will miss you, Doc," Joe said. "You have been an important part of this town and our family for a long time."

"I appreciate that. I'll always have fond m-memories of Fertile. I made m-many good and loyal f-friends. And it was h-here that I met the love of my life." He brought Caroline's hand to his lips.

The leave-taking was especially painful for April. She hugged Caroline and then Doc, trying bravely to keep the tears from overflowing.

"I wish the two of you a long and happy life. Don't worry about things here, Doc. Take care of each other and . . . be happy." April turned and bolted out the door.

She reached the steps on the porch,

paused and let the tears roll down her cheeks. They blinded her eyes, and she was grateful for the hand that came suddenly to her elbow to guide her down the steps. Joe didn't say a word until they were out on the street.

"You'll be all right. You'll do just fine."

"I'm not crying for *myself,* you ninny." She jerked her elbow from his grasp. "I know I'll be all right. I'll be just fine. I'm always just fine. No matter what happens, I'm just fine. Knock old April down, and, like a rubber ball, she bounces right up . . . just fine." Her heels clicked on the sidewalk as the words came spewing out. "Ask anyone, and they'll tell you that you can put your foot on her neck, but she'll get up somehow. You can drag her through the mud, and she'll come out clean as a whistle. She's a rebounder and doesn't need any help from the town jelly bean. You can take your sweet talk somewhere else."

His gaze flicked to her set, defiant face. "That was quite a tirade. Have you finished?"

She refused to answer him. They walked side by side past the barbershop, the mercantile and the post office. Outside the hotel, Joe took her arm to keep her from mounting the steps.

"I won't be back until late tomorrow night. If you need any help, call Corbin. He knows we are leaving in the morning."

"I don't think I'll need any help."

"You never know. Corbin's here, if you do. Are you taking everything over to Doc's in the morning?"

"If I leave anything here, I'll have to pay a day's rent. I'll drive my car over so I'll not have to walk through town carrying my ironing board."

"Doc told me what happened the morning Mrs. Poole died. I almost had a heart attack when he told me how close you came to being stabbed in the back with a butcher knife."

"But it didn't happen, thanks to Fred," she said with a shrug.

"I'd thank him, but I don't want to let him know that Doc told me his sister tried to stab you. Doc wants me to keep an eye on you."

"Good of him, but I don't need you to keep an eye on me."

"I'll come by Doc's as soon as I get back tomorrow night."

"I might not be there. I have a date."

"Oh, yes. I'd forgotten." It was evident that he hadn't. "Isn't it with Harold Dozier, the big-shot lawyer, who struts around town with a dainty little handkerchief stuffed in his breast pocket? I've often wondered if he ever blows his nose on it." He didn't even try to keep the sneer out of his voice.

"Why don't you ask him?"

"I just might do that."

"Well, don't do it tomorrow night. We'll not be back until late."

"Where are you going?"

"We've not decided yet. Maybe to Mason. Harold said something about St. Joe."

"St. Joe is a good sixty miles from here. You've no business going that far with a man you hardly—"

"And you've no business telling me what to do."

Joe looked at her mutinous face, then jerked her around to the side of the hotel where they wouldn't be seen by anyone on the street.

"You go to St. Joe with Harold Dozier, and you'll end up in a hotel room. Is that what you want?"

"Maybe," she said sassily.

"Damn you." He put his hand to the back of her head, grasped a handful of hair and tilted her face up to his. "I ought to kiss you senseless."

"Just try it and I'll bite you!"

"It might be worth it."

"Better yet, I'll scream rape!"

He laughed at that. She could feel the movement of his chest against the breasts crushed against him.

"Laugh, you jackass. And that's what you are. A big, fat jackass."

"I'm not fat. Julie is worried because I'm losing weight." He was grinning now: the slow, sweet grin she hadn't seen in a week. It angered her that she loved that grin and had missed it. It made her snap at him.

"I don't care if you're skinny as a bean-pole. You're still a jackass."

"Ah, honey." He lowered his head until his forehead rested on hers. "I've missed you."

"You've seen me every day."

"Yes, I have, and I could hardly keep my hands off you."

"That's a good line. Do you mind if I use it sometime?"

"Not as long as you're talking to me."

He bent his head and kissed her gently,

softly. She gave a high moan, reacting with panic.

"No! I don't want this."

"Yes, you do. You want it as much as I do." There was harshness in his voice.

"That's not true!"

His mouth dipped and covered hers with a hunger that silenced her, forcing her lips to open beneath his own. One hand moved to hold her neck in a viselike grip, tilting her head so she could not escape from his kisses.

All her resolve crumbled. She abandoned thought of everything but the sensation of being close to him and of the flurry of excitement his lips were arousing in her.

They strained together, hearts beating wildly, and kissed as lovers long separated. His hand roamed restlessly from her shoulders to her breasts. He began to tremble, and his kiss became deep, deeper, until they both were dazed and breathless.

"Don't do this to me," she gasped when he lifted his head.

"If you don't want it, why did you kiss me?"

"I . . . didn't . . ."

"You did. You know damn good and well

you did. Be honest with yourself. You liked it as much as I did." He was shaking, as if with a chill, breathing roughly, as if he had just completed a long run.

She stared at him, and he stared back as if he were not looking at her at all, but at something that suddenly made him go pale and haggard. She jerked away from him. Their eyes did battle for a space of a dozen heartbeats, then, dragging her back against him, he lowered his head and fastened his lips to hers again, kissing her bitterly, cru-elly—hard, unloving kisses that took the breath from her.

She struggled without success and finally surrendered to his superior strength. At last he lifted his head. His arms held her so tightly she thought she would faint, and her blood pounded in her temples. Then dismay crept into her mind when she realized how easily he could take over her life.

"You can't stand to have one get away," she accused hatefully. "It's a blow to your ego to have the new girl in town not want you." Sparks of anger glittered in her eyes.

Joe expelled a heavy breath, moved his hands down her arms and held tightly to her wrists. They stood like that for a long moment, his attention riveted to her anguished face.

"My God but you are blind . . . and stupid. You're the only person in the world I've cared about more than my family."

"No!" She took a deep breath and braced her shoulders defensively. She had gained a measure of control, and although her eyes were defiant, her mouth taut, there was an air of unconscious dignity about her poised head. "You only want a conquest. I won't let you hurt me." The words came out quietly.

She pulled her hands free and walked away from him, to round the corner and go up the steps and into the hotel lobby. The clerk saw her coming and slapped the key to her room on the counter. She grabbed it and without a word of thanks hurried up the stairs to her room.

April leaned against the closed door. Her head was pounding. She was unable to get her scattered thoughts together. She was confused, tired, and wanted desperately to have the hurt go away. It was as if her heart had been pounded to a pulp and her mangled emotions heaped on top. She felt limp and drab as a pile of wet laundry. She longed for bed but knew that it would be a long time before sleep would give rest to her mind.

April awakened feeling the heavy responsibility of being the only medical person in town. The mirror showed shadows beneath her eyes put there by a nearly sleepless night. She had been kept awake not only with thoughts of the clinic but with Joe's strange actions. She had tossed for hours recalling every word he had said. Some of them made absolutely no sense at all, especially the statement that he cared for her. Ha! He had a fine way of showing it.

When she left to get her car, she was surprised to see it parked in front of the hotel and decided that Joe must have moved it there last night or early this morning. She made several trips from the hotel room to her car before she was ready to leave. She placed the key to her room on the counter and asked for her bill.

"I trust that your stay here with us was pleasant." The desk clerk was a young man she had not seen before. "You're Miss Asbury, Dr. Forbes's nurse. My name is Dan Newbury. This is my first day on the job."

"It's nice to meet you." April took a bill from her purse. "Are you from here in Fertile?"

"No. I came from St. Joseph. The owner recalled the night clerk here and sent me over. I worked in his hotels in St. Joe."

"The night clerk was the owner's son?"

"Nephew."

"Welcome to Fertile, Dan. I hope you like it here."

"Thank you. I'm sure I will. I like being in a small town."

I thought I did, too, April said to herself on the way to the car. *Now I'm not so sure.*

At the clinic she opened the connecting door and stood in the middle of the room. It seemed so lonely. She wanted to cry but shook herself and opened the front door so she could unload her car. Later she stood at the counter in the kitchen and looked out the window while the coffee was perking.

Across the alley and down two houses was the tall two-story house where Miss Davenport lived. From its upstairs windows a person could see the back of this house as well as into the kitchen window. The busybody had kept track of what was going on here, probably with a spyglass. April pulled down the window shade until there wasn't even a crack of light shining through.

She was pouring a cup of coffee when the phone rang. Carrying the cup, she went into the clinic to answer it.

"This is Flora. Diane said Dr. Forbes is going to be away for a while. I'm surprised. Will someone be there to answer the phone at night?"

"I'll be here. Dr. Forbes went to visit his family in Tennessee."

"Diane said he'd been here in Fertile for a long time."

"Almost eleven years, I guess."

"We all feel so lucky to have you. I'm just surprised he left you here to run the office alone."

"I'm not alone. There are consulting doctors over in Mason."

"Well, some of us think it strange he just went on a vacation without saying anything about it."

And you're surprised. April was beginning to be annoyed. Then she was struck by an idea: a way to pay back a vicious, gossiping woman, and Flora was the perfect vehicle to carry the message.

"It wasn't exactly a vacation, Flora. I suppose I might as well tell you this. It's no secret. The doctor felt he had to leave town in order to keep his sanity. One of the ladies in town had chased him to the point where it was driving him to distraction. You might say she has run him out of town . . . for a while."

"Really? What in the world did she do?"

"Well . . . for one thing, she spied on him, front door and back. She even came into the clinic and tried to break into his private rooms through the connecting door because she thought he had a woman in there. She'd been after him for several years—bringing him cakes and pies—and even wanted him to fire me because she thought *I* was after him. Can you imagine?"

"For heaven's sake." Flora appeared to be flabbergasted at the news.

"He finally had to tell her that he wasn't interested in her and had absolutely no intention of making her his wife. Well . . . you know what happens when a woman is scorned. She spread all kinds of gossip about the poor man. He was so miserable he had to get away."

"Can you beat that? I know just who you're talking about. Now we know who to thank for running our doctor out of town."

"Maybe I shouldn't have told you this, but I didn't want you or anyone else to think that Dr. Forbes deserted his patients to go on a vacation without giving notice. The man was at his wits' end."

"You've sure set me straight. If you don't mind, I'll explain to anyone who I hear is wondering why the doctor left town."

"I don't mind, Flora. Everything I said is absolutely the truth." April crossed her fingers. *Almost the truth,* she said under her breath.

"Will Dr. Forbes be back?"

"I'm not sure. But Dr. Forbes is a very caring man and has provided medical care for the people in Fertile. A doctor in Mason will be coming over a day or two a week. I'll be staying here in Doc's house for the time being. In case of an emergency you can reach me here day or night."

April smiled after she had hung up.

There, Miss Hattie Davenport. Two can

play at your game. Rumor goes through Fertile with the speed of a cat with its tail on fire. Doc has enough friends in this town that you'll feel the consequences of your malicious actions.

Chapter 30

The news spread quickly that Dr. Forbes was out of town. No one appeared to be in a panic, only curious, because it had been quite a few years since he'd left town for any length of time. April answered questions, assured the ones who asked that a doctor would come from Mason on Tuesdays and Fridays and started an appointment list. Several of Doc's patients inquired about prescriptions. She referred them to Mr. Adler, the druggist.

She was able to "confess" to several ladies the "real" reason the doctor left town, telling the same story she had told Flora on the telephone. She never named names but gave out enough hints that the ladies knew the culprit could be none other that Miss Davenport. One of the women in her Sewing

Circle at church said that she never believed the stories the woman told about the doctor.

April had never been a part of such a scandalous thing as starting a rumor before, but she didn't feel the least bit guilty about it. Hattie Davenport deserved some punishment for the trouble she had caused Doc.

Julie Johnson came by shortly after noon. She had Joy and Sylvia Taylor, Thad's sister, with her. The girls were going to the Saturday matinee.

"When I was young, I'd go to the Saturday matinees to see the Little Rascals. I loved them. Still do." April smiled, remembering hurrying through her Saturday morning chores and then coaxing the dime from her grandpa. He always teased and threatened not to give it to her; but when he did, he usually gave her extra for popcorn.

"Today it's *Treasure Island*, with Wallace Beery and Jackie Cooper," Julie said. "Joy has read the book a couple of times. I hope she's not disappointed in the movie."

"How is Jack? Doc said he should be able to be up for a short time each day starting Monday."

"He's fine now. Ruby will be with him all

day today and tomorrow. He loves it." Julie laughed.

"He told me they are getting married at Christmas."

"Isn't it wonderful?" Julie's pretty face was wreathed in smiles. "I'm so happy for both of them. They've loved each other all their lives; but sometimes they didn't know it, and I was afraid they would kill each other before they made up."

"The rocky road of love." April was unaware of the wistful tone in her voice.

"What time was Doc's train leaving?"

April looked at her watch. "About now, I think. It's one of the reasons why they left so early."

"Then Joe won't be back until late."

"I expect not."

"I'll miss Doc. He's been a part of our lives for a long time. Joe thinks the world of him."

April reached for the phone when it rang, glad for the interruption. She didn't want to talk about Joe with his sister. It was Mrs. Colson, who had heard that Dr. Forbes had left town, and was worried she'd not be able to get paregoric for baby Lucille.

"Don't worry, Mrs. Colson. The doctor left

instructions for me to refill the paregoric one more time. He seemed to think Lucille should be weaned sometime soon. He said you could start giving her a little oatmeal and a few mashed vegetables such as potatoes and carrots."

"She's starting to drink milk out of a cup. She does pretty good but she still wants to nurse."

"Come in when you need the refill. The doctor said there was no charge. How's Emery?"

"Oh, he's fine. He keeps asking when we are going to see the pretty woman again."

"For that he might get two candy sticks." April found herself smiling when she hung up the phone. That one was going to be a charmer like Joe. She had tried to keep her thoughts away from Joe all day, but at times he just popped into her mind as if it were his right to be there.

She was glad to be busy, but each time the door opened, her heart picked up speed and her throat became dry. Her greatest fear was that someone would come in with a problem she couldn't handle.

In the middle of the afternoon she came from the back room to find Harold Dozier standing in front of her desk holding his hat in his hand. Today he wore a brown pin-striped suit and looked as if he had just come from a meeting with the governor.

"Is it true that Dr. Forbes has gone to Tennessee and left the town without a doctor?"

"It's true that he's gone to Tennessee, but he hasn't left the town without a doctor. A doctor will come from Mason two days a week."

"That's a fine kettle of fish. People can only get sick two days a week?" His tone of voice irritated her, and she answered him sharply.

"Many communities larger than Fertile have been without a doctor for years, and patients have to travel fifty miles to see one. You've been lucky to have had one right here in town this long."

Don't you dare say a word against Doc, you puffed-up horse's patoot.

Her tone of voice warned him that he was on thin ice. He immediately started to backpedal.

"I understand that even a doctor needs a vacation once in a while. He's been good for the town. We'll miss him."

"He is an excellent doctor who cares about his patients."

He was silent, then said, "I stopped by to find out if you were still at the hotel."

"No. I'll be staying here for a while."

"I'll pick you up at seven. Is that all right?"

"Fine. But I can't leave town now that the doctor is away."

"Oh? I'd planned for us to go to Mason, have dinner and maybe take a drive over to Walnut Grove and on to Calmar. There will be a beautiful harvest moon tonight. Perfect for a drive."

"I'm sorry if you're disappointed."

"There isn't really a decent place to take a lady to dinner here in Fertile. We could run over to Mason."

"What's wrong with Bergstrom's?"

He gave her a blank stare. "I could have something catered at my place."

"I suppose you could, but don't expect to have my company while you eat it."

"I guess you're right. This isn't Kansas City. Bergstrom's it is, then. See you at seven."

April gritted her teeth in frustration and asked herself why she had ever consented to go out with that dressed-up dandy. She

immediately forgot about him and the
evening ahead when a woman came in followed by a man carrying a crying child.

"We need to see the doctor."

"The doctor has been called away. What
seems to be the matter?"

"He's not here? Where is he? When will
he be back?"

"He went to Tennessee." April had to
speak loudly in order to be heard over the
child's screams. "What seems to be the
matter?"

"Where's the nearest doctor?" The man's
weather-roughened face was tight with anxiety.

"Mason."

"We'll take her there."

"Let me look at her. There may be something I can do to give her some relief."

"It would take hours to get to Mason in
the wagon, Roy."

"I'll get a car . . . somehow." He shifted
the child, a girl of about four years, to the
woman and started for the door.

"Wait. She's hurting. Let me see if I can
help," said April.

"You're not a doctor. We're just wasting
time."

"I'm not a doctor, but I've been a doctor's helper for years. Your child is suffering. I may be able to help her. If I can't, I'll lend you my car to take her to Mason."

"Let her, Roy. I can't stand to see my baby like this."

The father took the child back in his arms and followed April into the surgery. He kissed the little girl repeatedly and murmured, "There, there, puddin' pie . . ."

As soon as he placed the child on the table, she rolled to her side and drew her knees up to her chest.

"How long has she been like this?"

"Since the middle of the morning."

April pulled the child's dress up, unbuttoned her underwear from her shirtwaist and pulled her panties down. Her hand moved over the girl's stomach. It was hard as a rock. She refused to straighten her legs.

"When was her last bowel movement?"

"I don't know. She takes care of that herself." The woman's worried eyes sought her husband. "Do you remember seeing her go to the potty or squat in the yard?"

He shook his head.

"I think she's constipated," April said. "If we don't get her bowels to move, she could get a locked bowel, and that is serious. I'll put some warm oil up her rectum and see if we can get a movement."

April looked at both parents to see if they objected. When they said nothing, she filled a pan with hot water and set the bottle of mineral oil down in it. While the oil was warming she scrubbed her hands, then prepared the table by slipping a couple of folded towels under the child.

"What is her name?"

"Connie. Connie Harvey. We live about five miles north." Mrs. Harvey stood with her hand on her husband's shoulder. He had squatted down to murmur to the little girl. "She's a daddy's girl," Mrs. Harvey explained.

April brought out a glass tube with a rubber ball on the end and greased it with Vaseline. She filled the cylinder with the warm oil and inserted it into the screaming child's rectum. Slowly she released the oil.

"Hold your hand firmly against her lower abdomen and gently massage it." After several minutes, April set a granite chamber pot on the floor.

"Lift her onto it," she instructed. "If we can get a little out, we can give her an enema of warm soda water."

Mr. Harvey was on his knees holding the child—telling her that she was Daddy's big girl. The love the big gruff man had for his child was evident. April couldn't help but think of her own childhood and what she'd missed by not having a father to love her.

"I think she did a little," the man said after a while.

"Good."

With the help of Mrs. Harvey, April gave Connie two light soda water enemas. After the last one her little stomach was soft and she had stopped crying.

"Feeling better, puddin'?" Mrs. Harvey asked.

"See if this will make you forget about that old stomachache." April gave her a stick of candy.

"What do you say to the lady?"

"Thank you."

"If the doctor were here, he would recommend that you stop giving her a lot of bread or biscuits for a while. Get her to eat things that won't pack in her bowels, like fruits and vegetables. Dried apples and peaches are good. And watch her stool to be sure she has a bowel movement, if not every day, every other day."

"I don't know how to thank you. We were so scared."

"I'm sure you were. It upsets parents to see their children suffer."

"I don't know how we're going to pay, but we will," Mr. Harvey said when they were ready to leave. "Put it down on the books, and I'll be back."

"It will be a dollar, Mr. Harvey. Pay when you can."

"Thank you, ma'am, and I'm sorry I was sort of owly before."

"I understand. Bye, Connie. Come back and see me sometime when you're not sick."

After the Harveys had left, April entered the office call in the ledger with notes about Connie and the treatment she had given her. The next half hour was spent in putting the surgery back in order and ready for another patient. With that done, she sank wearily down in her chair and looked at her watch.

I would gladly give my eyeteeth not to have to go out with Harold.

There was nothing fancy about Bergstrom's restaurant. It was family-operated. Mrs. Bergstrom was the cook with the help of her daughter-in-law. Her daughters were waitresses, her son and husband scurried around removing dishes and seating the customers. Business was good on Saturday night.

April and Harold were the center of attention when they walked in. He spoke to several people only after they had spoken to him. April saw George Belmont and waved to him, then paused to speak to Fred, who sat alone at a table.

"Hello, Fred. How are you?"

Fred immediately got to his feet. "I'm doing all right. You? I hear Doc had to leave suddenly."

"Yes, he had to go to Tennessee." April felt Harold tug on her arm. "I'll get the rest of my things out of your house in a few days."

"No hurry."

April wanted to jerk her elbow from

Harold's grasp, but she did the polite thing and moved away with him.

Harold was unhappy about the table where they were seated because it was in the middle of the room. He apologized and said the next time they would dine at the Bistro in Mason. April didn't mention to him that there would be no next time.

The meal of meat loaf and scalloped potatoes was delicious, and April was hungry. She ate with relish, while Harold moved the food around on his plate as if he expected to find a worm. April thought the evening would never end.

When they left the restaurant, Harold asked her if she would like to go to the picture show.

"I'd rather not, Harold. This was my first day without Doc, and I'm really exhausted."

"Then we'll just ride around for a while and get acquainted. It's a pretty drive along the river road after you get past Shanty Town. Fertile would be a nice little community if not for the undesirables who live along the river. But I guess there must be a place for the shiftless and the ne'er-do-wells. It's the same in most towns."

"Why do you say that? I've met some

really nice people who live down there. Not all of them live there by choice. They're doing the best they can to get along."

"They're a bunch of ignorant troublemakers. The fools went down to Calmar to blow up the rock pile. It was stupid of them to try to take the law in their own hands. Look what one of them did to Jack Jones. Shot him for no good reason at all."

"You can't blame a whole community for the actions of one man."

"You know the old saying that birds of a feather flock together."

"That may be true about birds, but not necessarily about people." He had opened his mouth to argue when she said, "Harold, I'd really rather go home, if you don't mind."

"I mind, but if that's what you want." He drove slowly around the block and stopped in front of the clinic. Before she could get out, he placed his hand on her arm. "Sit with me for a while. It isn't every day I have the prettiest girl in town all to myself."

"Are you sure you don't need glasses?"

"You are beautiful. Haven't you looked in a mirror lately?"

"That's very nice to hear even if it's not true."

"The first time I saw you, I knew that you were the girl for me." He slid over in the seat and let his arm rest on the back behind her shoulders.

"You don't really know me, Harold."

"I know enough. You're pretty; you're smart; you stand head and shoulders above the yokels in this town." His hand had dropped to her shoulder and was pulling her toward him.

She resisted. "I don't consider the people here yokels."

"Compared to you, they are." He pulled her against him and bent his head to kiss her.

"Hey, wait a minute." She pushed against his chest but was no match for his strength.

"I've been looking forward to this for weeks." His hand grasped the back of her head, and his mouth smashed down on hers. His lips were hard, urgent. She tried to turn her head, but it was held in a vise. "Just as sweet as I thought you'd be."

"Let me . . . go!"

His mouth was on hers again, his tongue inside her lips against her clenched teeth. She moved her head from side to side in an attempt to dislodge him, but he was relentless. Finally he lifted his head.

"What's the matter with you?" he growled. "You're a nurse. You've seen plenty of naked men and know what they need when they're with a woman. Here, feel this." His hand forced hers to the erection between his spread legs. "You'll not be disappointed in that. Bet it's bigger than Doc's."

"You're disgusting. Let me go!"

He laughed. "You don't need to put on an act with me. I know you want it. I've lived in the city and know that nurses, pretty nurses, hand it out every day, if not to doctors, to their bed patients."

"That's not true!"

"Come on, now. You don't have to put on an act with me."

"If you don't let me go . . . I'll hurt you!"

He chuckled. "I could have a different woman in my bed every night. And I chose you for tonight."

His mouth moved across her cheek to hers and clamped over it. It was wet . . . sickening. April forced herself to relax for a few seconds, then knotted her fist and brought it down hard on his crotch.

"Ohhh!" he yelled and grabbed his member. The instant she was free of his arms, she was out of the car. "Bitch!" he yelled.

"That should tell you how much I *want* it, you small-town billy goat. You come around me again and I'll fix you good." She ran up the steps, unlocked her door, entered and slammed it shut.

She sagged against the door and rubbed the back of her hand across her mouth in an attempt to wipe away the taste of his slobbery kisses.

Chapter 31

April moved through the darkened house to the bedroom. Mechanically she unbuttoned her dress and changed into the nightgown she had thrown across the bed before she left the house to go to dinner with Harold. She desperately wanted to forget the whole sordid event, the hateful things he had said, the groping, his slobbery mouth . . .

She sank down on the edge of the bed. Hot tears burst from between her thick lashes. She could no longer hold them back, though she strained every muscle with the effort. She felt as if she were standing on the edge of a precipice, and if she moved, she would topple into oblivion.

It was too much to hold inside. Huge racking sobs came from deep within her and disrupted the silence of the dark room.

She couldn't have choked them down had her life depended on it.

She had been alone since her grandmother died, but she had never felt such overwhelming loneliness as she did now. It was as if she were entirely alone in the world without another human being to care if she lived or died. She collapsed back on the bed and cried because she faced a long, loveless, desolate future. The one person she had thought was right for her turned out to be not so right, after all. She vowed to never expose herself to the hurt again.

"What will I do in the years ahead?" she whispered into a silence that gave no answer.

Holding her hands to her face, she allowed herself a moment of self-pity. She felt as if she had been battered by a terrific storm, her insides torn apart with hurt. The family she had longed for was as remote as the moon.

She cried until her pillow was wet with her tears, then, exhausted, she dozed. She nodded off several times only to awaken again and find herself still crying. Later, much later, she awakened once more, but this time it was different.

Someone was kneeling beside the bed, murmuring endearments, wiping the tears from her cheeks with a warm finger.

"Don't be scared. It's me. Joe." The soothing, familiar voice brought on fresh tears.

"Why . . . are you here?"

"Why are you crying?"

"I don't . . . know," she sobbed.

When she was lifted and held close, she clasped her arms tightly around him. There was no question of her rejecting him. He was all that was dear and familiar to her, and he had cared enough to come. She burrowed her face into his shoulder, and soon it was wet with her tears.

"Shhh . . . don't cry. Hush, little sweetheart . . ."

"I'm so tired of being . . . alone."

"You're not alone, darlin'. I'm here. I'll always be here if you want me."

His fingers played lightly with the straggling wisps of hair that stuck to her cheek, then he caressed the nape of her neck. Soon the sobs that shook her were replaced with faint grieving moans. She felt drained and empty.

"Why are you here? How did you get in?"

"I'm here because I had to make sure you were all right. I got in with the key Doc gave me."

"I didn't hear you knock."

"I didn't. I was going to tiptoe in and see if you were all right, then leave. I couldn't leave when I heard you crying."

His gentle hands held her and rocked her as if she were a small child. She cried until she had no more tears and lay limp and lifeless against him.

"I'm glad you came," she whispered.

"Did something happen today to upset you?" His voice was close to her ear.

"Not really. I just don't know if I can handle this job. It's too big."

"Doc had enough faith in you to leave you to take care of his patients. He said you were the best nurse he'd ever known. And you had the best possible references from the hospital in Kansas City."

"But . . . what if I make a mistake?"

"It wouldn't be intentional. You'll do the best you can do, sweetheart. It's all anyone can do." He looped the hair behind her ear.

"I know how you feel, honey." His voice was the merest whisper. His thumb made a swipe beneath her eyes and wiped away the wetness there.

"You can't know how I feel. You've got a wonderful family who love you. You'll never be alone. They'll stay by you through thick and thin."

"You'll never be alone if you'll let me take care of you." His lips moved lovingly across her face.

"I . . . can't."

"You know that I have deep feelings for you. I think I've made it plain enough." His voice lowered into a husky, urgent whisper. "Is it that . . . you could never care for me the way I want you to?"

She wasn't dreaming this conversation, because she could feel his breath, cool on her wet face.

"I don't want to love you," she blurted. "You'll get tired of me and . . . go chasing around."

"Why do you think I will do that? Have I given you a reason to think I would be unfaithful to you?"

"You don't have to give a reason. You're

handsome, you flirt; you like women. They chase after you. It's enough."

"I don't understand. I'm glad you think I'm handsome. I think you're beautiful. But as for the rest of it . . ."

"My father was a handsome man. He liked to flirt and he liked women, lots of women. He flitted in and out of our lives when he was between women. He broke my mother's heart."

"And . . . yours," Joe added sorrowfully. "I'm sorry, sweetheart. I can only say that I'm not like your father. I've fallen head over heels in love with you, and if you'll trust me, I swear that I'll never betray that trust." His cheek was pressed tightly to hers as he whispered in her ear. "I've never been so miserable in all my life knowing that you were going out with Harold Dozier, a man who could give you everything, while I have only a heart full of love to offer you."

"If you loved me, why have you been so cold for the past week?" She pulled back so she could see his shadowy face. "You acted as if I was a . . . just a friend of Doc's."

"Not when I kissed you outside the hotel. When I heard that you were going out with Harold after the kisses we had shared, I thought you had been just playing around with the farmer who didn't even have a car to take you on a date. Then Doc told me that you'd never take me seriously. He said that you thought I was a flirt and a ladies' man. I was trying to reform so you'd see me differently." He pulled her back into his arms and held her tightly. "Dear Lord, it hurt."

"I just said that I'd go with Harold on the spur of the moment. I didn't want you to think I was one of the women chasing after you."

"Then tonight . . . knowing that you were with him . . . was like a knife in my heart. I wanted to kill him."

"So did I. I don't like him . . . at all."

"He can give you much more than I can."

"I don't care if he's rich as a king."

"Are you willing to take a chance on me?"

For an answer she moved her hand up to the back of his head and tugged.

"Joe . . ." His name came from her lips even as she was searching for his. "Kiss me . . . please . . ."

His lips, warm and gentle, explored her mouth, her eyes, her throat. She could feel his fingers on the rounded flesh of her breast, fondling the stiff peaks.

"Yes! Oh, yes." Her lips, soft and eager, sought his that were firm yet gentle, hardening with passion only at the insistence of hers. Something deep within her was stirring, bringing an ache to the nether regions between her legs. She moved restlessly, an unfamiliar hunger gnawing at her relentlessly.

"I've been in hell all day. I had to come—"

"You love me? You're not just saying that?"

"If love means thinking about you every minute of the day, wanting to be with you, worrying about you, scared to death that you'll see me as just an ignorant yokel, thinking I'll die if you don't love me back . . . then I love you, my sweet girl."

"Ah . . . Joe . . ." A sudden flood of tenderness overwhelmed her, and she turned her face to his and kissed his lips with sweet, lingering softness.

His lips covered hers, murmuring between kisses. "Tell me. Tell me what I'm dying to hear you say."

"I love you. Oh, I do. I was sure that you knew how I felt about you." The driving force of her feeling was taking her beyond reason, beyond herself and into a new dimension.

His mouth was sweet, his cheeks pleasantly rough against her face. Warm lips became more demanding, and long fingers entwined her tousled hair. His tongue circled her lips, coaxing them to open, and then darted inside to tickle every crevice of her mouth. Her skin tingled, her heart pounded in rhythm with his.

"I love you, Joe. Oh, I do love you." The taste of him, the feel of him, was so wonderful that she wanted to pull him inside her and keep him there forever.

The kiss lengthened. Her fingers moved, gliding over the firm muscles of his shoulders, slid inside his shirt and into the soft down on his chest, wanting to touch him and instinctively knowing it was what he wanted. Her fingertips brushed a nipple buried in the soft hair, passed by, but returned to caress it. His bare skin surprised her with its smoothness. His body answered the movement of her hand with a violent trembling. He drew his lips away and buried his face in her throat like a child seeking comfort. She held him to her and caressed the hair at the nape of his neck.

"Get in bed with me," she whispered.

He was still for a minute. Then said, "Oh, darlin' girl. Are you sure? I'll want to do more than . . . hold you."

"I want you to do more." She whispered the words so softly he wasn't sure that he had understood them.

"You're sure?" he asked again.

"I'm sure. More than sure."

He pulled his arms from around her and stood up. She saw him jerk off his shirt, his trousers, and kick off his shoes. She lifted the covers. The mattress sagged, the springs creaked under the extra weight. Then his arms reached for her, gathered her to him and held her tightly against his bare chest. His muscular legs entwined with hers.

"I've dreamed of this." He pulled her arms up to encircle her neck. "Hold me, sweetheart."

"I've never . . ."

His lips stopped her words. "We'll not do anything you don't want to do. It's heaven to be with you like this, holding you, loving you. I'll not ask for more. Even if it kills me." One of his hands slipped inside her gown and cupped her breast, his thumb stroking the hard point; the other hand caressed her bottom and pulled her tightly against the part of him that was throbbing painfully. He couldn't hold back a groan of pleasure.

"You want more," she whispered. "I feel you against me."

"Ah, sweetheart. I don't seem to have any control over it. The night of the flood, I was afraid you'd notice and be disgusted with me." His hand tugged at the neck of her gown. "Will you take it off?" he breathed in her ear. He could feel the fierce pounding of her heart. Her hands reached for the hem and lifted the gown up and over her head.

Seconds later he cradled her to him reverently. His warm, passionate kisses began on her lips and traveled over the side of her face to her ears and throat. His hand caressed every curve, every soft, graceful line, over her hips and down her thigh. He was tender and gentle and set her on fire with passionate kisses. She wanted to speak, to tell him what she was feeling, but she felt certain that he knew.

"Do you want more?" he whispered hoarsely. The part of him that throbbed so aggressively against her was large and strong like the rest of him.

"Everything," she replied against his lips and swallowed his joyous cry.

Deftly he rolled her onto her back and pinned her with the length of his long body. He was unhurried, tender, amazingly gentle. The stroking of his hands sent waves of pleasure up and down her spine. Her hands glided across his chest and down his shoulders with no thought as to what they should be doing.

She suddenly felt his fingers between her legs stroking the velvet lips. "Is this what you want, my darling girl?"

"Oh, Joe. Yes, yes, yes . . ."

His prowling fingers stroked her until she hurt deep, deep inside of her. She had thought about this but never dreamed she'd feel such exquisite delight. She moved uninhibitedly under his touch. So many new sensations crashed through her body and mind that she was unable to distinguish one from the other. It was all too pleasurable, too wonderful. To be with this beloved man like this was . . . was . . .

Dear God, it was heaven!

His hands gently held her legs apart. She became aware of a hard pressure against her, a slow, gradual filling of that aching emptiness. A sudden movement of his hips brought a pain-pleasure so intense that she cried out.

"I'm sorry . . . sweetheart. I'm sorry. I had to!" he whispered in her ear and lay still for a long moment.

"I know. It's all right. It's all right." She kissed his face with quick, passionate kisses and clutched at his buttocks to keep his throbbing warmth inside her.

"I hated to hurt you. I love you so much."

"I expected it to hurt . . . at first."

He began to move gently, carefully. "All right?"

"All right."

She lay still for a moment and then began to move, imitating him, finding her reward in the way his kiss deepened and his body trembled. She clung to him, aware only of this sweet, loving man and the wonder of his love for her. Then she became aware of the thrusting, pulsating rhythm that was pushing her toward a bursting, shivering height where nothing but the two of them existed.

"My sweetheart! My love . . ." His voice came to her as if from a great distance as they reached the summit. Then she was over the top, lost in a sea of sensation.

When it was possible to think and feel again, Joe's weight was pressing her down in the bed. She put her mouth to his shoulder, tasting the salty tang of his skin. He moved his head to kiss her lips, his mouth so tender on hers, so reverent, that it almost brought tears.

A wave of protective love washed over her. She wrapped her arms around him. Her lips sought his and kissed him desperately. He buried his face in the curve of her shoulder, and she held him there.

When he moved, it was only a fraction so he could whisper, "Did you like making love with me? It's only the first of many times."

"I loved it," she breathed. "I didn't have any idea that it would be so wonderful."

"It's only this wonderful with the one you love, sweetheart." He rolled, taking her with him, and they lay side by side, face-to-face, sharing small nibbling kisses. "If I had known what it was like to have you like this, feel your breasts against me, I wouldn't have been able to wait." His lips moved over her face and paused to tease her lashes.

"I never thought that this awful evening would have such a wonderful ending."

"It isn't over, love." He leaned back so he could see her face. She smiled, seeing that the old grin she loved had returned.

"You don't mean . . . ?"

"I haven't heard the train go through."

"What has the train to do with it?"

"It goes through town at four-thirty. That's when I'll leave so you'll not be labeled a scarlet woman in case Miss Davenport is up looking out the window."

"You don't have to leave. If Doc could keep Caroline in here for a week, I can keep you for a day. Tomorrow is Sunday. When you want to go, you can go out the clinic door. People will think you needed my special attention." She laughed happily.

"I'll never *want* to go, but I'll have to go out to the farm in the morning and do my chores. Remember Rolling Thunder? He gets mean when he's hungry."

"So we've got until the train goes through?"

"Ah, darlin' girl. We've got the rest of our lives if you say the word."

"What word?"

"Words. If you say you love me and want

to spend the rest of your life letting me love you, I swear that I'll take care of you and the babies we'll have."

"I love you. I want to spend my life with you. I want your babies. Lots of babies."

He was sure that this was the most glorious moment in his life. His arms crushed her to him. His kisses devoured her mouth. She could feel the thunderous pounding of his heart against her soft breasts.

"You won't regret it, darlin'. I swear it!" His voice trembled with emotion.

Nothing mattered from then on except satisfying their desperate need for each other. They swirled in a mindless vortex of pleasure created by caressing hands, lips and closely entwined limbs. When they were finally joined, it was forceful, ecstatic and more satisfying than the first time.

He murmured over and over that he loved her. He told her of the hunger that gnawed at him and the thirst for the mouth she offered so willingly.

They made love until sheer exhaustion sent April into a deep sleep and Joe into a void between sleep and awareness, dreading to hear the sound of the Union Pacific going through town. She lay molded to his naked body, her cheek nestled in the warm hollow of his shoulder. That this lovely creature loved him was nothing less than a miracle. He wanted to shout it from the housetops.

Oh, Lord. I want to give her the world.

Chapter 32

"Wake up, pretty girl." Joe spoke softly and placed tender kisses on her lips.

April opened her eyes and found his face just inches from hers. She stroked his cheek with her fingertips.

"Has the train gone through?"

"Hours ago. I couldn't leave you. I'll wrap a big, fat bandage around my hand before I leave. Miss Nosy Davenport will think I've had an accident."

She laughed happily. "It's daylight. Rolling Thunder will be getting mean." Her fingers slid into the hair at the nape of his neck. She was curled up in his arms, one leg sandwiched between his.

"I've been waiting for daylight. I wanted to look at you before I had to go."

His eyes held hers. There was something

in his face she hadn't seen before. Love. And it was for *her.* She felt wonderfully, gloriously happy.

"Tell me what you told me last night. I'm almost afraid to believe it." He pulled back his face, his eyes watched her closely.

"I . . . love . . . you." She spaced the words for emphasis. His lips covered hers before she could say more.

"That's what I wanted to hear. You are mine!" He looked as happy as a boy on Christmas morning. "When will you marry me? It better be soon because I'm going to sleep here in this bed with you every night from now on."

"Oh, my! That will make Miss Davenport very happy."

"How about Miss Asbury?"

"I'll be known as a fallen woman."

"Not for long. You'll be a respectable married woman."

"When?"

"Today. Tomorrow at the latest."

She laughed. "That's impossible."

"We'll talk about it when I get back."

"When will you be back?"

"Two hours at the most. I'll do my chores,

then go by the farm and see Jack. Pa does only what's necessary on Sunday."

"I'll cook—"

"I'd rather you stay right here in bed and wait for me."

"Oh . . . you!"

"Kiss me. It's got to last two long hours." His hand moved up and down her back and over her rounded bottom. The feel of her warm body against his and the scent of her filled his head. "I don't want to go. But knowing you'll be here waiting for me will make it bearable," he whispered and kissed her long and hard.

She returned his kisses hungrily, feeling the familiar longing in her loins, pressing against him, her breasts tingling as they had last night when he caressed them.

"I'll be waiting for you," she whispered and parted her lips for his kiss. His mouth covered hers and she clung to him, melting into his hard body. He kissed her quickly and pulled back.

"I'd better go while I can."

He dressed hurriedly, leaned over to kiss her again and was gone.

April didn't move until she heard the car start and drive away. Then she bounded out of bed and hurried to the bathroom. The cold, wet cloth felt good against her.

She could hardly contain her bubbling spirits as she looked in the cabinet and icebox for something to fix for breakfast. All she could find were potatoes, eggs, cheese and part of an apple pie. She hoped that Joe liked fried potatoes.

The phone rang while she was waiting for water to heat to make a cup of tea.

It was Mrs. Bailey, a mother with an eight-month-old baby.

"He has cried all night, and when he fills his diaper, its runny. I just don't know what to do."

"He's teething, isn't he?"

"Yes, his gums are white. He's exhausted from crying, and I'm exhausted from lack of sleep."

"Try putting some crushed ice in a cloth and let him chew on it. Sometimes that will give relief. You can also rub his gums with the flat end of a spoon handle. If he runs a temperature, call me back and I'll call the doctor in Mason, and I'm sure he'll want to see him. The doctor won't be here in Fertile until Tuesday."

"I'll try the ice."

She was frying potatoes when she heard the key in the lock, the door open and footsteps come toward the kitchen. Her heart quickened. As soon as Joe appeared in the doorway, she dropped the spatula and sped to his open arms. His smile reached all the way into her heart. He was her heart, her soul. He had become so dear to her that she would never be content when he was out of her sight.

"I could hardly wait to get back," he whispered against her mouth, then lifted her off her feet and whirled her around.

"I missed you!"

"Then you've not changed your mind about being Mrs. Jones?"

"Not on your life. I'm holding you to it!" She kissed his mouth. "But you'd better let me get back to the potatoes before they burn."

"I never thought I'd be jealous of a pan of potatoes!" he complained. Then the old devilish grin came back. "I'm even jealous of this." He plucked at her blouse. "It's closer to you than I am."

While eating the fried potatoes and eggs, April asked about Doc and Caroline.

"He telephoned his sister from Kansas

City to tell her they were coming. Isn't it something that you can talk over a wire all the way to Tennessee? Anyway, they boarded the train, but not before Doc took Caroline to a store and bought her a new dress, hat and coat. Doc was so proud to walk out in public with her on his arm, something he could never do here."

"I hope they will find a place where they can be happy."

"Doc is confident they will."

April and Joe spent the day being totally absorbed with each other. They sat on the couch, his arm around her, her head on his shoulder, and talked of everything that had taken place in their lives up to now. She told him about her father leaving her and her mother stranded in St. Louis and how they'd had to go home to her grandparents in Independence.

"He came to see us from time to time. It didn't bother him that my grandparents were supporting his family. Each time he left, my mother died a little, until there seemed to be nothing remaining for her. She went to bed one night and never got up. I've hated him ever since."

"Have you seen him since you grew up?"

"Once. Right after Grandmother died. He came to the house and thought he would move in and I'd take care of him. I told him that I had not had a father for twenty years and didn't want one now. He left, and I've not heard from him since and don't want to ever hear from him again."

Joe told her about his mother's dying when he was fourteen and how Julie had stepped in to take care of her brothers and sister. He told her that Ron Poole, Shirley's husband, had attempted to rape Jill and how Thad had fought with him.

"The poor girl!"

"Thad tackled him, and he was just a skinny kid himself. They rolled over near Thad's horse. When Ron tried to stab Thad with a knife, he stuck it in the horse instead. The horse kicked him. Ron lived long enough for us to get him home. Pa wouldn't have him in the house, and he died in the barn."

He was about to tell her something else because he wanted there to be no secrets between them when they heard footsteps on the porch, then a heavy knock on the door.

Joe groaned and grabbed April for a quick kiss before he let her leave his arms to open the door.

Fred stood there. His hat was set square on his head. He held a flat tin box clutched to his chest.

"Hello, Fred."

He jerked off his hat. "Miss Asbury. Ah . . . I . . . wondered if you would spare me some time." His eyes went past her when Joe came to stand behind her and put a possessive hand on her shoulder.

"Hello, Fred."

"Joe." Fred didn't show any surprise at finding him there. "I really do need to talk to someone . . . and . . . ah . . . I'm glad you're here, Joe. This concerns your family among others." He was clearly in an agitated state. His hands shook, his eyes darted from Joe to April.

"Come in, Fred." April held open the door.

"Thank you."

"How are things going, Fred?" Joe asked in an attempt to put him at ease. "I see you're making a few changes at the store. Took off that ragged awning for one thing. It helped the looks of the building."

"Shirley would never let me take it off because Ron had put it there."

"I heard that the store and house are yours now."

"Shirley made out a will the first year I was here, leaving the house and the store to me. I was surprised. I think she had forgotten about it." He stood holding his hat and the flat tin box. "I have something here you should see."

"Come into the kitchen and I'll get us some tea."

Fred hung his hat on the hall tree and followed April. He placed the tin box carefully on the table and sat down. Wearily he rubbed his face with his hand.

"I have wrestled with what I found in this box for two days. I don't know what to do about it, but something must be done. It affects too many lives."

"What is it?" Joe felt cold fingers on his spine. He feared it would have something to do with Julie and Joy. He sat down and reached for April's hand. She moved close to him, instinctively knowing that he needed her.

"First, let me tell you that we found the box about six years ago. It was behind a stack of shelves that we pulled out because the roof was leaking. Shirley took it, and I never gave it another thought. I found it again when I went through her dresser drawers looking for things to bury her in. I didn't get around to opening it until a couple of nights ago."

Fred lifted the lid on the box and let it fall back on the table. On the top of what looked like Kodak pictures and mementos was a small notebook. He took it out and handed it to Joe.

"It seems that my brother-in-law kept a record of his shameful activities. Your sister's name is there. I had planned to ask Miss Asbury's advice on how I should let your family know about this."

Joe took the book and began to read. A muscle ticked in his jaw when he read:

Julie Jones—July 1917—girl March 1918 named Joy. Below was written, *I couldn't have picked a better name myself.*

Joe cursed silently, remembering the day Julie, alone in the barn, gave birth to Joy. He forced himself to continue reading and was surprised by the number of names he recognized. In the back of the book he found a list of eleven children who lived in and around Fertile. Another list matched the boys and girls according to their ages.

"Mrs. Poole wrote this?" he asked.

Fred nodded. "Now that I look back, she was never the same after she found this box. She became increasingly bitter and harder and harder to live with. I think she hated all women." Fred lowered his eyes to the table. "Women seldom came to the house and never to visit."

"It wasn't the women's fault that her husband was a sick pervert," April said staunchly.

"She rented to Miss Asbury because I insisted. I thought it would be good for her to have a young person around. But it just made her more hateful."

Joe looked at the Kodak pictures and picked out one of Joy when she was about four years old, coming out of the church with Julie.

"I wonder how he got this picture. Good Lord." He picked up a picture of a young woman sitting on a step and flipped it over and read, " 'Ardyth Jenkins pregnant with my kid.' I knew Ardyth. When she was about fifteen, she drowned in the river. Everyone thought it an accident."

"He raped Sammy Davidson's mother a few months before your sister." April was scanning the pages of the notebook. "It seems that Mrs. Poole's plan was to try and make a match between her husband's children. She had Joy down here with Sammy Davidson. Richard Myers with the Bradbury girl."

April looked up at Fred. "Oh, my. She planned to get revenge by having the children each mate with their own brother or sister. But why take her hurt out on the children?"

"I don't think she was in her right mind," he said tiredly.

"I was there when the bastard died." Joe stared at the picture of Joy. "He died after he tried to rape Jill, who was about fifteen at the time. If Thad's horse hadn't stomped him, my pa would have killed him on the spot. As he was dying, he bragged about all the offspring he was leaving behind. I remember him saying that there were eighteen of them. He had the guts to ask to see Joy. He wanted her at his funeral. Pa said he'd see him in hell first."

Joe continued. "Julie didn't know who had raped her. He was always careful to blindfold his victims. No one knew what had happened to her but me and Pa and Jack, but we never talked about it. My mother was bedfast," he explained to April. "She died shortly after Joy was born and every-one assumed she died in childbirth."

"Poor Julie," April said. "All this time she's had to pretend that Joy was her sister and not her child. That must have been hard."

"Knowing Julie, I'm sure she told Evan before they were married." Joe picked up a picture of a barefoot boy and recognized Sammy. "Mrs. Poole was throwing Joy and Sammy together. Joy will be shocked to find out that he's as much her brother as Logan is."

"What a mess." Fred shook his head. "It's a relief to me to have someone else know about this. I just didn't know what to do."

Joe said, "Corbin and Doc were there when Ron died; and we all agreed that Mrs. Poole shouldn't have to suffer for what her husband had done, so we kept it quiet. The story that was put out was that his horse spooked, he was thrown and the frightened horse stomped him."

"The parents of these children should know the rapist was Poole. Then it will be up to them to tell the children if they choose." April's calm voice filled the silence. "What if Joy and Sammy had grown up and fallen in love with each other, got married and later discovered they were brother and sister? It would have destroyed them."

Joe looked steadily at Fred. The man had risen in his estimation. He could have taken this information and spread it all over town, yet he was here, exposing his sister's sick plan with the hope of fixing it.

"You should take this to Evan, Fred. He'll know how to tell Julie, and they can decide how to handle the rest of it."

Fred sighed. "I think you're right."

"If you want me to go out and bring Evan into town, I will. I'll think of some excuse."

"I would like to get this out of my hands." Fred went to the hall rack for his hat.

April and Joe went with him to the door. Joe's arm was around her.

"April and I are getting married," Joe said bluntly.

"I thought that was the way the wind blew. You're a lucky man." Fred smiled for the first time since he came into the house.

"I think so. Come back in a couple of

hours, Fred. I'll have Evan here. He may want to bring Julie, and he may not. It'll be up to him."

Later that afternoon Evan and Julie met with Fred. She told him how grateful she was that he came forward with the information about Ron Poole's offspring. She was shocked to read the list of names and realized she knew many of the children. What if two of them had married not knowing their relationship?

A heavy load would be lifted from her heart when she explained to Joy the circumstances of her birth. Not since before that terrible day when she was sixteen years old had Julie felt so happy. She had a wonderful, understanding husband and three beautiful children.

She could now put the past behind her.

Epilogue

June 1935

Dear April and Joe,

I take pen in hand to let you know that Caroline and I are settled here in Lahaina on the island of Maui. My friend has welcomed me into his practice, and Caroline and I are the proud parents of a son. Caroline has become acquainted with some of the native women. She loves it here and spends many hours going barefoot on the beach, collecting seashells and teaching her native friends to crochet. The sight of ships coming into the harbor never ceases to amaze her. We are happier than we ever believed possible. Write and tell us the news. I suppose you two finally figured out that you were in love.

Doc

August 1935

Dear Doc and Caroline,

Joe and I received your welcome letter. We are glad that you have found a place where you can live together as man and wife. Congratulations on becoming parents! This will probably not be much of a surprise to you, but Joe and I, Ruby and Jack were married in a double ceremony. Julie and Eudora wanted to have the wedding at the farm and we agreed.

Jack has gone back to work as Fertile's law enforcer. He and Ruby live upstairs in Mrs. Poole's house. I have a job now as a county nurse and we still live in your house. Joe and I have not decided if we will continue to live here or out on his farm.

Rolling Thunder has proved to be a good investment for Joe. He is gradually building up a good head of cattle.

When Fred was going through his sister's belongings, he found Ron Poole's record book. It listed all of his children and the names of the women he had raped. Fred gave the book to Julie and Evan. Julie explained the circumstances of her birth to Joy, and Joy showed more maturity than we expected. They left it up to her to tell Sammy. She did and both seem pleased to know they are half-brother and sister.

Marla Davidson ran off and left Sammy in the house on the river. Joe found the boy there alone, and now he's working and living with Jethro and Eudora at the farm. Jethro says he has taken to farming and is a good worker. Eudora now has him under her wing, and he adores her. All in all, things seem to have worked out fine for all of them.

Fred and Joe have become friends. Fred is a changed man now that he's out from under the thumb of his sister.

He's keeping company with Sarah Parker, and it appears to be serious.

Hattie Davenport got her comeuppance. Sarah and I spread word that you left town because of her pursuit. She lost most of her social standing in town after that.

Let us hear from you. You are missed here in Fertile. People keep asking if we've heard from you.

The postmaster tells us that this letter will probably reach you before Christmastime. We wish you a joyous Christmas and a Happy New Year.

From your friends in Fertile,

April and Joe